1.50

Trudi Pacter, a fo[...] -
time writer. Her [...]
Kisses, The Sleepi[...]l.
She is married to [...]r
time between Lond[...]

G000152537

Also by Trudi Pacter

KISS AND TELL
SCREEN KISSES
THE SLEEPING PARTNER
LIVING DOLL
YELLOW BIRD
WILD CHILD

For Nigel, my husband

TO LOVE,
HONOUR AND BETRAY

Trudi Pacter

POCKET
BOOKS

LONDON · SYDNEY · NEW YORK · TOKYO · SINGAPORE · TORONTO

First published in Great Britain by Simon & Schuster, 1996
This edition first published in 1997 by Pocket Books
An imprint of Simon & Schuster Ltd
A Viacom Company

Copyright © 1996 by Trudi Pacter

The right of Trudi Pacter to be identified as author of this work has been
asserted in accordance with sections 77 and 78 of the Copyright Designs
and Patents Act 1988

Simon & Schuster Ltd
West Garden Place
Kendal Street
London
W2 2AQ

Simon & Schuster Australia
Sydney

A CIP catalogue record for this book is available from the British Library.

ISBN 0-671-85445 3

Printed and bound in Great Britain by Caledonian International Book
Manufacturing, Glasgow

This book is a work of fiction. Names, characters, places and incidents
are either the product of the author's imagination or are used fictitiously.
Any resemblance to actual events or locales or persons, living or dead, is
entirely coincidental.

Chapter One

Sally . . . London, 1994

She saw her at the top of the stairs, and for a second she couldn't believe it. The dress was obviously Chanel and must have cost a fortune. It was made of some black silky material and emphasised the curve of her breasts and the way her waist swooped in. On a woman of thirty it would have been sensational, except Sally's daughter wasn't thirty. She was just fifteen.

Sally hurried across the hall to intercept her. 'What on earth . . .' she said. But the girl must have known what was on her mind, for she smiled sweetly and told Sally to stop fussing.

'Daddy bought it for me,' she announced. 'He wanted me to look great for his birthday, so we went down Bond Street and picked it out.'

Just for a moment, Sally felt like screaming. Annabel had been getting round her father since she was in nappies. She must have spun him quite a line to make him buy her this creation. She wondered how she was going to get her out of it.

'Would you like to know what I think about the dress?' she asked.

Annabel hesitated.

'Not really, but you're going to tell me anyway.'

You bet I am Sally thought, eyeing her daughter with as much disapproval as she could muster.

'It makes you look silly,' she said.

There was a silence while the girl took this in. And Sally could see she'd dented her confidence a little. Yet she couldn't resist one last protest. 'Daddy thought it was beautiful.'

'David would think you were a knockout in sackcloth,' Sally said, determined not to let her get away with it, 'so let's not talk about your father. Let's talk about the dress.'

She took a step back and regarded her daughter. She was pretty, that was for sure, but it was the sort of prettiness that could look cheap if she wasn't careful. There was too much bosom and blonde hair for the revealing dress David had bought her, and she wondered what on earth he was trying to turn her into.

Then she thought, what do men know?

'It's not such a bad dress,' Sally pronounced finally, 'In ten years time you could just get away with it.'

'Why not now?'

'Because it's too sexy and you're too young to put yourself on display like that.'

She saw Annabel pout.

'Is this your way of telling me to change into something else?'

Sally started to feel indignant.

'You're not exactly stuck for choice.'

'I am for this party. The whole world will be here, all Daddy's friends, all the people he does business with. He told me yesterday there was a chance Mick Jagger might show up. And now you're telling me I've got to turn up in some horrible cheap item.'

Sally reflected on how much she had spent kitting her daughter out. There were uniforms for her expensive private school, her riding gear, her tennis gear and all of it was in addition to her other demands. If Annabel didn't pick up at least one new outfit from the King's Road every week, she thought her world was coming to an end.

I spoil her, Sally thought. And David's just as bad. Taking her out on shopping sprees to Chanel isn't doing either of us any favours. Pretty soon she'll be so out of control, she'll be telling me what to wear.

2

Thinking about her own wardrobe suddenly gave her an idea. She couldn't come up with another Chanel dress, but there was more than one designer label hanging in her closet.

'Forget the horrible cheap item,' she told her daughter. 'I've probably got something you can wear.'

Annabel was doubtful.

'You're miles older than I am, Mummy. Anyway we don't go for the same things.'

Sally looked at her thoughtfully.

'You're telling me you wouldn't consider anything by Donna Karan?'

She saw her hesitate and because she knew her daughter so well, she knew she was mentally reviewing the contents of her wardrobe.

'You wouldn't be talking about a pants suit with a tuxedo jacket, would you?'

'I might be, why do you ask?'

'Because if you were, I could be persuaded to part with this dress.'

Sally sighed.

'Get upstairs, will you? The suit is in the spare closet at the back.' She paused before adding, 'And get a move on. I don't want you parading in front of my mirror for hours. The guests will be here any minute now.'

The notion that she was about to be inundated with nearly a hundred party people made Sally get a move on herself. There were still things to be done and she hurried through to the drawing-room to see how far the caterers had got.

The sight that greeted her made her relax a little for the room had been rearranged exactly the way she'd instructed. Her good antiques had been pushed discreetly into corners, along with the cluster of little tables she normally had dotted around. Now there was just a big bare space with nothing to impede her guests apart from the grand piano in the window. She made a mental note to tell one of the waiters to put cocktail mats on its top. She didn't want people leaving wet rings behind on the mahogany.

She was about to hurry through to the kitchen and fire off another dozen orders, when she decided enough was enough. She'd been working all day long organising this evening. She'd put on this kind of show millions of times before, and she knew that now, at the eleventh hour, there was nothing more she could do.

Sit down, she told herself. You've earned it. Then she thought of David, whose birthday all this was in aid of. We've both earned it, she thought. She took a glass of champagne from a silver tray, which was on a table ready for the the party to begin.

Who would have imagined, she thought, toasting herself, that people like us could have put on a spread like this. It was something that went through Sally's mind every time she put on a party. For she had never stopped being grateful for whatever luck had granted her all the splendour around her. She had never forgotten that, not so many years ago, she and David had come down from Manchester with only their dreams and their ambition to sustain them.

We had my savings as well, she reminded herself. Without the money my grandmother left me, all the dreams in the world wouldn't have got us to where we wanted to go.

For David had wanted to set up his own public relations agency. He had worked nearly ten years in somebody else's agency and now he needed to prove himself. He needed to show her and his family that he was as good as he always boasted he was. And she had given him the wherewithal to do it.

She'd also worked alongside him in the agency in the early days. And she hadn't regretted any of it, for David had come through.

He was marvellous with people. It was his talent, the reason he'd chosen public relations in the first place. For he could talk anyone into anything.

The clients he started with had followed him out of his old agency because of this gift of the gab. And the new clients, the ones he hustled at parties and over lunch, came to him for the same reason. There was a brilliance about her

4

husband, a glamour, that pulled people into his orbit and kept them there.

Sally smiled to herself, my money and David's brilliance. The combination was unbeatable. And then one day, my money didn't matter any more. David earned it back a thousand times over. He earned it back enough to let me have Annabel and move here to this house. This castle, this fortress.

She realised she was becoming fanciful and put it down to the champagne. Then she thought, the hell with it, and drained the rest of the glass. If she couldn't be fanciful on David's birthday, when could she be?

She stood up, thinking she might get a refill, when she saw David come into the room. He was wearing a dinner jacket and his hair was brushed back and she couldn't help thinking how much like Michael Douglas he looked. He was far handsomer than any of her friends' husbands and there were times when it made her feel insecure. She would wonder if she was pretty enough, or smart enough. But tonight, she had no such worries. She had spent all afternoon at the hairdresser's; she was looking good and she knew it, so she hurried over to David and kissed him.

'Happy birthday,' she said.

He kissed her back with the kind of warmth she had come to expect. Then he held her away from him and scrutinised her.

'You'll do,' he said approvingly. 'I bet the dress cost a bob or two.' It was by one of the new English designers she always thought was too young for her. But her husband's eyes told her otherwise.

'It cost a fortune,' she said, enjoying his admiration. 'But then so did everything else tonight.'

It crossed her mind to bring up Annabel's dress. Then she thought, why spoil things? I can handle my daughter perfectly well on my own. Aloud she said:

'Have you seen the buffet now the caterers have finished?'

He grinned.

'Have you seen the guests?'

5

'Guests?' she protested, 'what guests? We're not expecting anyone for half an hour.'

'They're here all the same. The boring little man who makes kitchen equipment is in the hall getting sloshed with one of the waiters. And Lord Durham and the current ladyship are in the kitchen picking over the buffet.'

Sally felt a moment of sheer panic.

'Do you think we should get out there and do something?'

She saw the laughter in her husband's eyes.

'I don't think so,' he told her. 'They seem to be perfectly happy as they are.'

He picked up a bottle of champagne and started uncorking it.

'The best thing we can do right now is to have a quiet drink together, before the fun really starts.'

By the time they finished the house was filling up. It happened in the space of five minutes. Where there had been one or two people, there were suddenly dozens, as if some invisible signal had been given for proceedings to start. It was early autumn and already the women were wearing coats, throwing them carelessly to the hired butler as they passed through.

Sally watched them, searching the crowd for someone she knew. Her real friends seemed to be thin on the ground. All she could see that night were clients, potential clients and clients' wives. Her heart sank. Give them half an hour, she thought, and the men would be huddled together talking business, leaving me to take care of the girls.

And they thought of themselves as girls, even though most of them would never see forty again. They wore girlish clothes and had girlish opinions and every time Sally made an effort to talk to them she felt she was drowning in a sea of inanity. For these women were like sponges. Talk to them about the latest play in the West End and they swallowed up all her comments and observations and added nothing to what she said. Ask about their children and they looked vague and occasionally worried, as if a detailed discussion might reveal their true ages.

Once when she was still learning to play the company game,

6

she made an attempt to talk about the corporations their husbands owned. But she soon learned it was a pointless exercise. These women simply weren't interested in how their money was made. Their concern was spending it . . . on hairdressers and restaurants and places to park the yacht during the summer.

Sally had once spent an entire dinner party listening to some client's wife explaining the merits of leaving the yacht in Cannes harbour as opposed to St Tropez. Afterwards when she moaned about it, David turned the whole thing into a joke.

'That woman's husband spends half a million with us every year,' he pointed out. 'For that kind of money you can try to look interested when she talks about her yacht.'

He was right, of course. David had a job to do and so did she. And if hers wasn't as much fun as his, then she'd just have to learn to live with it. Chatting up wives, she decided a long time ago, went with the territory.

The sound of the front door pulled her back to the present. This would be the last of her guests tonight and she wondered who the latecomer was.

Then the door opened and Diane walked through.

Sally felt a rush of warmth as she went to greet her oldest friend. Neither of them bothered with the statutory air kiss. They simply enveloped each other in a bear hug that went all the way back to their days in Manchester when they had shared a flat and an office and a life.

'So you finally got here,' Sally exclaimed, disentangling herself. 'What kept you so long?'

Diane made a face.

'The office. What else?'

Sally regarded her friend and felt slightly impatient with her. She was such a beauty with her long, dark hair and china-white skin. What on earth was she doing spending all her time at the office?

'You work too hard,' she chided her. 'You should get out more.'

'I don't want to get out more,' Diane told her. 'I like what I do.'

7

It was a classic understatement. Diane didn't just like managing a group of fashion boutiques. She loved it and lived it, to the exclusion of almost everything else. Even tonight when all the other women were here with their husbands or boyfriends, Diane was on her own.

Sally shrugged. There was no point in nagging her about missing the boat. It was a boat Diane clearly didn't want to catch. So she went back to safer ground.

'How's my account doing?'

It wasn't her account at all, of course. It belonged to the agency. But she called it 'her account' because she was the one who had talked Diane into handing it over two years ago. The question made Diane smile.

'Your account's going great guns. Did David tell you we're opening up in Edinburgh next year?'

'David doesn't tell me anything these days.'

'Well, he should do. It's going to be our best branch.'

Sally thought for a moment. 'If Edinburgh is going to be such a big deal,' she said, 'surely you'll need some sort of promotion?'

'I've been thinking along those lines already,' Diane laughed, 'but no-one's actually come to me and asked to do anything.'

Sally looked at her. 'Then I'm asking . . .' Before she could go any further, she saw David coming towards them.

'I heard that,' he said. 'What vital thing is Sally asking? She looks as if she's got the light of battle in her eyes.'

Sally saw Diane looking worried. 'We were just talking about the account.'

'And Sally asked you something,' David prompted.

Diane sighed. 'I told her about Edinburgh and we were tossing around the idea of spending money on a launch.'

David raised his eyebrows. 'And I thought you were having a girlish gossip.'

Sally linked her arm through David's. 'We were having a girlish gossip. Only business is much more interesting than talking about the hairdresser.'

She heard her husband sigh, and wondered what was bothering him.

'Sally darling, I do wish you'd stick to the hairdresser.'

'Why so?'

'Because it makes better party conversation. I'll deal with the business in the office.'

His tone was light, but there was no mistaking the dismissal in it. She'd wandered onto David's patch and he clearly didn't like it. She looked at Diane and saw the worry was still on her face. So she backed off, slipping her arm out of David's.

'I think I'm going to leave you both to it,' she said reluctantly. 'I know when I'm not wanted.'

Chapter Two

Sally had worked the room thoroughly the way she always did. She knew who was drinking too much, who was feeling shy, who wanted to talk to David. She'd smiled till she thought her face would crack and she'd laid on the charm so thick that she felt sure someone would notice and call her a fraud. Only no-one did.

They were enjoying themselves, working up an appetite for dinner. And now the whole thing looked under control, Sally gave a silent signal to the head waiter to open the doors to the dining-room.

The party was in its second stage now, the eating stage. For the next half hour she stood back while her guests filed through and helped themselves to the cold buffet. She had ordered lobster and asparagus, poached salmon and dozens of native oysters which had just come into season. When she got the bill, she thought she'd gone over the top. She'd worried about it for days afterwards. Only now she realised her fears had been for nothing.

David's important clients were beside themselves with delight when they saw the spread. There were exclamations and little expressions of greed that only the truly wealthy make over other people's food. She waited for the glow to come over her. The glow that always enveloped her when she had produced a really successful evening. Only she didn't feel it.

She realised she was still smarting from David's dismissal of her. He shouldn't have done that, she thought. He shouldn't have made me look like a fool in front of Diane. And she wondered what had got into her husband. He might not have treated her like an equal, but he always made it clear he loved her. Until recently, when he'd started behaving totally out of character.

There had been a client dinner a couple of months ago when he'd come down on her like a ton of bricks for daring to butt in on his business, though at the time she'd only been trying to save David's face.

It had been a terrible evening, she remembered. A doomed evening when nothing went right at all. She supposed a lot of the problem was the pressure they were under. For the man they were trying to impress had the power to increase the agency's turnover by half a million. Chandos had been shortlisted, along with one other agency for a big American hotel account. And the clincher had been dinner with the owner, who had come over specially to vet them.

She'd done her best for David that night, booking them a table at Claridge's and spending all day getting ready so she would look like the perfect company wife. She'd even come on like a company wife, asking after the client's wife and family. It had been her first mistake.

The hotel chief, whose name was Brad Hastings, seemed reluctant to answer her question. He was a big bear of a man with a mane of greying hair and surprisingly gentle eyes. As far as Sally was concerned he seemed the archetypal family man, so she was confused when she couldn't draw him out. She was about to have another go at him, when David took hold of her arm and drew her into a corner.

'Weren't you told about Brad's wife,' he hissed at her.

Sally shook her head.

'Well you should have been. The whole family was wiped out in some sort of robbery in New York. He hasn't been the same since.'

Sally looked across the bar where Brad was talking earnestly to Jeremy, their managing director. Why didn't Jeremy put me in the picture? she wondered. It was the first thing he should have done. But there was no time for recriminations. The evening was in full swing, so she walked back into the fray and steered the conversation towards dinner.

Claridge's was famous for its cuisine, she informed the American. They were all going to be in for a treat. At last she seemed to be saying the right thing, for Brad brightened up considerably and for the next ten minutes regaled her with tales of his experiences in London restaurants. It seemed someone was always booking him into places at the worst possible times. Either the chef was off that day. Or a visiting football team had taken the place over and drowned out all attempts at conversation.

Sally laughed when she heard his parade of disasters and assured him he was in better hands tonight. She had been supporting Claridge's for years now and they wouldn't dare let her down.

Ten minutes later, she wished she hadn't opened her big mouth. For Claridge's had let her down. They had somehow contrived to give them a table in the corner right by the kitchens. She supposed it wasn't as bad as sitting next door to a football team, but it came a close second.

'I had no idea they would put us here,' Sally whispered, wishing the ground would swallow her up.

'Well they did,' David said, looking like thunder, 'so we'd better make the best of it.'

As soon as the wine arrived, the atmosphere started to mellow a little. If she concentrated hard, Sally could almost convince herself that she couldn't see the endless streams of waiters going back and forth to the kitchens. Only she noticed that David was having a hard time coping with it. His eyes kept straying to what was happening a few yards away and she could see it was putting him off his pitch.

Normally at business dinners, David was brilliant at presenting the agency. Aided and abetted by Jeremy, his managing director, he could convince almost anybody that he knew more about their account than anyone in London. Only now he was having trouble. He started talking about hotels, but he got the most basic things wrong. Sally had nearly landed a hotel account in the early days and she winced every time David made a mistake.

In the end Brad leaned forward and enquired where David had done his research.

'It sounds to me,' he said gently, 'as if you got your hands on some out-of-date material.'

Sally felt herself choking on her wine. The evening had gone from bad to worse. If somebody didn't do something soon, the whole thing would be a write-off. In desperation she dredged her memory, trying to recall just one detail of the hotel account she had chased all those years ago. And to her surprise her memory came up trumps. As no-one else seemed to be saying very much, she started to feed what she remembered into the conversation.

She realised she was on the right track when Brad didn't interrupt her. David hadn't managed to get two sentences out without putting his foot in it, but she was getting on famously. Brad seemed to like what she had to say.

He didn't actually buy anything. That would have been hoping for too much. But he was interested.

'Do you work in your husband's business?' he asked her curiously.

For a moment she didn't know what to say. Would David want her to lie, so they could get the account? Or should she level with him? In the end she decided on the truth.

'David and I started the agency together, but I left a few years ago to have a baby.'

It had been more than a few years ago, but Brad didn't have to know that. She looked across at David to see if she'd said the right thing. To her surprise she could tell nothing from his expression. His face seemed to have set into the bland mask he put on for difficult clients and even she couldn't seem to get a reaction out of him. Eventually it was Brad who broke the silence.

'David must have been reluctant to let you go,' he observed. 'You're a very bright woman.' After a pause, he went on: 'Tell me, would you consider going back to work if I gave Chandos my account?'

This time David found his voice.

13

Sally's not for hire,' he said. 'She belongs in Oxford looking after the family.'

All of a sudden she felt let down. One minute she had been flying. The next the ground had been cut from under her feet.

She wondered if Brad thought she was some kind of idiot, but he didn't seem to. He simply smiled at David and looked regretful.

'If you ever change your mind about your wife,' he said, 'you know where to find me.'

'You shouldn't have done that,' David said when they got into the taxi outside the hotel.

'I shouldn't have done what?' she asked, wondering which particular *faux pas* he was going to pull her up for.

'You shouldn't have taken over with Brad Hastings. It was totally wrong.'

Now Sally was all at sea. She could understand him complaining about the terrible table. The way she had put her foot in it over Brad's wife was also reasonable cause for angst. But saving the situation from complete disaster, stopping David from looking a fool; this was something he should have been applauding.

'What's the matter with you?' she said crossly. 'If I hadn't done my stuff, you would have ended up with egg all over your face.'

David didn't say anything for a moment. He just stared gloomily out of the window at the rain flooding down on Park Lane. Finally he found his voice.

'Has it occurred to you that I couldn't give a damn about Brad Hastings's account? When everything started to go wrong and he made that crack about my research, I knew I had to cut my losses and get out. I would have done too, if you hadn't played the account exec.'

Sally was momentarily speechless.

'But Brad liked what I had to say. It was the old Metropole presentation and it made us look as if we knew what we were talking about.'

She heard David sigh.

'I know what it was,' he told her. 'I was there when you put it together. But you shouldn't have dug it up without telling me. It makes me look as if I don't know what's going on.'

Sally looked at her husband hunched up in the corner of the back seat and realised she'd hurt his pride. She made an attempt to move closer to him, only to be greeted by his back. Oh dear, she thought. I'm going to have to humour him.

I'm sorry I was a bit heavy handed tonight,' she apologised. 'But Brad spends a lot of money on PR and I wanted us to stay in the running.' She paused, catching her breath. 'We could still pull it off, if you let me get involved.'

This time David turned round and faced her and she saw he was scowling.

'There's no way you're getting involved,' he told her. 'I didn't like you working in the first place. And I'd hate it now.'

And that was the end of it. She'd tried to talk him round, but David didn't want to hear her. In his eyes she was his wife, and her place was at home. There was no room whatever for manoeuvre.

Chapter Three

She was still thinking about David when she felt a tap on her arm and saw Diane standing in front of her.

'You look a bit sour,' she observed, 'is anything wrong?'

Sally tried to cover up with a social smile, but Diane knew her too well for that.

'Out with it,' she said, 'I'm not going anywhere till I know what's on your mind.'

She sighed.

'It was just something David said . . .' She realised she had her friend's full attention for Diane's eyes grew very wide.

'You didn't have a fight before the party, did you?'

'Nothing as dramatic as that. We're still speaking to each other. Just.'

'What do you mean . . . just?'

Sally led her over to the window where they wouldn't be overheard. Then she did her best to explain herself.

'It's to do with the agency and the way David starts behaving when I talk about it. You saw him do it just now. He treats me like a moron every time I open my mouth.'

Diane smiled.

'No he doesn't. He treats you like a wife.'

Sally looked at her friend and thought she was going to explode.

'I was a person before I was a wife,' she said indignantly. 'Or maybe you didn't notice.'

Diane put an arm out to steady her, as if physical contact would diffuse some of her anger.

'I know how much of a person you were and still are,' she said softly. 'But people change when they get married. Your life doesn't revolve around the agency the way it used to. And why should it? You've got Annabel and David and the house on your hands.' She paused, choosing her words carefully. 'If I were you I'd leave the business to David. It's something he does very well.'

Sally felt in some subtle way that she was being excluded. Her best friend and her husband inhabited the precious little world of work and anybody who didn't clock in nine to five somehow didn't count.

But she did count. She founded Chandos alongside David and she was damned if she was going to be pushed to one side.

'This may come as a surpise to you,' she said tightly, 'but I was every bit as good as David in my day.'

'So why did you quit? Why didn't you go on being good?'

The question took some of the wind out of her sails.

'Annabel came along,' she said.

As if on cue, there was her daughter standing right in front of her, wearing the skimpy Chanel dress she'd expressly asked her to change out of. I should smack her, she muttered under her breath, except it probably wouldn't make any difference. Aloud she said:

'Annabel darling, come and say hello to Diane.'

The girl slouched across the room until she stood in front of them. It was obvious she had been avoiding them, for she couldn't quite meet her mother's eyes. Sally was about to raise the subject of the dress when Diane beat her to it.

'Where did you get the sexy dress?' she asked

Annabel had the grace to look embarrassed.

'Daddy bought it in Bond Street.'

Diane raised an eyebrow.

'It doesn't look like a Bond Street dress to me. I'd say it was nearer Soho.'

She deserved it of course. Her daughter had no business

17

running around half naked at a family party. Yet she felt oddly sorry for her. Sixteen-year-olds had no defence against sophisticates like Diane. All thoughts of smacking her went right out of the window. Instead Sally stepped forward and put an arm round Annabel.

'What made you decide against my trouser suit?' she whispered.

Annabel looked slightly guilty.

'I did try it on,' she admitted, 'but it swam on me. I looked like a soldier in a musical comedy.'

Sally stifled a smile.

'So you decided to look like a sexpot instead.'

She saw the desperation in her daughter's eyes.

'What else could I do?'

'Nothing, if you're happy with it.'

'But I'm not happy with it.' Annabel shot a look at Diane. 'People are saying I look cheap.'

'I didn't say cheap,' Diane cut in, 'I said you looked like you belonged in Soho. There are some very expensive hookers around that neck of the woods.'

But Annabel had had enough. Turning to her mother she said, 'I think I'll go up and get into a pair of jeans.'

Then before Sally could say anything, she turned tail and headed out of the door.

Sally looked at Diane.

'I guess I should thank you for that. I wouldn't have had the heart to be so tough.'

Diane shrugged.

'It's easy for me. I don't have to live with her.'

Without their having noticed it, the room had gone quiet. As they registered the silence, they saw David standing in front of the ornate Victorian fireplace. He was obviously about to make a speech and Sally began to feel curious about what he would say. At one of their business parties he would have praised whichever client the do was in aid of. Only tonight was in aid of David himself, and he could hardly blow his own trumpet, however attractive the prospect was.

Sally listened intrigued while David ran through the usual preliminaries. He thanked the caterer, his guests for coming. Then he read out a couple of telegrams and came to a halt.

'There's only one person I want to talk about tonight,' he eventually went on, 'and that person is my wife.'

Sally looked up to see all eyes were on her. She started to feel rather small. I've been carping on about David slighting me all evening, she thought. And now he gets up and makes a speech about me. He started to talk again and she focussed on what he was saying.

'I suppose you're all expecting me to say it was my brilliance that put us on top. But that isn't quite true. The reason I've succeeded at all is entirely due to my wife. All through the lean years she stood by me without a murmur of complaint. When I missed dinner five times in a row because of a late meeting, Sally understood. Because Sally understands the business.'

She held her breath. He's going to tell everyone how we started Chandos together, she thought. But it was a vain hope. Tonight David seemed more interested in boasting about her home-making abilities.

'Everyone here knows that my wife's parties are second to none. But they don't know about her other talents. Sally is the only girl I know who can rustle up a dinner for ten in two hours. Organise a box at at the Opera at a minute's notice. And look as if she's just stepped out of the pages of *Vogue* no matter how hard I push her.'

Despite herself, Sally was flattered. Over the years she'd worked like a dog to make David and the agency look better than they were. And now he was acknowledging it.

She might have gone on basking in David's praise, if she hadn't seen Annabel slide through the door. She was looking desperately for someone she knew and Sally raised a hand and signalled her to come over.

Annabel looked grateful and pushed her way through the crowd until she was standing beside her.

'Do I look better now?' she whispered.

Sally smiled. She had changed into her model teenager outfit

– faded jeans and a soft cashmere sweater Sally remembered buying for her last birthday.

'You look perfect,' she whispered back, conscious that the hurried conversation was interrupting David. But she didn't care. All her teasing and bullying and careful handling of Annabel had produced this result. The one she'd wanted all along.

It was at that precise moment she realised that bringing up Annabel was by far the most challenging job she had done in her life. Bringing up Annabel and making a home for David. As achievements went, they weren't all that remarkable. They'd look terrible on a CV. But it was what she was happy doing.

She remembered her earlier conversation with Diane and realised she had got things out of proportion. There was nothing wrong with being a wife and being treated like a wife. And the hell with my past triumphs, she thought. I might have been brilliant in my day. But my day is long gone and it's high time I accepted it.

She reached out for Annabel's hand, feeling reassured at the way the girl clung to her. This is where I belong, she told herself. I'm needed here to provide love and support and back-up for my family.

She wondered why she had ever doubted it.

Chapter Four

It was well past midnight before the last guests went, leaving the house in a shambles.

Sally surveyed the wreckage of her drawing-room and wondered why it was always this way. No matter how many helpers she hired, not one of them stayed late enough to clear up afterwards. She supposed it was something to do with their unions. Absently she began to pick up glasses and empty ashtrays. David stopped her.

'Don't you think you've done enough?' he chided.

She made a face.

'I hate to leave it like this for Mrs Swann to face on her own.'

'It's what I pay her for,' David sighed, despairing at his wife's concern for domestics. He suspected she tidied before and after someone came to clean and he decided that tonight he'd had enough of it.

'Look,' he said, as patiently as he could, 'why don't I get us both a drink and we'll have it in the study.'

'But darling, it's almost one o'clock.'

He thought about it for a moment, then he said, 'I know it's late, but there's something we have to talk about.'

She looked weary.

'Are you sure it can't wait till tomorrow?'

He was briefly tempted to give in to her. He was definitely past his best and what he had to say required all his powers of persuasion. Then he thought, no. I've already put this off too long. If I don't tell her now, I'm never going to. He put his arm round her shoulders and led her into the book-lined study.

'Sit down and I'll organise the nightcap,' he told her. Then he disappeared next door, returning with two brandy snifters and a bottle of Hine.

'Sorry I couldn't find anything grander, but Mrs Swann seems to have hidden the Armagnac.'

Sally grinned lazily and snuggled deeper into the leather wing chair.

'I wouldn't worry,' she told him, 'I've drunk so much tonight, I probably wouldn't know the difference.'

She watched as David uncorked the brandy and poured them both a measure. They had done this after parties for years, sitting up till all hours discussing their guests and whether they had achieved what they had set out to do. Recently they seemed to have got out of the habit, and she was glad she had let David persuade her to stay up. She took hold of the glass he held out to her and warmed it in her hands.

'What was it you wanted to talk about?' she asked curiously.

David didn't answer her for a while. Instead he walked over to the ornate teak desk Sally had given him for some past birthday, and settled himself behind it.

'Darling, you're not going to like what I've got to tell you.'

'Tell me anyway,' she said.

He held the brandy balloon under his nose, inhaling the perfume. She thought he was going to gulp it straight down, only he changed his mind and put it on the desk.

'I'm leaving,' he said.

At first she couldn't comprehend what he was saying.

'Where will you go at this time of night?'

'I don't mean I'm going right now. I'll pack my things in the morning.'

She felt the dark, masculine study closing in on her. And she wondered if she was really awake, or whether this was some nightmare brought on by too much rich food.

'I don't understand,' she said faintly. 'Why would you want

22

to leave me? You were saying a couple of hours ago what a great wife I am.'

Sally cast her mind back to the party and wondered if she was going mad. David had been so exuberant tonight, drinking champagne and making speeches. Surely she would have noticed if anything had been wrong. She looked at her husband behind his oversized desk and realised she hadn't been watching him closely enough. If things had been normal they'd have been drinking their brandy curled up together on the sofa, not sitting miles apart from each other like strangers. She thought about going over and putting her arms round him, but her instincts told her it was too soon. She needed to get to the bottom of this sudden declaration before she made any moves at all. He hadn't made any reply to her question, so she decided to push him a little.

'How can I be a great wife one moment and an abandoned one the next?' she said, trying to keep it light. Then she wished she hadn't, for she saw there were tears in his eyes.

'It's not your fault.'

'If it's not me,' she said softly, 'what the hell is it?'

'Everything else in my life. The office. The pressure of keeping up this house. The pressure of just being me. The pefect Mr Fixit, pouring champagne for all comers.'

'But you loved all those things. And you're good at them.'

He took hold of his brandy then, downing most of it in one gulp.

'I'm not good at them. Not any more. All I am is one big phoney pretending to be something I'm not. Tonight's performance was all part of the act.'

Sally thought of asking if the little speech about her was a fabrication as well, but she resisted.

Instead she said:

'Suppose you tell me about what's bugging you before it drives us both insane.'

For a moment David didn't say anything. He simply put his head in his hands and stared down at his desk. Just as she was about to prompt him again, he started to speak:

'A few months ago, maybe it was as long as a year ago, I discovered I wasn't enjoying the business the way I used to. The clients started to get on my nerves; I resented their demands. A couple of times I got close to losing my temper in meetings. At the time I thought I was getting overtired. So I took a holiday.'

Sally looked at him.

'The package to Mauritius last winter. Is that what you're talking about?'

He nodded.

'It didn't work though. The minute I got back to the agency all the old feelings came back. It got to the point where I couldn't stand lunching and listening to all the usual platitudes being trotted out about the business. You probably don't remember, but agency lunches are like a kind of ritual dance.'

She cut across him then.

'I do remember. I remember you dancing with the best of them and winning the biggest prizes. You were marvellous, David. The best public relations man ever. You only had to go to a party and accounts would fall into your hands.' Sally paused, then she said, 'What happened to you?'

For the first time since they started the conversation, he made an attempt at a smile.

'I got bored, I suppose. Bored and disenchanted.'

'So you're going to run away from everything,' she said. 'Is that it?'

'No, it's not it. And I'm not running away.'

'Then what are you doing?'

'I'm taking a break and going away for a while. Jeremy can handle the agency perfectly well without me. And I daresay you'll be pleased to get me out of your hair.'

She tried to smile, but it didn't quite come off.

'Why would I be pleased? We've been together for nearly twenty years. I'm used to you. More than used to you. I've come to depend on you being around in my life. I don't know what I'd do if you weren't there.'

'You'd manage. You've got your friends and the tennis club.

And there's Annabel of course. She'll keep you running around, if I know my daughter.'

Suddenly Sally realised that David was serious after all. He wasn't just complaining about being overstressed. He was doing something about it. And that something clearly didn't include her. She fought down rising panic, knowing that if she broke down now, she might lose everything.

'How long are you thinking of going away from me?' she asked, doing her best to keep her voice under control.

The question caught him off balance and he played for time by pouring them both another drink. When he finally answered her, he couldn't quite meet her eye.

'I haven't made any definite plans,' he told her. 'I want to travel around for a bit, get some space around me so I can decide what I'm going to do with the rest of my life.'

Sally looked at her husband, wondering what had happened to change him so. Until now their lives had been happy enough. The old passion they had shared at the beginning had died out, but that happened in every marriage. Love changes, she reasoned. It changes into friendship and trust and the deep-down security of knowing there is one human being you can really count on.

She began to realise that David was slipping away from her. If he really did go travelling she knew she wouldn't be able to count on him any more. He'd be like an animal set free, an animal who no longer knew its home. The panic she'd tried to force down overwhelmed her. She got up from her chair and went over to where he was sitting.

'Don't leave me,' she begged. 'Take me with you. I'd go anywhere, do anything, as long as we could be together.'

He put his arm round her waist and drew her close.

'You wouldn't, you know. You think you could cope with something different to the life you've built around you, but it's not possible any more. You're not the little girl I married. You're the wife I talked about tonight at the party.'

'I could change.'

He looked at her affectionately.

25

'Why would you want to do that? You've earned this lifestyle, this house, the designer dresses. You're comfortable around money and I've no intention of making you uncomfortable.'

She moved away from him now, aware he was trying to get round her.

Experience taught her that if she let David have his way, he'd end up persuading her that a separation was what she really wanted, when it was the last thing on her mind.

'I can do without the designer dresses,' she said. I haven't had them for all that long, whatever you say.'

She saw she was banging her head against a brick wall, for David looked adamant now.

'It still wouldn't work,' he said sadly. 'We've grown too far apart.'

The feeling of unreality she felt earlier came back to her. For she didn't know they'd grown apart. In her ignorance, she imagined they were closer than ever. She felt tears trickle down her cheeks and she made no attempt to stop them.

'I thought we were so happy,' she sobbed. 'I thought you loved me.'

He got up and went over to her, cradling her in his arms while she cried it all out. Then when it was over he took her by the hand and led her over to the sofa where they always sat.

'I'm not such a bastard,' he said, settling her down beside him. 'I meant everything I said in that speech tonight. You've been a wonderful wife and we've had a great life together.'

She looked at him bitterly.

'So why do you want to throw it all away?'

David sighed.

'Because I've changed.

'How have you changed?'

He looked rueful.

'I've Grown up, I suppose. When we first got together I was so lost I needed someone to lean on and look after me. And you were there and I loved you for it.'

There was a small leaden silence.

'And now you've grown-up you don't need me anymore.'

She saw the regret written across his face and realised she'd got to him. In the old days, the days before today, she would have apologised for the barb, sworn she didn't mean it. Only she did mean it, and she had no intention of taking it back.

'Stop being angry with me,' he begged. 'I can't bear it when you're angry.'

'You might have thought of that before you decided to leave me.'

'I did think of it. I stayed awake at night worrying about how you'd take it and whether you would fall apart.'

She smiled grimly.

'Well I'm still in one piece. Though it's no thanks to you.'

The space between them was so cold it could have frozen solid. Nothing and no-one could have got through it. Except David and David's determination. For in the middle of everything, he reached out for her, pulling her close and kissing her full on the mouth.

She pulled away.

'What did you do that for?'

'Affection, fondness. I couldn't bear to see you so sad.'

'So you thought a little sex might cheer me up?'

He looked at her in the intimate way he always reserved for their private moments.

'It always has done.'

She should have got out of the sofa there and then and marched up to the spare room, locking the door against him. Only she couldn't. Her limbs were suddenly made of lead and a curious inertia came over her, halting the slightest movement. All she could do was watch while David unhooked the front of her expensive dress and slid his hands inside it. Her breasts responded instantly, hardening at the tips as if his touch was precisely what they were waiting for. How my body betrays me, Sally thought. I tell him I hate him for what he's doing and all the time I can't wait for him to go on.

And she couldn't. He had parted the front of her dress now and the whole thing had fallen around her waist without her

27

making the slightest effort to gather it together again. There's no hope for me, she thought. I've been loving David and wanting David for too many years to turn it off like a fax machine.

He seemed to sense this, for he was gently pulling her out of her dress. And she knew that if they went on like this they would end up making love right there on the library floor.

She knew David knew it too, for all at once he grinned.

'Why don't we finish what we started? Nobody's going to walk in on us.'

All at once she didn't care any more. The party, David's shocking announcement, her sense of desolation suddenly disappeared. All she could feel was David's hands on her body. David's breath on her neck.

She started undressing him, loosening his belt and unzipping his fly until the hardness of him was in her hand. She got rid of her gown and all the extravagant lacy underpinnings that went with it. Then she lay down and parted her legs and waited for David to come to her.

He took his time. Tonight David wanted to play all the games she thought they'd abandoned years ago. He roused her with his fingers. After he'd finished, he roused her with his tongue. Then just when she thought she'd faint with desire, he mounted her and went inside her.

For a moment she tensed, then their own familiar rhythm took over and she lost herself in him.

David packed two overnight bags the following morning. Then he brought Sally a cup of tea in bed and told her he would send for the rest of his things. She propped herself up against the pillows, listening to what he was saying and wondering if he really meant it.

They had slept in each others' arms all night. And when she had woken in the early hours and started to cry, he had wiped her tears away and told her there was nothing to worry about. He would always look after her.

Now in the cold light of day it didn't look as if he had meant that at all.

'What have you decided to do?' she asked, looking fearful.

'I thought I'd stay in the London flat for a bit while I sorted things out.'

That sounded ominous, Sally thought, taking a sip of her tea.

'What are you sorting out exactly?'

David sat down heavily on the end of the bed.

'Chandos has got to go on functioning,' he told her, 'whether I'm there or not. So I've got to revamp the team and tell the clients I'm leaving them in good hands.'

She put down the tea on her bedside table, slopping it in the saucer.

'So you are going then?'

'I didn't say I wasn't.'

She rubbed last night's mascara out of her eyes, realising too late that she looked like hell.

'So you didn't mean what you told me in bed.'

For a moment he looked worried.

'I say a lot of things in bed. What are you talking about?'

Sally looked at him, wondering if he had the slightest inkling of the promise he had made.

'You said you would always look after me.'

She waited for him to deny it, only it didn't happen. Instead he reached out over the coverlet until he found one of her hands. Then he held it in his, squeezing it to reassure her.

'I will always look after you,' he told her gently. 'Why do you think it's so important the agency goes on running? The money Chandos makes will keep you and Annabel in this house.'

She felt obscurely disappointed.

'It's not going to keep you in this house though, is it?'

He let go of her hand and stood up.

'Sally, we went through all that last night.'

'And you think that's enough,' she said bitterly. 'You think that pathetic little goodbye speech is enough to shut me up. Well its not. We've been married to each other half our lives. I need a bit more convincing before you serve me with my severance papers.'

She'd put him on the spot. She could see from the nervous

tic that had started up under one of his eyes that David was beginning to feel as lousy as she was. Good, she thought. He can't just walk out of here as if it was some kind of luxury hotel. David must have realised this, for he sat down on the bed again.

'I can't go over the whole thing again now,' he said, looking sheepish, 'but you're right. We have to talk some more.'

She looked at him.

'Do you want to come down here again?'

He shook his head.

'It would be easier in London. Why don't we have dinner in a week or so when we've both calmed down a bit?'

Chapter Five

Diane

Diane normally had a sales meeting on Fridays. Only this Friday's meeting had been unexpectedly cancelled, so before she could get tied up in something else, she grabbed her bag and told her secretary to hold all calls. She would spend the rest of the day strolling round the West End checking out Browns and Ralph Lauren with a brief look in at the Chanel boutique. She needed to know what the competition was up to and today was a heaven-sent opportunity.

By five thirty she'd seen all she needed, so she hailed a cab in Piccadilly and directed the driver to the tree-lined street in Kensington where she lived. As soon as she opened the door of her flat she knew the cleaner had been. The mail was neatly stacked on her coffee table and there was a huge bunch of flowers standing in a vase in the hall. She fought down a feeling of annoyance. Martha was always doing that, adding little touches in an attempt to turn the flat into a home.

And there was no point. This place wasn't a home. It was a pad for a successful career woman. She picked up the flowers from the Italian marble table and carried them through to the kitchen. Then she opened the fridge, extracted a bottle of cold white Soave and padded back into her inner sanctum.

There was something almost monastic about the room where she lived. Everything was painted white. Even the floorboards were white, with the starkness relieved by pastel-coloured Chinese rugs. When she had first moved in she had told her decorator that she wanted it to look like a penthouse in Manhattan, and he had taken her at her word. All her furniture had been specially imported from Milan and looked as if it belonged in a museum. The pictures were splashy and modern and came from Amsterdam by way of New York. And the whole place had a stillness about it, as if somebody had sprayed it with hair lacquer, setting its gloss for ever.

She had lived here in solitary splendour for ten years, ever since she came to London. And she had never doubted the rightness of her surroundings. They exactly reflected all the things she wanted to be when she left the provinces behind her.

Manchester, she thought, remembering. The arse end of the world. Then she started to feel guilty. It wasn't that bad, she thought. It only felt that way because I was struggling to make my name in fashion. And it was tough going on a provincial paper. She recalled the stodgy tweeds she had to push, and the local tacky boutiques and she winced. If I'd stayed I would have got nowhere, she thought. I had to leave newspapers, even though I loved them.

She had begun to work for the Chic boutique group in the early eighties, when women were being taken more seriously in business. It meant uprooting and moving to London.

And it was at that moment she decided to change herself. She had always been tall, pale and dramatic, like the heroine of a Verdi opera. But she knew none of that would cut any ice in the big city. The town was awash with ambitious beauties. And she needed more than that, which is how she found style.

She started with the apartment, spending more than she could afford on a trendy decorator. Then she revamped her own look. She lost ten pounds on a crash diet. Then when she knew she could carry it off, she paid a visit to Armani in Sloane Street, adopting the designer's mannish jackets and pencil pants as her new uniform. The managing director of Chic boutiques picked her out in her first week.

'Who the hell is that?' he demanded.

The head of marketing, the department for which she worked,

mumbled something about her coming from some provincial paper. But the top man wouldn't be fobbed off with her CV. This creature didn't look like a journalist from the sticks. She could have been a top model or a pop star. And because appearances counted for everything in fashion, he decided to give her a chance.

She was given a small project that all promising newcomers were put to work on. Her brief was to come up with a range of clothes for school leavers. And the man she answered to showed her where to find all the background she needed. She was taken across to the files, where all the old teenage collections were stored. But Diane wasn't in the least bit interested. She had no use for other people's old ideas. What she needed was inspiration.

So she went exploring. First she checked out all the junior departments in the big stores. Then she checked out the teenagers themselves. She wandered around Brixton and Clapham and the World's End of the King's Road. When her curiosity was satisfied, she went to work on a series of sketches. In retrospect what she was creating was the forerunner of punk.

The head of marketing wasn't the least bit impressed. To him the images of ripped jeans and studded neckbands were ugly and unwearable. And he forbade her to show them to anyone else. Not that she listened. She went straight to the managing director's office before anyone could stop her. Then she demanded that Simon Moyses look at her work.

He nearly didn't. If there was anything the managing director hated, it was aggressive women. Then he looked at Diane and for the first time he saw how frightened she was. Behind all that bravado she was a terrified little girl, and he let his guard down.

'You can present your work for twenty minutes,' he told her. 'Then it's over. I haven't got time for hysterical juniors.'

His words propelled her into action. Within minutes her sketches were all over his desk. And Simon looked at them in amazement. Her ideas were very raw, but there was something fresh here, something that would capture people's imagination. For a moment he was tempted to give her a chance and try out her line in his Chelsea store. Then he reconsidered. Chic didn't go in for the youth market. Their customers were high-earning career women in their twenties and thirties. He sighed, hating to let her down, hating to admit the whole excercise had been a test of her potential. So he hedged.

'Let me think about these ideas,' he told her. 'I'll get back to you.'

He didn't, of course. He put the whole problem back to his marketing director, who told Diane her project had fallen on its face.

'I did warn you,' he said, 'but you wouldn't listen.'

This time Diane did listen. And what she heard was that she had failed. She had gone out on a limb for something she believed in, and nobody had given a damn. She thought about handing in her notice and going back up North. At least she could get a well-paid job there working on a paper.

If Simon Moyses hadn't got back to her in a week, she might well have carried out her threat. Only Moyses had her number. He knew how highly strung creative people could be. Particularly the good ones. So he had his office get hold of her before she could do anything silly. There were three new projects on the stocks. He needed her input on every one of them.

Diane smiled at the memory of how she had been. How intense I was then, she marvelled, how pushy. I bet this apartment suited me down to the ground. She regarded her expensive, uncomfortable furniture and realised with regret that she was growing out of it. She didn't have things to prove any more. And she wondered if it was time to move on.

She might have thought about it for longer if it hadn't been for the answering machine. She wondered why it hadn't caught her attention earlier, for the red light was flicking on and off in a frenzy. Diane normally got one or two messages during the day, but the way the machine was going, it looked as if all her friends had decided to call at once. She got up from her squashy leather sofa and switched the tape back to start. Then she began listening.

The first message hadn't registered. Whoever had called heard they were through to a machine and put the phone down. Diane felt irritated. It was 1994 for heaven's sake. You would have thought by now people were used to talking to tapes.

The next caller was Sally. Not the usual, boisterous garrulous Sally, but a nervous Sally, hesitating over every word.

'You're not there . . . I rang your office and you weren't there either . . . er, when you get back could you ring?'

She probably rang before, Diane thought, and aborted at the last minute. The bleep sounded and Diane listened for the next message. It was Sally again. Only this time she knew what she wanted to say.

'I think I'm in trouble,' she said. 'I need to talk. Please call when you get this message.'

The next one was Sally sounding nervous and leaving the time she called. The next was Sally sounding desperate. The next was Sally sounding suicidal.

Christ, thought Diane, she must have been ringing all afternoon. She got up and hurried over to the phone, dialling Sally's number from memory. It was picked up on the first ring.

'Diane,' said Sally.

'How did you know it was me?'

'Instinct I suppose. You're always there when I need you.'

Diane sighed, and wondered what she'd done to be lumbered with the role of big sister. It was fine when they were young together, but those days were long gone.

'You'd better tell me what the problem is,' she said as kindly as she could. 'You sounded like a crazy woman on my answerphone.'

There was a small silence.

'I am a crazy woman,' Sally said, 'David walked out on me on Monday.'

'After all these years, I can't believe it. You must have got it wrong.'

'I wish I had but David sounded so sure of himself. He even said . . .' Sally started crying then and Diane realised she was never going to hear the full story unless they were face to face.

She listened while her friend poured out her misery. When

there seemed to be a pause in the sobbing, Diane came back on the line.

'Darling,' she said, 'I'm coming down to Oxford. We can't talk like this.'

'I know. When will I see you?'

She thought about jumping into her car and going right then, but the idea of the weekend rush put her off.

'Can you hold out till tomorrow, say lunchtime? I promise I won't be any later.'

She heard Sally blow her nose.

'I've gone all week without talking to anyone. Another day isn't going to make any difference.'

Diane got down to the white-painted manor house slightly before two. She hadn't meant to be so late, but the weekend rush went on longer than she expected. Every road out of London was jam-packed with families hurrying to get a breath of country air before they had to turn their cars round and head back to the pollution. And she didn't get clear of the traffic until she was on the outskirts of Oxford. From there it took her another half hour before she reached the Robinsons' leafy suburb.

By the time she pulled into their front drive, she was feeling guilty and pressured. Sally's in trouble, she thought, and all I do is get caught in a traffic jam.

She ran up to the front door, pealing on the bell with all the urgency she felt. Then Sally answered it and Diane did a double take. She didn't look like a woman who had been deserted by her husband. Every blonde hair was brushed neatly into place. Her make-up was flawless. And she'd done herself up in a cashmere lounging-suit, which made her look like a rich woman on a cruise.

'Have I come to the right place?' she asked in mock surprise. 'I expected the wreck of the Hesperus.'

'If you'd arrived yesterday, you might have found it,' Sally told her, 'but I've pulled myself together since then.'

Diane took her hand and squeezed it. 'I'm glad,' she said, 'though you might tell me what's been happening.'

Sally led her friend through the cavernous hall and into her pine-clad kitchen and poured them both a glass of wine. It was a cosy room backing onto a rose garden and Diane wondered how anyone could feel any real pain in these surroundings.

Then she heard the whole sorry story and realised she was being cavalier. For Sally had gone to bits when David walked out. Whereas most wives might have smashed the best china or done a little damage to the husband's remaining possessions, Sally did neither. She simply folded up and retired to bed.

Diane went back over the years they had known each other and realised this was completely out of character. Sally had always been the pragmatic one. She was the one who cried at setbacks.

'What on earth possessed you?' she demanded. 'David's only a man, after all.'

For the first time Sally looked indignant.

'To you he's only a man, because you've got a job and a life you can call your own. David is my life.' She looked rueful. 'Or should I say, he was my life. With him gone everything collapses.'

Diane leaned forward and took Sally's hand in an effort to comfort her.

'It only collapses if you collapse,' she said softly. 'You got out of bed didn't you? So there must be hope.'

Diane's hand was like a life raft and as she clung onto it the last few days replayed themselves in her mind. Her memory of them was crystal clear and the irony of that made her smile. The good things that happened to her never registered like that. When she tried to recall them, all she could see was a happy, muddled jumble of people and places. It was only the days she spent grieving in bed that came back to her at all vividly.

She slept a lot, she remembered. And when she wasn't sleeping, she watched television. Every now and then David would come into her mind, but the thought of him gave her such pain that she blanked him out. Only she couldn't hide from him all the time. During the nights she would dream he was still there, sleeping soundly beside her. Then she

37

would sit up in a cold panic and wonder if she was losing her mind.

Annabel noticed the change in her almost at once and wanted to know what was wrong. So Sally said she had a bug and it seemed to satisfy the girl. It wouldn't keep her quiet forever, Sally knew that. But it bought her time.

A few days later she took a look at herself. She was in the bathroom when she saw her reflection quite by chance, and it stunned her. For the woman staring back at her wasn't her at all. She looked old. It wasn't that she hadn't got make-up on or that her hair needed washing. Her eyes looked old. There was a disillusion in them that hadn't been there before and she knew that if she was going to face the world at all, she would have to find a way to hide it.

She had no idea of how long she stood in front of her mirror, thinking of ways to put herself back together. But when she'd finished, she went to work and by the end of the day she was almost normal again.

Anyone looking at her would be distracted by the glossy make-up and the way she wore her clothes. As long as they didn't look into her eyes, nobody would notice there was anything different about her at all.

Diane's voice brought her back to the present.

'Let go of my hand,' she said. 'You're killing me.'

Sally looked down to see she was making a good job of crippling her friend.

'I'm so sorry,' she said, relaxing her grip, 'I got carried away.'

Diane looked at her.

'How long has it been now since David left?'

'I don't know. About a week I suppose.'

'And does Annabel know what's going on?'

Sally wrinkled her brow.

'I told her David was away on business. I didn't want to upset her until I absolutely had to.'

Diane looked at her friend in despair.

'But you do absolutely have to. David's not going to come running home announcing he's changed his mind.'

'He might.'

There was a silence.

'What makes you say that?'

Sally wondered how much to tell Diane. To an outsider, even a close outsider like her, things did look pretty final. But she knew different. She knew that underneath all the confusion and the air of finality, there was a faint ray of hope.

How do I explain about the love-making, Sally thought frantically. How do I tell Diane that men like my husband often say things they don't really mean because they're going through a hard time.

'David's had a lot of hassle at the office,' she said, as if it explained everything. 'He's not himself at the moment.'

'You mean leaving you is just an aberration?'

'I'm pretty sure it is.'

She saw the doubt on Diane's face and ploughed on.

'David did something after the party he would never have done if he was serious about leaving me.'

Diane put down her glass of wine and the curiosity on her face made Sally feel embarrassed.

'What was it?'

There was no ducking out of this confession now. She'd dug herself in too deep, so she took a deep breath and said:

'He made love to me actually.'

If Diane was surprised she didn't show it. Instead she took a sip of her wine and absorbed this new part of the puzzle, mulling it over. Finally she said:

'Men sometimes do that when they're leaving you know. It happened to me once years ago. I think there's something about losing you forever that frightens men and turns them on at the same time.'

There was the slightest of hesitations.

'But David's not losing me forever. We're having dinner together on Saturday.'

'David's doing what?'

'I just told you. He's taking me out to San Lorenzo to talk things over. Maybe to patch things up.'

Diane didn't say anything. Instead she stared moodily at the table. Why does David have to prolong the agony, she wondered. Why does he have to lead Sally on with love-making and little dinners, instead of making a clean break of it? She sighed. It would all come to nothing, of course. And poor Sally would be on the floor again.

She wondered whether to put a stop to the whole charade and tell Sally what was really going on with her husband. Then she thought, what's the point. What's the point in hurting her even more?

Chapter Six

Diane, Manchester, 1974

It was raining the way it always did in this town. Solid, relentless curtain rods pouring out of greyness and splattering the roads and the pavements with puddles the size of lakes.

Diane sighed. The prospect of waiting for a bus to take her into Manchester filled her with gloom. The service from Sale was erratic to say the least and she had visions of huddling under an umbrella while her new boots got soggy in the downpour.

It was the boots that decided her. She had got them from one of the little designer shops in the centre of town. And just the memory of what she paid for them made her wince. Even with her discount, they were way beyond her means. And now she was going to get them ruined, unless she took action. She dialled the mini-cab number the office used and the minute the operator picked up the call he recognised her voice.

'Let me guess,' he said, 'you're either late for conference or you don't fancy waiting for the bus.'

Diane thought of saying something sharp to put him in his place. Then she looked out of the window and realised she needed him too much.

'I've got to put a story together for the early edition,' she explained hastily, 'so I can't afford to hang about.'

'Whatever you say, Diane. Would fifteen minutes be alright?'

She told him it would and put the phone down before the

operator could ask her any more questions. She had been here six months, and already the chumminess was beginning to drive her mad. Everyone from the mini-cab firm to the man on the front door of the Express building where she worked wanted to know her business. She'd be going up in the lift, fretting about a deadline and the man who pressed the buttons would tell her to cheer up. And if she ignored him, if she ignored any of them, they just pressed on with their friendly, intrusive questions until she was ready to scream.

In Surrey, where she grew up, people just didn't behave like that. Her mother taught her from an early age to keep a distance between her and what her family considered to be inferiors. They were mainly local tradesmen who were always addressed by their surnames: the postman was Mr Wells; the cleaner, Mrs Shepherd. First-name terms were reserved for equals, though Diane often worried who was and who wasn't. Daddy, she knew, was an accountant and therefore a professional man. But where did that leave their neighbours who owned a chain of dry cleaners? Or Mummy's best friend, whose husband had a construction business?

In the end she worked out her parents' criterion: people who had as much money as they did were regarded as equal.

It was a crude rule, but it seemed to work. For when she started her first job on a women's magazine everyone called her Diane, even though she was only an assistant. And everyone called the head of the typing pool Mrs Grant.

She worked her way up the fashion department, thinking she knew exactly how the world worked. Then she landed this job on the *Express* in Manchester, and everything was turned on its head.

The front doorbell went and she pulled on her raincoat and made to leave. It's ironic, she thought, this is my first really big job. I'm the fashion editor up here, yet everyone I meet treats me as if I'm their wayward daughter.

She stopped worrying about it when she saw the time. It was ten forty-five and the traffic was reduced to a one-lane crawl all the way to the University. At this rate, Diane thought, I won't be in Great Ancoats Street until lunchtime. She started to panic. She hadn't missed morning conference since she started the job. There had been one or two tight moments when she overslept, but she always managed to make it just before the editor closed his door.

This morning will be the exception, Diane fretted. There will be a gap where I'm meant to be sitting and all hell will break loose. They'll probably put one of the junior feature girls in my place and once that starts I might as well hand in my notice and be done with it. She was so wound up that she didn't notice where they were until the car pulled up in front of the black glass Express building.

For the second time that morning she looked at her watch and realised she was going to make it after all. It was eleven fifteen. She had precisely quarter of an hour to spare. With a sigh of relief, she jumped out of the cab, handed the fare through the window and pushed her way through the huge chrome doors.

By the time she got to the open-plan office on the fourth floor she had shed her raincoat and umbrella and managed to slide a comb through her hair in the ladies room. I look the part, she thought. Now all I have to do is act the part. She opened her desk drawer and started to go through her notes.

Every morning at eleven thirty, Diane and all the other heads of department sat in with the editor to decide on the next day's paper. Because they produced the Northern edition, there was always a running fight between local material and national news and features. The local coverage of the North was not published unless it was considered equal to the news from London. There have to be easier ways of making a living, Diane thought, though at that precise moment she couldn't think of any. Instead she gathered her papers together and joined the group converging on the corner office.

As she came through the door, Diane saw Bob Anderson was already behind his desk poring over layouts. His concentration was so intense that he didn't look up until everyone was seated in a semicircle in front of him. Then he finally dragged himself away from what he was doing and regarded the group. He was a heavy man with the red face of a drinker and pale, cunning little eyes that seemed to see round corners. Diane sensed he already knew what was on the schedule she held in her hands, even though she hadn't discussed it with him. She wondered if the others felt the same.

The features editor went first. He had an interview with a television actor who was doing a play for Granada. He also had a number of local round-ups, but the actor was the best thing he had and he pushed it for all he was worth.

That day he was lucky. London was planning to run an interview with an obscure art-movie director and the television star won hands down. As a bonus for saving the day, Bob Anderson let the features department get away with a single-column piece on a local fly-fishing competition and everyone started to relax.

The editor was in a receptive mood now. There was a chance they might all get their stories into the paper. Their optimism was rewarded. The picture editor managed to replace the London spread with some candid shots of the newly returned prime minister, Harold Wilson in his native Yorkshire. And the news editor scored with an exclusive on the Maze prison riots.

Now it was her turn and Diane was relieved she had something decent for a change. A local designer had just signed a contract to supply a national high street store group, and she had the first interview together with sketches of the new collection. She expected Bob to go overboard for it. Everyone else in the room seemed to like the story. Only the editor hesitated.

'I don't see it on the fashion pages,' he said finally. 'It's more of a news item.'

Diane stiffened, for she knew exactly what was coming next. Sophie Angel in London had something he liked better. She resigned herself for the inevitable.

Except it didn't come. Instead Bob leaned forward and said:

'I've got a fashion spread that will knock everyone's socks off up here.'

Diane wondered what on earth it could be. Fashion, fashion that knocked your socks off, only really happened in capital cities. She wondered if there was something going on she didn't know about. Maybe Bruce Oldfield was opening in the North, or one of the Paris designers. She shrugged off the idea. If that was happening she would have heard about it.

She saw the editor reach inside his desk and produce a set of pictures. Then he picked them up and handed them over to her. Diane did her best to control her expression, for they were some of the dowdiest shots she'd ever seen. They were all showing off some kind of tweed and it appeared as suits and hacking jackets and long lumpy skirts. She looked up.

'What's the story?' she asked. 'Is there a big name behind the designs?'

The editor shifted in his chair.

'Not exactly,' he admitted.

Now she was struggling for inspiration.

'Are they terribly cheap, is that it?' she asked, 'or is it a local firm making it into the big time?'

Anderson dismissed her questions with an irritable little wave.

'I don't get involved with frocks,' he said, 'that's what I employ you for. Why don't you be a good girl and ask the PR for all the details. His number is on the back of the pictures.'

In that instant Diane knew what was going on. Some pushy public relations man had managed to button-hole Bob Anderson. He probably did it at the golf club or at some boozy civic reception. Diane could almost picture it. Her editor would be propping up the bar and telling dirty stories and very casually one of his entourage would draw him to one side:

'There's a chap I want you to meet. He could be useful to the paper.'

The old man would fall for it, of course. It was easy to lead him on when he'd had one too many. And the slimy toad of a PR man would sell him whatever bill of goods was going that day. Clearly when Bob ran into him he was trying to get a plug for these awful tweeds.

She turned over the pictures to find out who the shyster was and discovered his name was David Robinson and he was a director of an outfit called Omega. She dimly recalled seeing

Omega's name linked with an international cosmetics company and a high-class handbag manufacturer.

It's just my luck, Diane thought, that I have to get landed with the dud.

She could have dropped the pictures straight into the fashion page and called it a day. It wasn't her fault they were bloody awful. The blame lay entirely with her editor. Then she thought, who is going to know that? My readers won't have a clue. And my rivals will think I'm losing my touch. She looked at the glossy ten by twelves spread out over her desk and knew she had to do something about them.

Wearily she picked up the phone and dialled Omega's number. David Robinson came on the line the minute she asked for him.

'You want some details about the tweeds,' he said all brisk and helpful.

Not so fast, Diane thought.

'I want to see the tweeds before we go any further,' she told him. 'I was thinking we might do our own pictures.'

'That's a great idea. How soon do you want them?'

Diane thought for a moment. There wasn't enough time to reshoot and make tomorrow's paper. It would have to be held over for next week.

'If you send a messenger over in the next couple of days, that should be OK.'

The tweeds were there two hours later, and Diane felt vaguely irritated. She knew the PR man was only trying to be helpful, but his efficiency was a pressure all in itself. She told her secretary to take the clothes through to the studio, then she got on with what she was doing.

Three days later Diane took a good look at the tweeds and found they were better than she expected. The publicity photos had made them look lumpen because whoever shot them was trying to make some kind of fashion statement. The models were posing they way they might have done for Chanel, and that was all wrong. These were good tweed suits, nicely made

46

and unpretentious. If she showed them for what they were, Diane thought, she might have something worth putting on her page.

She got hold of Amanda Williams, Manchester's top model agent.

'Have any of your girls got county connections? You know, stately homes in Cheshire, that sort of thing.'

The agent thought for a moment.

'There's no-one on my books,' she said, 'but one of my assistants has a father who hunts.'

Diane began to think she was wasting her time, but she gave it one last shot.

'The huntsman,' she said, 'does he keep his horses anywhere we can photograph?'

Amanda laughed.

'You bet he does. Lord Fordham's horses are stabled in his own yard. At the back of the manor house.' After a pause, she went on, 'I'd have to ask Gilly if she can talk her father into letting you use it. What's the job?'

Diane told her about the tweed suits.

'If we put them in the right setting on the right girls, we might get something good.'

The following week *Express* fashion devoted itself to the county look. Aristocratic-looking girls nuzzled up to horses, sat in front of roaring fires, strode out through windblown fields. It was the kind of thing Ralph Lauren was starting to make his name with and the response was surprising.

Everyone wanted the high-born country lady look. Diane's tiny department was deluged with readers's letters wanting to know where they could buy the clothes in the pictures. And it wasn't just letters. The phone never stopped ringing, which is why Diane answered her own line when David Robinson called.

She had made up her mind that once she'd got rid of this job, she'd have nothing more to do with him or Omega Public Relations. Yet here he was on the end of her phone, chattering on as if he was her best friend.

'What you did for my tweeds was fantastic,' he enthused. 'The client doesn't know what's hit him. How clever you are.'

She decided to put a stop to his burble. It might go down well with her editor, but she'd heard too much of it to be impressed.

'Why don't you save your thanks for Bob Anderson,' she said drily. 'He got your client in the paper. I was just doing my job.'

For one wonderful moment during the silence that followed Diane thought she'd got rid of the pushy David Robinson. But she was out of luck. He came right back on a different tack.

'I suppose you hate me, don't you?'

'Hate's a bit strong. Let's just say I don't have time for people who go over my head.'

Again he didn't say anything, and when he came back on the line, his voice was softer, as if she'd winded him.

'You're quite right, of course,' he told her. 'I should have come to you first, but Bob's an old friend and I took the lazy way out. Will you accept my apologies?'

Diane didn't have much choice really. She was hardly going to tell him to go to hell.

'I don't mind calling a truce,' she said cautiously.

'Good,' he replied, 'Then you'll let me take you out to lunch.'

She sighed. There was no way she was going to get out of this one. She might as well give in gracefully and get it over with. She picked up her diary and started turning the pages.

'How about the week after next . . .'

She had chosen to meet him in the Piccadilly Hotel because there was something anonymous about it that appealed to her. There were places like this in every big city, multi-storey citadels built of chrome and glass that catered for businessmen on expense accounts. And that's exactly what David Robinson was, a businessman trying to make the most of what she suspected was a tenuous connection. He deserved exactly an hour of her time before she made her excuses and left.

Diane arrived in the American-style lobby of the Piccadilly on the dot of one and made her way directly to the bank of lifts. There was one free almost immediately and she got in and pressed the button for the top floor, which was taken up almost entirely by the main restaurant.

As she walked into the bar area, Diane scanned the crowd. It was packed that day with a visiting convention of insurance salesmen, all wearing little badges saying who they were. The whole length of the bar was occupied, and even the tables by the windows which were usually free were not so today. Diane inhaled the thick cigarette fug around her and began to regret choosing this place. Who was she punishing, she wondered, some PR man who wouldn't know the difference or herself? She began to struggle her way through to the restaurant entrance, when she felt a hand on her arm.

'Diane Craven,' said a familiar voice. She looked up and there he was.

She hadn't prepared herself for the fact that David Robinson might be in any way remarkable. In her mind's eye he was a middle-aged executive in an off-the-peg suit. Yet this man didn't answer to the description at all. He was a few years older than she was with a shock of dark hair and a lazy, sensual face that made her think he may have Italian ancestry. Yet it wasn't his good looks that impressed her. Newspaper offices were littered with glamorous young men. What got to Diane was how finished David was, as if some stylist had been instructed to produce the perfect gentleman, from his handmade shoes to his Rolex watch, and this was the result. She took a step backwards.

'David Robinson,' she said faintly, 'I'm glad you got here first.'

He didn't stand on ceremony. Instead he propelled her out of the smokey bar and into the cavern of a restaurant. It was as deserted as the bar was full, yet she felt ill at ease. Normally she wouldn't have noticed the garish carpet or the plastic fitments, but on David Robinson's arm it all registered.

She had insisted on this big, brash salesman's mecca and now she was marked with it. The man with her would judge her to be at home in places like this and she groaned inwardly. How could I have been so stupid, she thought.

49

The head waiter descended on them the minute they got in the door, apologising for the big party in the bar.

'They are lunching in a private room,' he told them, 'so you won't be disturbed.'

David grinned.

'Good,' he said. 'I've got a lot to say to this lady.'

It was the sort of remark that set her teeth on edge, yet he said it with such sincerity that she couldn't hate him for it. For a moment she almost believed that David really did want to be her friend. Then he asked the waiter to bring them a bottle of champagne and she came back to reality. This was a PR man spending his company's money to impress her. She had to hold onto that.

'Tell me about your agency,' she said, 'I hear you handle more interesting accounts than Scottish tweed.'

David regarded her.

'I can send you the client list, if you want, but I didn't invite you to lunch to sell Omega.'

'Then why are we here?'

'I told you on the phone. I made a blunder by going to Bob with a story and I wanted to put it right.'

The champagne arrived, accompanied by two huge leather-bound menus and Diane waited until the waiter had gone away before she spoke again.

'You put things right when you apologised on the phone,' she told him. 'I don't need a grand gesture.'

He picked up one of the crystal flutes and put it in her hand.

'Drink this,' he said, 'and stop being so prickly.'

'I wasn't being prickly.'

'Yes you were, you've been hell from the first minute I spoke to you in your office. It's like dealing with an iceberg. Your husband, poor man, deserves an award for bravery.'

She willed herself to stop smiling.

'I don't have a husband.'

'I can't say I'm surprised.'

She started to giggle, the tension inside her ebbing away with her laughter.

50

'Why are you so rude to me?' she demanded. 'Nobody speaks to me like that.'

'Someone needed to,' he said gently. 'It's my guess you've been hiding behind your London manners ever since you came to this town.'

She remembered her irritation with the over-familiar taxi drivers and the pushy doormen. Everyone was trying to make her welcome and all she could do was shut them out.

'How do you know about it?' she asked.

He picked up his champagne, downing half the glass in one swallow.

'I'm in public relations,' he told her. 'It's my job to know.'

After that it was easy. David wanted to know all about her. He wanted to know what her father did and where she went to school and why she chose to go into journalism instead of settling down and getting married.

And she told him the whole story. All her family had been suburban and she had grown up in a house on the edge of a golf course outside Woking.

'I didn't have a miserable childhood,' she admitted, 'but it was so safe and so predictable that I felt stifled. Daddy had only had one job all his life, as a partner in a firm of accountants, and he thought everyone else should behave like him. He genuinely thought all I wanted was to marry some solid citizen and raise a family.'

David looked at her.

'Wasn't that on your agenda at all? I thought that was what most girls wanted.'

She considered for a moment.

'Don't lump me together with most girls. My parents did that and they made a mistake.'

She remembered the first time she mentioned staying on at school to her father. He'd hit the roof because he didn't believe she should be wasting her time studying something she would never use. Instead he wanted her to take a course at the Cordon Bleu so that she would be an asset to her future husband.

It was then she decided there wouldn't be a husband. Or if there

51

was, he would happen in the dim and distant future, after she'd managed to break away from the dismal greyness into which she had been born.

She turned down the Cordon Bleu course and the offer of secretarial college, insisting on taking her A Levels. In the end her parents caved in and she surprised them both by getting top grades in four subjects. Her teachers wanted her to go to University, there was even a chance of Oxbridge. But she knew better than to push her family into that. There would be war if she even thought about it.

So she started to apply for jobs instead. Her father knew nothing about it until she had been accepted as an assistant on *Style* magazine. She got the job on the strength of her A Levels and the fact that she was prepared to accept a miniscule salary. Because she knew she'd have to live at home until her prospects improved, she played the whole thing down.

'It will keep me occupied until I find a husband,' she told her parents.

And they swallowed it because they had no choice. They lived to regret it. For Diane climbed the ladder quickly. Escape from Woking was all the incentive she needed and she networked frantically, getting to know all the women's editors on the big magazines. Six months after she started on *Style*, she was headhunted to *Tatler* to work in the fashion department. She started to make her name there and if she had chosen she could have become one of the formidable names in fashion. But it was an insular world, as narrow and restricting as Woking, And Diane had fought too hard to leave one ghetto to be trapped into another.

Then she heard on the grapevine that there was a job going on the Manchester *Express*, and she applied for it immediately.

'I knew it would probably be difficult making such a huge move,' she told David, 'but I had to do it.'

'And was it difficult?'

She looked at the elegant, sexy-looking man sitting opposite her and thought it might have been a piece of cake if she'd known him all along.

'It was a wrench leaving London,' she admitted, 'but I'm glad I got away. At least up here, the parents can't wheel on one of their suitable young men.'

They had just about finished lunch and Diane glanced at her watch and saw it was gone three. She was an hour over the limit she had set herself, yet she didn't feel badly about it at all. For quite unexpectedly she realised she was falling in love.

Chapter Seven

Diane waited all week for David to call her, and when he didn't she took her courage into her hands and called him. It didn't get her very far. David was pleased to hear from her, but in a hurry.

'I'm rushing into a meeting,' he told her. 'I'll get back to you.'

Then when he didn't get back and Diane called again, he was full of apologies.

'I'm off my feet,' he said by way explanation, 'we've just landed a big new American client and it's all systems go.'

They talked about the new account; then Diane started on her own office gossip and he cut her off.

'Someone's just come in to see me,' he told her, 'I have to go.'

'When am I going to see you?' she asked, knowing how desperate she sounded and hating herself for it.

'When I get back from the States. They're sending a group of us over to meet the new client. I'll call you the minute I get home.'

She wondered if he was doing it on purpose, giving her the come-on over lunch, then suddenly backing off. Men had played with her like that before, thinking this form of deliberate cruelty turned her on. The problem is, she thought ruefully, it does turn me on. Every time some man plays me for a fool, I come running after him like a hungry puppy. She hoped against hope that David wasn't that kind of man, that he was simply as busy as he said he was.

Three days later she realised she was hoping for too much. For it was then she saw David in a local steak house. She was standing at the bar waiting for a table when she recognised David in the middle of a big party and she knew she couldn't stay.

'We've got to get out of here,' she told her companion. 'I'll explain later.'

Cissy Grey, who ran the woman's page on the *Mail*, knew an emergency when she saw one and got up immediately.

'You look as if you've seen a ghost.'

'Not a ghost. Just a lying bastard of a man.'

They got out into the street and Cissy hailed a taxi.

'There's an Indian place near here where you won't see anyone. Then you can tell me what all this is about.'

Cissy was one of the few friends Diane had made in Manchester. She was small and blonde and looked like Barbara Windsor, and because of it men didn't take her seriously. They would date her once or twice, then drop her when something classier came along.

In a way that was what drew Diane to her, for she had the same kind of bad luck with men, though for totally different reasons. For Diane was only interested in men who didn't want her. She had been so terrified of being pushed into the arms of a suitable husband that she avoided decent men like the plague. She could cope with a shallow shit who wanted a fling, which she did, regularly, right to the bitter end, when she came and cried on Cissy's shoulder.

Tonight the blonde knew they were in for a long session, so the moment they got into the Indian restaurant, she came to the point.

'Who was he, then?' she asked.

Diane looked pained.

'Someone I met ten days ago. He came on very strong over lunch, so I thought he was interested.'

'Only he wasn't?'

Diane signalled the Indian waiter to bring them some drinks.

'I called a couple of times and he was always rushed off his feet. Then he said we'd get together after some trip he was making to the States.'

She paused while the waiter delivered the white wine to their table and uncorked the bottle. Then she said:

'David was meant to be in the States when I saw him tonight. And I felt so stupid about the whole thing, I got up and ran for my life.'

Cissy leaned forward, considering what she had been told.

'If you called this man, I can only guess he's in the fashion business and it was something to do with work. You wouldn't have picked up the phone otherwise.'

Diane smiled.

'You can stop fishing,' she told her friend, 'his name is David Robinson and he works for Omega PR.'

'That David Robinson. No wonder you're having trouble.'

Diane was intrigued.

'I didn't realise you knew him.'

'I don't know David. Nobody does. The guy is a complete mystery.'

'Come off it, I saw him with a group of friends just now.'

Cissy prayed for patience.

'I'm not saying David doesn't have friends. He probably knows more people than you and I put together. But they don't mean anything to him. They're there for a purpose: to help David, and as long as they're useful he lets them stay around.'

Diane remembered how eager David was to know her when she was promoting his tweeds.

'I suppose I was useful to him for a bit,' she said ruefully.

'And you'll be useful to him again,' Cissy told her, 'so don't think you've seen the last of David. The next time he needs you he'll be all over you like a rash.'

She knew her friend was trying to warn her off, but Diane couldn't put David aside so easily. She had known him for the length of a lunchtime, yet he had managed to convince her that he was the only man who was capable of understanding her. It was nonsense, of course. She knew that, but part of her was bewitched so she went on asking Cissy about David.

It turned out she'd come to the right person, for Cissy and David had grown up together. Her family, like his, were wealthy and Jewish and lived in prosperous Broughton Park.

'Looking at it now,' she told Diane, 'it was a real ghetto. But when we were little, Broughton Park just seemed to be the best place in Manchester. It had bigger houses than anywhere else. Lots of my friends' parents had swimming-pools. And everyone knew everyone else. You couldn't walk down the street without bumping into somebody you knew.'

Diane looked impatient.

'How did David fit into all this?'

Cissy smiled.

'Like a glove in the beginning. His father was, and still is, a big force in the rag trade. The family had been at it for generations. And David, being the eldest of three brothers, looked set to inherit the family factories. He probably would have done, if it hadn't been for his mother.'

As Cissy talked about David, a vision of Rose Robinson came into her mind. She was a tall, rather imposing woman with none of the warmth you normally associate with Yiddisher mommas. Cissy and her friends always used to say she modelled herself on the Queen Mother, for there was a grandness about her.

She wanted David to be grand as well, Cissy thought. That's why she insisted he went to public school. As she remembered it, the idea of sending little, chubby, eager-to-please David to some stuffy English institution seemed even more ludicrous today than it had done all those years ago. But Rose wouldn't be budged. She'd even chosen Stowe, because they took in Jewish boys.

And in the end David went, because he didn't want to let her down. To start with he didn't fit in at all. His Manchester accent set him apart as much as his Jewishness. And he was mercilessly teased by the other boys, who imitated the way he talked, and made sly jokes about his not going into chapel for prayers.

In his first year, David begged his parents to take him away. He'd trail home every holiday looking haunted and unhappy. And

Albert prevailed on his wife to see reason. But she wouldn't be moved.

'David will learn to be like the others,' she predicted. 'It's what I want for him.'

And she got her way in the end. For in time David's natural survival instinct took over and he adapted to his new world. He lost most of his Northern vowels, and he began to adopt the arrogant, slightly hectoring stance of the privileged upper classes. Rose thought it was wonderful. As the change in David became more apparent, she was all over him, praising him to the skies. In her eyes David could never do any wrong, but now he had this glossy new exterior he assumed the status of a minor god. This did not bode well for the family business. For as a minor god, David had no intention of dirtying his hands in a factory.

When he finally left Stowe, David announced he wanted nothing to do with the rag trade. Instead he was going to drop out for a year and back-pack across India. Albert was all for letting him go, thinking the experience would be so horrible he'd come running back to Manchester begging to be taken into the family fold. But, as always, he allowed himself to be prevailed upon by Rose.

'Use your influence to find him a decent job,' she instructed.

And when Albert said he had no influence, she pointed out that he had a lot of pull in public relations. He used a promotions outfit called Omega to push his fashion lines. And to date he was their biggest client.

Somewhat unwillingly, Albert paid a visit to Eric Peebles, Omega's managing director, and asked his favour. Peebles obliged on condition that if David turned out to be a no-hoper, he could get rid of him after six months. The two men shook on it, then Albert went home to complete the negotiation by persuading David to stay in Manchester. It wasn't difficult. As always, Rose smoothed the path, telling David what a big success he was going to be as a PR man.

'With the polish you got at Stowe,' she told him, 'you'll run rings round everybody at Omega.'

Cissy shuddered slightly thinking about Rose. She was such

a pushy woman, so dedicated to shaping her favourite son that she didn't stop to think what damage she could do to him. It was one thing, she thought, to give David self-confidence, but to convince him that he was invincible was another. If anyone believed that about themselves, they became arrogant at best and dangerous at worst. To her certain knowledge, David was guilty on both counts.

She saw Diane looking at her and came back to the story she was telling.

'As you've doubtless realised, David was a big success at Omega. He had a knack for the public relations game and quite soon Eric Peebles was talking about keeping him on and making him a junior partner.'

'I bet his mother was pleased.'

'She was actually, though I doubt if she would have been quite so excited if she'd known just how her David had pulled it off.'

Diane looked puzzled.

'What do you mean?'

'I told you David was a user,' Cissy said, 'but what I didn't mention is that he has no conscience about the people he uses. He's quite capable of cutting any of his friends into tiny pieces without giving it a moment's thought.'

'Aren't you being a bit hard on him?'

There was a short silence while Cissy turned it over in her mind.

'Maybe I am,' she said after a bit, 'but I don't think so. Joe Slackman doesn't think so either.'

'Who the hell is Joe Slackman?'

'Somebody that David trod on. If you want to know about it, call him at Omega. He works there and he's a friend of mine. Just mention my name.'

Joe Slackman was a hard-working, efficient executive who was never going to get anywhere. It wasn't that he didn't have flair. He knew his trade as well as the next man. But he lacked the one thing that David Robinson had in spades. He lacked motivation.

Diane realised this when she met him after work in a wine bar near the station. He was a slight man in his forties with thinning hair and sloping shoulders that he made no attempt to disguise with fancy tailoring. If he'd smartened himself up, Joe might have passed for attractive, but he didn't see the point in trying any harder than he had to, and Diane imagined it had been his downfall.

After twenty minutes with Joe, she realised she had been wrong about her last assumption. Joe's downfall at Omega had been largely due to David. Though getting the whole story out of him was not easy. She tried flattery and all the other tricks in her journalist's armoury, but Joe was a proud man and couldn't be cajoled into demeaning himself.

So finally Diane did what she should have done in the first place. She told him the truth. She'd fallen for David and he'd let her down. Her admission of weakness seemed to unleash something in Joe. For he too had been taken in by David and the shared experience made them co-conspirators.

Where Joe had been hesitant at first, now there was no stopping him. And Diane realised he needed to talk about David, as if confessing his experience would somehow cleanse him of it. She listened spellbound while Joe told her about his first encounter with David.

He had been at Omega for only a matter of hours when he came into Joe's office.

'I'm starting here as a trainee,' he explained, 'and I need somebody to show me the ropes.'

Joe should have smelled a rat there and then, but he didn't. He offered to help him. And the next thing he knew, David was sharing his office and his secretary and picking through his files. But he was subtle about the way he moved onto Joe's territory.

For the first month he courted Joe, running his errands and asking his advice. Occasionally he would persuade him to lunch in the local pub. And when David had Joe to himself he would subject him to an almost non-stop barrage of flattery. In the end he had Joe believing that he was some kind of guru in the PR business. And it was his mission on earth to impart his wisdom to David.

It took two months for David to drain Joe. After that he had a working knowledge of how to run an account. All he needed now was something to cut his teeth on. So he went to Eric Peebles, Omega's managing director.

It wasn't as easy as he imagined to get his first break. Peebles had been suspicious of David from the moment Albert Robinson had strong-armed him into taking him on. He wasn't inclined to hand over any of his hard-won business for some junior to make a mess of. So he tried to fob him off with excuses.

'You need to watch some of the others. See how they take meetings. Learn how they fill in a contact report. You've got a long way to go before I let you do anything.'

This didn't suit David at all. He was all set up and raring to go, so he did a sneaky thing. He persuaded Joe Slackman to let him help out on one of his projects. In the short time he'd been there, David was fully conversant with everything that went over Joe's desk. So he knew where the older man was being pushed and what he had no time for.

The project he took over was a development for a chocolate bar a major manufacturer wanted to market to young mothers. What they needed was some kind of device that made it different from everyone else's chocolate bar. And Joe, who had had the project for three weeks, had come up with nothing. So David went to work. He read all the research and checked out all the competition. Then he went out for a walk and applied his mind to the problem. When he got back to the office, he was greeted by a desperate-looking Joe.

'The chocolate bar people are coming in first thing tomorrow. So you'd better tell me how far you've got.'

David looked at Joe.

'I've got no further than you did. Though if you let me come to the meeting I can snow them with all the research I've done. It will make us look as if we've been hard at it on the business.'

Joe didn't have any alternative but to let him have his way. He was running out of time and the only member of the agency who could talk chocolate bars was standing in front of him.

The two men went into the meeting at nine the following

morning. Because it was an important piece of business, the agency had made their boardroom free. And they all took their places round the big mahogany table. Joe, as the senior man, sat at its head, where he kicked off the presentation. He talked in a roundabout way about the project and the problems it posed. Then when he started to run out of steam, he handed over to David who did as he had promised. He laid bare everything he knew about the confectionery market. Only he didn't just parrot facts, as Joe had expected. He had his own views on the current market trends, and he could see from the rapt expressions on the clients' faces that they endorsed those views.

Joe let David have his moment in the sun. He had done his homework, but there it ended. He didn't have the experience to take the project any further. He was just about to cut in on him, when David announced he had formulated a plan for the chocolate bar.

Joe's head began to spin. There had been no mention of any kind of plan when he had talked to the boy before the meeting. He wondered what he was playing at.

He didn't have to wait long before he found out. For David was up and running, putting forward a proposal that was so simple he could have kicked himself for not thinking of it in the first place.

The essence of David's plan was to give away a toy with each chocolate bar. It would be a cheap plastic thing, small enough to be included in the packaging. Yet the quality of the toy was unimportant. What made this a killer idea was the double benefit. The young mum would be giving her brats two treats in one. It had to make this bar a winner. He was so bewitched by the idea that he quite forgot to weigh in with his opinions. Instead he let the head chocolate man build on the plan. And after that he had lost control of the meeting.

Afterwards Joe wondered if that one moment of weakness lost him the account. Then he looked at David and saw the victory written all over his face and realised he had lost it well before then. The boy had planned to steal the business from him the moment he offered to help him out. And he knew he should never have trusted him.

After David landed the chocolate bar account, Eric Peebles decided to give him his own office. This was just as well, for the atmosphere between Joe and David was bitter. The older man knew he had been used, but there was nothing he could do about it for David didn't need him any more. Now his feet were on the ladder, he didn't need to curry favour with anyone except clients and potential clients. He built up his existing business, chivvying extra brands out of the confectionery manufacturer at every opportunity. Then he started looking around.

'David had this fantastic network of friends and acquaintances,' Joe told Diane. 'He was quite shameless about the way he used them to get business. He didn't actually care whose feelings he hurt or who he trod on as long as there was an account at the end of it.'

Diane looked at Joe, and wondered why she was never attracted to this kind of man. He was solid and dependable and would never do anything to upset anyone, yet it was the David Robinsons of this world who always got her attention.

'David must have made a lot of enemies along the way,' she said.

Joe shrugged.

'It didn't seem to bother him. He was in such a hurry to succeed that he didn't really notice that most of the other executives at Omega gave him a wide berth. Nobody would come within a hundred miles of him in case he pulled another fast one and made off with a piece of their business. Not that he needed to use those tricks anymore. After two or three years he pulled in so many accounts, he had one of the best lists in the agency.'

Diane smiled.

'His father must have been thrilled to bits.'

'Not really. Albert only got him the job as a temporary measure.'

They had managed to get through a bottle of wine, but there was more to tell, so Joe signalled for a replacement. When it arrived and both their glasses were full again, he went on with the story.

'There was no doubt in Albert's mind that eventually David

would come to his senses and want to work in the family firm. It was his heritage, after all. So when he didn't, Albert got very angry. We heard on the grapevine that he'd gone to Eric Peebles and tried to get his son fired. But he didn't get away with it. By then David was handling so much business, it was easier to get rid of Albert.'

For the first time since they had met, Joe smiled. As if the friction between father and son gave him some kind of comfort.

'What did Albert do about the situation?' Diane pressed.

'There was nothing he could do. But he got his revenge in a very personal way. In the long run it probably damaged David more than anything else he could have done.'

Joe paused and took a sip of his wine.

'It happened at the firm's Christmas party. Albert decided to pop in that year. As he was such a big client Eric Peebles couldn't exactly stop him.

For a while it didn't look as if Eric had anything to worry about. Albert was on his best behaviour, chatting up all the secretaries and promising to give the agency more business. Then he spotted David and everything changed. He called his son over and in front of everyone he gave him a dressing down. He not only criticised his clothes and the way he'd combed his hair, but threw in the fact that David had stayed out till the early hours every night that week and worried his mother sick.'

Diane remembered how in control David had been when she met him.

'How did he handle being humiliated?' she asked. 'He must have hated it.'

Joe shrugged.

'He didn't how any emotion at all. He just stood there quietly and took the whole thing on the chin. At the time, I thought he was being weak. Then I thought about it and realised he was being his usual artful self. David had been fighting his father long enough to know where they both stood. Albert was the old lion demonstrating he was in charge. And David was in the background taking pot shots at him. I think David always knew he would win in the end. But he was prepared to bide his time before moving in for the kill.'

Diane looked concerned.

'Surely David didn't have to kill his father?'

She realised she had made him laugh.

'You don't know the law of the jungle. Unless David neutralises his father, or moves away from him, there's no way he can hold his head up.'

Diane thought about David for a long time after she had left Joe. She had searched him out in order to rid herself of David, thinking that having the low-down on him would break the spell. Only it hadn't. If anything she was more fascinated by him than ever. She had expected a rising young man, but not a driven one, and the sheer cold brilliance of his ambition drew her to him. She had fought to make her mark in the world, just as he had, and she felt a kinship with him.

If I'm not careful, she thought, I could make an even bigger fool of myself than I have already.

Chapter Eight

David's nerves were on edge. This was the third time in a week he had heard mention of her name and it unsettled him. He had no intention of getting involved with Diane Craven, yet try as he might to put her out of his mind, he kept tripping over her.

Joe had talked about her in the pub at lunchtime, saying how much more attractive she was in the flesh than in her by-line picture. And when he'd asked how Joe had met her, the older man had been momentarily embarrassed.

'Actually she was fishing for information about you. You must have made quite an impression when you took her out to lunch.'

If he hadn't been so irritated, he might have been flattered. But girls like Diane turned him off. There was something unfeminine about these eager beaver little career women. They were so anxious to prove themselves that it completely escaped their attention they were with a man and should at least make the pretence of deferring.

He decided the best way to get rid of Diane was to meet her face to face and tell her the truth. She wasn't for him. He'd do his best to let her down lightly of course. There was no point in blowing his connection with the *Express* fashion page. But he couldn't put up with her hounding him either. So he decided on a strategy. He would buy her a drink somewhere expensive. Then before she got the wrong idea, he would tell her he was in love with someone. He was seeing three girls on a casual basis; any one of them would make the perfect alibi.

Now it was settled in his mind, David's confidence started to return. He actually put in a call to the *Express* first thing the following morning. And when he got through to Diane, he acted as if he had never ignored her. He expected her to be cool with him, but he found just the opposite.

Diane was thrilled to hear from him and was surprisingly available when he suggested a drink. She was free almost any night the following week and he arranged to meet her on Monday. The sooner the better, David thought. The woman's eagerness was beginning to make him uncomfortable.

He arranged to meet her in the bar of the Midland because there was something reassuring about that hotel. It was solid with a kind of quiet luxury that suggested old money. And he knew that when she was surrounded by all the oak panelling and thick carpets, there was no way Diane could throw a scene.

At six on the dot, David was sitting at his favourite table nursing a whisky and soda. He noticed with satisfaction that the place was almost deserted. Even if Diane did decide to get difficult, no-one would be there to see her.

At six thirty David was still sitting there. He was onto his second whisky and there was no sign of his date. She's been held up at the paper, he thought. Journalists were always doing this to him, rushing in late babbling excuses about last-minute changes. He pulled out a copy of the evening paper from his briefcase and started to read the headline on the front page. It was juicy political scandal and he found it riveting. It was only when David reached the sports page that he finally glanced up. The bar was getting full now and he saw that all the other tables were occupied by residents and businessmen on their way home from the office.

Where is Diane, he wondered with mounting irritation. I've been sitting here nearly an hour and there's no sign of her. He decided to call her office. If she wasn't at her desk, somebody there would know where she'd got to.

After what seemed like an eternity, David got through to the sub-editors' desk where he was informed that the fashion department had gone home. He decided he wasn't going to be fobbed off so casually.

'I'm looking for Diane Craven,' he said, 'she's got to be around there somewhere.'

The voice on the other end of the line sounded unimpressed.

'No she hasn't,' it said, 'Diane's away in Paris all week at the fashion shows.'

David was astounded. Diane must have known she was going to be away when she arranged to see him. So she'd deliberatley stood him up. A feeling of dismay came over him, followed swiftly by an unfamiliar longing. When she was chasing him, Diane held no appeal for him whatever. Only now she had decided to stop, he was disappointed.

Over the weeks he had come to accept the woman had a crush on him. Part of him enjoyed it in a perverse way. He was almost looking forward to seeing the hurt in her eyes when he turned her down. Except it wasn't going to happen because she'd done it first.

He went back to his table and ordered another whisky. Then he observed what he was doing in a detatched sort of way. He was getting pissed in an expensive bar because some girl he didn't even like had decided to teach him a lesson. I must be going mad, he thought gloomily.

David found none of his regular girls interesting any more. He'd take them out to dinner the way he was expected to. Then, instead of feeling the usual excitement as the end of the evening approached, he would get restless. He wanted sex, David always wanted sex, but not with the girl he was with. Not with any of the girls on his list.

What he wanted, or rather who he wanted, was Diane Craven, and he hated himself for it. In David's life he liked to be the one who chose, who made the decision. Only now the decision was being made for him by the sort of pushy career girl he had been avoiding all his life.

By the end of the week, he realised he was going to have to see her again. For the thought of her was driving him mad. What he wanted from Diane, he decided, was one really spectacular night. He wouldn't need to see her after that, because the spell would be broken and he could go on with his life.

Now he knew how he was going to deal with Diane, David felt better about things. All I need to do now, he thought, is to pin her down. He thought about phoning her at the office. Then he rejected the idea. This girl knew far too much about playing games. The first thing she'd do when her secretary said he was on the line would be to put the phone down. I can't have her turn her back on me a second time, David thought. There has to be another way.

He went through every permutation he could think of. Bumping into her at lunch – no, too informal. Inviting her to a press party – no, too obvious. But the press party idea had mileage. If the event was glamorous enough, if there was something in the story which might provide a break for her, then she would come, particularly if it didn't look as if he was doing the inviting. He did the rounds of his colleagues, finding out what was coming up. In the process he found Sam Steeples.

Steeples was a has-been Hollywood star who was doing a detective series for the local network. Everyone would rush to interview him. Stars, even has-beens, were pretty thin on the ground in Manchester. And Diane would be at the front of the queue.

There was only one problem. The executive who was handling Sam Steeples was none other than Joe Slackman. And he was going to find it difficult to get any favours out of him. He called Joe on his internal phone and asked if he could see him. But somehow Joe always seemed to be too busy. Finally, in desperation, he walked into Joe's office unannounced.

'To what do I owe this pleasure?' Joe asked, pretending he had entirely forgotten that David had been calling him three times a day.

It didn't phase him in the slightest.

'I've come to talk about the Sam Steeples party,' he said, getting straight to the point.

Joe looked curious.

'What about the Sam Steeples party?'

David hesitated for a moment, wondering whether to bring up Diane's name. Then he thought, no, I'll find out more about it first.

'Have you promised the big interview to anyone,' he asked innocently.

Joe grinned.

'I've promised it to everybody . . . *The Sun, The Star, The Mirror, The Mail.* They're all coming.'

'But there has to be an exclusive.'

Now Joe looked genuinely baffled.

'Why?'

'Because otherwise you'll get a gaggle of little news stories and nothing of any substance.'

Joe looked at David.

'You're up to something, aren't you?'

He thought for a moment.

'I bet you've promised Sam in depth to a friend of yours.'

David put on his most winning smile, which didn't fool Joe for a moment.

'Would I do a thing like that?'

'Yes you would, so you might as well tell me who the lucky journalist is and have done with it.'

David's smile receded like the sea at Blackpool.

'I haven't actually spoken to her yet. But I think Diane Craven would do a good job.'

There was a short silence.

'On you or on Sam Steeples? I know you've got the hots for her.'

'OK so I've got the hots for the girl,' David said, irritated beyond measure. 'Is that so terrible?'

Joe got up from his chair and started pacing around the office.

'Give me one good reason why I should want to improve the quality of your life. You haven't done me any favours in your brief career.'

David smiled.

'That was a long time ago. You can't still hold it against me?'

Joe stopped churning up the carpet for a moment and regarded his old protégé.

'Why can't I still hold it against you?' he demanded. 'You played very dirty when you were a little boy. I might have lost my job if I hadn't looked out for myself.'

'But you did look out for yourself and you survived.'

Joe looked weary.

'All the more reason why I shouldn't go along with you.'

David was desperate now. This was the only party for six months where he could get anywhere near Diane.

'I'm not going to poach Sam Steeples from you, if that's what you're worried about.'

'Damn right you're not. As long as I've got something to do with it, you won't get anywhere near him.'

David plonked himself down in a chair and ran his hands through his abundant black hair, as if he was in genuine turmoil. There was something terribly childish about the gesture and for an instant Joe saw a little boy hiding behind the grown-up suit. If I deny him this favour, he thought, if I deny him Diane, it will be a bit like taking his lollipop away or swiping his toy train set. For no matter how high David climbed, this protégé of his would always be a child. He looked across and saw he was still sulking and he started to wonder if David could do him any more damage. In the state he was in it looked unlikely, so he decided to take a chance.

'You can stop the histrionics,' he said gruffly. 'I'll arrange for Diane to do the big interview with Sam.'

David looked up in disbelief.

'You really mean that?'

'I really mean it. Now get the hell out of my office before I change my mind.'

71

Chapter Nine

There was something not quite right about the story. In the first place she shouldn't have been offered it. She ran a fashion page, yet Joe Slackman was handing her an exclusive interview with a television actor.

'Why don't you offer it to our showbiz editor?' she asked Joe. 'It's much more his kind of thing.'

But Joe wouldn't be persuaded.

'We're looking to appeal to women with Sam Steeples. He's potential heart-throb material, so your page is perfect for him.'

'My page is strictly fashion.'

'So bend the rules. You've got the readers we're after. And we've got the story every national is hot for. It's got to make sense.'

Diane's head started to spin. This was one of the silliest propositions she'd had in a long time, yet she couldn't tell Joe what to do with it because Sam Steeples was news. In the end she accepted it on condition her editor agreed to make her page over.

He did, of course. When faced with a real story Bob Anderson would ditch a fashion page any day of the week. So Diane rang Joe back and told him she was available whenever Sam was ready.

She expected to be asked along to Steeples's hotel suite before the launch party at a nightclub. It was par for the course with this kind of interview. But the actor was busy with rehearsals and costume fittings.

'The only way we're going to pin him down,' said Joe, 'is to get him to talk to you during the party. There's a suite of offices just behind the club. So you could both go in there for half an hour.'

Diane's heart sank. All the other papers would be there and when they saw her sneaking off with their prime target, they'd do their damndest to sabotage her.

'Can't you find another way?' she asked.

But Joe couldn't and she was stuck with turning up at the nightclub and brazening things out.

She decided to go early in the vain hope that the competition would roll up when the action started. But she was out of luck. Everyone else had the same idea and when she walked in she saw a thick little knot of reporters and photographers huddled around the bar. As yet they hadn't spotted her, so she decided to keep a low profile and find out what the hell was going on.

There was no sign of Sam Steeples, which made her feel better. But there was no sign of Joe Slackman either, which made her feel nervous. He should be here, she thought. Lying in wait to whisk me through to his specially reserved office suite. She did a quick circuit of the club, losing herself in the throng of dancers, so nobody would pick her out. Only she wasn't stealthy enough, for she heard someone behind her call her name.

Diane turned round to find David standing there holding two glasses of wine. He gave her one, then led her away from the dance floor to a table in the corner of the bar.

If her mind hadn't been on the story, she might have felt nervous seeing him again. But all she could think about was the competition on her heels and the imminent appearance of Sam Steeples.

'Is Joe here?' she asked David, glancing nervously over her shoulder to see if the gang had seen her yet.

'Joe sends his apologies, but he's going to be late. I'm holding the fort until he gets here.'

She breathed a sigh of relief.

'So you know where to find Sam.'

She was slightly dishevelled, David noticed. Her thick black

73

hair which was pulled back when he met her was spilling over her shoulders tonight. And she was wearing a tight dress which flattened her bust and pulled her in at the waist. She doesn't look like an editor, he thought. She looks like a girl and it confused him for a moment. He decided to play the public relations man until he knew which way things were going.

'I left Sam in his hotel room twenty minutes ago,' he told her. 'Now you've arrived, I'll get my assistant to call and tell him to come down.'

Once more she looked over her shoulder at the journalists who seemed to have spread along the length of the bar. One of them waved at her and she smiled back briefly. Then she turned to him.

'How are you going to work this?' she asked urgently. 'If Sam walks in here now, they'll be all over him.'

David smiled.

'I'm not entirely stupid. Sam has strict instructions to come in the back entrance and go straight to the office we've organised for your interview. When its all over, he'll come into the club and throw the others a few bones.'

She looked at him with deep suspicion.

'I don't like the sound of that at all. I know what this pack can do when they're after a story.'

David sighed. He knew them as well as she did. If they decided to, the fierce-looking thugs at the bar could make a three-course meal out of Sam's few bones.

'You're worried they'll scupper your big interview?'

'What do you think?'

David considered for a moment. It wouldn't be difficult to send the actor straight back to his hotel after he'd seen Diane. Sam would probably be relieved to get off the hook so easily. But would Joe approve of those tactics, he wondered. He realised he probably wouldn't. It would not only alienate all his chums on the tabloids but deprive him of half his coverage.

Diane guessed what was going through his mind and she smiled at him encouragingly. It wasn't exactly a come-on, but it was a faint ray of hope and it was exactly the motivation David needed.

'I could head the boys off,' he said finally. 'It won't be easy, but I could do it.'

'That's great. But you don't have to stick your neck out.'

There was a silence. Then David said:

'I do, you know. I want us to be friends.'

So that's the game, Diane thought. You give me an exclusive and we can pretend that all your lies and running away didn't really happen. She wondered if she could bear to be hurt by this man a second time. Then she looked at David across the darkness of the nightclub and caught some of his intensity.

He wanted her. She knew that now. Just as she knew she was going to take another chance on him. They'd been circling around each other for long enough now. There was only one conclusion to this dance . . .

She turned to him.

'I've decided to accept your kind offer,' she said.

They stared at each other for what seemed like hours but was probably only minutes, each of them engrossed in their own secret thoughts. Finally it was David who broke the spell.

'We'd better get a move on if you want to do this interview. Sam will be here any minute.'

She got up from where she sitting.

'What happens afterwards?'

'Afterwards I send Sam back to his hotel and buy you a drink. How does that sound?'

'Interesting,' Diane said.

Joe Slackman arrived at his press party to find the journalists in a state of mutiny. They had been waiting around for nearly two hours with no sign of Sam Steeples and they wanted to know what was going on. A florid-looking man from the *Mirror* grabbed hold of Joe the minute he walked in the door.

'Where are you hiding Sam?' he demanded. 'We know you've got him somewhere.'

Half a dozen of the others joined in the inquisition, accusing

75

him of inviting them under false pretences – or worse, setting them up for someone else to steal the story from under their noses.

Joe felt a moment of pure panic. This wasn't how it was meant to go at all. When he got there he expected Sam to be holding a press conference, with David in the background fielding the difficult questions. David, he thought. That's who I've got to find. He'll know why this party is falling apart.

He found him sitting at a table in the corner of the bar. At first glance he seemed totally relaxed, sipping a Perrier and talking to his assistant. But Joe knew him better. David was smoking, something he only did in moments of extreme crisis and he knew then he was in deep trouble.

'David,' he said, pulling up an uncomfortable little wooden chair, 'would you like to tell me what's going on? I nearly got lynched when I walked in.'

David stubbed out his cigarette in the overcrowded ashtray in front of him.

'I had to keep Sam away from here tonight, otherwise we would have lost our exclusive.'

Joe grabbed hold of an open bottle of wine and splashed it into a dirty glass.

'Come again,' he said.

The resident DJ chose that moment to turn up the sound system and David had to lean halfway over the table to make himself heard.

'It's Diane Craven,' he shouted. 'She started kicking up a fuss when she saw the other pressmen. The bitch threatened to take her page away unless we neutralised the others.'

Joe looked incredulous.

'So you let her push you into removing Sam? I don't believe it.'

Then he remembered how keen David had been to impress Diane. He was so intent on getting her into bed that he would have moved heaven and earth to give her what she wanted. She didn't push David into this, Joe realised. He did it of his own accord. He looked across to the bar into the angry faces of his precious contacts and suppressed an urge to throttle David.

'I don't suppose it would do any good to ask where Sam is right now?'

David looked sheepish.

'He took off for Liverpool I think. He's got friends there.'

It was a lie of course. Sam Steeples was probably tucked up in his hotel room or boozing in the Granada pub. But there was nothing he could do about it without making a scene.

Joe suddenly felt weary. It had been a long night and the last thing he needed was a shouting match with David. In fact the last thing he needed was aggravation of any kind. He pointed to the mob at the bar.

'You created this problem,' he said grimly, 'so you talk your way out of it. I'm not going to tell them what happened to their big story.'

David looked contrite and got out of his seat. Then he elbowed his way through the mass of gyrating bodies who all seemed to be bobbing up and down in unison. The music which was blasting out at high decibels seemed to hypnotise the dancers, and David wondered if he had ever found this sort of thing fun. When he wanted to seduce a girl, he took her to a restaurant where he could talk to her, and he wondered if it had been such a good idea to give Diane champagne here. Only airheads flourished in this atmosphere and Diane was hardly that.

David sighed. He was stuck with this club, whether he liked it or not. Just as he was stuck with explaining himself to a mass of angry pressmen. He had reached the silver horseshoe that was the bar and winced slightly as he looked into mirrored surfaces reflecting neon light. This is Manchester at its worst, he thought, noisy and brassy. The barman was hovering right by him, so he leaned over and had a word in his ear.

'Get the DJ to turn it down,' he instructed, 'I'm going to make an announcement.'

The hacks had seen him now and as he edged his way towards them, he rehearsed his excuses. The best he could come up with was that Sam had been taken ill. So he went with it, embroidering the story with descriptions of a killer migraine headache.

At first none of them believed him. So he just went on repeating himself, over and over again until the sheer strength of his will beat them into the ground.

'Sam is wiped out,' he told them, almost believing it himself. 'Give me a break and try to show some human feeling.'

The ringleaders, the thug from the *Mirror* and his friend from the *Star*, started to back down.

'When will he be himself again?' they wanted to know.

'You could call tomorrow and I'll have an answer for you.'

It seemed to satisfy them, though David knew that when they nursed their hangovers in the morning, Sam Steeples would be old news. He turned to face the mob one last time.

'I'm keeping the bar open for another hour,' he told them. 'After that it's everyone for himself.'

There was the general moaning he'd come to expect, but there was no real energy in it. The boys, as usual, had accepted defeat philosophically and were already ordering another round. He left them to it after that, hurrying back to his table where Joe was waiting.

'How did it go?' he wanted to know.

'Piece of cake,' David said, sitting down and ordering another bottle of wine.

But Joe wasn't interested in drinking with him.

'I'm off home,' he said shortly. 'You can wind things up here.'

David thought of talking him out of it. Then he remembered what he'd done to Joe tonight and knew it would be no good. He'd used up every scrap of credibility he ever had with this man and he wasn't going to get any more chances with him. So he gazed mournfully after his retreating back and wondered if Joe went in for revenge.

He might have gone on worrying about the situation, if his assistant, Mary Rose, hadn't joined him. Without asking, she picked up his cigarettes and helped herself. Then she took hold of a glass and held it out to be filled.

A few years ago she and David had had a brief fling and even now she never let him forget it. He reached for the wine bottle and wondered how much longer he would put up with this behaviour. If Mary Rose started acting possessively in front of Diane it could ruin everything. He looked at his watch.

'Have you checked on how the interview is going?' he asked. 'They've been at it for over an hour.'

Mary Rose swallowed some of her wine, then she lit the cigarette. Finally, when David was about to run out of patience, she spoke.

'They've finished,' she said. 'I thought I told you.'

'When did they finish?' he pressed.

'About half an hour ago, why?'

He was about to tell her he was expecting Diane to join him, but he decided against it. Instead he said:

'Have you any idea where they are?'

The girl looked bored. As far as she was concerned her job was over when the interview ended.

'I think they both left,' she told him, 'does it matter?'

David sighed. Of course it bloody mattered. He hadn't put himself on the line providing a big story for Diane to rush off into the night.

'Diane didn't tell you where she was going?' he asked.

Mary Rose puckered her brow, as if remembering the last half hour was an effort that was beyond her.

'I don't think she did,' she replied, 'but I'm not absolutely certain.'

It was then David decided Mary Rose had to go. He would replace her with one of the male graduates who were currently flooding the job market. What he lost in sex appeal, he'd make up in efficiency.

'Why don't you go home,' he said wearily. 'I'll see everyone out.'

She looked reluctant.

'We normally do that together after a press party.'

'Not tonight,' he said firmly, 'there are a couple of people I need to talk to in private.'

She shifted out of her chair with a great show of reluctance. It wasn't like David to dismiss her like this. Dimly, in the back of her mind, she realised something was wrong. She thought about making another protest, but David was too fast for her. Before she could open her mouth, he was helping her on with her coat and propelling her towards the door.

'Go and get your beauty sleep,' he told her. 'I'll see you in the morning.'

He sat on his own for a long time after Mary Rose had gone. The music was less frantic now and the couples on the dance floor were beginning to thin out. Even the press contingent had decided to call it a night and as the club got quieter and emptier, a sadness settled around David. He had had such high hopes for tonight. He was so certain that Diane would fall into his arms. Now she had disappeared and he felt faintly ridiculous. She made a perfect fool of me, he thought. She probably knew all along she was going to dump me once she had her story, and I didn't even see it coming.

He emptied the last of the wine into his glass, and decided that career women, all career women, were bad news. They were so used to competing with men that they saw them as adversaries even when the business game was over.

The last person had left the club and now he was alone with the bartender and the cleaners. Someone had turned the lights up, revealing shabby paintwork and a carpet that had seen better days. And he felt a sudden hopeless rage at being stuck where he was. As long as he stayed in Manchester he would be holding parties in places like this and in the end it would rub off on him. He would end up like Joe Slackman, spent and cynical before his time. He decided then he wanted better for himself. He wanted better and he would get better.

He gathered his things together and was preparing to leave, when he heard a door open. The club was closed and he tensed himself to face a burglar or a mugger high on drugs.

Then he saw Diane come into the bar. She was still wearing her tight dress, only now her make-up was smudged under her eyes and her hair was pushed back into a bunch. He got up and hurried over to her.

'What the hell are you doing here?'

She summoned up a faint smile.

'I thought you were expecting me.'

'I was expecting you two hours ago, not now in the middle of the night.'

She collapsed onto a bar stool and it was then he saw how bone weary she was.

'I need a drink,' she told him. 'Does your offer still stand?'

He called the bartender and asked for two brandies. When the man refused him, he put a fifty-pound note on the counter.

'I know you're closed,' he said, 'but I paid for tonight and I'm prepared to go on paying.'

He saw him hesitate for a moment, but the money was too much for him. Without saying another word he pocketed it and produced the drinks. David slid a glass towards his companion. Then he said:

'Are you going to tell me what happened tonight?'

She nodded.

'I went back to the paper,' she told him. 'I realised you weren't going to hold the hacks at bay for more than one night, so I had to file my story for tomorrow's paper.'

'Why didn't you say?'

Diane took the brandy balloon in both hands, warming the liquor inside.

'There wasn't time for long explanations. I needed to get on with it.'

It was at that precise moment he should have told her to get lost. He didn't need a woman who put her work before everything else in her life. He looked at her.

'The *Express* is very important to you, isn't it?'

'It's all I have.'

Now he was irritated beyond measure.

'It's all you're going to have if you insist on behaving as if nothing else existed.'

She put her drink down and got up.

'I didn't come here for a fight. I could have got that at the office.'

David watched as she lifted her heavy holdall onto her shoulder and buttoned her jacket. Any minute now she'd be gone for good. And all of a sudden he couldn't let her do it. His hand reached out and took hold of her arm.

'Don't leave,' he said. 'I've been waiting for you all night.'

He wasn't quite sure how it happened, but one moment he was tugging at her sleeve and the next she was in his arms and he was kissing her. Out of the corner of his eye, David saw the bartender looking at them as if they were the late late show. Gently he pulled away from Diane.

'It's time we moved on,' he told her, 'before we get a bigger audience.'

Chapter Ten

David and Diane found his car in one of the back streets behind the club. And she wasn't surprised to see it was an 'E' Type Jaguar. His rich daddy would have given it to him and she felt obscurely jealous. Her parents didn't go in for extravagant presents. Since she left home, they barely acknowledged her at all. And she knew until she did the right thing and presented them with a husband, they'd keep their distance.

She looked across at David as she climbed into the front seat. There was no danger of him turning into a husband. He probably wouldn't stay the course as a boyfriend – she'd known men like him before. You're in this for a quick thrill, she thought. I'm a big, exciting challenge to you. And when you've had your fill of me, you'll be on your way.

He'd started the car now, reversing into an alleyway behind them, before turning onto the road and putting his foot down. The streets were empty now and David took full advantage of it. By the time they were heading out of the city, the clock was touching eighty miles an hour and she started to feel lightheaded.

What the hell does it matter if this isn't the real thing, she thought. David is what I want this minute. I'll worry about tomorrow when it comes.

He lived in Didsbury, better known as bedsitter land. Except David's block didn't have the run-down appearance of most of the conversions. Somebody had built this with the intention of turning it into flats. And it hadn't happened that long ago either, for there was a smell of fresh paint in the hallway, and the lift was one of the new electric ones that operated silently. She had a bet with herself that David's apartment would be the penthouse. And when she walked into the long, low lounge with its huge picture window, she knew she had been right. His parents had bought him the pad to go with the 'E' Type and she wondered how many girls had been bowled over by this show of opulence.

She saw David looking curiously at her.

'Don't you like my home?'

She pulled herself together.

'I'm impressed out of my mind. Most of the bachelors I date live in pigsties.'

'Most of the bachelors you date don't have their mother coming round for a weekly inspection. She'd make my life hell if there was an ashtray out of place.'

There was something smug about the way he said it, as if he was born to live in a palace. She was overcome with a savage urge to mess things up a little. She wanted to see him with his hair ruffled and his tie undone and she walked across the room to where he was standing. She saw she was nearly as tall as him and this realisation empowered her.

Instead of waiting for David to make the first move, she put her hand out and touched his face, tracing the outline of his lips with the tips of her fingers. He took her hand in his then, pulling her towards him.

As they kissed, she put her tongue in his mouth. Diane had never been this forward before. Yet instead of feeling ashamed, she was overcome with a tingling excitement. She wanted to sink herself into this man, drown herself in him and she started unbuttoning his shirt.

His chest was covered in crisp black hair and he smelt of some expensive aftershave. She looked up into his face to see the effect she was having on him. And as she did so, his hands went to the zipper at the back of her dress.

She had no idea how it happened, but one minute she was standing up and in control. The next she was on her knees in

84

front of David, with her bra round her waist. She saw his flies were undone and she realised what he wanted her to do. She should have put a stop to the action there and then. She was an emancipated woman, not some slave girl. Yet her body seemed to have a mind of its own.

Instead of getting to her feet, she saw herself tugging at his trousers until they were round his knees and his penis was in her face. She put her hands around the stem of it, feeling its rhythmic throb. Then as if it was pre-ordained, she took the swollen pink tip between her lips and started to circle round it with her tongue. He started to move the length of it in and out of her mouth and she knew that if they went on like that, he would spend himself and there would be no pleasure at all for her.

So she pulled away and stood up.

Then David took her hand and led her over to the sofa, where he sat down and pulled her on top of him. They were both naked now and she was straddling him, sitting in his lap like a cheap floozie. Seeing her like that drove his desire to fever pitch and he found her entrance and pushed himself into her, and the act of love seemed to bring her alive.

It was like nothing he had ever experienced before, for the women he was used to were soft and passive. They didn't ride him or use him like this one did. They didn't rake his back with their fingernails. They didn't scream their pleasure when their climax came near. Coupling with Diane was like coupling with some wild thing. And though he despised himself for it, he couldn't get enough of her.

They made love nearly all night, acting out fantasies he'd only seen on dirty films. And in the morning he felt sick and ashamed and hungrier than ever for her.

I can't let it end now, he thought. I have to see her one more time.

He asked her to have dinner with him that night, expecting her to cancel all her plans. She surprised him by turning him down. It was as if she was aware of the hold she had over him now

85

and was playing it for everything she could get. A wiser man would have cut his losses there and then. But where Diane was concerned, David seemed to have lost all sense of reason.

He waited for her to let him know when she was free again. And when she was he took her to the fanciest restaurant in town, where he plied her with *foie gras* and the best red wine in the cellar.

Any of his regular girls would have been impressed out of her mind, but Diane was very cool about the whole thing. She didn't exactly say that her job made her used to this kind of thing, but she didn't have to. He knew what she did and it made him feel powerless.

That night he nearly threw in the towel. It was on the tip of his tongue to put her in the car and drive her home at top speed. Then he remembered how it had been between them that first time, and he was curious to know whether it had been an illusion, a figment of his over-heated imagination.

So without asking her, he drove them back to Didsbury. He expected her to protest that he was assuming too much. But Diane didn't say a word. She simply followed him into the lift and remained silent until they were inside the apartment.

For the first time in his life, some of David's self-confidence deserted him. He wanted Diane. It had become a permanent ache in his loins. But he didn't know how the hell to put it. It crossed his mind to tell her he loved her. But Diane was too canny, too street-wise to fall for that kind of lie. He sighed. Maybe a cup of coffee and a brandy would help things along.

'I'll go and get us something to drink,' he said, beating a retreat into the kitchen.

He had no idea how long he'd been standing there fiddling with the gold-embossed coffee cups. But suddenly David was aware Diane was in the room. He turned round and saw her in the doorway. Then he did a double take. For she was completely naked except for her high heels and the thin gold chain she wore around her neck.

There was something cheap about her, the way there had been the last time when she straddled him so shamelessly. And the whole weight of his puritanical upbringing commanded him to walk away from Diane.

'What the hell do you think you're up to?' he said roughly.

'I'm tempting you.'

'Don't you think it's up to me to make the running?'

Now she smiled, slowly and lazily. He was reminded of the lionesses in the local zoo. It was clear she didn't give a shit who made the running. This woman was on heat and she was going to have what she wanted, whatever it took. Just for a moment he wondered if she would devour him. Then he caught the scent of her and he found himself responding.

He had to touch her now. Just once, just to remind himself how her skin felt. So he reached out and put his hand on her small, pert breast feeling the nipple harden in anticipation.

The words were out of his mouth before he could stop them. 'You're no better than a whore.'

'Thats what you want,' she said smiling. 'In your secret schoolboy dreams, you want to roll around in the dirt with a whore like me.'

As she talked she was loosening the top of his trousers. And all of the sudden he was seized with a terrible rage. Diane was playing with him, manipulating him like a puppet. And he knew he had to put a stop to it.

He pushed her frantic, exploring hand away from him. But he was too late, he was hard as a rock and the invitation of her nakedness overcame him.

He put his hand between her legs, feeling for her entrance. Then without asking permission, he took his cock and pushed it inside her.

A long time later, when they were in bed, he turned to her and asked the question that had been driving him mad for days.

'What the hell is going to happen to us?'

She pushed a snarl of black hair out of her eyes and looked wary. 'What do you want to happen?'

For the first time ever he was lost for a reply. So in the

end he came out with the truth. 'I want this to go on,' he said.

'You mean the fucking?'

'Do you have to be crude.'

'Of course I do. Thats what you like about me.'

Chapter Eleven

They were both too busy to see each other every night. But somehow as the weeks wore on they found the time. David would turn up at the *Express* unexpectedly on his way home from work, and whisk her off for supper – or Diane would show up at one of his press parties and they would both leave the moment they saw the chance.

It was as if they were permanently hungry for each other. And no amount of feeding the obsession did any good. The more they were together, the more they wanted to be together. And in the end, David tackled the situation head-on. 'It would be a lot easier for both of us if you moved in with me.'

They had been seeing each other for three months when he came up with the idea and Diane automatically backed off. 'I don't shack up with men for the sake of convenience.'

David looked at the fierce dark girl lying in bed beside him and wondered how the hell he'd got involved with her.

'There's nothing convenient about you,' he said affectionately. 'You don't cook, you don't do what you're told and half the time you're more involved with your job than you are with me.'

'So why do you want to live with me?'

He sat up now and looked distracted. 'Because I can't live without you.'

'You're just saying that.'

He got out of bed and started pacing around the room and she could see from his tortured expression, David was trying to find a way to explain himself. In the end he said: 'Its no use, you're too English to understand. You're too frightened of your emotions.'

'You're telling me Jews never get frightened?'

Now he looked exasperated. 'Of course we do. I'm scared all the time when I think about you and the way I feel. But it doesn't stop me from wanting to commit.' He took a deep breath, 'The difference between you and me is that I'm tougher. I grew up being shouted at and criticised every day of my life. So I learned how to handle being humiliated.'

She looked at him standing naked in front of her and felt a rush of tenderness. He was so brave, this man of hers. Brave and foolhardy.

She made one last attempt at reason. 'It's one thing that you were humiliated by your parents when you were little. But you're not a child anymore. You're a fully grown man with a fully grown girlfriend waiting to move in. How will you handle that if the family doesn't approve?'

He looked stubborn. 'They will approve,' he told her. 'It's just a question of explaining it to them.'

Chapter Twelve

Ever since he left home, David had a ritual he had never broken:
On Friday night he went home to Broughton Park to celebrate
the sabbath with his family. For twenty four hours he was the
devoted eldest son, walking with his mother to synagogue on
Saturday morning; listening to Albert's problems in the factory,
over lunch; talking football and girl problems with his two
younger brothers.

In a strange way he enjoyed playing this unfamiliar part, for
he knew it wasn't going to last. On Saturday night he could climb
back into his fast sports car and disappear back into the life he
had made for himself in the city.

Though there was one hurdle he had to climb before he did
so. His mother's inquisition.

As regular as clockwork, two or three hours before he was
due to leave, Rose would sit him down with a cup of tea
and ask him if there was anyone he was seeing. It was an
oblique question, but David knew his mother well enough to
understand the sub-text. She wanted to know if he was dating
a girl. She wanted to know if she was Jewish. And if that was
the case, she wanted to know when he was getting married.

The whole routine irritated him beyond measure, but he
humoured his mother. Because he loved her. And because deep
down he knew that as the eldest son he had an obligation to the
family to do the right thing . . .

Until now, of course, he never doubted that he would. In his
mind some suitable girl with the right parentage would come

along and that would be that. Except it hadn't worked out that way. He was head over heels in love with a non-Jewish career woman. And whether his mother liked it or not, he was going to make his intentions clear about her.

His chance came, as he knew it would, when his mother took him aside for the third degree. She always sweetened the pill by taking him into the garden. As if the sight of the close-cropped lawn and the ornamental flower beds would somehow put him in a more receptive mood.

She'll have her wish today, David thought, pouring himself a second cup of tea. I've never been more receptive in my life. And before Rose could ask the familiar question about him seeing someone, he beat her to the punch.

'Mother,' he said, 'I want to tell you about a girl I'm interested in.'

He had his mother's full attention now. 'Who is she?' Rose wanted to know. 'Do I know her parents?'

'She's not from around here.'

'That doesn't mean I won't know her family. We have meshpurcha in London as well you know.' She was all done up in her sabbath best. The suit was from Chanel and to match it she wore a mass of costume jewellery pearls and clinking gold chains.

David looked at her and wondered if this was the moment to come clean about Diane. Then he thought, why not? She's got to know sometime. 'Mother,' he said softly, 'there's not much chance of your knowing Diane's family. She isn't Jewish.'

There was a cold silence. Rose was disappointed, he knew that. But he also knew that given time he could talk her into seeing things from his point of view.

'How did you get involved with this . . . girl?' his mother said finally.

'She's not a girl, I already told you she's called Diane.'

'I don't care if she's called "Mary mother of God",' Rose replied with some vehemence. 'As far as I'm concerned, she's a waste of time.'

He looked at his mother in amazement. Throughout all his boyhood, she had never showed the slightest bit of emotion.

The shouting and screaming was his father's department. Rose always managed to keep schtum whatever the problem.

This has really unsettled her, David thought. I have to do something to calm her down. 'Would it do any good if I brought Diane home to meet you? At least you could see she hasn't got two heads.'

She fiddled with her elaborate beads. 'There wouldn't be any point. I can take your word for it, she passes muster.'

David sighed. 'Anyone would think I was rushing Diane to the altar. She's just a girlfriend, I don't see what all the hostility is about.'

Rose got up from where she was sitting and started ripping out weeds from the flowerbed in front of them. She did it in a kind of frenzy, as if it was David's head she was tearing out of the earth.

'It always starts out with the shiksa being just a girlfriend,' she said half to herself. 'Then she turns into a habit and if we're not careful she starts to get accepted in the family.' She turned to David. 'Before we know where we are, you'll be setting up home together and the marriage will be just a formality.'

He knew he was in a corner then, for as always his mother had second guessed him. She had been doing it all his life, plucking ideas out of his mind when they were half formed and turning them into finished scenarios.

When he wanted to run away from school, she had known it before he did. And because she was one step ahead, she had managed to thwart him. He looked at his mother with a mixture of love and loathing. If she had her way, he and Diane would be finished. And he felt a brief moment of pure panic.

He had to get away from Rose, he decided, before she could do any more damage.

He didn't tell Diane about the conversation with his mother. It would only hurt her, he rationalised. And there was no point in rocking the boat. Given time, he would work on Rose, leading her gently round to his point of view. But it would take cunning and a great deal of patience. So he kept everything up in the air and hoped against hope he would get away with the balancing act.

He hoped in vain. For towards the end of the week, when he was thinking about going home again, Diane asked him a question.

They were having dinner in a local Italian Bistro and she hit him with it just before the waiter brought the coffee. 'David,' she said apropos of nothing, 'are you ashamed of me?'

The pasta he had just eaten lay heavy in his stomach. 'Of course I'm not. What makes you think that?'

There was a silence for a moment, then she said, 'You told me a couple of weeks ago, you'd sort things out with your parents. But nothing seems to have happened . . . so there has to be a problem.'

He wondered whether she was going to give him a hard time. Then he looked at her nervously tearing the paper napkin into shreds and he realised Diane wasn't in the mood for a fight. She simply wanted to know where she stood, so she could make her own plans. And the panic he felt when he left his mother came back in spades.

Once she knows its hopeless, he thought, she'll start to lose interest. All her plans for moving in will go on hold. And she'll start spending more time in the office. He reached across the table and took the torn napkin out of her hands.

'Stop boxing at shadows,' he said gently, 'There isn't a problem.'

'So why don't you take me home at weekends?'

David sighed. Diane was uncannily like his mother when it came to pushing him into a corner.

'I will take you home,' he promised, 'but let me talk to my father first. He's been away, so I haven't have the chance.' It wasn't strictly true. Albert had been in Manchester all week. But Diane didn't know that. So he could go on juggling his options for a few more days.

He took a totally different line with his father. Where he had dressed Diane up as important when he spoke to Rose, with

Albert she was just a girl who was giving him trouble. 'She's making a row because I don't take her seriously.'

Albert gave his son an appraising look. 'And meeting us will make a difference?'

'She says it will.'

Neither of them said anything for a moment, then Albert asked the big question.

'I suppose you're sleeping with her?'

David spread his hands and looked helpless. 'What do you think I'm doing with her?' It was a plea for understanding. A male cry from the heart. And it got the response he was angling for. His father clapped a hand on his shoulder and muttered something about being young himself once.

They walked for a few minutes in a companiable silence. Then David said; 'So it's alright to bring her home next week?'

'Have you talked to your mother about it?'

David looked unhappy.

'I mentioned it . . .'

'. . . And she made your life a misery,' Albert finished for him. 'It's par for the course with Rose. She's set her heart on you ending up with a Princess.'

'But I'm not ending up with Diane.'

'I know that and you know that, but there's no point in trying to get it through your mother's head.'

He thought for a moment. 'I'll try to make her behave when you bring the girl. But meet me halfway will you? Tell her we'll see her for sunday lunch. There's no point in upsetting your mother on a Shabbes.

If David's father hadn't taken it into his head to drop into his son's office four days later, things might have turned out differently. As it was, Albert Robinson walked through the door just before lunch to find David flirting with a good-looking dark-haired girl. At least he assumed that was what his son was doing, for the girl was perched on his desk and from where he was standing she was showing a great deal of thigh. He decided to spare David any embarrassment by ignoring the girl. She was probably some cheap little typist who didn't know who the hell he was anyway.

Before he got to David, Albert had been in a meeting with the managing director and now he was anxious for his son to know what they had been discussing.

'I'm thinking of putting some more business your way,' he said without preamble. 'I've got a new line that needs promoting.'

To his surprise, David didn't look as eager as he expected. Instead of coming straight back to him, he whispered something in the dark girl's ear which caused her to slide right off his desk. As she did so, she revealed the fact that she was wearing stockings attached to a garter belt.

For a short moment, Albert envied his son. In his kind of business there was an endless supply of willing bimbos ready to open their legs whenever he said the word. He thought about chatting her up himself, but he resisted. There were more important things on his mind.

'What do you think about me giving you a new account?' he demanded. 'Or are you doing so well it doesn't matter to you?'

David started to look frazzled.

'Of course it matters to me,' he said. 'It matters to the whole agency. You're a very important client around here.'

The older man was somewhat mollified and to show he forgave David, he started bombarding him with questions. He wanted to know what ideas he had for an up-market range of sportswear. And when David didn't come through immediately, he pretended to sulk, wondering aloud how this son of his could justify the salary he was earning.

The two men played this game quite often and Albert knew that any minute now this clever boy of his would talk his way back into his good graces. To his surprise, David didn't say anything. Instead the girl with him spoke up.

'You need to sponsor something – a football team or a car rally. Once you get your name associated with a sport, you're halfway there.'

If it had come from his son, maybe he would have gone for

the idea. But this tramp had no place poking her nose into his business.

'I'm not paying to talk to the office help,' he said rudely.

The brunette looked at him sharply.

'I'm not who you think I am.' She extended a hand. 'The name's Diane Craven. I do the fashion on the *Express*, so I know what I'm talking about.'

Albert Robinson did a double take.

'Isn't David bringing you to lunch on Sunday?'

She nodded looking faintly smug. 'We should have a lot to talk about.'

Over my dead body we'll have a lot to talk about, the old man thought savagely. When David told me about you, I had a feeling he was doing the wrong thing. And now I've seen you, I know he is.

He was about to say something discouraging.

Something that would make her feel she was wasting her time trying to get near him and his family. Then he looked at David.

The boy was gazing at Diane with an open admiration he'd never seen before. Albert's heart sank.

So that's why she was being pushed under his nose, he thought. Rose was right all along. David's got plans for this one.

The three of them made polite small talk while Albert considered what he was going to do about the situation. He'd already realised there was not much chance of frightening her away.

This was a tough little customer with her eye on the main chance. The entire family could huff and puff on Sunday and it wouldn't make the slightest bit of difference. She'd just get his son on one side afterwards and the stupid idiot would do anything she wanted.

There has to be another way to outsmart this bitch, Albert thought, before she really gets her claws into David.

Diane bought a leather trouser suit for her visit to Broughton Park. It was by an Italian designer and cost far more than she could afford, but she knew she had to look the part for David's parents. So she dipped into her savings account and hoped she was doing the right thing.

She realised it was one of her bigger blunders when she met David for lunch.

They usually went to the Midland on Fridays because it was flashy and expensive and it made David feel better about leaving her over the weekend. The fact that he wasn't leaving her, but taking her to meet his parents on Sunday should have alerted her to trouble.

Only she wasn't expecting trouble. So she dressed herself up in her expensive new outfit and presented herself at David's table on the dot of one.

The first thing that was different was that he didn't notice her. Usually when she was wearing something new, he fell over himself with compliments and flattery. Now he seemed to look straight through her when she sat down.

'Is there something on your mind?' she asked him.

'Not really.'

He took hold of the carafe of wine on the table and poured her a glass.

'Here, have something to drink.'

There was something abstracted about him, almost as if she was a tiresome client he had to appease for the sake of the agency. And she wondered what had got into him. She took a sip of her drink, then she turned to him.

'At least I thought you might have noticed the outfit.'

He looked at her properly then.

'It's very nice,' he said without much sincerity in his voice. 'Did you get it for anything special?'

Now she began to feel really impatient. 'I told you about ten times I was buying something to meet your parents.'

'And this is it?'

She nodded.

'I hope you didn't blow everything you've got,' David said.

A worry appeared on the horizon of her mind. It was only a tiny suspicion, but as she thought about it, it gained momentum. There was a problem with Sunday, a thorny problem which

David was trying to avoid. She'd known him long enough to understand his evasions. For David didn't confront trouble head on. He approached it obliquely, giving little hints that things were not what they should be. Today, she realised, he had been avoiding her eye ever since she walked in. And now the remark about her outfit clinched it.

'I won't be wearing this to Broughton Park, will I?' she said.

He had the grace to look embarrassed.

'There's been a mix-up. My mother forgot to mention that we've got cousins from Israel arriving this weekend. There's a whole mob of them and they'll be running her off her feet.'

'You're telling me I'll be in the way?'

'Darling, try to understand. It's enough of a strain for my mother to meet you as it is.'

Now she was totally bemused.

'You didn't tell me that before. I thought your family wanted to know me.'

David poured some more wine into his glass.

'Of course they want to know you,' he said huffily. 'It's just difficult this weekend.'

She suspected he was lying. The whole excuse was too pat, too thought out. So she gave it the acid test.

'How long are your cousins staying?' she enquired.

'Around three weeks. Why do you ask?'

Diane smiled, hoping it would mask the unsureness she felt.

'I thought we could make a firm date with your parents after they'd gone.'

David didn't exactly squirm, but he looked so uncomfortable that she almost suggested he paid the bill and called it a day.

'You don't want to make a date, do you?' she said.

'I'd love to make a date, but it's just damn difficult to pin everyone down.'

She listened while he trotted out his excuses. His parents were going away after the cousins left. When they came back there was some Jewish festival. Then his cousin was getting married.

Diane let him prattle on till the end of lunch. Then she looked at her watch and said she had to be back at the office early.

At any other time, David would have made her stay, tempting her with brandy and *petits fours*. Now he seemed to be relieved to get rid of her. She wondered what had got into him.

David didn't call her after the weekend. It took three days until she heard anything at all, and when they did speak he sounded busy.

Diane was reminded of the first time David had tried to get rid of her. His technique hadn't improved since then and she decided she didn't want to spend the next few weeks listening to his lies. So she ended things.

'If I'm not good enough for your family,' she told him, 'I'm not good enough for you.'

She expected him to make a token protest, yet he didn't fight at all.

'We'll talk in a week,' he told her, 'when you've cooled down.'

Except she didn't cool down. When David called she avoided him. Diane estimated David would keep trying to contact her for another few weeks, but it was too much to hope for. His calls died out after ten days, leaving her insulted.

Months later, when the hurt had faded, Cissy told her why he had walked away.

'Albert Robinson was going to pull his new account out of Omega, if David didn't give you up. So lover-boy did what was in his best interests.'

Diane felt bitter. I should have seen it coming, she thought. If I hadn't been so in love with David, I could have predicted it.

Chapter Thirteen

Sally . . . 1994

When Sally knew she was loved, she took the way she looked for granted. When she went to the hairdresser's she knew she would come out tinted exactly the right shade of blonde. When she put on a suit or a dress from her vast wardrobe of this season's clothes, it went without question they would make her appear thinner and more elegant. She never worried that her shoes were the wrong shape or her stockings were the wrong colour. She was supremely sure of her taste.

Then David walked out and Sally's carefully built façade began to crumble. Now whatever she did to herself was somehow wrong. Worse, she was starting to look her age. Sally cursed the unfairness of time and nature. When she needed to present herself at her most alluring, she looked middle-aged and suburban.

She thought ahead to the evening when she would see David again. He had chosen San Lorenzo for their first real talk since the break-up. Now she reflected on the cruelty of his choice. For the Italian restaurant on Beauchamp Place was the haunt of the beautiful people. Willowy models and jet-set playgirls used it as a meeting-place. Up against that kind of competition she didn't stand a chance. David would take one look at her and the last thing he'd want to do was come home.

She pulled herself up short. This whole business was getting to her, making her negative, and tonight that was the last thing she could afford. One of them had to believe their marriage was worth saving. One of them had to fight for the house, the daughter, the years they'd invested in each other. With a sigh she sat down in front of her dressing-table and started to put on her make-up.

Sally arrived at the restaurant slightly before nine and was relieved to find she was the first one there. It gave her time to scramble down two flights of stairs to the tiny cramped ladies room where she could put on fresh lipstick and fluff her hair out. As always, there was competition for the mirror and it took twenty minutes before Sally emerged, ready for whatever the evening and her husband had in store for her.

He was there when she got back, standing by the bar and chatting up the head waiter. She noticed he'd ordered his usual bottle of champagne, which was ready in an ice bucket. Her heart lifted. David only ordered champagne when he wanted to win someone's confidence. It's not going to be so bad after all, she thought, coming up behind him and planting a kiss on his cheek.

'My lovely wife,' he said, 'come and share this expensive bottle.'

They chatted companionably, David telling her an outrageous story about a client who was always slow with his payments.

'Jeremy and I decided to punish him until he paid up,' David told her.

'We pretended to stop working for his company, sending him copies of letters cancelling his promotions.'

Sally was intrigued.

'Did it work?'

'Like a charm. The quarterly check arrived in the next post.' He grinned and signalled the barman to refill their glasses.

'The one thing I won't miss is worrying about my clients not paying on time. Jeremy's inherited the whole headache and good luck to him.'

Alarm bells sounded in Sally's head. This wasn't the way it was meant to go at all. They were having dinner tonight to talk things over. The jury was still out. Or was it, if

102

David was getting rid of the business? She took hold of her champagne.

'You're going too fast for me,' she said, attempting a smile. 'I thought you hadn't taken any firm decisions yet.'

Until that moment she had imagined he was relaxed. Now she saw he had been acting all along, for the smile disappeared along with his charm.

'I decided what I was going to do a long time ago,' he said harshly. 'And you're not going to make me change my mind.'

The ground was giving in front of her now, but she hung onto her resolve.

'So what am I doing here if you've no intention of listening to me?'

'You're here to help me wind up this marriage.'

The way he said it made it sound as if their seventeen years together was just another business concern. And part of her started to hate him.

'How do you wind up a marriage?' she asked savagely. 'Do you bundle me and all our memories into a filing-cabinet and label it dead?'

He ran a hand through the barbered black hair.

'You're getting hysterical. I didn't come here for a fight.'

I bet you didn't, she thought. You chose this place because you knew I wouldn't dare make too much of a scene, not in front of all the supermodels and their flashy boyfriends. She was tempted to go ahead anyway. Then she remembered their daughter, a daughter who would suffer if she told David to go to hell. So she took a deep breath and decided to play it his way.

'If we're going to end this marriage,' she said as evenly as she could, 'what do I get out of it?'

She saw him start to relax and knew she'd hit on the right approach. David was on familiar territory when he was talking about money.

'I told you I'd make over my share of the agency already. But if you agree to everything quickly, then I'll throw in the house as well.'

It occurred to her that she was entitled to the house anyway.

103

But she kept quiet about it. What Sally needed to know now was how far David had got with his termination of their life together.

'Have you talked to a lawyer yet?'

'I sat down with Fred Davis last week and worked out a few details.'

He reached into his inside pocket and produced a neatly folded document.

'You might want to run your eye over this and tell me what you think.'

It was all so neat and organised, it took her breath away. All last week she had been agonising over how to save her marriage while David had been ending it behind her back. She looked at the folded divorce agreement in her husband's hands. He wanted her to read it before they'd even sat down to dinner, and something in her rebelled. He could have his bloody divorce, if that's what he wanted. But she'd agree to it in her time and on her terms. She took the papers and tucked them into her bag. Then she said:

'I'm sure they make fascinating reading, but right now I'd rather see a menu.'

There was a deliberate rebuke in her voice and it had the desired effect. The charm he had so suddenly abandoned earlier on snapped back into place.

'Darling, I'd forgotten you needed feeding. Forgive me.'

Within minutes one of the Italian waiters was escorting them down the slatted wooden staircase into the main restaurant. Sally noticed they had been given the most visible table, the one Ivana Trump always sat at. But it gave her no pleasure, for she knew that the table, like the restaurant itself, had been chosen with the express intention of keeping her quiet.

Somewhere in the middle of dinner, when the pasta and all the salads had arrived, Sally realised she wasn't going to eat anything. So to fill in the space between them – the space that was threatening to become a gulf – Sally took the divorce papers out of her bag. It was all as David had explained.

And his generosity astounded her. David was in such a hurry

to get out of the marriage that he was willing to hand over everything he had.

She looked up from what she was reading.

'Are you sure you want to give me all this?'

He shrugged.

'It's only fair. Your money put me in business in the first place.'

He paused. 'You and your money.'

She felt a stab of bitterness go through her. In all their years together, David had never even acknowledged her contribution to their fortunes.

Now he was leaving her, it was all he remembered. She looked at him.

'How are you going to live without Chandos to support you?'

David considered this.

'I'll find something.'

'But what will you find? You can't live in limbo for the rest of your life.'

Two impossibly elegant Italian women were coming down the staircase. For a moment David seemed distracted by them. At another time, Sally might have felt ignored, but now it hardly mattered. David didn't want her any more. Whoever he looked at was none of her business. She signalled the waiter to clear away the plates, and she saw she had her husband's attention again.

'You asked me something?'

She shrugged.

'I wanted to know where you might be. I'm sure Annabel will want to keep in touch.'

To Sally's surprise, David looked furtive. As if she was asking him for something he was doing his best to keep hidden.

'I've no idea where I'm going to be,' he told her finally. 'So it's no use leaving telephone numbers and addresses. But I will be in touch. You can rely on that.'

Just for a moment Sally wondered what the hell was going on.

'Is there something you haven't told me?' she asked. 'Something I ought to know before you disappear from my life?'

David shook his head.

'You know all there is,' he told her.

She was not convinced. Hours later, when she was driving home, she was tortured by nagging doubts. David's up to something, she thought. If he'd been playing it straight, he would have haggled over the divorce like any other errant husband.

She wondered if there was another woman in the picture, someone he had to keep so secret, so secret that he wouldn't even part with a telephone number. The thought made her feel so sick that she had to stop the car and rest her head on the steering-wheel.

A few days later she heard from the family solicitor. It was a long letter on the same lines as the one David had shown her over dinner. Attached to it was another note from Fred Davis himself.

Dear Sally,
As you can see David has played fair by you and I know he would appreciate it if you returned the compliment.

So be a pal and don't dither. David is in a hurry to wind up his affairs, so we would all like it if you made up your mind quickly.

If there's anything in the attached that you disagree with or want to discuss, give me a call.

He'd signed it with love and Sally resented his easy familiarity. It made her feel like a brainless housewife who was being despatched and patted on the head at the same time.

She thought about hiring her own lawyer to deal with Fred Davis, but she knew she was being unrealistic. Lawyers cost money and she didn't need anyone in her corner to fight a perfectly reasonable agreement. It was going to be a friendly divorce. Now all she had to do was explain what it meant to Annabel.

As she wondered how her daughter was going to cope with this upheaval, she realised she hadn't told her anything about

106

it. She'd been putting it off in the hope that it would go away. Except it wasn't going away and she had a letter to prove it.

She thought about her cherished, over-indulged daughter. This will be the first major disappointment in her life, Sally realised. She's not going to take it lying down.

She broached the subject of David as soon as Annabel came home from school. When Sally was in, the two of them usually had tea in the over-furnished drawing-room. Over the years it had become a kind of ritual, a sort of stage tea, with tiny crustless sandwiches and elaborate French pastries. Neither of them actually ate anything. But the fact that they could lent the occasion a kind of phoney importance.

It was the one time in the day when Annabel was treated like a grown-up and Sally was glad she had made this effort for her. It built her confidence and her self-respect, though when Sally started to talk about David, she wished her daughter had a little less of either for Annabel made no effort whatever to understand the situation.

'Daddy would never just walk out,' she said when she heard her parents were divorcing. 'You must have done something to drive him away.'

Sally did her best not to look shaken.

'What on earth are you talking about?' she demanded.

For a moment Annabel was silent. Then she started talking about a schoolfriend with a similar problem.

'Mary's parents are splitting up because her mother has a boy-friend. I don't think he was all that important. From what I heard it was just a fling, but it completely destroyed Mary's father.?'

'And you think I've done the same thing?'

Now the girl started to look uncomfortable.

'What else could it be? Daddy was devoted to us.'

It occurred to Sally to suggest that David was the one with a bit on the side, but she resisted. This split was going to damage her daughter enough as it was. She leaned forward and poured them both fresh tea. Then she went and sat beside Annabel on the sofa.

'Darling,' she said, 'I can promise you I was never disloyal to your father.'

The girl looked spikey and rebellious. If Sally hadn't been so concerned about the situation she would have been tempted to grab her by the shoulders and shake some sense into her.

'How can I believe what you say?' she demanded.

'I loved your father. He was the centre of my whole life.'

The anguish in Sally's voice pulled Annabel up sharp.

'Poor Mummy,' she said. 'I had no idea.'

Sally laughed harshly.

'I don't think David had either.'

Chapter Fourteen

Sally . . . Manchester, 1976

Sally couldn't believe she had landed the *Express*. She had written to all the national papers as soon as she left University but she didn't think any of them would take any notice. There were too many graduates like her. All looking for jobs in the media, all offering nothing but their degrees and their enthusiasm. Only the *Express* had taken her seriously. They had a graduate training scheme in their provincial offices and she was offered a posting in Manchester.

She told her mother the minute the letter arrived at their house in Highgate. She wished she hadn't. As always, Freda was anxious for her.

'You don't know Manchester,' she said, 'or newspapers. You'll be like a fish out of water.'

Sally sighed. She loved her mother dearly but they didn't share the same vision of the world. Freda wanted her to do something worthy. Medicine or the law would have suited the family down to the ground. But Sally wanted to be creative and she stuck to her guns.

'I won't be like a fish out of water,' Sally said as patiently as she could. 'I've been away at University for the last three years and there haven't been any problems.'

Freda looked adamant.

'You were a student then, living a student's life. Now

you'll be with journalists and riff-raff and it won't suit you at all.'

Sally was tempted to tell her mother about some of the riff-raff that hung around the campus, but she had unnerved her enough for one day. So she hugged her tightly, knowing that affection always reassured her.

'I'm going to love the *Express*, Mummy,' she said. 'And if I don't, I'll turn round and come right back home again.

She remembered her promise to her mother when she walked into the Manchester offices of the *Express*. For when she saw where she would be working, she felt like turning tail and heading straight back to Highgate.

She was shown to the floor where she would work, a big shabby open-plan area with rows of desks lit by bare neon strips overhead. Everywhere she looked there was debris. Old newspapers competed for floor space with used carbons. And in the air there was the stench of cigarette smoke.

The messenger who escorted her from the front hall led her up to a middle-aged man in his shirtsleeves who was engrossed in a pile of proofs. He looked up, irritated as she approached.

'You must be the new trainee,' he said extending a hand. 'I'm Ron Clegg, deputy news editor. You'll be answering to me for your first six months.'

Sally gazed at him wide eyed.

'Then what happens?'

The newsman scowled.

'I'll tell you when I find out what kind of reporter you make.'

He sat her down at one of the long desks which seemed to be occupied by six other people. Then he cleared a space in front of her and put down a pile of newspapers.

'Work your way through these,' he told her, 'until I come out of morning conference. Then you can tell me if you see anything worth following up.'

She saw the other reporters looking at each other and grinning and she felt like an idiot.

110

'What's so funny?' she demanded.

The boy sitting next to her swung round in his seat.

'You're new, aren't you?' he enquired.

She nodded.

'Well, the first thing you've got to do is pay no attention to what Clegg tells you. The follow-ups have already been decided on by Clegg's boss and when the little man comes out of conference we'll all get our orders for the day.'

Sally looked nonplussed.

'So I shouldn't go through the papers?'

Her companion laughed.

'You should have seen them hours ago, when they came up. But you've just started. You'll learn the routine.'

She sped through the papers as fast as she could and when she looked up, she saw a group of executives spilling out of a big office at the far end of the room. Ron Clegg and a tiny, raddled-looking man were making their way over to the reporters' desk. Sally felt a thrill of expectation. I'm going to be given my first story, she thought. I hope I'm equal to it.

She needn't have worried. Sally's first story really wasn't a story at all. She was sent down to the town hall to go through the voters' lists until she found a number of addresses of known political activists and rabble rousers. A major exposé on racial unrest in the city was being prepared by the newsdesk, and Sally was a small addition to the investigation team. At first she felt honoured to be included, but as the week wore on she began to feel less like a newshound and more like a dogsbody. As well as the town hall, she was sent to the local courtrooms to pore over their records. And when she'd finished down there, the public library was her next port of call.

At the beginning of her third week, Sally went to see Ron Clegg.

'When do I get sent on a real story?' she demanded. 'I'm beginning to feel like a clerk.'

Ron looked thoughtful.

'So you want to try your wings.'

He handed her a piece of paper, with a scribbled address on it.

'In an hour or so the police are going to evict the family who live there. They're all squatters, Liverpool Irish I would think. There could be trouble.'

Sally felt excited.

'Do you want me to bring a photographer?'

The desk man shook his head.

'Get a quote from the injured parties and one from the law and phone it in.'

The address Sally was given was in the old part of town behind the University. She took a bus as far as she could. Then she asked for instructions from passers by.

She walked for about an hour before she found the street she was looking for; the crumbling brick terraces all looked the same to her. At some point it started to rain and Sally started to wish she'd worn something more sensible than this season's maxi-skirt with the high platform heels she'd bought from Biba.

She stuck out like a sore thumb in these streets, an open invitation to any lout who wanted to rob her and leave her for dead. She was starting to wonder whether she should head back to the office when she found she was standing outside the address Ron had given her. For a reason she couldn't fathom, there was nothing going on. There was no sign of a policecar, or even a policeman. So she went up to the door and rang the bell. Nobody answered it. She went on pressing the bell for a good five minutes. Then she tried the knocker, to no avail. So she went next door and found a neighbour.

'I'm from the *Express*,' she said nervously, 'I was told there was going to be an eviction at number thirty-two.'

The old woman who answered the door looked at her curiously.

'I think you've been told wrong,' she said. 'The people who lived there left last week.'

Sally did a double take.

'Do the police know?'

The door was starting to close in her face.

'You'd better ask them, I'm not here to do your job for you.'

Now it was starting to rain in earnest, soaking the expensive fabric of Sally's skirt so that it clung to her. Next time she thought savagely, I'll wear a raincoat and wellies and the hell with trying to impress the office.

She eventually found the police station tucked away in a side-street behind a pub. To her relief, the desk sergeant took pity on her. When she enquired about the eviction, he went and consulted his records and came back to her in minutes.

'We'd scheduled an eviction,' he told her. 'You were right about that. But I've no idea why your office sent you out. These things very rarely happen.'

Sally was confused.

'Why is that?'

The policeman gave her a funny look.

'What have you been doing all your life? Squatters don't hang about waiting for us to throw them out. They stay on till the last minute, then they vanish.'

She realised she'd been made a fool of. Ron Clegg knew all the time that she would come back empty handed. But why had he done it to her? Why had he made her tramp through this rough neighbourhood in the pouring rain for nothing? Sally decided to ask a few questions when she got back to the office.

The newsroom was deserted when she finally walked in. All the reporters were either out on stories, or they'd gone to the pub. Ron and his news editor had followed their example for all she could find was a mournful-looking desk man munching his way through the sandwiches his wife had packed for his evening shift.

She considered marching over to the pub and tackling Ron there and then. Then she realised her suit was still wringing wet and she probably looked like a scarecrow. I'll go to the ladies loo, she thought, and patch myself up. Then I'll go and find Ron.

The sight that confronted her in the mirror was worse than she imagined. Her wavy blonde hair was drying out into a halo of frizz and the make-up she put on that morning had all been washed away by the downpour. She took hold of her skirt and squeezed the soggy material.

'Don't do that,' a voice said behind her, 'you'll ruin the whole hang of it.'

Sally looked up to see a good-looking dark-haired girl a few years older than she was.

'What are you,' she asked crossly, 'some kind of authority on women's clothes?'

The girl smiled.

'You guessed right. I do the fashion page.'

At another time Sally might have been impressed. But right now she was damp and cold and mad as hell at the entire newsdesk.

'How lucky you are,' she said, running her hand through her ruined hair. 'I wish I had your job.'

'I bet you do, I hear you've been getting the run-around.'

To Sally's astonishment, she found she was beginning to cry. All the frustrations of the past three weeks seemed to well up inside her and come spilling down her cheeks. She groped around in her bag for a tissue, but her companion beat her to it.

'Here,' she said, handing over a pack of Kleenex, 'get it all out. It will make you feel better.'

Sally dabbed at her face.

'The only thing that will make me feel better is to kick Ron Clegg where it hurts.'

Diane Craven smiled.

'It's not worth it,' she said. 'He'll only get his revenge by sending you out on more wild goose chases.'

Sally looked at the fashion editor in genuine suprise.

'How do you know I was sent out on a wild goose chase?'

'Trainees always are. It's meant to toughen you up.'

'Or kill us.'

Diane laughed.

'You don't look the type to go under to me. I'd put my money on you surviving the newsdesk.'

*   *   *

114

To Sally's surprise, she did survive. The next morning she came in all spruced up and put herself at Ron's mercy for the second time that week.

This time he came up with a doorstepping job. A local newsreader had run off with a married councillor and holed up in a remote cottage in Cheshire. Sally was despatched along with the rest of the provincial papers to wait for them to appear and make a statement.

The group of them hung around in the cold for most of the day. And when the light began to go the man from the *Mail* suggested they all retired to the local pub. The thought of a country inn with a big roaring fire was too much to resist. Then Sally thought about Ron Clegg and his merry men. If she came back empty handed from a real story, there was no telling what the consequences might be.

She turned to the other reporters who were starting to climb into their cars.

'I'll stay around here a bit longer,' she said. 'If anything happens, I'll come and get you.'

They told her she was an idiot and she'd probably die of exposure. But it made no impression on Sally. If she had to wait around all night, she was going to get something out of this.

Around nine, when she started to think the others were right, the front door opened a chink. Sally rushed up the front path to be confronted by the newsreader looking pinched and worried.

'I see the animals have called it a day,' she said.

Sally rubbed her hands together and stamped her feet.

'Not this animal.'

The newsreader raised her eyebrows.

'Which paper are you from?'

'The *Express*, though if you make me stand on your doorstep all night, I won't live to work for anyone.'

Now the door opened fully and she was ushered in.

Sally's interview with the runaway newsreader Jean Ogden appeared on page three the following morning. The rest of the pack who had gone to the pub called her a prize bitch for keeping the story to herself. But Sally didn't care. She'd given up a warm fire and a glass of wine for her exclusive. There was no way she was going to spoonfeed it to the guys who hadn't.

She got a reputation for being tough. She wasn't a particularly talented journalist and most of her stories were rewritten by the sub-editors. But Sally was persistent.

She chased ambulances and fire engines as if her life depended on it. When she was sent to wait outside a jail for a newly released prisoner, she turned up at dawn to be sure no-one else got to him first. And when a famous local artist turned nasty and refused to speak to the press, it was Sally who legged it up to his house on the moors and threw herself on his mercy.

Her ploy worked. Rowan Williams was so impressed with her determination to see him that he invited her in and spent all evening talking about his controversial new exhibition.

In a way her success was her undoing. For she had to live up to it. When she came back with the Rowan Williams story, the editor was so excited that he decided to promote it to a feature page. Sally was panic stricken. She was about as capable of writing a feature as she was of winning the pools. It was simply beyond her, but when she told Ron Clegg, he refused to believe her.

'I'll fix you up with a quiet spot away from the rabble. Once you start to concentrate you'll be surprised what you can do.'

Sally looked at Ron in despair. No, she thought, the only one who'll be surprised is you. And when you see my copy, I'll be going home on the next train.

Diane was surprised to see Sally perched at the end of her desk. She was sitting there, hunched over her machine and gazing into space. Diane guessed she was about to produce a big story. Normally she would have been irritated by this intrusion into her space. But she had a soft spot for the gutsy new reporter, so she wandered over and asked if she could do anything to help.

Sally looked up from her blank sheet of paper.

'The only thing that would help,' she told Diane, 'is if you sat down and wrote this for me.'

'You can't be serious.'

'I've never been more serious in my life.'

Sally rubbed her hands across her eyes. It was the unselfconscious gesture of someone who hadn't bothered with make-up that day. Diane noticed how scruffy the girl was looking. She puts all her energy into holding down her job, Diane thought, and she neglects herself totally. She remembered the first time she ran into her when she was looking like a drowned rat and she realised then she would have to take her in hand.

'You'd better tell me what the story is about,' Diane said, 'then I'll see if I can do anything.'

She was rewarded by a look of total gratitude, followed by a fevered scramble through her notes.

'I did an interview with Rowan Williams that they want me to make into a feature. But I can't do features.'

She stopped and looked embarrassed. 'Actually I can't write.'

Diane sighed. Half the staff of the paper couldn't write, but they didn't go around admitting it. She paused, wondering whether to caution her about it. Then she realised that the girl was not in a fit state for a lecture.

'Have you typed up your notes?' she asked.

Sally nodded.

'Then you'd better hand them over,' she said, 'and I'll do what I can.'

An hour later Diane handed the finished feature over to Sally.

'Give it to Ron,' she said quietly, 'and tell him you wrote it. I've put your name at the top.'

'But I didn't write it.'

Diane looked at her.

'You did all the work. If you hadn't got to Rowan Williams the feature wouldn't exist.'

She saw the girl looking doubtful, so she gave her a push.

'If you don't hand it in now,' she urged, 'you'll miss the edition.'

* * *

The two of them became friends after that. Whenever Sally wasn't out pounding the streets for the newsdesk, she'd wander over to where Diane was sitting and they'd sneak down to the office canteen for a cup of coffee and a cheese on toast. If it was lunchtime, they'd go further afield to the smart shops in Deansgate where they'd windowshop and dream of the days when they could afford to blow a month's salary on a dress.

Without realising what they were doing, they both fell into step with each other, each providing what the other needed. For despite the hustle of their working lives, deep down they were lonely. Sally was lonely for her parents and the friends she had left at University. Diane was simply lonely for David, who she hadn't managed to get out of her system. Only when they were together, sharing gossip and secrets, did the loneliness vanish.

All through the long hot summer of 1976, the two women forged their friendship, often spending weekends together if neither of them had a date or a party to go to. In a way it was inevitable they would end up sharing a house together, though Sally had to be pushed into it.

In her first few months in Manchester, Sally had found a home in one of the numerous little boarding-houses in the University district. She had a landlady who looked after her and a place to lay her head, and that was all she thought she needed – until Diane set eyes on the place. She had driven her there one Sunday night after they had had dinner together and Diane couldn't believe what she saw.

'You're not planning to stay here for any length of time, are you?' she asked.

Sally looked surprised.

'Why not?' she said. 'It's cheap enough and I'm not here all that much.'

'That's not the point. If you live like an animal you'll start to behave like one. And I don't suppose you want to end up like the rest of the hacks.'

Sally thought about the rough crew who she was starting to spend time with. They all drank like fishes, even the women, and when they weren't in the pub, they were in cheap curry houses.

She thought about her fastidious mother and the well-kept house in Highgate. She wasn't born to this life, but it was all she had right now. She turned to Diane.

'I didn't ask for a sermon. Anyway I can't afford anything better.'

'You could afford to share a flat.'

Now Sally was really cheesed off.

'Who do I know with a spare room?'

Diane thought about telling her to go through the ads in the evening paper, but realised Sally would never get round to it. She considered her immaculate little house in Sale. She had lived alone there quite happily until David came into her life and got her into the habit of sharing. Now he'd gone, she was lonely and she wondered whether to admit it to Sally. She decided to take a chance.

'If you're interested, I've got a room going free in the house I rent.'

'Wouldn't I get in your way?'

Diane laughed.

'You probably would. But I'd be glad of the company.'

Sally looked around the digs she had taken for granted all these months and suddenly noticed how tatty everything was. The walls in the room where they were sitting were blackened and scorched from the constant coke fires, and the sofa sagged in the middle. She had never set eyes on Diane's house in Sale, but she had a shrewd idea it was a damn sight better than this.

'I'm paying thirty-five pounds a month here,' she said. 'How much more would you need?'

Diane thought for a moment.

'Thirty-five pounds a month would suit me fine. When do you want to get out of here?'

'How about tomorrow?'

The minute she walked through the door, Sally knew she had come home. There was nothing grand about the place. It was just a little suburban terrace, the same as all its neighbours. But that's what she liked about it.

There was a front parlour with an old-fashioned three-piece suite. A little alcove at the top of it contained a proper wooden dining-table. And down the hall was the biggest country kitchen Sally had ever seen. Whoever lived here last must have knocked two rooms into one, for there was enough space to hold a dinner party for twelve.

Diane had added her own little touches when she moved in. She had picked up a Welsh dresser at a sale and had stripped the kitchen table down to its original wood. And one of her contacts at Lewis's had provided chequered curtains and an eye-level oven, all at cost price. The kitchen was by far the best room in the house, and Sally knew they'd spend most of their time there.

She was spot on. Whatever time either of them came in, they always ended up there, drinking a glass of wine or a cup of coffee and going over the day. Sally had never learned to write, despite all Diane's efforts to coach her. But since she had moved in, she seemed less worried about it. She had a life now, as well as a job. And she had a best friend to watch over her.

Over the months, she realised that Diane was having an influence. She had made her grow her hair out of the bob she always wore, and when it was long enough, Diane sent her along to her hairdresser's for a proper make-over. Now her hair waved around her shoulders and she liked the effect. It made her feel female, so she looked to her new friend to revamp the rest of her. She realised she was changing when the other reporters started treating her differently.

In the old days she had been one of the boys, standing her round in the pub more often than she had to. And she always found her own way home. Now she was treated like somebody special.

Brian Smith, the good-looking young deputy sports editor, started taking her to lunch, and after that to dinner. But he wasn't her only admirer. A man she met round at Cissy's who worked for the local television station called regularly, as did a local footballer she interviewed.

From being a hag-ridden reporter, Sally had suddenly turned herself into a party girl. And she appeared to thrive on it.

Then Diane started to hear stories about her. At first she didn't give them too much attention. Any new girl in town was bound to get herself talked about. It went with the territory. But as the weeks wore on, the same piece of gossip seemed to come up.

Sally was a tease. She would date a man a couple of times, giving him all the time-honoured signals. Then, when he came to making a pass, she would turn him down flat. According to Brian Smith, who buttonholed Diane in the office pub, Sally didn't even go in for kissing. She would simply freeze the minute he came within range.

'She made me feel that wanting her was somehow unnatural,' Brian said.

'I went around for days afterwards, wondering if there was something wrong with me.'

The conversation with Brian worried her. Diane had known him for years, ever since she had joined the *Express*. As far as she knew, there was nothing amiss with him. He was attractive and sexy and certainly didn't deserve to be kicked out of bed.

Diane decided she'd better have a talk with Sally. The following night she got her chance. Diane had been washing her hair and watching television, when she heard the front door open. Minutes later Sally came into the room. She was not her usual groomed self. Her lipstick was smudged and she looked as if she'd been in a fight. Diane got up and went over to her.

'Are you OK?' she asked, concerned.

It was then she saw Sally was close to tears.

'I could do with a glass of wine,' she said.

Diane thought quickly. If she remembered right, Sally had been spending the evening with a man she had met at the weekend. The plan was to see James Loughran conducting the Hallé orchestra, then have dinner. But something had gone horribly wrong.

She took a tissue out of her pocket and wiped away a smear of lipstick from her chin. Then she saw it wasn't lipstick at all. It was blood. Someone had hit her on the jaw and she knew without having to ask who had done it. She led her over to one of the overstuffed armchairs, and sat her down.

'If I were you, I'd ditch the glass of wine and have a hot drink. If you stay there, I'll make some tea.'

Half an hour later, when Sally was looking normal again, Diane decided to find out what on earth had happened. She put her cup down and looked at her flatmate.

'Your date hit you about, didn't he?' she said.

Sally looked nervous.

'How do you know?'

'It's difficult not to know when half the men in this town are moaning about what a tease you are. If you want my honest opinion, I'm surprised you don't get beaten up more often.'

Her head came up then, the way it always did when she was angry.

'You're enjoying this, aren't you?'

Diane sighed.

'No, I'm not enjoying it. I'm hating it. When I took you in, you were a normal happy girl who liked her job and got on with everybody. Now you've turned into an accident zone and I want to know why.'

Sally didn't say anything for a bit. She just sat curled up in the armchair, sipping her tea and looking sad. Finally she broke the silence.

'I didn't mean to provoke any of them, you know. All that happened was that I couldn't give them what they wanted.'

'Then why did you go all out to lead them on in the first place?'

'Is that what they told you?'

Diane got up and went over to Sally, putting an arm round her for reassurance.

'I didn't talk to all of them. I got nobbled by Brian Smith in the pub, who told me he thought you fancied him and was all disappointed when he got it wrong.'

'He didn't get it wrong,' Sally said. 'I got it wrong. I always do.'

Diane looked at the girl she'd taken into her home and realised there was a whole side of her she didn't know. I'd better get to know it, she thought grimly, before Sally finds herself in any more trouble. She got up and poured more tea. Then she turned to Sally again.

'Suppose you tell me why you're so frightened of sex. That is the problem, isn't it?'

Sally nodded. 'It's been like this ever since I was up at Reading.'

Diane waited for her to go on, but the words seemed to have dried up. So she prompted her. 'Something happened at Reading. Something bad.'

She'd hit a nerve, for Sally looked tearful again.

'I don't think you want to hear about it. It's not a very nice story.'

'Try me?'

With an effort, Sally cast her mind back to her second term at University. She was still a virgin then, though she was doing her best not to be. She had made an arrangement with her best friend, who was in the same boat, that she was going to get rid of her innocence on her nineteenth birthday. They'd both read all the sex manuals and had come to the conclusion that there was no point in wasting it on a student of her own age. What she needed was an experienced man of the world. Someone who could initiate her gently and thoroughly into life's greatest mystery.

So she chose Brendan Grey who took her English literature class. She guessed he was at least forty. He had been married, although he and his wife were living apart. Not that it was his marital state that encouraged her, it was Brendan himself. For he had bedroom eyes. Some evenings after classes he would buy one or two of them a drink in the local and she was conscious of his eyes fastening on her. They were very dark eyes, wicked eyes. And she knew that while he was talking about Thomas Hardy, he wasn't thinking of the novelist at all. His mind was on undressing her, conjuring up ways to make love to her. And she was glad she only had to wait another week for her birthday.

Brendan was suprisingly easy to seduce. All she had to do was tell him she was nineteen that day and wanted to celebrate with a drink, and he was all hers. He took her to a bar in town, near

123

to where he had his flat. And when they had got through their first bottle of wine, Brendan asked her if she was hungry. She was. And he suggested that if she was prepared to take the risk, he would cook her dinner.

His eagerness made her smile. She'd risk him cooking dinner alright, because she knew if she played her cards right, they wouldn't go anywhere near the kitchen. His eyes were already starting their journey down her body and she knew if she didn't get him out of the bar quickly, she'd die of impatience.

The apartment was roughly what she had expected. There were books everywhere – on the chairs, the tables, the sofas, even the floor. Sally had to heave the Complete Works of Shakespeare onto a free surface before she could sit down. Then Brendan was sitting beside her and she stopped worrying about the clutter. She imagined it would take some time to warm him up. After all, Brendan was much older than she was, and a full professor. There had to be rules about the sort of thing she had in mind. He caught on very quickly.

'We'll be more comfortable in the bedroom,' he told her.

And she leapt out of the sofa and practically dragged him there.

Everything changed after that. She expected him to caress her with his hands, the way he had been doing with his eyes. But it didn't work out that way. As soon as they got into the bedroom, Brendan told her to get undressed. He said it in a very matter of fact way, as if he was her doctor instead of her lover to be. But her curiosity was stronger than the warning bells in her head, so she did what he asked. When she was completely naked, he told her to lie down on the bed. And it was then she noticed, Brendan hadn't taken off his clothes. All he had done was loosen his trousers and she felt a moment of disquiet.

'You are going to make love to me?' she asked nervously.

And he smiled and said that was the general idea.

He climbed on top of her then and she closed her eyes anticipating his hands on her skin. Except there was nothing. Brendan's hands were parting her legs and her eyes came open to see he had his cock in his hand. It was huge and red and swollen like a monstrous salami and she knew there was no way he was going to fit it inside her.

'You can't,' she said.

But he was already between her legs and she struggled to get free. He pinned her down then. One of his big, heavy arms went right across her throat so she couldn't move anymore. Then she felt it. He was pushing his cock inside her, impaling her on it as if it was some dangerous weapon. And the pain cut through her.

He went on hurting her for what seemed like hours, grinding away at her as if she wasn't a person at all. She was a thing, an object he used to put his cock inside. And she felt sick with shame. Dear God, she said in silent prayer, if this ever finishes I won't let another man touch me as long as I live.

Afterwards, when Brendan climbed off her, there was blood everywhere. And she looked down and saw it was coming from her. So this is what I was saving it up for, she thought bitterly.

Sally looked up to see Diane staring at her, and her memories receded, bringing her back to the present. Here she was in the flat she shared in Sale, nursing a swollen jaw as a penalty for not parting her legs.

'So you see,' she said, 'why I can't get it together it with my dates.'

Diane felt slightly sick. Sally was paying the price for a rape that happened years ago. She had branded all men as monsters who wanted to attack her. She could not see them as affectionate friends who wanted to please her. Diane realised then she wanted to do something to change Sally's perception. She wouldn't talk her round in an evening. But if she just set her on the right course, things might change for her.

Diane got up and walked through to the kitchen. When she returned, she was carrying a bottle of good red wine and two glasses.

'I think we deserve this,' she said. 'Though I do wish you'd told me about your problem before things got out of hand.'

Sally grinned.

'You mean you could have saved the claret for a dinner party?'

'I mean I could have stopped you getting into trouble.'

'How could you have done that?'

She thought for a moment.

'For a start,' Diane said, 'I would have clued you up about men.'

She paused and went on:

'Most of them don't expect instant sex from their dates. They'd like it, of course. If you look hot to trot, they're not going to pass up the opportunity. But given the chance, they'd just as soon get to know you first.'

Sally looked doubtful.

'Are you sure?'

'Put it to the test. Next time someone asks you out, resist dressing up to the nines, and come on like a friend. You might have a better time.'

It took more than one evening for Sally to get her nerve back. Now when somebody asked her out, she turned them down flat, preferring to sit at home and play Rod Stewart or Cat Stevens on Diane's record player.

Not that Diane let Sally put her head in the sand. When the two of them were home, she would sit Sally down and they would go over the whole thing again, analysing it until all the shame and all the fear were put into the right proportion.

After three months, Sally started to make small sorties into the real world. She went to the odd party and had coffee with a man who seemed interested in her.

Diane watched Sally find her feet again and felt a sense of relief. She had been worried about her, more worried than she cared to admit. There was a time when she even wondered if she needed professional help to get her over the trauma. But her counselling seemed to have put her on the right track.

Just before Chistmas, Sally marched into the kitchen where Diane was attempting to cook a dinner party and announced she was seeing someone.

'I met him at a dinner party,' she said, 'and we've been dating ever since.'

126

Diane pushed aside a pile of overflowing saucepans and gave Sally her full attention.

'How long have you been dating?'

Sally looked slightly embarrassed.

'Only a few weeks, but I think it's serious.'

'What makes you think that?'

Now the coyness was gone, replaced by a big smile.

'Because he isn't trying to push me into bed. He knows I'm inexperienced and he respects it.'

Diane felt a moment of anxiety for this new friend of hers. She didn't know of any man alive who would go on keeping his distance indefinitely.

'What will you do if things hot up?' she asked cautiously. 'Assuming the new boyfriend isn't gay, he's going to want more than a platonic friendship in the end.'

Sally thought about it for a bit, then she poured herself a glass of wine.

'He's definitely not gay,' she said, taking a sip. 'So if he wants something more, I suppose I'll cope.'

Diane sighed. As affairs go, it didn't sound like *Gone with the Wind*.

Chapter Fifteen

It was Cissy's idea to throw a party. She was leaving Manchester for a big job in London on a glossy magazine and she wanted to say goodbye to all her friends.

'Everyone expects me to throw a booze-up in a wine bar,' she told Diane, 'but I want to do better than that.'

The two girls were having a drink after work in Yates's Wine Lodge, an old-fashioned Irish bar with sawdust on the floor. It faced the Express building and Diane often used it to see friends and contacts. Now as she looked down the long narrow bar, she understood what Cissy was saying. If she had her goodbye somewhere like this, it would be very jolly but it would be anonymous. All Cissy would remember of it would be bodies jam-packed against each other in a wreath of cigarette smoke.

'Why don't you throw the party at your flat?' Diane asked. 'At least it would be more personal.'

Cissy considered this.

'It wouldn't work,' she said finally, 'I need a place twice the size to fit in all the people I know.'

'So borrow my house.'

Cissy looked at her.

'Do you mean that?'

'I wouldn't have offered if I didn't mean it. We can get Yates to provide the wine and you and I can do the food.'

Cissy took the bottle of wine off the counter and filled up both their glasses. Then she said:

'I love it, though I'm not keen on cutting up a million

sandwiches. Can't we rope in that flatmate of yours to lend us a hand? She's wonderful in the kitchen.'

She saw Diane hesistate.

'Sally isn't around that much at the moment. She's seeing someone and spends every spare moment she gets with him.'

'Does the mystery man have a name?'

Diane shrugged.

'I'm sure he does, but Sally isn't mentioning it at the moment.'

She caught the expression on Cissy's face.

'Give the kid a break. Remember what it was like when we started having affairs. We were so nervous it was all going to finish in five minutes, neither of us breathed a word until we were practically living with the man.'

Cissy extracted a cigarette from the pack on the bar and clicked her lighter at it.

'I suppose you're right,' she said, 'but Sally could have chosen a better moment to fall in love.'

Cissy threw her goodbye on her last Saturday night in Manchester. As Diane predicted, Sally was not at home all day, but she wasn't missed. She was too inexperienced to understand half the things they were talking about, and in a way Diane was pleased she was making herself scarce. She was truly fond of her new flatmate, but in many ways she was still a child and there were times when Diane needed to be around grown-ups.

The two old friends managed better than they'd imagined. By seven o'clock the furniture was pushed back against the walls, all the food was piled high on the kitchen table, and the wine had finally arrived.

Exactly one hour later Cissy appeared in a silver chain-mail dress and impossibly high stilettos. Diane thought she looked even more like Barbara Windsor than ever, but she kept her opinion to herself. This was her big night, and no-one was going to take it away from her.

People started arriving around nine. A group of Cissy's colleagues from the *Mail* turned up first, clutching goodbye presents which they insisted she opened on the spot. Diane cleared a space while this was going on and started getting drinks, continually interrupted by the doorbell. The Granada crowd pushed their way in next, closely followed by a crowd of hacks and sub-editors from half a dozen different papers in the city.

In what seemed like minutes, Diane's huge kitchen filled up and overflowed into the hall. Somebody had turned on a record of the Rolling Stones and as if by some hidden agreement, the front parlour turned itself into a disco. Before Diane could decide whether or not she was pleased with this turn of events, she was grabbed by a good-looking television presenter and pulled into a dance.

It was getting on for midnight before she began to wonder what had become of Sally. She had seen her first thing in the morning before she rushed out and had made her promise to bring her new man to the party. Sally seemed fine about it then. Only now she wondered if the girl had had second thoughts. She decided to go through the house to make sure she hadn't sneaked in the door without her noticing. And she was glad she did, for when she reached the kitchen, her flatmate was standing there, clutching a glass of wine and talking ten to the dozen to a couple of young men she didn't recognise.

I wonder if one of them is the new boyfriend, Diane thought, making her way over to where Sally stood.

'Glad you finally made it,' she said, linking her arm through hers.

Sally grinned.

'Sorry we were so late, but we got hung up with some friends. I thought they'd never let us get away.'

Diane noticed the girl was looking radiant. It wasn't what she was wearing. Her high-necked woollen dress was a little demure for a party. It was her face that gave her away. She had the hopeless, slightly lost look of someone who had been overtaken by love and didn't quite know what to make of it. Suddenly Diane had to know who was responsible for this.

'Aren't you going to introduce me to your new boyfriend?' she asked.

Before Sally could say anything, Diane heard a familiar voice.

'I think,' said David Robinson, 'our hostess and I have already met.'

She'd kept out of his way for nearly two years, so he shouldn't have had any effect on her. But his eyes and the way he smiled did something indescribable to her stomach.

It's still the same, she thought. I still want him more than any man in the room. Then she realised too late what a fool she was. Sally was standing beside him, wearing that possessive look new girlfriends always sport at parties.

'So you're Sally's big secret,' she said weakly.

She expected him to look embarrassed, then she remembered he was in PR.

'You make me sound like a prize that somebody's won in a raffle.'

'I wouldn't call you a prize,' she said grimly.

She saw Sally looking worried and realised she shouldn't be conducting this private war in front of her. Only it was too late to stop now. David was wearing the savage look with which she was only too familiar.

'What would you call me,' he said softly, 'or rather what do you call me?'

She wanted to hit him. She wanted to hit Sally too, so that they would both experience some of the pain they were now visiting on her. But if she did, she'd only end up looking like a woman scorned. So she did nothing. In the end it was Sally who broke the deadlock.

'David didn't tell me he knew you,' she said, looking unsure of herself.

Diane softened. None of this was Sally's fault. The poor kid had no idea what was going on. She decided to put her in the picture, before things got out of hand.

'David and I were an item,' she said shortly, 'but it's been over for years.'

She didn't wait to listen to Sally's protestations. The two of them could have it out another time. Right now all she wanted to do was put as much distance between her and David as she decently could. So she fixed her gaze on a group of friends across the room, then with the skill born of long practice, she edged towards them.

Sally turned to David.

'Suppose you tell me what all that was about?' she said.

David thought he'd got Diane out of his system. It had been a long time and a lot of girls since she climbed out of his bed. But he had been fooling himself. The minute they ran into each other, the old feeling came back in spades. It was her fault, of course. She knew just how to pull his strings.

A challenging look and a barbed remark was all the ammunition she needed that night. If Sally hadn't been there, they would have had the mother and father of all fights and probably ended up falling into each others' arms.

He sighed and pushed the door open to his apartment. It was no good, he thought. She wasn't for him, not by any stretch of the imagination. His father had put him right about that, and though he resented it bitterly, the old man had a point. David walked across to the bar and poured himself a whisky, then he walked over to the window and looked out into the rainy Manchester night.

Albert's words came back to him then.

'You're on the way up,' he had said. 'Anyone can see that by the time you're thirty, you'll be running your own show. But you won't do it with a wife like Diane. She's been around too many men and she's got herself a name for it. She'll only end up disgracing you.'

The thought of Diane destroying his career made him shudder. So he took a gulp of his drink and did his best to banish her from his mind. But she wouldn't leave him alone. Images of their love-making, erotic and disturbing, came back to haunt him. Diane was as dangerous as cigarettes or cocaine, he thought ruefully. You thought you'd broken the habit, but one whiff and you're hooked all over again.

I'm better off with a girl like Sally, he decided. At least I know where I am with her. Except that he didn't, not as of tonight. For when he'd hustled her out of Diane's house, she'd given him a very bad time. It was suprising for her really. Until that moment the girl had been a pussycat. He had defended himself with his usual energy, but nothing he could say seemed to wash any more. The pussycat had grown claws and she refused to believe that he had no idea where he was going tonight.

'You knew bloody well you were going to bump into your old flame, who just happens to be my dearest friend,' she had screeched at him. 'What the hell do you think you're playing at?'

He had placated her as much as he could, taking her to one of his favourite Italian bistros and plying her with wine and copious amounts of their best cognac. But she didn't seem satisfied. In the end all he could do was bundle her back in his car and drive her back to Sale.

David drained the rest of his drink and considered pouring another. It had been a tough night. Tougher because he had not been able to silence Sally the way he usually silenced his girlfriends. He couldn't make love to her.

But now that he came to think about it, that was one of the main reasons he liked her. She didn't share her favours around half the town. In fact to his knowledge she'd only been to bed with one man in her life, and that suited him down to the ground. For when he finally conquered her, he knew that the only tricks she practised would be his tricks. She wouldn't make him her slave, the way Diane had done, because she wouldn't know how to.

He smiled. Sally with a little care and attention would become his creature, his sole invention. He made a note to call her the following day. After a decent night's sleep she would be in her right mind again and willing to listen to reason.

He rang her at the office three times before he finally got through. And when she answered, she sounded distant, as if he was a stranger instead of the man she had been seeing non-stop for three weeks.

133

'I really can't talk to you now,' Sally told him in a fluttery little voice that didn't sound like her at all.

David cursed under his breath, She was still in a state about last night. He decided to ignore it.

'I haven't got time for a chat either, so why don't I just pick you up after work as usual?'

The fluttery little voice went up two octaves.

'Don't do that, I won't be there.'

'Why won't you be there?'

'Because I don't want to see you any more.'

'Damn and blast,' he cursed out loud this time. 'It's that bitch Diane, isn't it? She's been telling stories and putting you off me.'

'She's done nothing of the sort, and don't call Diane a bitch.'

David decided he was in a no-win situation. In the mood she was in, Sally wasn't going to come clean about what was going on. The best thing he could do was to let her stew a little.

'Why don't I call you in a week when you're feeling better?'

He heard her hesitate and knew he had her on the run. If Sally was serious about calling it a day, she would have slammed the phone down by now.

'What's the matter?' he asked. 'Don't you want to leave things for a week?'

The question seemed to concentrate her mind, for when she came back on the line she was spitting mad.

'You can leave it for as long as you like,' she said. 'I couldn't care less.'

David decided Cissy would probably know what all the fuss was about. If she hadn't already left for London. He took out his diary, located her home number and rang her. To his relief she picked up the phone immediately.

'David,' she said, sounding surprised. 'I didn't expect to hear from you. You're not ringing to thank me for the party, are you?'

134

'No, I'm not ringing to thank you for the party. The party was a bloody disaster.'

He heard her giggle.

'You're talking about the touching reunion you had with Diane?'

'That touching reunion, as you call it, cost me my girlfriend.'

She didn't say anything and for a moment he thought she'd broken the connection. Then she came back again.

'If I was staying in Manchester I might be tempted to get involved with your drama. But I'm off to the big city in a couple of days, so count me out.'

David stared at the instrument in his hand in utter frustration. Cissy was the one person who could intervene for him. She could even fit it in before she left. But she wasn't playing. He decided to approach her from a different angle.

'As you're going out of my life, at least let me buy you one last drink.'

To his relief she fell for it.

'I'm pushed for time,' she said, 'so I can't meet you. But you can come up to my flat after work if you like.'

David arrived at Cissy's tiny, purpose-built apartment on the dot of six. He had gone to the trouble of bringing a chilled bottle of champagne, knowing it would soften her up. It did more than that. It helped her out, for Cissy seemed to have put everything, including the contents of her fridge in a series of giant packing-cases.

'We'll have to drink out of toothmugs,' she said, 'it's all I seem to have left.'

David looked at the shambles all around him and remembered another time, years ago, when Cissy would have died rather than let him see her like this.

'Is there anywhere where we can actually sit down and have a conversation?' he asked desperately.

'There's the bedroom,' she said casually, too casually, and he knew immediately what was on her mind.

Cissy didn't want a goodbye drink. She wanted a goodbye fuck and it was in his interests to go along with her. At least he would have her full attention while it was going on. And afterwards, when she was relaxed and receptive, she would tell him what he wanted to know.

He opened the champagne in her tiny kitchenette and half filled the toothmugs she supplied. Then, with no ceremony at all, he walked through into her bedroom. He knew the layout of her apartment from the days when they were together and he didn't pretend it had slipped his mind.

'I see you've painted the place since I was last here,' he observed.

'Are you surprised? It was a long time ago.'

He sat down on the queen-sized bed.

'It doesn't seem to bother you as much as someone else I could name.'

Cissy looked uncomfortable.

'It was different for Diane. You were in love with each other.'

For a moment he felt haunted. It was bad enough coming face to face with Diane and wanting her all over again, but being reminded of how much she meant to him once was too much.

'We've been history for two years,' he said. 'You would have thought everyone would have forgotten by now.'

'You haven't forgotten.'

'Is that what everyone thinks? Is that what you and Diane have been telling Sally?'

She put a hand out to steady him.

'Don't be silly,' she said softly. 'Diane is a realist. She knows you'll never come back to her.'

'So why is Sally acting as if I'm still Diane's property? You've probably heard she won't come near me.'

Cissy withdrew her hand and retreated to the edge of the bed.

'You might try and see things from someone else's point of view for a change. Sally is devoted to Diane. She owes her more than she can ever repay, so she's not going to want to hurt her feelings by running around with someone she was crazy about.'

He attempted a laugh.

'You're not trying to tell me women are loyal to each other, because I won't believe you.'

Cissy sighed.

'What do you know about loyalty? You've been betraying your friends all your life.'

The wine was starting to taste sour in his mouth and he realised he'd had quite enough of it for one day. He looked at Cissy, self-righteous in a shapeless track suit, and knew he'd had quite enough of her as well.

'It's time I was going,' he said, putting his glass down.

Then he looked up and changed his mind. For Cissy had taken off her sweatshirt and was wriggling out of the pants. Now he remembered what it was he liked about her. The woman was made for sex. She even wore the old-fashioned underwear that made her look like a dirty postcard.

He went across to where she was standing and unhooked her bra. Then he cupped his hands under her breasts and started to suckle her. She made no secret of her enjoyment thrusting her hips against him and making little moaning sounds in the back of her throat. So he edged her towards the bed and started undressing himself.

They were both totally naked now. Then David glanced down and saw Cissy had left on her suspender belt. She'd done it to please him because she knew it turned him on. And he suddenly felt in control again. Cissy might shout at him for being heartless, but when the chips were down, nobody was going to judge him too harshly, no girl anyway.

In the end, all girls really wanted was sex and affection. And if you gave it to them they didn't stay mad at you for long.

Chapter Sixteen

Three weeks later, Sally rang him at the office. She did her best to pretend it was a business call and she was following up a story for the *Express*. But David knew her better than that.

She missed him. It was in her voice and in the way she was so pathetically unsure of herself that she couldn't even remember the details of the press release he was meant to have sent her. In the end he put an end to her misery by asking her round to his office.

'We can talk about the story then,' he promised her. 'And if you come at six, I could give you a drink, if that doesn't put too much of a strain on your principles.'

She accepted a little too quickly and David realised that his theory about women had been right all along. They might look out for each other in the short term, but when push came to shove, they looked after themselves.

Sally missed having a steady man in her life, because she was the kind of girl who needed that sort of prop. She might work for a living alongside Diane, but her career didn't fill her life the way it did for Diane. He suspected it was because Sally wasn't as sure of herself as the other girl. Journalism, he knew, would lose out to the first available man who came along and asked her to marry him. And she would settle down quite happily to a life of raising children and making a home.

She'll be good at it, too, he thought, remembering the odd occasion when they stayed in and Sally cooked for him. She seemed to have a talent for concocting quite elaborate meals without any fuss at all. And she cleaned up afterwards. On a couple of occasions he had been impressed to find his kitchen was as immaculate as the daily had left it when they came in.

He pulled himself up with a start. There was no point in getting carried away with the idea of Sally. Part of him still belonged to Diane and until he could claim it back, he wasn't free to think about the future.

Sally arrived on the dot of six, looking slightly bedraggled. She had lost weight, David noticed, and it didn't suit her. The whole point of Sally, the reason he had been attracted to her in the first place, was her rounded femaleness. Marilyn Monroe must have looked like Sally when she was very young. It was an earthy milkmaid kind of look, except that now she had fined down, she looked more like a waif and stray.

He suddenly felt immensely protective towards her, for he realised she must have suffered during their break-up. So he sat her down and opened his last bottle of champagne which he had been saving to impress a potential client.

Sally looked so grateful when he handed her a glass that his heart opened to her. Diane or even Cissy would have seen right through his entire act. They probably would have chided him for acting like a phoney. Sally would never do that because she had no interest in finding him out. She accepted him on face value and that made him feel safe, safe enough to tell her how he felt.

'I missed you,' he confessed.

She smiled over the rim of her glass.

'I missed you too, but you probably know that.'

He had no idea what they talked about after that, except that the conversation was easy. There were no embarrassing questions about Diane, no going over the past, no recriminations. After half an hour, David was so relaxed that he enquired if she was free for dinner.

She was, so he took her to a quiet little place round the corner from where he lived. David's instincts told him this was the right night to be close to home, for Sally was unlikely to be this receptive to him ever again.

His instincts proved right. When he casually suggested she came back to his flat for a nightcap, Sally agreed without her usual reticence. Tonight she seemed to want to do the things that pleased him. And he guessed that if he wanted to make love to her, she wouldn't put up more than a token resistance.

He decided to take things slowly. She was still an innocent and the wrong move could easily frighten her. So when they got back, he made a great fuss of lighting a fire and setting the sound-system. He needed her to feel at ease with him. When she kicked off her shoes and curled up on the sofa, David knew he was getting somewhere.

For an hour or so, he let her drink the coffee he had prepared while he sat at her feet and listened to her talk. She had never really opened up about herself before, but the atmosphere was having an effect on her. For no apparent reason, Sally wanted to talk about her family and childhood. David made no move to stop her, for the truth was that what she had to say intrigued him.

He had her down as a middle-class girl from a predictable English background, and she turned out to be nothing of the sort. Her father George was a cellist who played in the London Symphony Orchestra. And her mother was an intellectual with ambitions to retreat to some academic backwater where she would be left in peace with her books. It wasn't to happen for when Freda met George there was a moment of spontaneous combustion and the two decided they had to spend the rest of their lives together.

Unfortunately Freda's parents got in the way of their marriage. For Freda came from orthodox Jewish stock and marrying out of the faith was unthinkable. In the end, of course love had its way and Freda and George eloped.

'From that moment on,' Sally said, 'my mother's family never spoke to her again. As far as they were concerned, she was dead. And even when I was born, they didn't come round.'

As David listened to her story the pieces of the puzzle started to fit together. He had always wondered why a modern girl with a high-flying job could be so unworldly. Now he knew she had a strict Jewish mother it was perfectly understandable.

She would have been brought up to put men on a pedestal, which explained why she needed him so much and why she never criticised him.

But it was still beyond him why Sally was still acting like a virgin in her twenties. None of the Jewish girls he grew up with had any truck with the old-fashioned notions of purity.

He decided it was high time Sally came into the twentieth century.

He was still sitting on the floor and very casually he took hold of the foot nearest to him and pulled it closer. Then, almost as if he was thinking of something else, he began to caress her instep. At first she tensed, as he knew she would, then gradually he felt the beginnings of relaxation. She was getting used to the touch of his hands on her, and he knew it was time for the next stage.

He eased himself onto the sofa so he was sitting next to her. Then, very lightly, he ran his fingers across her temples and into her hair. Her skin felt like silk, smooth and flawless, and he knew that when he finally undressed her, her body would feel exactly the same. He fought down the urge to take her clothes off there and then. Instead he leaned forward and kissed her full on the mouth.

They had kissed before, chaste goodbye pecks; but this was in another class. For he pushed his tongue between her lips in an explicit declaration of desire. Her reaction surprised him. He had expected some sort of a struggle, but it didn't come. Instead, she returned his kiss with a passion of her own.

And David realised, Sally was hungry. She had flirted with the idea of sex all her adult life, but she had been so scared of giving herself that she bottled all her feelings. Now she had stopped holding back and for the first time in his life, David felt responsible for what he was about to do. He knew that tonight would change her. She would start to become a full-blown woman tonight, by his hand. And instead of scaring him, he found the prospect a turn-on.

As they kissed, he started to undo the buttons holding her blouse together. She was wearing a bra, of course, and with a skill born of long practice, he released the catch at the back.

Her breasts spilled out into his hands, and he was thrilled by their lushness. With her clothes on she had looked like a waif, only now he was releasing her from them, he discovered she was quite the opposite. Sally might have lost weight, but her breasts hadn't and there was a pert roundness to her belly that reminded him of an Indian dancer.

He was suddenly overcome with the desire to see her naked. Gently he pulled away and started unwrapping her. First he undid her skirt, sliding it down over her hips. Then her tights came off, followed by her blouse and her redundant bra. If she had been any other girl, he would have automatically stripped her of her panties with no ceremony at all. But he knew it was her last protection, so he took his time. Moving close, he took the heavy breasts in his hands; then he leaned down and started kissing her nipples.

Sally let out a long sigh, and for no reason he felt sorry for her. Until this moment none of the men she had known had given her the briefest moment of pleasure. And he vowed to make it up to her. His hands moved to the lace panties and they came off with no trouble at all. So he slid his fingers between her thighs. She was wet already. And he took his mouth away from her breast and kissed his way down the length of her body.

He stopped then, in case he was going too fast for her. Then she opened her legs a little and he realised he wasn't. She wanted his tongue inside her and he gave himself up to her scent and her moisture.

He made love to her three times that night, and every time she climaxed, he saw her come a little more alive. Her transformation filled him with wonder. He had never really created anything in his life. Not even his career compared with this. For he had never controlled his career the way he controlled this woman.

When she was in his bed, Sally would feel how he wanted her to feel, react how he needed her to react. And he suspected her dependence on him could become addictive.

Just before he fell asleep, Diane came into his mind. He often remembered her after he'd made love, only this time the spectre of her didn't bother him at all. It was then he realised he had finally broken her spell.

It was time he took Sally home to meet his parents. They had been sleeping together nearly a month and she was starting to get nervous again. She was obsessed with the idea that she was somehow betraying Diane. And nothing he could say would convince her otherwise. Sally had even stopped going back to Sale, and he kept finding things of hers in his cupboards.

He didn't really mind her moving in of course. She had a talent for making him comfortable and there were times when he wondered how he ever did without having his breakfast brought to him in bed, or having his coffee ground fresh from the roast bean. Living with Sally was almost like living back home in Broughton Park, with one improvement: his mother wasn't on at him the whole time.

The thought of his mother brought him up short. He had never really lived with a girl before. If Rose discovered this, there would be hell to pay. So he decided to bring things out into the open, only this time he didn't make a big deal of it. He simply called Rose and told her he was bringing his girlfriend home for Shabbes.

His mother protested of course.

'I'm not having a shiksa in my house on Shabbes,' she told him.

David came right back at her.

'I'm not bringing one,' he replied. 'Sally's mother is as kosher as the Beth Din.'

He didn't see any point in mentioning that Sally's father wasn't of the same origin. And to his relief, Rose didn't press him. She was so excited that he was finally bringing home what sounded like a suitable wife, that she didn't subject him to her usual cross-examination.

Instead, she told him she would be making up the bed in the spare room, unless he had any objections. David knew it was her way of finding out if he and Sally were lovers and he

143

decided then and there that he wasn't giving either of his parents the satisfaction of knowing. If they wanted to judge Sally, they could judge her on how she looked and sounded. It was more than enough ammunition for a first meeting.

As it was, David needn't have worried about Sally making a wrong impression. From the moment she arrived in Prestbury, bearing flowers for Rose and chocolates for Albert, she was an instant hit. It was as if she knew the way his parents minds worked and she played on it.

Friday night dinner was praised to the limits. The egg and onion, the boiled chicken, even the heavy lokshen pudding, all seemed to be childhood favourites of Sally's and she wanted to know exactly how Rose had prepared them. It went on like that all weekend and David started to despair of Sally.

She's gone right over the top, he thought. Mother will either think she's on the make or stark staring mad. Only the girl seemed to have a hypnotic effect on his mother, so much so that on Sunday evening the two women cut dinner short and disappeared into the kitchen to talk recipes.

As soon as Rose left the table, David's two younger brothers took it as a signal to disappear as well, leaving David alone with his father. He felt instantly uneasy. Albert already had that look on his face, the intimate cunning look he used when he wanted to have a man to man confessional.

David took out a pack of cigarettes and lit one, hoping to create a diversion, but his smoking habit had ceased to irritate his father. He didn't flap his hands about in front of his face. He didn't even pretend to have a coughing fit. He simply leaned forward across the table and fixed David with his eye.

'So,' he asked.

David drew on his cigarette.

'What are you talking about?'

'You know damn well what I'm talking about. I want you to tell me about the girl.'

'Her name's Sally.'

'OK, Sally. I want you to tell me about Sally.'

They could have gone on like this for hours, sparring with

each other and saying nothing that really mattered. But David was bored with the game. If Albert wanted the low-down on Sally, he could have it.

'She's only half Jewish,' he said.

The abruptness of the statement didn't have the least effect on Albert.

'From what I hear it's the right half. So if you wanted to make plans we wouldn't have any objections.'

David groaned inwardly. As always his future had already been decided for him. No wonder Rose had fallen for Sally's clumsy flattery. His parents had probably held a family conference on her merits and drawbacks. And the chips had fallen in her favour.

'I don't have any plans,' he said sullenly, 'except to go on as we are.'

'You mean dating?'

'I mean Sally's moved in with me.'

That stopped Albert in his tracks, David noticed. And he felt a moment's satisfaction. It didn't last longer than that, for his father was back on the offensive before he could light another cigarette.

'Why do you have to do this to me?' he said. 'Why can't you just settle down and get married like normal people?'

David felt his stomach go into knots.

'I've hardly known Sally for any time at all,' he protested.

'You've known her long enough to ruin her for anyone else.'

David thought about the glow he had brought to Sally, and how he had achieved it.

'I haven't ruined her. I've made her into a woman.'

He saw the look of disgust on his father's face and realised he had gone too far. Albert's generation still considered sex as a means of procreation. The fact it might be enjoyable was not something you talked about. He considered pouring himself another glass of wine, before he returned to the battle. Then he thought, what's the point. I'm not going to win tonight, so I might as well call it a day. He pushed his chair back in an effort to leave, but Albert motioned him to stay where he was.

'I can't make you do the right thing. I can't make you do anything any more. But I can make you listen to reason.'

He paused, weighing up what to say next.

'Getting married is a big responsibility,' he said finally. 'I do understand that. A girl like Sally will want babies and a proper house and it could end up costing you a packet.'

David started to feel impatient.

'What exactly are you trying to say?'

'Just that I could make things easier for you.'

'You're not offering to lend me money?'

The old man smiled.

'Not for babies and houses. That's for you to take care of. What I want to do is put up a lump sum to set you up in a business.'

'A public relations business?'

'What else are you good at?'

For a moment David couldn't believe what he had just heard. For years now he had dreamed of running his own agency. He had the talent and the contacts, but try as he might there was no way he could find a backer. On the few occasions when he had sounded out his bank manager, he always got the reply that he was too young and had no experience of running his own concern. And no amount of hard-sell on David's part could change his attitude.

Now his father was handing him everything he wanted on a plate, with one proviso: he had to marry.

He started to feel as if he was being slowly suffocated. The last time his father had interfered in his private life, he had ended up leaving the only girl he had ever cared for. And he had taken a vow, there and then, that he would never be bullied into anything again. He saw his father looking at him and realised he had to give him an answer.

'I'll think about it,' he said.

David was very quiet on the drive back to Manchester. While Sally prattled on about his mother and what an easy time she

146

had had, David looked sour and hardly answered her. Finally when they got to the flat, Sally turned to him.

'There's something wrong, isn't there.'

He looked irritated.

'Of course there isn't. You did very well over the weekend.'

She picked up her overnight bag and carried it into the bedroom. When she didn't come out for a good twenty minutes, David decided to find out what was holding her up.

Sally was sitting on the bed when he came through the door. And from the look of her, she had been crying. All his resentment was suddenly wiped away.

'What is it?' he asked, hurrying over to her.

She wiped her eyes with the back of her hand.

'It's nothing.'

'It's not nothing. I've done something to hurt you and I want to know what it is.'

The concern in his voice started the tears all over again, and it was a good five minutes before he got any sense out of her at all.

'You didn't enjoy me getting on with your mother,' she said finally. 'I suspected it at the time. And when we were alone I knew I was right.'

For a moment David felt helpless. He had wanted her to cultivate his parents. It had all been part of his plan. But Sally had succeeded too well. And now he was being virtually blackmailed into marrying her.

'I was proud of you this weekend,' he said with as much sincerity as he could muster. 'I just wasn't all that thrilled with my parents.'

She looked surprised.

'What did they do wrong?'

'Nothing I really want to talk about now.'

She didn't say anything for a moment, and when she turned to him again he noticed a new determination in her face.

'I think you have to talk about it if it's anything to do with us.'

Suddenly he was exasperated. First his family were turning on the pressure, now his girlfriend was getting into the act. He got up from the bed and walked across the room to the window.

'OK, I'll get it over with,' he said harshly. 'My parents would like to see us married instead of living together.'

He expected her to reject the idea out of hand. He had made it quite clear he wasn't exactly in favour of the idea. But Sally didn't do what he wanted at all.

'I think your parents have a point,' she said.

'It would be nice to be married. The relationship would mean something then.'

'You're saying it means nothing now?'

She thought about it for a bit.

'Just about,' she said finally.

Then she got up and went over to the wardrobe. Without saying a word she started to take all her clothes off the hangers.

'Now what do you think you're doing?'

'What does it look like? I'm moving out.'

She stalked past him and headed for the bathroom, and before he could stop her, all her bottles and jars were being piled into a big plastic bag.

'Can't we talk about this?' he asked.

Sally shook her head.

'We have talked about it and I know where I stand.'

'And where's that?'

She was standing in front of his built-in cupboards, heaving out two suitcases and David was surprised how much of her life she'd managed to infiltrate into his.

'You've turned me into a mistress,' Sally said, opening the cases and throwing in everything she had to hand, 'and I don't see any future in it.'

So that's what she wanted – instant promotion to the matrimonial bed. And if he wasn't playing, then it was goodbye. He was tempted to tell her to go to hell, then he saw how ridiculous he was being. He was fond of Sally. He liked her in his life. He enjoyed the way she looked after him. If he had been left to his own devices he would probably have ended up asking her to marry him anyway.

So why am I letting her walk out? he wondered. Because I'm mad at my father for trying to push me into something I wanted to do all along?

He went over to the suitcases and slammed both their lids down. Then he took hold of Sally and propelled her towards the bed.

'What are you doing?' she demanded.

'I'm going to make love to you,' he told her, 'and if I can convince you it means something, then I'll probably ask you to be my wife.'

Chapter Seventeen

Now they were getting married, both families had to be told. Sally rang her mother the next day and got the response she predicted.

'Why didn't you tell me you had a serious boyfriend?'

She was tempted to be chippy and say it wasn't any of her business, but she stopped herself. She wanted Freda to be happy for her, so she told her all about David and what a splendid husband he was going to make. And when she finally put the phone down there was a semblance of peace. Her parents wanted to meet David of course. And they wanted to say hello to the future in-laws, but the ice was broken.

David's parents were less surprised with the news. Albert knew his son well enough to realise he wouldn't say no to being backed in a business. But he was still relieved that his eldest had decided to come into line.

As far as both sides were concerned, David and Sally were as suitable a match as they could have hoped for, and they set about discussing where the marriage should be held and when the date should be.

Sally was slightly overwhelmed at the swiftness of events. One minute her life was her own, the next, it seemed to belong to everyone but her. Both sets of parents assumed she would give up her job as soon as she was married. And when she said she wouldn't do it, there were cries of horror all round.

'But what about babies?' her mother demanded. 'You can't work and have children.'

At this point she stopped being polite.

'Of course I can work and have babies,' she said crossly, 'only right now I don't have any plans to start a family. And if you're talking to my prospective in-laws, you can give them that message.'

She slammed down the phone after that, half expecting her mother would call her right back and return to the attack. She didn't. Rose didn't call her either and Sally realised she had scored a small victory.

'The minute I stood up for myself,' she told David when they got home that night, 'everyone backed down.'

David grinned and poured her out a glass of wine.

'Here's to you winning all your fights,' he said, raising his own glass.

'What do you mean, all my fights? Isn't one enough?'

'You've got to be joking. Weddings are a battleground. Wait till you start on the guest list.'

Sally looked at him, worried now.

'Our friends aren't going to be a problem, are they?'

'I can name one who will be.'

It was then she thought about Diane. She'd managed to put her out of her mind for weeks now. Avoiding her in the office and not going back to the house they shared. But she knew she was fooling herself. Diane was her dearest friend. She deserved better than being cast to one side, just because a man got between them.

I'll have it out with her, Sally promised herself. I'll come clean about David and make her understand that I didn't decide to marry him to hurt her.

She decided to drop round to the flat on Sunday evening, the time when Diane washed her hair and did her ironing. They could be informal with each other then, though there were bound to be harsh words. Sally pulled herself together. I have to face that possibility, she thought, just as I have to face Diane at work.

The next morning she was sitting on the newsdesk in one of the rare moments between stories. And before she could change her mind, she got up and walked over to the fashion department.

Diane was on the phone, deep in conversation. Out of the corner of her eye she saw Sally and motioned her to sit down. Then she put her hand over the receiver.

'What is it?' she asked. 'I'm in the middle of an interview.'

For a moment Sally felt like an unwelcome intruder.

'I was thinking of dropping over on Sunday, if that's alright with you.'

She saw Diane hesitate as if she needed to say something important to her. Then the moment passed. Whoever it was on the end of the line had prior claim on her attention.

'Sunday would be fine,' she said absently. 'Are you thinking of staying for supper?'

'If it won't put you out.'

The fashion editor raised her eyebrows.

'Why should it? You live there as well.'

Then before Sally could say anything else, Diane went back to her interview and she could see she had been dismissed.

I can't blame her for not falling over me, Sally thought, as she made her way back to the newsroom. I haven't been the most loyal of friends.

Sally spent the rest of the week in a state of nerves. She had no idea of what she was going to say on Sunday and as it got closer she got more and more twitchy. David noticed the change in her immediately.

'What is it?' he wanted to know. 'Are the parents getting to you?'

'It's not the parents,' she said miserably. 'I can cope with them. It's Diane. I'm going to see her on Sunday.'

David looked at her.

'You don't have to do it on your own, you know. I can come with you.'

She dearly wanted to say yes, come along, make it easier for me. But she kept her mouth shut. What she had to say could only be said between the two of them. David being there would simply make things worse.

'I'm a big girl,' she said, 'I don't need my hand held.'

*　　*　　*

She got to the terraced house in Sale at around seven. Because she knew this would be her last visit, she came with two large suitcases for her things. Diane didn't seem surprised when she saw them.

'I thought you'd have packed up sooner,' she observed. 'It must be difficult having only half your clothes.'

Sally put her cases down in the hall.

'It hasn't been easy,' she admitted, 'but I held back because I didn't know what to say to you.'

Sally realised she wasn't the only one who wasn't looking forward to this evening. Diane looked weary and somehow older than she remembered. She suddenly realised that if she didn't have a glass of wine, she'd never get through this evening.

She led the way down the hall, hoping against hope that the half case of wine she'd bought two months ago was still there. She found all six bottles on a shelf in the pantry. So she took two of them out and carried them through to the kitchen where Diane was waiting for her.

'I thought we might have some of this before supper,' she said.

For the first time since she arrived, Diane smiled.

'Since when did we need a drink to make it easier between us?'

'Since about three weeks ago,' Sally said, 'when David came back into my life.'

Diane reached into a drawer and found a corkscrew.

'You're right,' she smiled, 'go and find some glasses.'

For a while they talked about nothing very much. There had been some changes in the office, with a new deputy editor arriving from London, and they were both intrigued about how he would make his mark. Diane talked about a call she had had from Cissy in London. And when they had thoroughly dissected Cissy's new job, they got round to talking about what was on both their minds.

'So you decided to move in with David,' Diane said.

Sally took a deep breath.

'I couldn't help it, I was in love with him.'

For a split second neither of them said anything. Then Diane waded in.

'I think I knew all along how you felt about David. It was hard not to.'

'So you aren't angry with me?'

'Of course I'm angry with you. I'm angry with you both for going behind my back. But I'll get over it.'

Sally's heart sank. If Diane was all shaken up because she was living with David, how was she going to take it when she told her they were getting married? She decided to go straight for it and take the consequences later.

'There's something you don't know.'

Diane looked up from pouring the wine.

'What don't I know?'

'We've decided to get married.'

All the colour drained out of her face. One minute Diane looked normal, the next she could have been a ghost. And Sally started to feel wretched. She could have coped with recriminations, but this silent suffering was something different. She went over to where she sat and put her arms round her.

'I had no idea it would do this to you.'

Diane started to tremble all over.

'I don't think you really knew how I felt about David. What we had wasn't just another affair for me. It was the most important thing in my life. And when it finished I had no idea how I was going to survive it.'

Sally started rubbing her friend's shoulders, trying to get the circulation going so she'd stop this awful shaking.

'But you did survive,' she said. 'You went on and had other boyfriends. I've even met some of them.'

'They weren't David and they didn't make me forget him.'

'Why didn't you tell me all this before?'

'I did in a roundabout sort of way, but you weren't paying attention.'

She wasn't either, for try as she might there was no way she could have stayed away from David. Even if Diane had threatened suicide, she would have still gone back to him.

She wondered if there was any future for her and Diane after this.

The older girl must have read her mind, for she straightened up and pushed Sally away.

'It's been a shock,' she said, 'and I've taken it badly. But I don't hate you for marrying David. Someone was going to do it eventually.'

'Does that mean we can still be friends?'

Diane made a face.

'I won't come to the wedding, if that's what you mean. And I won't visit you and David in your married bliss afterwards. But we can still see each other from time to time.'

The way she said it made Sally realise things were ending between them. They'd probably still have the odd drink after work, but the trust had gone. And with it some of the warmth. She no longer had an older sister to look after her now, because she'd chosen David to look after her instead.

She hoped he was worth the sacrifice.

Chapter Eighteen

Sally . . . 1995

A week before he left them for good, David asked his daughter to have lunch with him. Annabel viewed the invitation with deep suspicion. He wasn't planning to meet her at any of the places where they usually went. Fortnum's soda fountain and the Hard Rock had been cast aside for Claridge's.

'Why would he want to take me to a stuffy old-fashioned hotel?' she asked her mother. 'I'm not one of his clients.'

Sally privately shared Annabel's opinion, but she knew better than to say so.

'Daddy feels comfortable in Claridge's,' she told her daughter. 'If you go along with him you'll make it easier for both of you.'

She did as she was told, turning up at one o'clock to find the lobby packed full of American tourists. They all seemed to be vying for the attention of the porters who were running around the street looking for taxis. Rich idiots, she thought sulkily, pushing her way through to the palm court. Why can't they find their own taxis?

Her father hadn't got there yet, so she found herself a table outside the restaurant and ordered herself a glass of white wine. She wasn't really allowed a grown-up drink yet, but at that moment she couldn't care less. Her father was taking her out to lunch to give her the same tired old excuses he had given her mother. He would probably say he wanted his space and she needed a drink to cope with that because she knew he would be lying to her. Nobody walked out on their whole life unless they had something better to go to. Daddy was keeping something back and the realisation made her love him a little less.

In fact when he came walking towards her five minutes late, she didn't think she loved him at all.

'Darling,' he said, catching sight of her drink, 'it's a bit soon for that, isn't it?'

She made a face.

'I needed it.'

He didn't argue with her. Instead, he ordered a glass of Chablis for himself and asked her if she'd seen the menu yet. She shook her head and five seconds later two leather-bound tomes, heavy as encyclopedias, came winging their way to their table. Because she couldn't think of anything else to do, Annabel opened the one nearest to her and started flicking through it. The starters had a whole section to themselves, and at a quick glance, she didn't think she fancied anything she saw. It was all so messed about and she wondered what her father saw in this place.

'Do you think they could manage a steak and chips?' she asked cautiously.

David laughed and took the menu out of her hands.

'At these prices, they could manage anything you wanted.'

He took over after that, summoning the waiter and organising the kind of food she was familiar with. It choked her up to see him do it, because she knew it wasn't going to last. The days when her father treated her to extravagant lunches were drawing to a close. And the resentment she had felt earlier came back in spades.

'Why are we doing this?' she asked, when the waiter finally left them.

'Because I love you and I'm concerned for your future.'

She looked him straight in the eye.

'Pull the other one. You don't give a damn about me and you know it.'

She'd hit him on a raw spot, for his face looked pinched and grey and he didn't say anything for a bit. Finally Annabel had to break the silence.

'What's the matter? Did I get too near the truth?'

He drew away from her and took a sip of his wine.

'How much longer are you going to go on shouting at me?' he asked.

It took the wind out of her sails. She expected him to defend himself or at least put her in her place. But he did nothing of the sort. He just sat there and looked sorry for himself. So in the end she relented.

'I'll stop being angry, if you're straight with me.'

'I've always been straight with you.'

'No you haven't. You haven't told me why you're leaving Mummy.'

He looked at her reproachfully.

'You've hardly given me the chance.'

At that moment she realised that her father was going to level with her. He was going to admit to something tawdry in his private life and she began to wish she hadn't started this. For now it had come to it, Annabel didn't want to know if her father was having an affair with someone. It frightened her to think someone she had never met could destroy her home and her security. So she turned to him and said:

'You don't have to tell me any secrets if you don't want to.'

Some of the grey left his face and he took hold of her hand.

'I think it's time you knew what's going on. It's why I brought you here.'

Annabel started to panic.

'Can we have something to eat first?'

'Of course we can.'

He led her past the crowded tables, full of businessmen and elderly lunching ladies, until they got to a little dais right at the top end of the restaurant. It was a separate section, up three stairs, where people could say what they liked to each other without the risk of being overheard.

She was tempted to run out of this gilded, grown-up room

before it was too late, but couldn't. The waiter had already pulled her chair back and was busily arranging the napkin on her lap. So that's why he brought me here, she realised. I could escape from the Hard Rock, or even Fortnum's. But in this stuffy place, I'm a captive audience.

The food started to arrive then – chilled melon and asparagus out of season. Despite herself, she dug into it. She didn't feel like eating. She didn't even want to be here. But whatever the deterrent, her appetite never failed her. They were halfway through lunch when her father brought her back to the reason why they were there.

'There's something I want to tell you,' he said.

She was so nervous that the words came out of her mouth of their own accord.

'I don't want to know if you've got a girlfriend,' she said.

David stared at her in suprise.

'If it hurts you, I won't talk about it . . . But you have to know that some time in the future, when everything's settled down, I'm going to think seriously about getting married again.'

'You're going to think about it, you're not going to do it?'

He put his hand on her arm, then he said:

'I wouldn't marry anyone before you had the chance to meet her first.'

Annabel's heart was in her mouth.

'Will that happen soon?'

David smiled.

'I shouldn't think so. Your mother probably told you, I'm going abroad for a while. There's a man in Paris who wants me to set up a business for him, and if I can't think of anything else to do, that's where I'll probably end up.'

He said it all very casually but Annabel wasn't deceived. Daddy was going to live in Paris. He'd probably been planning it for months. Just as he'd probably been having an affair for months. But there was one fact that was missing.

'Why doesn't Mummy know any of this?' she demanded.

David looked at his daughter.

'She will when you tell her.'

* * *

Annabel got home to find her mother on the phone. She was talking to one of her women friends and she could tell from the way the conversation was going that Sally was being let down.

Ever since Daddy left, Mummy was finding she wasn't welcome anywhere. Friends she usually had dinner with as a matter of course were suddenly too busy. And when Annabel asked her what was going on, her mother had looked sad.

'There's no place in my world for a woman without a husband. It makes the other wives nervous.'

She didn't ask her mother why, but she could guess. In her short experience, married people had such shaky arrangements that anyone who was unattached was a danger. The woman who was giving her a hard time on the phone right now was probably worried sick her husband would start making eyes at Sally if they were left alone for five minutes.

The whole thing disgusted her. Why did any of them bother to get married in the first place if they had no intention of sticking at it? She went over to her mother who was putting the phone down.

'Another nervous wife?'

Sally made a face.

''Fraid so. But that's old news. Tell me what your father had to say over lunch?'

Annabel hesitated. Her mother's whole world had come to pieces in the last few weeks. If she told her it was all because of some woman who had stolen Daddy from under her nose, she wouldn't be best pleased. The news may very well tip her over the edge. So she told her half the story.

'It looks as if Daddy is going to be living in Paris.'

Sally looked interested.

'How come?'

'Some man he knows wants to set him up in business there.'

'It doesn't surprise me. He had to have something else lined up, or he wouldn't be able to leave us his share of Chandos.'

There was a moment's hesitation. 'So it doesn't bother you?'

'Of course not. I might be disappointed with your father, but I don't want him to end up in the gutter.'

Annabel made to leave the room. Mummy might feel forgiving at this moment. But when she knew the whole truth, she'd probably change her mind.

Annabel always thought she knew her parents. Her father was a high-powered businessman who spoiled her rotten when she managed to get round him. Her mother was simply the perfect match for her father. Because as well as being glamorous, she was totally organised. She had never known a moment when Sally hadn't been perfectly in control – until this moment, she thought, for almost overnight her parents had become different people. Daddy had stopped behaving like a tycoon and was confiding in her as if he was her best friend instead of a parent. And Mummy had lost her way. The whole thing made her very uncomfortable even though her good sense told her that people were only human.

The truth of it was she didn't want her parents to be human. She wanted them to be parents, which is why she kept putting off telling Sally about her father's girlfriend. It was bad enough seeing her wandering around the house like a sleepwalker. But if she was really hurt, there was no telling what she would do. I don't want to see her pain, Annabel decided. I've got my own to deal with.

Things might have gone on in the same way for months if her mother hadn't asked her the one question she was dreading.

'Darling,' she said when they were having tea one day, 'when you saw your father, did he mention anything about a girlfriend?'

Annabel started to get worried.

'Have you heard something?'

'Her mother smiled.

'Not really. It was just a suspicion I had. I was never really convinced about your father's reasons for leaving.'

So Mummy wasn't so stupid after all. In a way Annabel was relieved about that. It took some of the responsiblity away from her. After all, how could she hurt her mother with a secret she already knew about? She decided to test the water.

'Would you be very upset if Daddy did have someone else?'

Sally thought about it.

'I don't think it would give me any sleepless nights, if that's what you're asking. I've been through all that already.'

The girl wondered if she really meant what she said. She'd seen her mother acting terribly bravely in front of her, then when she'd gone past her bedroom she'd heard her crying.

'Are you sure you wouldn't mind?'

Too late, she saw Sally was on to her. She put down her tea and gave her daughter one of the stern looks that Annabel had come to recognise as meaning trouble.

'There's something you haven't told me, isn't there?'

The girl decided there was no point in holding out any longer.

'Daddy did mention something about a girl . . .'

It was then she knew her mother wasn't going to fall to bits, for she looked fierce enough to kill.

'Did your father tell you anything about her, her name for example?'

Annabel looked shamefaced.

'I didn't really give him the chance. I was so gobsmacked, I didn't want to know any details.'

She thought her mother was going to box her round the ears. She thoroughly deserved it. Instead she took her in her arms and held her tight.

'Poor baby,' she said, 'what a nightmare this has been for you.'

There was something horribly final about knowing the truth about David. Before, she had been able to dismiss her suspicions as the ramblings of a jealous wife, a jealous, discarded wife. Now there was no doubt about it. Her husband had a girlfriend. He had probably left her because of the girl and all the hurt she'd felt at the very beginning came flooding back.

After all these years, she thought bitterly, he couldn't be

straight with me. He had to make up some ridiculous lie about the business being too much for him. And when he couldn't hide behind the lie anymore, he had to involve our daughter. This last blow was the hardest to bear. For using Annabel as a go-between was the final trashing of their marriage. David told our child, she thought, that he didn't love me any more. He loved somebody else. And he expected her to understand, and pass on the message.

She wondered if her errant husband had any idea of the damage he was doing. Annabel was still a child, for heaven's sake. She was still young enough to believe in gallant knights and happily-ever-after. Only what was she going to believe in now? And who was she going to trust now that all her dreams had been shattered?

Worrying about Annabel got her moving again. Before then she had felt so sorry for herself that she had let everything go, taking refuge in her big house and pulling up the drawbridge as if it was some kind of citadel that could protect her from the world.

Now she knew she was being selfish. OK, so her husband had left her. Her married friends were rejecting her. She was a big girl, wasn't she? She could cope with those calamities.

But her daughter was a different story. What Annabel needed more than ever was to feel safe again. To know that although her whole world had been turned upside down, life still went on.

So she set about cleaning up her act. She started by turning out all the reminders of the past. The heavy, old-fashioned oil paintings that David had made her hang in the drawing-room were taken down. In their place she put modern pictures she'd collected from local galleries over the years.

While she was about it, she closed up the dining-room. There would be no more entertaining clients. And there so few friends around now that laying out the silver didn't seem worth the effort. From now on, she would eat in the kitchen. They would both eat in the kitchen, and for no good reason she felt a profound sense of relief. Pretending they were grander than they were had been David's game – a game necessitated by business, but David's game nonetheless. And she was glad to be free of it.

Now she turned her attention to herself and she realised she hadn't been to the hairdresser's for far too long. Her red-gold hair was going grey at the roots and she knew it was time to pay a visit to Daniel Galvin in London.

She had been changing her hair colour since the early days of her marriage, using it as a way of cheering herself up. After Annabel, when she had the baby blues, she had gone from her natural dark blonde to raving titian. And when she turned forty, she celebrated the event by reverting back to her original blonde. Now she realised it wasn't enough. She needed another dramatic change, so she rang the salon in George Street and made an appointment for as soon as she could.

Sally realised she had done the right thing when she finally saw what the tinter had done. She had been sitting all day with silver paper wrapped around her hair and when everything came off, she stared in astonishment at her reflection. For she had turned into a tiger lady, streaked and dangerous looking. She wondered what the people she knew would say. She smiled. It had to be more complimentary than what they said before. She regarded herself in the mirror again. At least nobody would feel sorry for her looking like this, she thought. She walked through the salon to get her coat, and as she passed the reception desk, she was stopped by the girl behind it.

'It's Mrs Robinson, isn't it?' she asked.

Sally nodded, expecting compliments. Instead the girl looked as if she wanted the ground to swallow her up.

'Do you think . . . I mean, would you mind settling your bill?' she stammered.

Sally stared at her in astonishment.

'I don't do that,' she said. 'You always send me your account.'

Now the receptionist was really in trouble. She hunched up over the appointments book and started fiddling with her biro. Finally, because she knew she couldn't go on like this much longer, the girl came to the point.

'We stopped your account last month.' she admitted.

'Why on earth did you do that? You'll be saying next my cheque bounced.'

There was a silence while the girl looked nervously at her.

'Actually, Mrs Robinson, it did.'

Sally was suddenly irritated. The hairdresser should have told her, or at least dropped her a line. As for the bank, they seemed to have forgotten their job. She decided a strong phone call to the manager was in order the minute she got home. She looked up to see the girl behind the reception desk had developed a nervous twitch. Poor thing, Sally thought. She's been told to strong-arm me into settling up and she's terrified of getting into a row. She pulled out her wallet.

'I've got Barclaycard or American Express,' she said. 'One of them is bound to solve your problems.'

When Sally got back to Oxford, she was ready to do battle with the bank. But no sooner had she walked through the door than the bounced cheque went straight out of her mind, for the sounds that greeted her in the hall sounded like the outbreak of war.

She identified one of the voices as belonging to her daughter. The other she couldn't place. But whoever it was seemed to be at the end of her tether.

'I can't do it, and I won't do it,' she heard the woman's voice insisting. 'I don't care if your mother is upset.'

Sally hurried towards the drawing-room, judging the fracas to be happening there. And she was greeted by the sight of Annabel and the woman who did their flowers glaring at each other over a vase of tired-looking blooms, obviously the ones ready for replacement. Sally wondered why she wasn't at work doing just that, instead of arguing with her daughter.

'Might one of you tell me what's going on?' Sally demanded, walking into the room.

The two women looked up startled and it was Annabel who broke the silence.

'Dawn says she's not bringing any more flowers this week.'

Sally did her best to remain neutral.

'Why is that?' she enquired.

Again it was Annabel who answered.

'She says we haven't paid her bill, but I think she's making it up.'

A shiver of alarm went up Sally's back. She had just come from a confrontation like this. She turned to Dawn.

'Maybe you'd like to tell me how we managed to avoid paying what we owe?'

The girl gave her a look reminiscent of the receptionist at Daniel Galvin.

'The cheque you sent me,' she stammered, 'was returned by the bank and my boss said we couldn't give you any more credit until you paid off the last lot.'

'He's right,' Sally said crisply. 'I'd do the same if I was him.'

Now Annabel intervened.

'There's been a mistake,' she said. 'There must have been. We've got plenty of money to pay our bills.'

Sally thought quickly. Before David left, he had gone through her budget most carefully with her. The cheque he delivered into her account every month wasn't as big as it once was. But it was still sizeable. And it was certainly enough to pay Daniel Galvin and the flower lady. She turned to her daughter, putting an arm round her shoulders.

'Stop fretting,' she told her. 'Some half-wit at the bank isn't doing his job properly. I'll go and sort him out first thing in the morning.'

Chapter Nineteen

Sally expected to do battle with the kind of bank manager she'd been dealing with all her life – a meek little man with a limp handshake and a mouthful of apologies. So what she was confronted with unnerved her.

For the manager turned out to be a woman, and she wasn't the least bit meek. Her name was Rosemary Gray and she had taken over the branch six months previously. She delivered this information in a clipped county accent while thumbing through the file in front of her. Sally was in no doubt at all that the file contained everything there was to know about her financial affairs and she felt her confidence returning. When the new manager found everything in order, she might look a bit less forbidding.

Sally watched as Rosemary Gray extracted copies of three letters.

'These were all sent in the last ten days,' she said.

Sally was astonished.

'I haven't had any of them. What address did you send them to?'

The manager looked at the first letter.

'Maida Avenue, London, West Eleven. According to our records, all our correspondence goes there.'

Sally sighed. Of course the bank wrote to the London flat. It was easier for David to pick it up from there and take it into the office for his secretary to deal with. Except David wasn't there any more. And the London flat was no longer rented to them. Sally regarded the woman sitting opposite her.

'Things have changed in the last few months,' she told her. 'From now on, everything comes to our Oxford address.'

'I take it we have that on record?'

Sally nodded.

'Good,' said the manager, 'now we've got rid of the paperwork, we can tackle the real problem.' She stopped short, seeing the confusion in Sally's face. 'Of course, you haven't seen the letters,' she said, pushing them across the mahogany desk. 'Why don't you go through them? Then we'll talk.'

Sally was lost now. She expected to march in and make a row about the bounced cheques, after which she would sweep out to a chorus of grovelling apologies. Instead of that, this stranger was telling her she had a problem.

She grabbed hold of the letters. It didn't take long to see what her problem was. Her account had been in the red for nearly two weeks now. No wonder her cheques were being returned. She looked up.

'This isn't possible,' she said. 'A cheque comes in every month from my husband's company. I should be in credit.'

Rosemary Gray looked troubled. Then she picked up her internal phone and asked for the accounts department.

'I'm calling about Mrs Robinson's monthly payment. When did it come in last?' She listened for a while, then she nodded. 'That's right, Chandos Public Relations.'

Sally watched a cloud grow across the manager's face.

'Are you sure about that?' she heard her ask. The answer must have been in the affirmative, for Rosemary Gray put the phone down.

'I'm afraid I've got some worrying news,' she said. 'There hasn't been a cheque from Chandos for two months now. Perhaps you should talk to your husband.'

Sally was completely numb.

'I can't talk to my husband,' she said in a whisper. 'He left me and went abroad.'

Just for a moment the stern-looking woman in front of her seemed to soften. There was a glimmer of concern in the cold blue eyes. But it was too good to last. As soon as Sally started to hope she might offer to help her, the professional mask snapped back into place and Rosemary was all business again.

'I'm sorry about your husband,' she said briskly, 'but there must be somebody at Chandos who can tell you what's going on.'

Sally thought about Jeremy Ross who was running the company now. He would know why there had been no money for two months. It was then she realised that the mistake hadn't been with the bank as she'd first thought. The mistake had happened back at Chandos. She was after all the major shareholder in the company and entitled to her share of the profits. If she wasn't getting it, she wanted to know the reason why.

It was harder than she thought to pin Jeremy down. He was always in meetings or out at lunch. Sally started to wonder if all his clients had such a difficult time getting hold of him.

It bothered her, for David had always been available. No matter where he was or what he was doing, David would always come to the phone. And she knew Jeremy should be doing the same. If he went on behaving like this, the business was bound to suffer.

Just as she was beginning to lose patience, he finally got in touch. It was at the end of the day and Jeremy sounded tired and rather the worse for drink, so she didn't waste time making smalltalk.

'I want to know about my money,' she said, getting right to the point. 'There hasn't been any for two months.'

Jeremy didn't sound in the least bit surprised.

'There's a reason for that,' he said, a bit too smoothly. 'Why don't I come down to the house and explain the whole thing to you?'

Alarm bells sounded in Sally's head. She had never liked Jeremy at the best of times, and the thought of him drinking her whisky and making himself at home while discussing her affairs did not appeal to her. It was too easy to tell lies in the comfort of a drawing-room. And her life depended on knowing the unvarnished truth.

'There's no need to drag all the way to Oxford,' she said,

matching his glibness. 'I'll be in town tomorrow, so I can come into the office.'

There was a moment's hesitation, then he said:

'What kind of time do you have in mind? I'm pretty booked up right now.'

But Sally was listening to no more excuses from Jeremy.

'Then unbook yourself,' she said crisply. 'I'll be with you on the dot of eleven thirty.'

'Make it twelve thirty and I'll buy you lunch.'

She was tempted to tell him to stuff his lunch. What she needed was to be in the office looking at the accounts. There was something fishy about Jeremy's non-payment. If it had been a simple mistake he would have told her about it on the phone instead of offering to see her face to face.

'I'll tell you what,' she said, 'I'll meet you at the office first. Then when we've sorted things out, we'll grab a bite to eat.'

He was enough of a public relations man not to be phased by her, or at least not to show it if he was.

'I'll look forward to that,' he said, putting the phone down.

Chandos's offices were at the top of St Martin's Lane, near the London Coliseum. It was a modern building that had been recently reconstructed and the architects had been generous in their use of glass and chrome.

It suited a public relations agency perfectly, Sally thought, as she walked into the spacious reception area. She hadn't been there since David walked out on her, but there hadn't been any appreciable changes. The lobby was still plastered with enlargements of all the national papers carrying the agency's most famous press campaigns. And on a far wall, framed in silver, were a series of industry awards.

Sally was curious about the awards. If David wanted to go on earning his living, she thought he would have taken them with him. Then she remembered Annabel telling her about some business scheme he was pursuing in Paris. She shrugged. Maybe David's new partner, whoever he was, didn't need proof of his achievements.

She walked up to the horseshoe-shaped reception desk and did her best to attract the attention of a flashy blonde she'd never seen before. The girl was in the middle of a phone conversation and clearly objected to the interruption, for she banged the receiver down and glared at Sally.

'Who was it you wanted to see?' she demanded.

Sally felt nervous. If she was thinking of bringing her business here, she would think again after talking to this girl.

'I have an appointment with Jeremy Ross,' she told the receptionist. 'He's expecting me.'

The blonde dialled an internal number and talked to the secretary on the other end. Then she asked Sally to take a seat until someone came to get her.

Sally thought of saying something rude to put this creature in her place. For she had been coming to this office for years now, walking through the lobby as if she owned it and taking the lift to wherever she wanted to go.

It's ironic, she thought, now I do own Chandos I get treated like a trespasser.

Yet there was something to be said for her new anonymnity. For she could observe what was going on and know that what she was seeing was not some show put on to impress her. The rude receptionist had been an eye-opener. Maybe if Jeremy kept her waiting for a while, her eyes would be opened further.

She tucked herself into a corner and kept looking at the lift, knowing that it was just before lunchtime and the executives would be on their way out. Five minutes later the doors opened, disgorging a group of three young men. They had obviously been at some presentation, for they were talking about it.

Sally heard the client's name mentioned several times. Despite herself, she was shocked. It had always been an unbreakable rule in David's day that clients were never talked about outside the first-floor offices. Yet here were a group of Chandos's executives discussing one of the company's bigger accounts without giving a damn who overheard them. I have to tell Jeremy about this, Sally fumed. He's letting the company go down the drain.

Because she was so angry about what she'd seen, Sally had quite forgotten what time it was. Not until she had glanced at

171

her watch did she realise that she had been kept waiting for nearly half an hour. She got up from where she was sitting and went back to the desk. This time the vampish-looking blonde had been joined by a girl she knew.

'Mrs Robinson,' she exclaimed, 'how long have you been waiting here?'

Sally looked grim.

'Too long.'

Her friend turned to the other girl.

'Have you any idea what you've done? Mrs Robinson's married to the man who owns the place.'

'Owned the place?' Sally said softly. 'David made it over to me.'

Her remark had the desired effect. The receptionist scampered over to the lift and disappeared in a frantic search for Jeremy's secretary. Five minutes later, she reappeared with the girl in tow.

'Mr Ross sends his apologies,' she stammered, looking sheepish, 'but he was tied up in a meeting.'

Now Sally had quite run out of patience. This was the tenth time she'd heard this excuse in forty-eight hours and she wondered why the girl couldn't think of a new story. She was about to say so, when she stopped herself. It wasn't the secretary's fault she was being messed around. The culprit was Jeremy, so she sat on her temper until she reached his office. She was just about to push her way through the door, when the secretary stopped her.

'Mr Ross isn't in there any more.'

'Then where on earth do I find him?'

Sally thought the girl looked shamefaced.

'He moved to Mr Robinson's suite after he went away.'

She should have known of course. Jeremy was the boss now. He looked like the boss when she came through the door. The tight, slightly shiny off-the-peg suits he used to wear had been replaced by something that looked suspiciously Savile Row. And he'd been to the barber's recently. The limp blonde hair that habitually trailed over his collar was short and dapper and it gave him a new authority.

In the past, Sally had seen Jeremy as her husband's puppet, making up in manners what he lacked in brains. Now he answered to no-one and she wondered how he was handling the challenge.

She walked over to the big cosy armchair David always kept in front of his desk and found it had been replaced. Now there was a spindly, French-looking chair and she glanced around to see what other changes had been made. The desk was different, Sally saw that immediately. Jeremy must have substituted his for David's. And there was a bar in the corner she'd never seen before. He must have seen her noticing it, for he moved forward and opened the walnut cabinet that concealed a fridge.

'How about a glass of champagne before we move on?'

Sally positioned herself on the uncomfortable new French chair.

'I'd rather talk about business,' she told him.

Jeremy shrugged.

'You won't object if I have a glass?'

Before she could reply, he removed a bottle of Laurent Perrier from the top shelf and expertly uncorked it. Sally began to feel uncomfortable. There was something too practised about the way he did it. She suspected Jeremy had been opening quite a number of champagne bottles in this office since David left. She waited until he poured himself a drink before she made her move. Then she said:

'You were going to tell me why you haven't been paying me.'

Jeremy pursed his lips.

'It's not a permanent thing,' he said eventually. 'When business gets better, you'll go back to normal.'

Sally stared at the dapper little man in his expensive new suit.

'Would you mind telling me what's happened to the business?' she asked.

'It's changing,' he responded after some hesitation. 'When David left, a couple of the big clients got edgy. They were used to dealing with him and they found it hard to accept anyone else.'

He paused, wondering how to go on.

Then he said:

'We did our damndest to convince them it was business as usual, but they didn't give us a chance.'

Sally remembered the rude girl on the reception desk and the loose-mouthed executives.

'Maybe you didn't give yourselves a chance?' she said. 'It doesn't looks as if anybody's trying any more.'

Jeremy began to look uncomfortable.

'How the hell do you know whether I'm trying or not? You've been here five minutes and already you're passing judgement.'

Sally suddenly felt weary.

'It's a bit hard not to pass judgement when you're doing so badly you can't deliver my share of the profits.'

They locked eyes across David's old office and Sally wondered how Jeremy was going to talk his way out of this corner. She didn't have long to wait, for he came back at her with the full weight of his charm.

'Darling Sally,' he soothed, 'you've got yourself into a panic over nothing. What's happening here happens to agencies all the time. Somebody leaves and for a little while everything looks uncertain. Accounts walk out of the door, there's a slight cash-flow problem, but it's not the end of the world. This is a busy, aggressive agency and life goes on. This past week we pitched for three new accounts. One of them looks like a dead cert. Next week we're going after even more business. So you see there's nothing to worry about.'

There was a small silence.

'I'd still like to see the books,' she said. When David and I started Chandos, I kept a close eye on everything that came in and went out.'

He took hold of the champagne bottle and poured himself a fresh drink.

'Things have changed since you were around,' he told her. 'We're all on computer now.'

'I can read a balance sheet,' she insisted, 'whether it's on a screen or in a ledger.'

'Jeremy sighed.

'If you push me into doing this,' he told her, 'we won't have time for lunch.'

'No problem', she replied, 'I can do without lunch.'

It took Sally less than an hour to realise she was in big trouble. Four of David's most profitable accounts had walked out of the door when he had. None of them had given any notice, because David in his arrogance didn't believe a notice period was necessary. Now almost overnight there was less money coming in.

Jeremy's first reaction, Sally saw, was to borrow from the bank. Chandos was allowed to draw up to a hundred thousand pounds in an emergency, though David had never had to use the facility. The agency had been in trouble before, but new business always appeared to replace whatever had been lost.

So far Jeremy was into the bank for eighty thousand. Despite all his clever talk, there was no sign that things were going to get any better.

Sally hunched over the screen, staring at the figures until her eyes watered. According to her calculations, Jeremy had to bring in another million in billing if they were to break even. And she knew he couldn't do it. If he had been any kind of operator he would have brought in temporary projects to get them over the hump. It wasn't the best way to do business, but it was a survivor's way. A few one-offs would stop the rot until they could get business that went on paying every quarter.

Sally sighed. She could go on searching through the computer records, but she had seen enough. Jeremy had had nearly six months to put Chandos back on its feet and he had failed miserably. There would be no more money coming into her bank account, now or ever. She realised she had better face that straight away and find a solution. If she didn't, both she and her daughter would be on the breadline.

She decided to sell the house. It was such a simple answer, she wondered why she hadn't thought of it before. She and Annabel didn't need a big place in the country any more. I can sell up,

Sally thought, and move to a flat in town. Annabel can go to school there just as easily as she can here.

The prospect of returning to London filled her with an excitement she hadn't felt in years. In the early days of her marriage she had spent most of her time there and she felt at home in the city.

I wasn't a housewife then, she thought. I was a career girl who liked the buzz of fancy restaurants and all-night parties. She smiled at the recollection. Her party days were over now, but there were other things to discover. She would make new friends, divorcées like herself. And she would search out new interests and pursuits. I may have hit a bad patch, Sally thought. But I'm not finished yet.

Three days later she realised she was mistaken. She had contacted Rosemary Gray at the bank for the deeds of her house, only to find they didn't have them. She spent the next two days searching through every cupboard and every drawer, hoping to discover them tucked away in some dark corner. But she came up with nothing.

Finally against her better judgement, she called Jeremy at Chandos.

'Did David leave any of his personal papers behind?' she asked.

Jeremy hummed and hawed and finally admitted he didn't know.

'His desk is still in one of the offices,' he told her. 'And so far nobody has dared to take it over, so there could be something left in the drawers. Do you want me to go through it?'

Sally told him she didn't. The less this shyster knew about her personal affairs the better.

'I'll come up in the morning and look myself,' she said.

It was a wasted trip. David had cleaned out every drawer before he went. She couldn't even find a cigarette packet. She looked around the deserted office that housed old filing-cabinets and the big cosy armchair that Jeremy had discarded. They were using this space as a dump room and she was appalled at the waste. She had no idea what they were paying per square foot, but she knew it wasn't cheap and she wondered how many other offices were sitting empty like this. With a million pounds worth of billing missing, she knew this couldn't be the only one.

Depression swept over her. She and David had invested so much of themselves in this business. All their hopes and fears and energies had been absorbed by it. And when she left it to have Annabel, she still didn't entirely cut her ties.

Over the years she had made sure every one of their clients was cosseted and cared for. Those who liked music were taken to the opera every season. The racing fanatics were invited to the box she organised at Ascot. And she never stopped inviting them to her house. At least twice a week, she held dinner parties where they would meet whichever influential captain of industry or famous actor she could rustle up. Sally tended the clients the way a gardener cultivated his favourite patch. And they paid her back by staying loyal to David and the agency.

She got up from her husband's empty desk and made to leave. It had all been a waste of time, she told herself. All her lavish entertainment, all David's hard work and commitment had been cancelled out by six months of Jeremy. When she drove home that night, she knew that given the opportunity she could have cheerfully murdered him.

The letter was waiting for her on the mat when she got in. It was addressed to David, but she opened it anyway. Then she wished she hadn't, for it was from a mortgage company. Her husband was apparently five months in arrears to them and they were threatening to repossess the house. Suddenly the missing deeds began to make sense. David wouldn't have them if he owed money to a mortgage company. They would be safely hidden in the headquarters of the Chelsea Building Society.

She felt like a complete fool. All the time when she thought David had bought their house out of his savings, he hadn't at all. He'd taken out a loan on the property. And now he didn't have the funds in his bank account to pay it back.

Why didn't he tell me, she wondered. I'm not a child who has to be protected from the truth. Then she remembered how proud David had always been about taking care of her. As if he was Father Christmas or big daddy, shielding her from the harsh realities of life.

This was one reality she was going to have to face up to all on her own. She saw the letter was from a Mr Cotton, then she looked at the top of the page and saw that his personal extension number had been typed in next to the telephone number of the branch.

It was time to make contact, she decided. She needed to know exactly how much David owed to the Chelsea.

Mr Cotton, who asked her to call him Bobby, was very understanding. He'd been trying to get hold of David ever since he had defaulted on his payments.

'Where did you try to get hold of him?' Sally asked, already knowing the answer.

'We wrote to his London address.'

Sally took a deep breath.

'We don't live there any more.'

She was going to tell him the rest of the story, but she decided to hold her fire. Sally needed to get a little more information out of Mr Cotton before she put him completely in the picture.

'Tell me,' she said, before he could reply, 'how much does David owe you? I don't mean the arrears. I'm talking about the whole lot.'

There was the briefest of pauses.

'If you don't mind holding on, I'll find the file.'

Several minutes later he was back on the line.

'The grand total is exactly two hundred thousand and nineteen pounds,' he told her.

Sally did a fast sum in her head. If she sold the house quickly and took what she could for it, she would probably walk away with three hundred and fifty thousand. When she'd paid the mortgage back, she'd be left with around one hundred and fifty thousand to feed and shelter her and her daughter.

She'd had more than that when she and David started out together.

Chapter Twenty

Sally . . . 1977

Two months after Sally and David were married, David had a visit from his father. It was something he had been expecting for some time, for he hadn't forgotten the offer Albert had made to back him. If his father had been a different person, he might have quizzed him about it before now. But he knew better than to play into the old man's hands. When Albert was ready, Albert would come to him. And now he had.

To what do I owe the pleasure?' he asked, looking up from the presentation he was preparing.

'I was going racing,' he said. 'I thought you might like to come with me.'

He noticed then his father was wearing tweeds and a snap brim trilby and he felt obscurely irritated. He wasn't a little boy that came running every time Albert beckoned.

'Can't you see I'm busy?'

'Of course I can, but you'd be doing yourself a favour if you came with me.'

David sighed. Why was it that every time his father did anything for anyone, he had to make such a performance about it. It was clear he wanted to start discussing the new business. But why couldn't he ring up and ask him out to lunch like everybody else?

He put his presentation to one side.

'I can't come today, Pa, I've got a meeting I can't put off.'

'You'll be wasting your time. What you need to be talking about are your own interests.'

He knew it without having to be told. But he also knew that going to a presentation for the agency that employed him was a good idea right now. He had been talking hard to his two biggest clients and they were both intrigued that he might be setting up his own business. Nobody had made any definite promises yet, but that was a mere detail. David knew they would follow him because they didn't believe anyone else was capable of understanding them. They were on the edge, poised to end their contracts any time now. So if he suddenly started cancelling important presentations, somebody at Omega was bound to smell a rat. They'd know he was losing interest, which meant he was on the move, which meant they would start nailing down every piece of business he worked on.

No, he thought. Father can go to the races on his own today. I'll take him out to lunch when I've got something to tell him.

Two weeks later David met his father for lunch in the fish restaurant he usually favoured. Albert had a permanent table in the businessman's haunt where he would sit for hours with his cronies in the rag trade, haggling over some deal they'd all agreed on months ago. When David chided him about the time he was wasting, Albert would shake his head and look sad.

'You don't understand, David, haggling is part of the pleasure. If deals were agreed on in five minutes, I'd go into another business.'

I am in another business, David thought. And for the hundredth time that day he thanked his lucky stars he had managed to resist being bullied into the family firm. It would have bored him to tears and driven him mad at the same time. And he knew his father finally understood this – hence the offer to back him.

Today he was going to show the old man he was worth putting money into, for that week the two clients he had been chasing had finally agreed to follow him into his own agency. It was a major

180

triumph, as both accounts had the potential he was looking for. They wanted to expand their horizons beyond the confines of the North. And if David hadn't assured them he was looking to set up shop in London, they would probably have cast around for someone else who would service them nationally.

As he walked into the restaurant, he saw Albert was already there, drinking blackcurrant tea and picking his way through a plate of pickles. So he went straight over and planted a kiss on his cheek.

'Have I got news for you!'

Albert smiled and indicated the pickle.

'Tuck in and then we'll talk.'

David took a lump of sour cucumber and did his best to look as if he was enjoying it. He had never understood his father's love of traditional Jewish food. It had always given him a stomach ache and the moment he left home he cut blintzes and chopped liver and pickled anything right out of his diet.

Now he was going to suffer bad indigestion, but he decided it was worth it, so he turned to his father and said;

'Don't you want to hear what I've got to tell you?'

The old man sucked on his tea.

'Let me guess. Sally's pregnant?'

David fought down the impulse to hit him.

'Sally isn't pregnant. We've only just got married, for Christ's sake.'

'What's that got to do with it?'

At this rate they could go on all lunchtime debating whether or not they should start a family. David signalled the waiter, knowing the diversion of ordering would get his father off the subject of babies.

And it did. By the time Albert had argued the merits of herring as opposed to smoked salmon, he had quite forgotten what he had been talking about. David seized the moment.

'I want to talk about my new business,' he said.

His father nodded.

'I thought you'd get round to it. I suppose you want to tell me what ideas you've got for it.'

'I can do better than ideas. There are two solid bits of business waiting to follow me the minute I open my doors.'

He saw he'd said the right thing, for Albert suddenly started to listen to him. He wanted to know what the accounts were and how much commission they would deliver over the next year.

While they ate their soup, David did his best to inform his father. He told him about his restaurant account that wanted to expand. Then when he looked suitably impressed he moved onto his toy manufacturer who was in the process of launching a new boardgame.

'I can't tell you how much either of them are going to spend because I don't know how far along they are with their plans. But I can promise you, they'll deliver more than they ever delivered to Omega.'

'Because you're so brilliant, I suppose.'

David made a face.

'I wish.'

'What other reason could there be?'

He decided now was the time to put his cards on the table.

'Before now, they only needed promoting in the North. Now they're going all over the country.'

'They'll need a London agency then.'

David hesitated for a fraction of a second.

'Father,' he said finally, 'I'm planning to be a London agency.'

'Why would you want to do a stupid thing like that? You don't know the first thing about London.'

'I don't have to. I know my business.'

'You think you know your business. When you're in the thick of those London shysters, they'll cut you to pieces.'

David started to feel nervous. He suspected his father might have reservations about him moving South. But until this moment he'd had no idea how strong they were.

Their next course had arrived at the table. Leathery pieces of fried cod, stiff and unappetising. David pushed his away and focussed his entire attention on his father. Albert had to understand how important it was for him to start his agency in London.

'There's no way I can stay in Manchester,' he said, 'if I want to stay in public relations. It's a good town to learn in, but that's about all. The business we get up here is small fiddly stuff the national agencies can't be bothered with. I can't make my name on any of it.'

'You don't have to make your name. All you need is a decent living.'

Indignation took the place of his nerves. 'Is that what you want me to do?' David demanded. 'Make a living going nowhere?'

'There are worse things. You'll be near your mother. We'll both see our grandchildren growing up.'

And I'll stay tied to your apron strings, David thought miserably. If I know you as well as I think I do, you'll want a controlling part in any business you stake me in. And you'll be round every day telling me how to run things.

He suddenly saw that what looked like a generous offer a few months ago was just another one of his father's confidence tricks. If he couldn't push him into the family business, then he'd do the next best thing. He'd push him into a side concern where he would have full control over him. He saw his father looking at him anxiously.

'You haven't eaten your fish. Is there anything the matter with it?'

'Not really. I just don't fancy it.'

He made tut-tutting noises through his teeth.

'You always were picky – picky about what you eat and what you do and where you live. You were even picky about who to marry until I put you straight.'

Suddenly David had had as much as he could take. He stood up abruptly and made to leave the restaurant.

'I've got a meeting,' he said. 'I have to run.'

Sally was surprised to see David home so early. She was on late shifts all week and she'd almost written off seeing her new husband in the evenings. Yet here he was bearing a bottle of wine which he seemed more than anxious to open.

Sally sighed. There was no way she could join him in his

evening glass of wine and still turn up for work. She went into the kitchen and poured herself a cup of coffee which she put on a tray. Then she added a glass for David.

'I didn't expect you home so early,' she said, coming back into the room.

'I didn't expect it either until I spoke to my father.'

Sally put down the tray.

'There's nothing wrong is there? He hasn't changed his mind about the new business?'

David looked at her.

'Father still wants to put the money up,' he told her in measured tones, 'but he'll only do it if I stay in Manchester. London's too far away for him to keep tabs on me.'

'But you've already landed two accounts.'

David looked grim.

'When my managing director finds out, I'll have landed the sack as well.'

'So you've got no option but to do it your father's way?'

He shrugged his coat off and flung it on the sofa. Then he got his glass and poured himself a drink.

'That's what it looks like.'

'But you'll be miserable. You hate taking orders from anyone.'

David gulped back half his drink, which seemed to regenerate him.

'There is another way,' he said quietly. 'I could go and look for a job in London. It won't be the same as starting my own thing, but at least I'll be free of my father.'

She thought about it for a moment. In many ways it was the ideal solution. She would be home again with all her old friends. And David? He'd be doing exactly the same thing as when she met him, but she knew that wouldn't do. David had bigger ambitions than to be a wage slave for somebody else. And he had come too close to realising his dream to be happy with second best.

She went over to where her husband stood and linked her arm through his. Then she led him over to the sofa.

'There's something I haven't told you,' she said.

184

For the first time that evening, David grinned.

'Let me guess. You're already married and I've made you a bigamist.'

'Don't be silly,' she said, 'this is serious.'

'Bigamy is serious.'

Sally set her face.

'So is a hundred and eighty thousand pounds – which is what I have waiting for me in a trust fund.'

For a moment neither of them spoke. Then David broke the silence.

'What do you plan to do with the money?'

'I was thinking of putting it into public relations, but I need a partner who knows the business.'

His instinct was to put his arms round her and cover her with love. Then he thought about the chance she'd be taking.

'I'm not the best investment in the market,' he admitted. 'With the wrong kind of luck, I could lose the whole lot for you.'

'If you had the right kind of luck, you could double it.'

He regarded the girl he'd just married with wonder. She didn't know much about what he did, but she didn't challenge him or bring him to book. Instead she accepted him entirely on trust.

'What have I done to deserve you?' he asked.

'It's not what you've done,' she smiled. 'It's what you're going to do.'

Chapter Twenty One

London . . . 1977

It hadn't been an easy move. David's parents made a fuss about their leaving – which she'd expected. As did her office – which she didn't.

Sally loved her job, but she was realistic enough to know she could easily be replaced. Only she was wrong. The news editor was distraught when he heard he was going to have to do without her.

'You're the best girl I've got,' he complained. 'I'll be lost without you.'

She still didn't quite believe him until she got a call from his opposite number in London, Jerry Kaye. 'I'm told you're leaving Manchester,' he said without preamble. 'Would you be interested in working for the paper in London?'

'Of course,' she told him, overjoyed, 'but why are you asking me?'

There was a long silence and Sally wished she hadn't been so curious. Finally Jerry came back on the line. 'Manchester tells me you've got guts,' he said shortly. 'Where I'm sitting, they're in rather short supply.'

David was thrilled when she told him about her new job. 'All we have to do,' he told her, 'is find us a place to live and we'll be set.'

What he wanted to do was take out a mortgage and buy

something substantial in Chelsea. But Sally had other ideas. She'd just put her life savings in David's new business, spending any more money seemed excessive.

So she twisted him arm and got him to rent a tiny flat in Redcliffe Square. It could only be reached by climbing four flights of stairs and when you got there the drawing room was about all there was to it. The bedroom and bathroom seemed designed for pygmies. And the kitchen could only take one person at a time.

David wasn't happy about it of course, but that didn't bother Sally. She knew if her husband hated the situation enough it would give him the incentive he needed to work his way out of it.

Not that David needed pushing. He seemed to spend all his time at his new agency – which they'd christened Chandos. The offices were only slightly bigger than their flat. And Sally started to worry about him. She wanted David to succeed, but she didn't want him to die in the effort. And with just one secretary and a glorified PA, it seemed likely that he might.

One evening, when she was clearing away the dishes after dinner, she decided to have it out with him. As usual he had staggered home around nine, too tired to do anything but eat and fall asleep in front of the ten o'clock news. And Sally was getting heartily sick of it.

'Don't you think you should take on someone else?' she suggested. There's too much to do for one person.'

David looked stubborn.

'I always managed to run my two accounts perfectly well on my own.'

'But you weren't building a business then.'

She thought about all the boring receptions they dragged themselves to in the hope of picking up a new contact, or a new client.

Every lunchtime and every evening David was out there, handing over his business card and doing his damndest to charm everybody.

'You can't do everything,' Sally went on, 'even if you think you can.'

He put his head in his hands in a gesture of defeat.

'What would you have me do?' he demanded. 'Waste more of your inheritance building up a staff? We don't have the space for anyone else. We don't have enough business either.'

Sally thought for a moment.

'What if I came in and lent a hand?' She saw the expression on his face, and hurried on before he could interrupt her.

'Look, I've been a journalist, so I do know how to talk to the press. And you can show me the rest.'

There was a silence for a moment, then David said.

'I thought you were going to stay with the *Express?*'

'I was, but I don't want it that much. It's more important that Chandos succeeds.'

David looked at his wife in despair. If he let her come in and be his dogsbody, she will have passed up a rising career. But if he didn't, she might just lose her investment.

'I shouldn't let you do this,' he sighed.

'I know,' Sally replied. 'But you can't stop me.'

They worked surprisingly well together, because Sally knew her husband's weak spots. He was brilliant when he was selling something. On his feet talking to a prospective client, David was one of the most mesmerising men she had ever known. But he was lousy at the boring bits. When she got stuck into his files, Sally saw David never sent his bills out on time. He didn't keep a proper record of his contacts. And he never checked in with them.

This is so sloppy, Sally thought. No wonder we don't attract any new business. She considered reviewing the situation with David. Then she realised she was being silly. Her husband lived on another plane, a higher, more creative plane. There was no way he would waste his time discussing bills and keeping files. It was up to her to do that for him. So she set about it with a vengeance.

After every party, Sally would quiz him about who he met.

Then when he was back in orbit, she would very carefully transfer all the names onto a ledger. Next to every name she would put a job description, or a note of how David could use them.

She planned to send out letters to them regularly every few months. If they'd installed a photocopier, or were shortlisted for a new account, the names on Sally's list would be told.

In six months the agency was working the way they both envisaged it. Their two clients were pleased with the service they were getting – even though half of it was provided by Sally. And they were starting to get asked to compete for accounts that were on the loose. All they had to do now was to land one of those accounts and they might start making money.

Except it never seemed to happen. So far David had been up for a garden furniture account, an interior design school, a chain of hairdressers and a major brand of dog biscuits. At least one of them should have come their way. But the answer was always the same: the potential clients liked David; they liked his ideas; but they'd never heard of his agency and they couldn't trust their precious account to an unknown boy from Manchester.

Every time the agency got turned down, David got a little more dejected and Sally found she had a full-time job just keeping his confidence intact. But she never doubted him for one minute. She believed in the man she married. She believed in his talent and his energy and his passion for the business of public relations.

Something is bound to turn up, she promised herself.

Something did turn up, though it wasn't what either of them expected.

David's parents decided to spend a few days in London to see how they were faring. And Sally's heart sank at the news. Albert hadn't been exactly supportive when they'd told him they were leaving Manchester. He even went as far as to pour cold water on Sally making over her inheritance to David.

'You must be mad,' he said. 'My boy is incapable of running a business on his own.'

If Sally hadn't be so anxious to keep the peace, they might have left for London without speaking to either of David's parents.

But she knew how important they were to him, so she bent over backwards to bring Albert round.

In the end she managed to make him apologise to David for doubting him. And by the time the four of them parted, they did so with tears and kisses. The old man even wished David good luck and Sally breathed a sigh of relief and made a promise to herself. The next time David saw Albert and Rose the new agency would be thriving and his entire family would eat their words.

If they'd waited another few months, Sally thought, we might have been ready for them. As it is, we're still living in two rooms. And David's agency is the size of a rabbit hutch. She was tempted to make David put them off, but he was so excited about seeing his parents again she didn't have the heart.

So she set about making the best of things. Instead of asking Albert and Rose to their flat, Sally booked an expensive fish restaurant in Soho. It was a haunt of successful media men with offices nearby and she hoped David would shine by association.

He didn't though. He was half an hour late because a client kept him behind in a meeting. And when he explained this to his parents, Albert just growled and said,

'That business you brought down from Manchester is never going to respect you until you show them you don't need them.'

'But I do need them?' David said. 'That business, as you call it, is all I've got.'

If Sally had been sitting nearer to him, she would have kicked him under the table. For until he got there she had been making a pretty good job of talking up the agency. She hadn't been specific, of course, but the overall impression was that new accounts were rushing through the door.

Now David had gone and ruined everything by telling the truth.

As she suspected would be the case, Albert seized on this. He wanted to know what was wrong with the agency. When David told him nothing, he refused to accept it.

190

'If you'd been doing well, you'd have more than the two piddling little clients you started out with.'

They both knew it of course. The fact that Chandos wasn't growing had been their sole topic of conversation for months now. But Albert airing it in public did nothing for David's temper.

'Have you got any idea how difficult it is to set up a new agency?' he demanded. 'It's not like the manufacturing business where you've got a product to sell. All I can sell is me and my ideas and my track record. And right now there are dozens of other public relations men trying to crowd me out.'

The old man didn't say anything after that. And Sally was grateful when one of the hovering waiters showed them to their table.

As they sat down, Sally prayed Rose wouldn't ask her if the place was kosher. To her intense relief she didn't. Though when Albert found his voice again, she realised she might have appreciated a discussion on kashrus after all.

For David's father hadn't been shut up by his son's outburst. His silence was simply due to the fact he was mulling over what to say next.

'There's no shame in failing,' he pronounced finally. 'Everyone does it when they start out. But you've got to be stong enough to admit you've got it wrong and do something about it.'

'Like what?' David asked accusingly.

Sally shot a look at David, willing him to keep a curb on his feelings. And when that had no effect, she looked pleadingly at her mother-in-law, hoping she might intervene.

In retrospect she realised that neither she nor Rose had the slightest effect on the two men. They were locked into a fight that had been going on since David's childhood and nothing other than a small earthquake was going to stop them from saying what was on their minds.

What was on Albert's mind was fairly predictable.

'I think you should cut your losses and come back to Manchester. You're a name in that town. You made your reputation there. There'll be no problem getting business from half a dozen people I could name.'

'You can only name them because they're friends of yours. And I don't do business by playing on past favours.'

Albert looked beady.

'So you've changed since you set up on your own. When you were working for Omega in Manchester you pulled in every favour that was going.'

David's lips pulled into a line and Sally knew the old man had got to him. He'll come back like a whiplash, she thought. But she was wrong. Before David could form a reply, Albert went on:

'Shall I tell you why you don't play the favours game any more? It's because you can't. Because you don't know anyone in London you can ask to help you out.'

David stood up then, pushing the table away so sharply that a bottle of mineral water tipped up and went all over Rose. Not that he noticed. Ignoring his mother's pained face, he grabbed hold of Sally's hand and dragged her towards him.

'Come on,' he muttered, 'we're out of here.'

They had both finished the only bottle of wine in the fridge, when Sally finally got up the courage to talk about what had happened.

Until she brought it up, she had listened to a monologue from David about his father. He had gone right back into his childhood, dragging up every injustice the old man had wished upon him. And in the end she decided she had had enough.

Albert wasn't a monster. He was bombastic and controlling, but underneath it all he loved his son and wanted the best for him. She knew David wasn't ready to hear that. So she did the next best thing. She defended what Albert had to say. Not all of it. She had no wish to see David give up and go back to Manchester. But Albert's last barb, the one that made David walk out of the restaurant, had an uncomfortable ring of truth about it.

'You can't blame your father for the fact you're not known down here,' she said gently.

David looked sulky.

'I can blame him for saying it.'

Now she rounded on him.

'No you can't. I've said it often enough. We both have. The clients won't give us a chance because you're not somebody in this town. You haven't got a name or a track record.'

'How can I make a name if nobody will consider us?'

Sally played her wild card then.

'You invent one.'

He wasn't sure if he was hearing right.

'Have you had too much wine, Sally?'

She laughed.

'I'm not drunk at all. I've been thinking about smartening up our act for a long time now, but I didn't know how to broach it because it's going to cost us money.'

She could tell David was hooked, because he stopped looking miserable and started listening to what she was saying.

'Tell me your plan for smartening up our act,' he said, 'and I'll tell you whether or not we can afford it.'

She got up and went over to where he was sitting on the sofa. Then she settled against him and started talking.

'My idea is we throw a party. Not some penny-pinching affair, but a fabulous extravagant bash that will impress the pants off everybody who comes.'

She drew breath, warming to her theme.

'I know it will cost a fortune, but I'd hire a room at the Ritz if we could get one and lay on champagne. I'd bribe a couple of famous faces to turn up. Or I'd spread money around the right agents. Then I'd go right back to my ledger. The one I've been building up with potential clients and useful contacts and I'd send out invitations to all the names.'

David put his hand on the back of Sally's neck and started playing with her hair. There was such passion in what she was saying, he found it was beginning to turn him on.

'What are you trying to achieve with this expensive party?'

She looked at him.

'I would have thought that was obvious. Only people who are

193

doing really well can afford to put on that kind of show . . . and if we convince enough people we're hot, they're going to want a part of us.'

It was such simple logic, David thought. Almost childish in its way. But people were childish. They loved show and tame celebrities. You could talk the best marketing game in the world, but without the necessary glitter it fell on deaf ears. He looked at Sally with a mixture of lust and real affection.

'Your idea has merit,' he told her. 'Do you think we could go on discussing it in bed?'

The party cost well over four thousand pounds and everyone from Elton John to Jean Rook was on the guest list.

'Do you'll think they'll come?' Sally asked fearfully when David plonked the list in front of her.

'For a glass of free champagne at the Ritz the world and his wife will turn up.'

Three weeks later, standing in the Marie Antoinette room in the grand hotel on Piccadilly, Sally remembered those words. For none of the celebrities on the list had made the party. All the clients and potential clients were there, nervously sipping their drinks. The press was out in force, gulping their free champagne. But unless a famous face walked into the room, Sally knew the party would never really take off.

The celebrities were a vital ingredient. They counted as much as the location and the temperature of the champagne and Sally started to send up a silent prayer, envisaging all the glittering names on the gold-edged invitation cards. If someone, even a star from *Coronation Street*, puts in an appearance, the agency would be in with a chance. But without that the press would start to leave and the room would thin out in no time at all.

She grabbed a glass of Moët from one of the white-coated waiters to calm her nerves. And it was then she saw Joan Collins.

She was standing just outside the door, dressed in a figure-hugging black suit with a mink coat flung over her shoulders. She looked exactly like all the pictures Sally had seen of her in the papers, yet it didn't stop the press corps from wanting yet another photo call. Joan must have known this, for the minute the cameramen appeared, she threw herself into half a dozen carefully rehearsed poses. It was as if she had a secret arrangement with all the pressmen present, for she seemed to know by telepathy exactly what they wanted and exactly how much time she should give them.

As the flashbulbs popped all around her, Sally started to relax. If Joan was the only celebrity to fall for David's con, it didn't matter. She was a big enough name to make the nationals tomorrow, as well as to make this party something to talk about, Sally thought. She hurried over to the waiter with the tray of champagne, grabbing a glass to thrust into the actress's hand the minute the session was over.

When Joan took the champagne from her slightly shaking hand, it was with the same composure as she did the photo session. Then she smiled pleasantly and walked over to a group of businessmen whom she seemed to know. Two of them were potential clients and Sally's confidence started to rise. The bluff was beginning to work.

Out of the corner of her eye she saw a crowd of what looked like body-guards at the entrance to the room. Then she saw the well-known face of a leading cabinet minister and she knew they were well and truly on the road. They had thrown away money they could ill afford to show people they existed. And nobody could doubt that any more. The buzz of excitement in the air was all the proof she needed.

Now it all depends on David, Sally thought. She kept a weather-eye on him all evening, and he seemed to be operating the way he always did at parties, spreading charm and his business card at every available opportunity. She wondered whether he had got any serious attention, or whether this would be like all the times when people promised him things without following through.

She got her answer towards the end of the party, when the crowd started to thin out. David and a bulky, prosperous-looking man were wishing each other a hearty goodbye.

'Look forward to Tuesday,' David said, clapping him on the shoulder. 'There's a lot to discuss.'

Sally grabbed her husband before he could disappear again.

'Was that a new account?'

David grinned.

'What do you think?'

Then he was gone, moving through the bright, fashionable crowd as if he had been doing it all his life.

'We're launched, she thought, feeling slightly weak at the knees. Albert Robinson, eat your heart out.

Things moved faster than even Sally believed they could. Several morning papers carried pictures of Joan Collins and one of them even mentioned Chandos by name as the organiser of the event. It was all they needed. The phones started to ring the following morning and they didn't stop ringing for the best part of the week.

There was a buzz around town that Chandos was hot and new and hungry and David didn't do anything to alter that impression. If anything, he enhanced it by pretending he was busier than he really was. Sally once heard him protest that he couldn't possibly see a potential new client because he was frightened he had an account that would clash with what was on offer. She was horrified, and said so the minute he put the phone down. And David just leaned back in his chair and looked pleased with himself.

'They'll come back to me,' he told her, 'and when they do, I'll be able to charge double the fees they had in mind.'

'But that's gambling,' she said. 'What if they don't come back?'

She could see she was irritating him, for he started flipping through the papers on his desk, as if she wasn't there. In the end she went back to her own office, wondering whether she knew David at all.

Before they'd gone into business together she thought she understood him completely. She knew what made him laugh and what made him relax. She knew which friends to invite when he wanted to impress, and who to avoid when he was feeling insecure. They were so much in tune that Sally could, and often did, choose his suits and ties and shirts without him even being there.

Now the tune had changed. She felt that David was a man she hardly knew. He was tougher than she'd ever imagined, playing fast and loose with his staff as well as the potential clients. It was as if people didn't really matter to him: they were all part of some game he was playing.

Sometimes, when she dared, she asked him where it was all going to lead. And on these occasions he looked suprised and said he thought she knew.

'You trusted me with all the money you had in the world. Don't you expect me to try and turn it into a big business?'

She very nearly told him, not if it was going to make him hard. But she bit her tongue before the words could come out. She realised even then how much succeeding meant to him.

The following year, when Chandos was ten times its original size, David decided Sally was wasting her time. She had proved she was an excellent backroom girl, but there were people he could hire quite cheaply to do her job. What he needed was a senior account handler and his wife was made for the job. She had a grassroots understanding of how the press worked. And because she had been at the agency right from the start, she knew the routine of the business.

It took a little fast talking to convince her she was up to the job he had in mind for her. But in the end she listened to reason. He was glad she did, for all his hunches about Sally proved correct.

She had a feeling for public relations. Clients liked her instinctively and when they got to know her, they came to rely on her. In just a few months he had managed to pass on a good fifty per cent of their most important business and she dealt with it like the trouper she was.

If he'd had more funds at his disposal, David probably wouldn't have given Sally as much responsibility as he had.

For in his opinion, she wasn't management material. She was too soft and too damned ethical to make anything of what she had. The sort of manager he had in mind for Chandos had to be prepared to delegate, something Sally was still too inexperienced to do. He or she also had to be capable of kicking ass, something totally beyond Sally.

There were times when he suspected his wife was frightened of her own shadow. Not that he could get impatient with her for it. He had fallen in love with her for those qualities he so despised in business.

He sighed and set his face. Until he could afford a proper number two, he was stuck with Sally. He was going to have to make the best of her.

Chapter Twenty Two

There shouldn't have been any trouble with Bobby Brown's restaurants. David had given her the account because it was so straightforward and predictable. The vegetarian chain had ridden the crest of the newly rising health boom and all the agency needed to do was encourage people to go on feeling good about them. So Sally was stopped in her tracks when she heard they were starting to poison people.

The news came via a frantic phone call from Tony Brooks the bluff Northerner who ran Bobby Brown's. When he first came on the line she could make neither head nor tail of what he was saying, as the man was babbling. But eventually she pieced together the story. An elderly pensioner was suing them after being taken ill in one of the restaurants. He'd been taking his grandchildren out for a birthday lunch and had collapsed when he delivered the children back to his daughter.

Sally wondered if it was a freak complaint. They got one of two of those every time the temperature rose. So she put it to Tony and got an earful for her trouble.

'The pensioner is the tip of the bloody iceberg,' he screamed at her, 'we've had three more people this week, all claiming food poisoning. When this hits the press they'll all go running for their lawyers.'

He was right, of course. The popular papers loved a juicy scandal like this, particularly when the victim was a frail grandfather. She could almost see the headlines.

'Pensioner in healthfood crisis.' 'Grandfather poisoned.' And if they were really unlucky, Bobby Brown's 'accused of negligence.'

In a matter of days the reputation they'd built up over the years would be torn to shreds. And then it would be goodbye Bobby Brown's. And goodbye to one of their major accounts. She knew she couldn't let it happen.

'Tony,' she said with more confidence than she felt, 'there is a way out of this, but it might take me a few minutes to work out what to do.'

She was busking of course. She didn't have the foggiest idea of how to deal with this kind of crisis, but she knew better than to let her client know that. Tony had been excitable and insecure ever since she'd first met him with David in Manchester, when they used to take him out to dinner and listen to his problems.

In those days he didn't have any problems, but he liked being stroked and reassured. And Sally was better at that than David. She would listen to his complaints for hours sometimes, while the dinner went cold on the plates because Tony was talking so hard. Afterwards, wrung out and dog-tired, she would wonder why she put up with this man. He was her husband's client, someone he should have dealt with during office hours. But David always talked her round.

'He trusts you,' David would say. 'When a client does that it's money in the bank.'

Sitting in her office today with the Bobby Brown's account falling about her ears, Sally wondered if David would still agree that Tony was bankable. She decided she'd better consult him fast. Her husband was the one person who would know how to get them out of this mess.

She got rid of Tony as fast as she could, leaving him with strict instructions not to talk to the press. Then she sped round to David's office. He wasn't at his desk, but his secretary was there.

'Where's David?' Sally demanded.

The girl looked suprised.

'I thought you knew about the presentation?'

'What presentation?'

'The one he's been working on all week. Canine petfoods.'

Sally let out her breath slowly. Canine petfoods, how could she have forgotten? If he landed this one they could double their turnover. But it was a long shot. It was more likely they didn't land it and because David was out of contact with his office they would lose Bobby Brown's instead. She groaned, remembering how big the account was.

'Where is the presentation being held?' she enquired, 'and did David arrange to ring in?'

The secretary looked impatient.

'David's in Glasgow and the answer to your next question is he rang in five minutes ago to say he was at the airport and on his way back.'

This was all she needed – a crisis she couldn't deal with and no David. She saw the girl looking at her curiously.

'Is there anything the matter?'

Sally shrugged.

'Nothing that an act of God couldn't cure.'

When she got back to her own office, Sally rang through to the switchboard and told them to hold all her calls. Then she closed the door and forced herself to sit down and evaluate the situation. She could do nothing but wait for David to get back at the end of the afternoon.

That was the most sensible course, for her husband was bound to have some kind of solution up his sleeve. But what if he didn't? What if Bobby Brown's problems stumped him as much as they were stumping her? All she would have achieved by waiting was to lose time. And Bobby Brown's couldn't afford to lose a second. Unless the agency had a plan of campaign worked out and ready to go first thing in the morning, the press would eat them alive.

For the first time since the balloon went up, she realised she was completely on her own. Bobby Brown's survival depended on her. As she considered this, Sally realised she felt exhilarated.

When she was working on the *Express*, she had loved the tough stories, the hard nuts no-one else could crack. Put her back up against the wall, and she was apt to come through with her best work. This isn't so different, she told herself. It's solvable, but not by everyone. It needs wangling, clever thinking. She wrinkled her brow and forced herself to remember all the disaster stories she had ever heard of. The newsdesk at the *Express* had one on their schedule almost every week. Someone had bought a pot of face-cream with glass in it. A brand of soft drink was found to be dangerous to children.

What they all had in common was a manufacturer who was at fault and a public that was outraged. At least that was the way she and the other reporters had been told to dish it up.

Did anyone get off the hook? she wondered. Was there a maker of face-cream who issued such a firm denial that they all backed off and left them alone? She racked her brains and came up with nothing. Those who sinned against the public good got it in the neck. And those who tried to cover it up usually ended up getting buried. Somebody must have survived, she thought. Every big company makes a mistake, but they don't all go out of business.

Out of nowhere an old news story popped into her head. It was about a super-glue that stuck children's eyelids together. She had been as outraged about the glue as everyone else. But the firm that made it did something to restore people's confidence in them. They issued an apology. Then they withdrew their glue until they could reformulate it.

At the time she thought the cost of the operation would sink them completely. But it hadn't happened. The company lost money for a while. Then the following year, they brought their glue back and went on doing business. People forgave them for their mistake, Sally reasoned, because they took responsibility for it. She knew now how she was going to deal with Bobby Brown's.

Tony didn't like anything she had to say. When Sally asked him to close his restaurants he refused point blank.

'I suppose you're going to tell me to cut my own throat next,' he said.

Sally prayed for patience. She had to make this client of hers understand what he was up against and sweet talking wasn't doing the job at all. So in the end she let him have it.

'If you don't do what I tell you, you might as well cut your throat. You'll be out of business within the month.'

'How's that?'

Tony sounded a little less confident than before and she decided to push her advantage.

'You don't really think anyone is going to eat in one of your restaurants when the media have finished with you, do you?'

'I thought people like you could stop the media.'

'No-one can stop the media when they've got wind of a scandal. The best we can do is soften the blow.'

'Shutting up shop is softening the blow? Give me a break Sally.'

'I am giving you a break and it's the only one you're going to get, so you'd better listen to me. First you make a statement tomorrow morning apologising for what you've done. Then you announce you're closing until you can guarantee no-one will get poisoned again. And to prove you mean what you say, you pay for an independent enquiry.'

For a moment nothing happened and Sally wondered whether she'd pushed Tony too far. Then she remembered he'd trusted her once and she prayed he hadn't changed.

He hadn't. When Tony came back on the line he was all questions. What he wanted to know was how they could possibly survive by admitting they were guilty. So she told him. She quoted the super-glue story word for word. She told him about a soft drinks company that put out a contaminated cola. And she told him how sorry they both were.

'Both companies grovelled to the public. They made asses of themselves. But they survived. If they'd claimed none of it was their fault, neither of them would be around today.'

She spoke with such certainty that Tony finally stopped arguing with her.

'It's going to take me a hell of a long time to convince our legal boys of your plan,' he conceded.

'Then you'd better get started now,' she told him. 'Bobby

Brown's is going on parade at nine o'clock tomorrow morning.'

It took Sally till the early evening to organise her plan of campaign. She arranged a suite of rooms at a local hotel to deal with the flood of enquiries that would come their way once the news was out. Two of her junior executives and her own secretary were seconded to man the phones.

And she worked out a long statement for Tony Brooks to deliver at the press conference she had organised. When she'd been through it with him, she sent out for all the facts she could find about vegetarian food.

Then she called it a day. All she wanted to do now was find her husband and go home. He should be back from Glasgow by now, she thought as she walked through to his office. But he wasn't. To make things even more difficult, the secretary had gone home, and nobody else in the office seemed to have set eyes on him all day. She rummaged through his desk for his diary. That should tell her something. It did. David was having drinks at the Savoy with a client and she was meant to be in attendance.

Damn and blast, she thought, David will give me hell for standing him up. Then she realised he probably wouldn't if he knew why she'd done it. She rang the hotel and got hold of her husband in the American bar. He was cool with her at first, but he melted quite quickly when she told him about Bobby Brown's.

'Have you done anything about the situation?' he demanded.

'Of course I have. I was waiting around to bring you up to date.'

David sounded grim.

'Stay where you are,' he instructed, 'I'll wind this up as soon as I can.'

She suddenly realised how tired she was and the vision of her flat swam invitingly before her eyes.

'Can't I tell you about it at home?'

There was a silence while David weighed things up. Then he said:

'I'd rather go through everything you've done in the office. I need to see it and, if needs be, to alter it.'

Sally started to wonder if she'd missed something.

'Be as quick as you can,' she said.

David was back at the office twenty minutes earlier than he promised. As soon as he got there he went over to Sally's desk and started reading through the material she had been preparing. He was surprised with what he saw. The statement she had written for Tony Brooks hit just the right note. It was more compassionate than Tony knew how to be, yet it wasn't grovelling. Sally knew what the press wanted to hear and had dished it up on a plate.

For a moment he was almost envious of her ability to communicate so effortlessly. He put the statement back on her desk and started leafing through a stack of reports she was putting together. He had no idea where she'd got her information, but here was a digest of vegetarian restaurants from the strict vegan rules to the preparation of food. He looked at her interested.

'Does Bobby Brown's operate like this?'

Sally pulled a face.

'More or less. I've checked most of it with Tony and he says we can go ahead and give it to the press.'

So she'd worked that one out as well, David thought. Snow the media with stories and information so that they don't go looking for trouble of their own. The entire operation had been handled so professionally that he might have masterminded it himself.

For a reason he didn't quite understand he felt obscurely annoyed with her. How dare she solve the first major problem they ever had all on her own? It made him feel redundant. As if all his experience and expertise counted for nothing because Sally could do without it now.

He looked at his wife and saw how utterly spent she was. And suddenly he felt like a heel. She saved the day, he thought, and all I can do is resent her for it.

'Why don't I take us out to dinner tonight?' he said, stifling his feelings. 'You look as if you could do with a bit of spoiling.'

Chapter Twenty Three

It was a bit like learning to swim. When you started, you clung onto the instructor, willing yourself not to go under and drown. Then the first time you reached the side of the swimming-bath on your own, everything changed – you didn't need anyone to hold you up any more. You could do it on your own, which is exactly how Sally felt after the Bobby Brown's crisis.

If David had been there to help her through it, things might have been different. But she had solved this one unaided. Bobby Brown's had come through the storm thanks to no-one but her. And it gave her the confidence she needed to do her job properly.

David was the first one to notice the change in her.

'Things must be going smoothly,' he observed. 'You haven't asked my opinion more than twice this week.'

'I've been rushed off my feet,' she told him. I'll try and keep you more in touch when things have quietened down.'

But she didn't get round to it. Every time she planned to sit down with David and go over her workload, something urgent came up and she was off again, rushing into meetings and client lunches.

She noticed a distance forming between her and David. Usually they would go home together every night. Now increasingly he found things to tie him up in the early evening: either he had to buy a client a drink, or he had to go to a party where he knew he could network and bring in new contacts. And Sally found herself alone at the flat, waiting in vain for David while she pored over contact sheets in preparation for the next day's grind.

They had moved to a new apartment in Little Venice and although it was far grander than anything she had ever lived in, it made her melancholy. The whole place with its views over the canal and expensive modern furniture wasn't intended for living in at all. David had bought it to impress his clients and when he wasn't there with her, she felt lonely. If she was honest with herself, she knew she should quit while she was ahead. The agency could well afford to replace her now – but she didn't want to go.

She had never really had any real success of her own. Her old job in newspapers, she realised, could have been done by any hack with the right kind of determination. But her job at Chandos was different. She really mattered here. The clients she serviced relied on her the way they used to rely on David. It made her feel good about herself – good enough to ignore the fact that her husband was drifting farther and farther away from her.

Sally was sitting in her office wondering how she was going to take her next meeting when David came bouncing through the door. Something good must have happened because he looked more cheerful than she could remember.

And when she asked him what it was, he looked mysterious.

'You'll find out when you come to lunch.'

She rubbed a weary hand across her eyes.

'When is lunch?'

'I was thinking tomorrow might be a good time.'

She was dumbfounded. Anyone who knew anything about public relations knew that a busy executive like her was booked up for weeks ahead.

Yet it didn't seem to bother him at all.

He simply expected her to cancel whatever important date she had because he needed her to applaud when he scored a victory. She imagined he had pulled in a prestigious new client and all at once she realised she was being dog in the manger about it.

'I'll rearrange my diary,' she told him before he could

twig what was going on in her mind. 'Where do you want to meet?'

David told her the Ritz and that pleased her. She'd been fond of the hotel on Piccadilly ever since that first landmark party. Maybe it will be lucky for us again, she thought.

She arrived at one on the dot. When the waiter showed her through to the mirrored restaurant, she scoured the room for a sight of David. He was in the corner underneath a big crystal chandelier. And to her surprise he was not alone. There was a man with him.

She knew David hadn't seen her yet, so she stood in the doorway and tried to place David's lunch date. He wasn't one of their clients, she was sure of that. So he had to be the new piece of business she'd guessed at when David came into her office looking smug.

What could it be? she wondered, looking over at the two of them. But the man's appearance didn't help her one little bit. He was thin and pale and wore his blonde hair long so it flopped over one eye. He could have been a dress designer or a merchant banker. And Sally decided she wouldn't accomplish anything more by standing there. It was time she went over and found out exactly what was going on.

She smiled and weaved her way through the crowded tables until she was standing right in front of the mystery man.

'Are you going to introduce me?' Sally enquired, turning to her husband.

David smiled.

'This is Jeremy Ross,' he said, 'our new managing director.'

For a moment she was so surprised that words failed her. What was David doing bringing in someone to run the company? Wasn't it something they did together? David mistook her silence for delight.

'I knew you'd be pleased,' he said, pulling out a chair for her. 'Jeremy is exactly what we need.'

Now Sally found her voice.

'I thought I was what you needed,' she said faintly.

David motioned the waiter to pour out the Chablis that was

waiting in an ice bucket beside the table. Then he turned to his wife.

'Darling,' he said, 'stop acting as if I'm pushing you to one side. Chandos is growing like topsy. Any minute now we're going to have to move offices again and hire more staff. So we have to have more weight at the top.'

Sally lifted the crystal glass and stared into it, wondering if she should make a stand. She knew nothing about this new managing director David had brought in to run their company. She had no idea of his track record or even if he was capable of doing the job. She took a sip of the dry French wine. 'Why didn't you consult me about this before?'

Before David could reply, Jeremy Ross cut into their conversation.

'I didn't know I needed your approval before I joined the board.'

Sally regarded the pale, foppish man sitting across from her and decided she didn't like him.

'David and I started this company eighteen months ago' she informed him. 'I put up the money and I'm responsible for nearly half of the accounts. Of course you need my approval.'

She looked at her husband.

'I assume getting me to agree to Jeremy is the reason for this lunch?'

David nodded.

'But I knew when Jeremy told you about himself that there wouldn't be any problems.'

She wasn't entirely convinced of this, but she went along with it for the time being. She turned to him:

'So put me in the picture,' she said.

He was more than prepared for her, and Sally suspected he had been rehearsing his speech all morning. He had been an account director at Shandwick, one of the biggest public relations outfits in town. His main business had been an international construction company which necessitated him flying all over the world. Jeremy Ross had cosied up to every major board director from Washington to Hong Kong. He was by his own admission a past master of shmooze and Sally recalled her first impression of Jeremy. She didn't like him.

While he carried on in detail about his career with Shandwick, she tried to analyse what it was that set her teeth on edge. He was well spoken, Eton educated with the appropriate polished manners that went with the expensive private schooling. And he was a good showman.

So why do I hate him? Sally wondered. Is it because eveything Jeremy says sounds so hollow? Or is it because David went over my head to bring him in? As the spiel came to an end, Sally decided to ask him the one question on her mind.

'Why would you want to leave a great outfit like Shandwick to join a tiny agency like ours?'

She should have known he would be prepared for that one as well. The answer came out slick and polished.

'It would take me years to become a partner if I stayed where I was. If I join Chandos it's automatic.'

Sally raised her eyebrows.

'How much of our equity is my husband giving away?'

For a second Jeremy looked furtive, so she glanced across at David and saw he was avoiding her eyes. She took a deep breath and repeated the question. This time she got her answer.

'I thought twenty five percent was in the right ballpark,' David said.

Her head started to spin. Twenty five percent was a quarter of everything they owned. And David was carelessly giving it away to some slick-talking salesman with a glamorous track record. David must have known what was going through her mind, for he began to justify the offer.

'I know its a bigger slice than you expected, but we have to invest in talent if we want to grow.'

Sally frowned.

'It's too much,' she said, 'I can't agree to it.'

She saw Jeremy looking at her. And for the first time she saw respect in his eyes.

'What percentage did you have in mind?' he asked her.

She picked up her glass, swirling the remains of the wine round and round while she thought. Finally she said:

'Ten per cent would be about right, with an option for the other fifteen based on your performance.'

Jeremy didn't bother to conceal his displeasure.

'I didn't think I was going to have to haggle for this job,' he said.

David was about to say something, but Sally decided not to let him. If she was going to have to suffer Jeremy Ross, then she would do it on her terms. Before her husband could open his mouth, she said:

'You don't have to haggle. The offer is ten per cent, take it or leave it.'

A heavy silence settled over the table and when Sally ventured a glance at David she saw he was looking like thunder. She was surprised to discover it didn't bother her. She had sweated blood building Chandos. David had too. And ten per cent of their sweat was all she was prepared to part with. It was Jeremy who eventually broke the silence.

'You drive a hard bargain, Mrs Robinson,' he said.

'Does that mean you're accepting the offer?'

He fumbled for a cigarette and Sally noticed that Jeremy's hands were shaking as he tried to light it.

'I'm accepting it,' he told her, 'but I want my lawyer to go over the contract before I sign anything.'

'That's OK,' Sally said. Then she turned to her husband. 'I take it you agree, darling?'

She expected him to squeeze her hand the way he liked to after a successful negotiation, only David didn't move a muscle. Sally had saved their little company fifteen per cent in equity and the man she married couldn't even be bothered to smile at her.

Chapter Twenty Four

When Jeremy moved into Chandos Sally knew she was going to be side-lined. I've been a stopgap all along, she thought bitterly. Even when I was making progress, David didn't take me seriously. And now he's got a second in command, he'll probably ignore me completely.

She was wrong about that. David started to pay particular attention to the accounts she was working on, earmarking the ones that took up too much of her time.

'You're overstretched,' he remarked one day when she got back from lunch later than usual. 'You could do with some help.'

Sally thought it was a casual observation and thought no more about it, until she was called into a meeting in David's office. Jeremy was there and in front of him was a list of all their clients pasted up on a piece of card.

'David and I have been talking about how we split things up,' Jeremy told her, 'and we both agree you've got too much on your plate.'

She started to interrupt, but David didn't give her the chance.

'This is for your own good, Sally. In a month or so, you'll thank me for making things easier for you.'

Sally didn't say anything. She just looked at her husband sending silent signals across the room to Jeremy and knew her worst suspicions were justified. The two of them had carved up the agency between them.

'Do I have a job left at all?' she asked brightly.

They both spoke at once.

'Of course you do.'

'Then maybe one of you will tell me what it is.'

Jeremy did the talking. She was to keep a cluster of small accounts which she normally delegated to a junior when she was busy. The main business was to go back under the overall control of David, with Jeremy doing the legwork. As the new managing director talked about the way the agency was going to operate, she started to feel furious. The whole business had been started with her money and her commitment. She had every right to tell them both to stuff it.

Then she saw David looking nervous. As if he expected some sort of showdown and she knew then she couldn't humble him in front of Jeremy. She'd have it out with him later, when they got away from the agency.

They had their first major row in the bar of the Connaught over a bottle of vintage Krug. At least Sally was rowing. David just went on behaving as if nothing out of the ordinary was happening. Her husband had virtually cut her out of the family business, yet he didn't seem to think it mattered.

'Most of the profits come to us anyway,' he pointed out after a particularly long outburst. 'I don't know what you're worrying about.'

'It's not just about money,' she said bitterly. 'You've taken away my reason for going on.'

He put a hand out and flicked back the fluffy blonde curls that had fallen into her face.

'I thought I was your reason for living.'

It stopped her short, for there was nothing she could say to that. David was her reason for living. It's just that she was finding wider horizons beyond him and she wanted to go on exploring them. She was about to tell him, when he interrupted her.

'Would you like to have dinner here?' he asked.

'I'd love it, but we'd never get a table.'

'Wanna bet?'

The diversion of summoning a waiter, who consulted the head

213

waiter, who hurried over to confer with David took her mind off her woes. They hadn't had dinner anywhere remotely glamorous for months now, and she missed the flattery and the attention. She would certainly be getting her fair share of it tonight, she realised, for the head waiter had managed to conjure up a table in the Grill. They would be dining with politicians and captains of industry. Despite everything that had happened, the notion excited her.

She saw David responding to the change in her mood, and for a moment she felt she had betrayed herself. Any other executive who had just been passed over would not be dining with the enemy. And if they were, they wouldn't be enjoying it.

Sally sighed. I'm not any other executive, she thought. I'm a wife as well. And it changes things.

He made love to her when they got home. It wasn't his normal, considerate love-making that she had come to expect. David was altogether more demanding tonight. The minute they got through the door he took her in his arms; for a moment she felt swept off her feet. David hadn't been this romantic in months and she savoured the moment, losing herself in his kisses. After a bit she felt his hands on the zipper of her dress and she realised things were getting out of control.

'We can't do it here,' she whispered.

David laughed.

'Who says we can't?'

He plonked himself down on the sofa and dragged her on top of him. She didn't quite know how it happened, but when they finally pulled apart her dress was gone and so were her panties.

'What are you doing?' she gasped.

'What does it look like?'

She was sitting in his lap, facing him with her legs pulled wide apart. And she was both shocked and wildly turned on. Ordinary married couples surely didn't get up to this sort of thing? Just for a moment she wondered whether he had done this with anyone else. Then she looked down and saw how hard he was and all of a sudden she didn't care. What she wanted was that hardness inside her. So she pushed herself down on him and lost herself completely.

Somewhere in the middle of it, she looked into David's face and felt that he was somewhere else, somewhere on a different planet. And she knew he wasn't thinking of her at all. He was thinking of some other girl. The one he had played this game with years before he met her. She called his name then, in an effort to bring him back to her. And he jerked his eyes open as if he was seeing her for the first time.

'Who was it?' she asked gently, when it was all over.

But he wouldn't be drawn. No matter how many times she questioned him, she met with a blank wall. So in the end, she allowed him to take her to bed where he slept all night with his arms tightly wrapped around her.

A month later to the day, Sally missed her period. She kept the knowledge to herself until she was absolutely certain there was no doubt about her condition. Then she broke the news to David, who reacted by sending Jeremy out to the off-licence to buy a bottle of champagne. The three of them drank a toast to the baby out of paper cups. Then because it was expected of her, Sally formally handed in her notice.

She had more important things to attend to now.

Chapter Twenty Five

London . . . 1995

Sally contemplated her future and didn't like what she saw. She had been brooding about it for nearly a week now, pacing up and down in her high-ceilinged drawing-room with its brocade curtains and expensive antiques.

She had created this room fifteen years ago when they moved in, haunting the sale rooms and the fancy interior design shops until she got exactly the effect she wanted. It had cost them a lot of money, even in those days; but now, Sally thought bitterly, the second-hand dealers would take the contents of this room for a knock-down price. She'd be lucky if she got more than ten thousand for everything in the house. Just for a moment, she wondered if it was too late to call a halt.

Then she pulled herself together. She was in a deep financial mess and only the sale of everything she owned was going to get her out of it.

Rosemary Gray at the bank had explained this to her very carefully when she finally went back there. The manager had examined the mortgage papers she brought with her and listened to a summary of the meeting she had with Jeremy at the agency. Then she pronounced judgement.

'You need a loan in order to live,' she told Sally, 'but I can only give it to you as a loan against the house, which of course you're going to have to get rid of.'

Sally had known this right from the start, but hearing it from her bank manager somehow made it official. She had to leave her lifestyle. All the memories and all the treasures she had collected over the years were now in jeopardy and the realisation threw her into a panic.

She had gone home and shut herself in. Then she wandered from room to room, touching a painting she had bought and haggled over in the Portobello Road, a collection of first editions David had given her, a Georgian desk, a diamond brooch.

It had taken her a week to say goodbye to everything and it hurt because she knew she was saying goodbye to a part of herself – the part that was loved and cossetted, the part that took fine things as her right. From now on, she would be making do, renting somewhere cheap in the suburbs and buying furniture at discount stores.

Her family would help of course. Daddy and Mummy would come through with one or two of the hideous Victorian pieces they loved so much. There would be the odd hand-out from an aunt or a cousin. And if things looked really dire, her parents might even suggest that she and Annabel come and live with them for a while. But she knew she couldn't handle that. She couldn't handle her mother's reproachful looks and subtle cross-examination. She'd want to know what had gone wrong with the marriage and why David had left her. And there was no way she could discuss it when she didn't know why it broke down in the first place.

She looked back over the years of her long, happy marriage, looking for cracks in the façade. But she could find none. David always seemed devoted to her and Annabel, spoiling them outrageously with gifts and holidays in the sun and everything else that money could buy. And she'd repaid him in kind. She never nagged him or turned him away in bed. She wasn't sluttish around the house. Nor was she extravagent. With the money at her disposal she could have filled her wardrobe with new designer labels every season. But she didn't do it because she respected her privileges.

She respected David. But he didn't respect me, she thought.

There was I, acting the part of the model wife, and he was sneaking off behind my back with some floozie. She wondered how she could have been so stupid not to have seen it. A sudden rage boiled up inside her, malignant and shocking. She had never allowed herself to feel this angry with David before, but now she gave full vent to her feelings.

None of this was my fault, she realised. I bent over backwards to be what David wanted me to be. I gave up my job and settled for being a home-maker. And the moment I did, I was patronised and dismissed, and I even put up with that because I didn't want to rock the boat. If I'd known how things would turn out, she thought bitterly, I might have stayed true to myself instead of selling out.

Suddenly a vision of herself as she might have been came into her mind. This new Sally had gone on working at what she was good at. She had stayed at the agency instead of quitting the minute she knew she was pregnant. And instead of giving way to David's and Jeremy's demands, she would have fought her corner and gone on fighting her corner till it was time to go home and have her baby.

Even then I needn't have stopped, she realised. I could have hired a competent nanny and gone back to the agency. She knew it probably wouldn't have been easy. David would have kicked up like hell. But when push came to shove, what could he do? She owned nearly half the equity in Chandos, so in the end he would have backed down and they would have come to terms.

The thought of what she had lost refuelled her rage so that she seethed and boiled and tried to kick holes in the exquisite oriental carpet under her feet. Yet instead of depleting her, her anger made her stronger. For now her vision was clear. If she went on like this, she realised, she might just find her way out of the muddle she was in. She might just think and scheme her way through it the way she always did in the old days.

What is my real problem, she asked herself, apart from losing David? And the answer came back loud and clear: losing the agency. For with Chandos in ruins she had less than nothing. The old Sally, the Sally she had been for years, was prepared to accept this fact. But the new Sally, the woman she was fast rediscovering, had no truck with failure.

It might be savable, she thought. There may be fewer clients, but they haven't all gone. What we have left, properly managed, could keep us afloat.

Now she wondered who would do it, for Jeremy was clearly qualified for nothing apart from propping up a bar. Her mind went back to the nucleus of executives she had seen coming out of the agency lift. At one time any one of them might have had the makings of a leader. But since David had left they had become loose-mouthed and sloppy. They need to be shaken up, she thought. Shaken up and cleared out along with Jeremy. But whom would that leave, apart from her?

And then she had her answer. It was such an obvious one, she wondered why it hadn't occurred to her before. She was the only one left now who gave a damn about the agency and whether it survived or not. She knew its dynamics. She knew most of the clients. In her day she'd even kept the books. So what's wrong with me taking over? she asked herself.

Just for a moment the old Sally reared her head again. I can't do it, she thought. I'm a middle-aged housewife who doesn't know a laptop computer from a hole in the wall. The young men in the agency would laugh at me, make mincemeat of me. Then she remembered that that was how she had been frightened out of her job the first time round – by men laughing at her, taking away her confidence. That isn't going to happen again, she vowed, her resolve hardening. Now I've found myself again, nobody is ever going to tell me I'm incapable of doing something that's second nature to me.

I own Chandos and I call the shots now. And if the people that work for me can't live with that, they can always hand in their notice.

Now Sally knew what she was going to do, she was tempted to share her plan with Annabel. But something stopped her. Her daughter had been moody and difficult ever since David's departure. If she pushed some half-baked scheme on her, she would risk unsettling her even more. No Sally thought, I'll wait until I'm certain I'm going to pull it off. Then I'll tell her.

She turned her attention to the business in hand, phoning Jeremy's secretary and demanding to be sent a list of the accounts they still had and the ones that were on notice.

When the accounts arrived in Oxford the next day, they made depressing reading. Out of dozens of clients, many of whom Sally had known personally, there were only three she could count on: Harvest Restaurants and Inca Toys, because they'd both come down with David from Manchester; and Chic boutiques because of her friend, Diane. She made a mental note to sound out the first two as soon as she could. Then she turned her full attention to Chic.

From the look of it, the account made up nearly half her billing. And she breathed with relief that her livelihood was in the hands of a friend. She could prevail on a friend. She could sit a friend down and state her case. If she needed to she could go on her knees to a friend and beg for a stay of execution.

Dear Diane, Sally thought. How hard I've tried your patience over the years. When you took me in, I repaid your kindness by walking off with the love of your life. And now I'm going to ask you to stake your reputation on a dying agency. Yet she knew Diane would give her a fair hearing, for she didn't seem to harbour any bitterness for what had gone before.

She cast her mind back three years to the moment Diane had come back into their lives. David had run into her at a party. Not that Sally got to hear about this immediately, for David, she discovered, was still consumed with guilt over Diane – so much so that he pocketed her business card and put the entire encounter out of his mind. It was only weeks later when Sally was taking his suits to the cleaners that she found the card and asked him about it.

'Diane,' he said, looking stricken when she brandished the card in front of him.

'I saw her a month ago at the French Embassy, but I didn't tell you about it, because I didn't want to get involved.'

'Why ever not?'

'I couldn't cope with all those hurt feelings, I suppose. Anyway a lot of water has gone under the bridge since then.'

It would have been easy to forget the whole thing and throw the card into the dustbin. But Sally couldn't forget how much Diane had meant to her. Back in Manchester they had been closer than sisters, and she knew she had to see her again. She looked at David cautiously.

'Would you mind if I rang her at the work number I've got here? Now she's in London, I thought maybe we could have lunch.'

She saw her husband looking quizzical.

'Do what you like,' he said, 'as long as you leave me out of it.'

So she had. She rang Diane at Chic and was greeted with cries of disbelief.

'It's been so long,' she exclaimed, 'I can't believe it's really you.'

Sally smiled, remembering how hard it had been to pin Diane down. She always seemed to be travelling and attending conferences. And in the end she'd had to barge into her office and drag her out. It had been worth it though. They had so much catching up to do that when they finally emerged from the restaurant where they'd had lunch, Sally was surprised to see it was after four.

'Oh dear,' she wailed, 'You'll be in trouble with your boss now, and it's all my fault.'

It was then she learned something new about her friend.

'I am the boss,' Diane told her quietly.

At first she didn't believe her, but after a bit of explaining the truth finally sank in. Diane managed, virtually single-handed, a country-wide chain of fashion boutiques.

'Who does your public relations?' she asked before she could stop herself.

Diane smiled and told her it was a dreary old-fashioned agency she was thinking of getting rid of. Sally realised she couldn't keep this sort of news to herself. David might not want to know Diane these days, but Sally reckoned he'd certainly want to know her business.

It wasn't hard to talk him round. In fact pursuing the Chic account was the thing that brought the three of them together again, for public relations was neutral territory. David could talk marketing to Diane without the least risk of embarrassment. And it cancelled out the past. Diane was so in love with her new job that nothing else seemed to matter to her. The fact that David had let her down all those years ago was of little consequence now. She'd finally found something to take the place of a man and she revelled in it.

In the end, though, it wasn't David who talked Diane into handing over her account. Sally did it over lunch one day, twisting her arm to give the agency a six-month trial on a new fashion line.

And it had worked brilliantly, so brilliantly that the rest of the account followed shortly afterwards. Though by then, both David and Diane had quite forgotten that the whole thing had been Sally's doing in the first place.

Chapter Twenty Six

By Diane's reckoning, Sally would have her divorce papers by now. And the knowledge depressed her as she knew it was the reason they were having lunch today.

Sally had called her after a three-week silence to announce she had booked a table at Langan's and she hoped she would be able to meet her.

She wants to talk the whole thing out again, Diane thought. She'll go back over her marriage wondering where she went wrong. Then if I'm really unlucky, she'll have too much to drink and end up bursting into tears. Diane sighed and applied more lipstick before getting up from her desk and slipping on her jacket. There was no way out of this scene, no matter how hard she tried to avoid it. The best thing she could do was to go to Langan's and get the whole thing over with.

When she arrived at the barn of a restaurant in Piccadilly, she saw Sally had been the first to arrive. She was sitting at one of the big circular tables in the window, totally wrapped up in the *Evening Standard*. She was even smiling faintly and Diane felt relieved. If she could be amused by something she read in the paper, she wasn't a total lost cause. She went over to the table and Sally looked up almost immediately.

'You're here,' she said, 'come and sit down and have a drink.'

Diane considered a Perrier, then she thought about Sally's divorce papers and decided on a Bloody Mary.

'What are you having?'

'Just a plain tomato juice. I need my wits about me right now.'

She raised her eyebrows. Since when did Sally need to think clearly when she was whinging on about David?

'I suppose the lawyers have sent you the final papers?' she asked testing the water.

Sally looked vague.

'They came a couple of weeks ago. Everything seemed to be in order.'

'So you're not worried about it being final then?'

For a moment Sally didn't say anything. 'If you're asking if it was a horrible shock, it was. But I'm over it now, anyway there are worse problems than David to deal with.'

She was intrigued.

'Like what?'

'Like Chandos.'

Diane started to listen. One of her juniors had told her something was wrong at the agency, but she hadn't taken any notice. Now Sally was telling her the same thing and she needed to know what was going on.

'What's the problem?' she asked, thinking it wasn't going to be half as tedious as the diatribe she was expecting about the divorce papers.

When Sally started laying it out in front of her, Diane realised she had been wrong. What she was hearing wasn't tedious. It was nothing short of terrifying.

'When did you know Jeremy was running the agency into the ground?'

'When he stopped paying me my monthly cheque.'

So the company was running out of money, Diane thought. Pretty soon they wouldn't be able to afford to pay for the autumn campaign, and then she really would be in trouble. She looked across at Sally.

'I hate to do this to you, but I think I'm going to have to pull my account.'

'Don't do that. At least not until you've heard me out.'

'There's nothing you can tell me that will change my mind. If I don't move quickly, Chic is going to suffer.'

'Not with me running the agency.'

Diane did a double take.

'Not with you doing what?'

Sally caught her friend's shocked expression and decided she needed something stronger than a tomato juice after all.

'I just said I was coming back to run Chandos,' she said, signalling the waiter for a glass of wine. 'It's not such a terrible idea.'

Diane looked at Sally and wondered if David leaving her had addled her brain.

'You have to be out of date,' she protested. 'How can you even consider going back?'

'I don't have any choice,' Sally told her. 'I either take hold of the reins again, or I watch while my whole life goes down the chute.'

She turned to Diane.

'Did you know my house was mortgaged? So even if I sell, I'll still end up with next to nothing.'

Diane didn't say anything for a moment. Instead she thought about David. He couldn't have known what was happening to Chandos. If he had, he would not have left Jeremy in charge.

She sighed. The very least he could do now was to come home and put things right.

'Have you told David any of this?'

Sally shook her head.

'I can't do it.'

'Why not, he's the best chance you've got.'

Now Sally looked adamant.

'David isn't the best chance I've got. I'm the best chance I've got.'

She paused for a moment, wondering whether to tell Diane what was going on in her mind. Then she thought, we've known each other for so long . . . Why not?

'When David dumped me,' she said, turning to her friend, 'something changed inside me. I was crying too much to notice it at first. But when things went from bad to worse I suddenly got a grip on myself. It was then I realised that David had never been my best chance. How could he be while he had his interests at heart, not mine. All through our lives together we did things David's way. And I always somehow managed to come off slightly worse. It made me realise that in the end the only person you can trust is yourself.'

'But have you got what it takes to dig yourself out of this hole?'

Sally's chin came up.

'I had it once,' she said, 'and I haven't changed all that much.'

She looked very determined as she said this. Despite herself, Diane started to feel a grudging respect. Sally had been such a worm for so many years and now she was finding herself it was all her friend could do not to stand up and cheer.

Then Diane thought about herself and her career and realised she was being sentimental. If she had any sense at all, she would tell her friend goodbye and move the account as soon as she got back to the office. She turned to Sally.

'I don't suppose you can give me any guarantees you're going to stay in business?'

She shook her head.

'All I can do is get rid of Jeremy, which is going to save us a packet. With him out of the way, I stand a good chance of stopping the rot and getting us back on course.'

Diane did a swift calculation in her head. In a month's time they would be laying plans for the autumn promotion. Once that started they'd be committed till the end of the year.

'Do you think you can stay afloat till Christmas?'

'We've still got the bank behind us, so I don't see why not.'

Diane pondered on the riskiness of business. Everything she did depended on the goodwill of somebody else. She was banking on Sally surviving long enough to see her promotion through. Sally was relying on her backers not pulling the plug until she got back on her feet. It was all a pack of cards that could be knocked over in a minute by the stiff breeze of bad luck.

She thought about the way life had treated Sally and realised the stiff breeze had turned into a howling gale. Everything she touched seemed to be doomed to failure and she wondered if she could afford to take this gamble.

Sally looked at her friend and realised what was going through her mind. It had been optimistic to imagine that Diane would support her. For she was a bad bet whichever way you looked at it.

She stared into space, preparing herself for the inevitable turn-down. Then she saw someone she recognised. He was sitting two tables away looking more like a grisly bear than ever.

Brad Hastings, she thought, the man with all the hotels. She had met him with David when the agency was chasing his business, though on this occasion her husband had failed to impress.

She cast her mind back to the disastrous evening a few months ago when she had started out by putting her foot in it and David had finished the job by demonstrating he knew nothing whatever about the hotel business. She'd made a half-hearted attempt to rescue the evening, by parading what she knew about the subject. But David had well and truly scuppered her rescue attempt by telling Brad Hastings there was no way he'd allow her to work for him or anyone else.

I hope he hasn't seen me, Sally thought, panicking slightly. The last thing I need right now is to go over old failures. But she was out of luck. For the burly American had spotted her staring at him and was getting out of his chair.

The first one of them to acknowledge him was Diane, who stuck out her hand and said her name as if she was announcing herself to royalty. She even told him where she worked and what she did which seemed a bit excessive to Sally who looked at the floor and hoped she was going to get away with a quick hello. But Brad wasn't put off so easily.

'Sally Robinson,' he said in his East Coast burr, 'is your old man still keeping you out of trouble?'

Diane looked questioningly at both of them, and Sally felt bound to explain.

'When David was with the agency, the three of us had dinner.'

Now it was Brad's turn to look questioning.

'I didn't know David had left Chandos.'

'He went a couple of months ago,' Sally admitted reluntantly.

'So who is running it now?'

She started to feel hot under the collar. It was all very well confiding her intentions over lunch but she wasn't ready to broadcast them to all and sundry. Diane was though.

'Sally is thinking of stepping into the breach,' she said, 'though I'm doing my best to talk her out of it.'

'Why would you want to do that?'

Diane pulled a face.

'She's been away from public relations for a long time.'

Brad considered this information.

'I don't think it matters all that much,' he said eventually. 'Sally still makes more sense than anyone else in her business I've talked to recently.'

Then before Diane could say anything more, he turned on his heel and went back to his lunchdate.

Diane was momentarily speechless, then she turned to Sally:

'I think I owe you an apology,' she said.

'Whatever for?'

'Underestimating you. That man who just looked you up is one of the biggest movers in the States. If he thinks you're an operator, then I guess I've been wrong all along.'

Sally looked at her.

'Does that mean I can keep your account?'

There was the briefest of pauses, then Diane said:

'You can have it till after the promotion, but on certain conditions. I don't want any changes in the account team. And if I hear a whisper the agency isn't paying its bills, I won't hesitate to walk away.'

Sally allowed herself the tiniest of smiles.

'I take it that's a yes.'

*　　*　　*

Whenever fortune smiled on her, Sally automatically expected to celebrate her good luck. So when she and Diane parted outside Langan's, her thoughts turned to Bond Street. All her wedding anniversaries had been marked by gifts from Asprey's and Cartier. On birthdays she got a handbag from Chanel or a designer outfit from Browns.

Now she had reached another landmark in her life, she wondered what to collect as a suitable reward. An idea came to her. She would walk round to Gucci and pick out a fine leather briefcase. She would carry her papers in it when she went to meetings. And every time she unclipped the expensive gilt clasp she would remember today and glory in the fact that she could beat the odds when she put her mind to it.

It took her five minutes to get to Gucci, and another twenty before she located the type of briefcase she wanted. Then she saw one that seemed perfect. It was made in the softest calfskin and all round the edges there was a gold trim. No-one carrying this could ever be mistaken for a suburban housewife. Just touching it transformed her into the high-flying executive she wanted to be. So she opened it and rummaged inside for the price tag. The sight of it sobered her up – it was nearly a thousand pounds.

A few months ago the price tag wouldn't have bothered her. She would have just handed over her American Express card and told the assistant to wrap it up. Only now she hesitated, for David wasn't picking up her credit cards any more. When the account came in, she would have to consult her monthly budget and calculate how much money she would have left when she paid it. She knew then that the briefcase was out of the question. The small loan Rosemary Gray had given her didn't run to this kind of extravagance. It barely covered the lunch she'd stood Diane in Langan's and she wondered how she could have been so stupid.

I'm still behaving like a rich man's wife, she thought, expecting to pick up trophies every time I've been a clever girl. She sighed. The way things were now, cleverness was an end in itself. She won her battles to survive, not to look good to her friends. She turned to the shop assistant who was waiting for her decision on the briefcase.

'I'll think about it,' she said.

When she got back to Oxford, she didn't immediately make herself a cup of tea the way she usually did. Instead she went straight to the phone and started calling the last two clients on her list. Steven Frank at Inca Toys and Tony Brooks who ran Bobby Brown's.

Tony Brooks came straight through to her as soon as she told his secretary who she was. He'd heard she and David had split up and he seemed concerned about her. For a moment she felt vulnerable, discussing her private affairs with a business associate. But there was no avoiding it. So she told Tony as confidently as she could that she'd got over David, and he seemed to believe her. When she said she was coming back to the agency, he didn't sound as shocked as Diane had been; he sounded relieved that he wouldn't be dealing with Jeremy any more.

'Come and see me at the end of the week,' he told her. 'We can do business together.'

He hasn't forgotten, Sally thought when she put the phone down. He's still grateful to me for saving his business all those years ago when food poisoning nearly closed them down.

Steven Frank hadn't forgotten her either. Like Tony, he was pleased she was back at Chandos and they made a lunch date for three days hence.

After that she decided she deserved her tea, and while she was making it she thought about what she had achieved. She knew both Steven and Tony would back her for a few months anyway. Both accounts had come down from Manchester with David, and even though Jeremy had made a muddle of them, they'd stick around out of loyalty. She was so busy mulling over her plans that she didn't hear Annabel come in.

'Hi, Mum,' she said, 'I can see I've got here at the right time. I'm dying for tea.'

Sally grinned. She could move mountains, but unless she

kept her daughter fed and watered, none of it would be worth anything.

'How do you feel about me going back to work at the agency?' she asked, testing the water.

Annabel looked up from cutting a slice of cake.

'Why would you want to do that?'

'Because Jeremy doesn't seem to be doing all that well for us.'

She saw her daughter looking aghast.

'You don't really think you can do better, do you?'

For a moment Sally looked grim.

'I'm going to have to,' she said, 'we're nearly broke.'

Annabel was just about to take a bite out of the sponge slice, when she changed her mind.

'Why didn't you tell me about this before?' she demanded.

'I haven't known about it for very long.'

'But now you do know about it, what's going to happen?'

Sally saw how frightened Annabel was and cursed herself for springing the news on the girl without any warning. If David had been around she might have had the time to sit her down and explain things properly. But David wasn't around. She was all on her own now, fending for herself and her daughter as best she could. She fought down the feeling of desolation which threatened to creep up on her every so often.

'Nothing bad is going to happen, darling,' she said, going over and putting an arm round the girl. 'The only one who is going to lose out in this situation is Jeremy.'

She arranged to fire her managing director in the bar of the Connaught because it was too public a place to make a scene. She was glad she'd decided on this course of action as soon as she walked in and saw him sitting in one of the little round tables by the window.

He reminded her more of a ferret than ever. His eyes were pink from too much drinking and too many late nights, she noticed that when he lifted his drink to his lips, his hand was shaking. I wouldn't trust him to run a piss-up in a brewery, she thought savagely, let alone take care of my precious business.

When he saw her, Jeremy jumped out of his seat and gave her a peck on the cheek. Then he wanted to know whether she wanted a glass of champagne. She said she wouldn't and settled for a glass of white wine. Then she leaned back in her seat and waited to see how Jeremy was going to handle this meeting.

By rights, he should be nervous, she reasoned. He must know she was onto him by now and she braced herself for the barrage of excuses that Jeremy always used to protect himself. They came on cue, the minute her wine arrived.

'I suppose you want to know why I'm still not paying you anything,' he began.

Sally didn't say anything, so he ploughed on.

'Things have been slower than I expected. Bobby Brown's has cut right back and Inca is dragging its feet on my new proposals.'

Sally looked at him.

'I know,' she said. 'I talked to them both this week.'

'What the hell were you doing that for? The clients are my business.'

Jeremy's voice had gone up a couple of octaves and the middle-aged couple sitting three tables away looked round in curiosity. With an effort Sally kept her voice down. 'Now you're talking about what is and what isn't your business, can I remind you that I own most of the shares.'

Jeremy looked resentful.

'But I still run the company. David left explicit instructions.'

'David left,' Sally said flatly. 'So it doesn't matter any more what he wanted.'

For a moment she thought he was going to hit her, for his normally pale face went bright red and she saw veins standing out on his forehead. She put out a warning hand.

'I wouldn't get too excited. There's worse to come.'

He took a gulp of his whisky and it seemed to calm him, for when she looked again the oily charm was back in place.

'If I didn't know you better, I'd suspect you were thinking of making a comeback. That's why you were getting cosy with my clients, wasn't it?'

She paused.

'How would you feel about me coming back to Chandos?'

It was unfair of her to play with him like this, but Sally couldn't resist it. She still hadn't quite forgiven him for pushing her out of the company, all those years ago. And now, just for a minute or two, she wanted her revenge.

Jeremy pinched his face into a smile.

'So you are coming back, I might have suspected it.'

'You still haven't told me whether I'd be welcome.'

She saw his mind struggling with itself. Half of him, she knew, longed to tell her that she was an upstart with no place in Chandos. But the other half needed to go on working.

'I think we could work out something together,' he eventually said. 'You weren't a bad executive in your day and you could be quite useful on certain types of business.'

'When I last looked, there weren't too many types of business left.'

Jeremy did his best to keep his smile looking fresh.

'I was thinking about Bobby Brown's,' he said hurriedly. 'You worked on it once.'

She didn't bother to conceal her contempt. 'The restaurants aren't spending at the moment. You'll have to do better than that.'

He began to sound slightly less confident. 'Maybe we could try to squeeze some more business out of them?'

'Like what?'

'I don't know, I don't handle the account.'

Now Sally's voice was icy.

'I would have thought it was your business to know what Bobby Brown's had on its agenda. Isn't that what managing directors do?'

Jeremy played for time by calling the waiter over and ordering more drinks. But there was no escaping Sally. She was leaning forward in her chair expecting an answer. He decided to fob her off with a lie.

'There's nothing doing at Bobby Brown's. The company's been stagnating for a couple of years now.'

'That's not what Tony Brooks told me.'

'Tony Brooks will say almost anything to a pretty woman. He was probably dangling a new promotion in front of you to get you into bed.'

Sally decided she'd had enough. The man had dug a deep enough grave for himself. It was time she gave him a decent burial.

It had been surprisingly easy to get rid of Jeremy. Sally had been expecting an ugly scene followed by threats to disturb the staff at Chandos. Instead the first thing he had asked about was his redundancy. He was on a three-month contract and he was more than anxious to be paid out. Sally remembered the grasping, almost pleading expression on Jeremy's face as they went over the terms of his notice. He was willing to return his shares in Chandos in exchange for his office computer, his fax machine and the six crates of booze he had stashed in a side office.

Sally gave in to his demands. As far as she was concerned she was getting the company back on the cheap, because Jeremy thought it was on the verge of folding up. She hadn't been annoyed by his lack of faith. She had simply been relieved that the situation had resolved itself so easily. She wondered how the rest of the pieces of the puzzle would arrange themselves.

She would have to take over the reins at the agency now, which meant being there every day. Suddenly her protected existence in Oxford looked very temporary.

When she started on her present course she had only the vaguest idea of where she would end up. But now it was coming clearer. If she was going to stand any chance at all, she was going to have to move to London. It would have to be a cheap district, Shepherds Bush or the back end of Fulham. And the thought of living in the hassle and grime of the capital filled her with trepidation.

She had started in London as a girl, of course, but things were different then. She was braver when she was young. She hadn't had her independence eroded by years of being looked after in a comfortable marriage.

Scenes from her past life flashed in front of her. She was back in her grand dining-room in Oxford hosting a dinner party for twenty. David was at the head of the table, dispensing a rare claret. And neither of them gave a moment's thought to what the event was costing them.

She moved focus and saw herself in her huge landscaped garden. It was a summer day and she was pruning the roses and wondering what designer creation she would be wearing for David tonight. Everything I did, she thought, included David. He was the main ingredient in my life. I didn't make a move without consulting him. The irony of it suddenly came home to her. For here she was taking over the agency single-handed as well as moving to some grim London suburb.

And David didn't know a thing about it. She wondered what else she would be doing without David's permission.

Chapter Twenty Seven

Diane . . . 1995

It was raining in Paris. A thick fine drizzle that blurred the outlines of the Sacré Coeur had forced the tourists into the cafés.

David watched them as they filled up the tables around him, dumping their coats and umbrellas in unsightly heaps. There was something depressing about Saturdays, he reflected. Even without the rain the town would be packed with windowshopping suburbanites spending their wage packets on greasy hamburgers and cheap red plonk. One of the drawbacks of living in a big city was having to share it with the sort of people he wouldn't give houseroom to.

For a moment David wondered how he had ever existed in Manchester. For this crowded grey town with its rain-slicked streets didn't seem all that different to him. I was miserable in Manchester, he thought, and I'm miserable here. For two pins I'd be happy to pack the whole thing in and head for home. Except he knew he couldn't do that. His elegant Oxford farmhouse and his comfortable marriage were relegated to the past now. He'd cashed them in for a love affair.

David finished his glass of mineral water and realised he was feeling sorry for himself. It wasn't just the love affair that had uprooted him. He was sitting in Paris because he'd been offered the chance to make some real money.

He remembered the day the offer landed in his lap. His girlfriend was giving him hell because he couldn't afford to leave Sally, then all of a sudden his problems were at an end.

A big conglomorate wanted him to sell their hair-care range in Europe. They dressed the job up of course. He would be responsible for the manufacturing operation. And they would give him a fancy title. But at the end of the day what Chemico wanted was a salesman. And they were prepared to pay half a million dollars a year for David's gift of the gab.

It was money that decided him. If he was pulling down that kind of salary, he could afford to pay Sally off with his agency and walk away from his old life altogether. I'll be a free man, he told himself, in a new city with a new girl.

The trouble was that the sales pitch hadn't lived up to its promise. He wasn't going to start earning big bucks until the factory was up and running. And that was months away. So all he did all day was hassle the French workmen and make endless phone calls to America. What made it worse was that the woman he loved was having second thoughts about leaving her job. He sighed. It would all work out in the end. By the spring the money would come rolling in and he could move out of the poky little flat on the 6th Arrondissement.

I'll buy a penthouse on the Avenue Foch, he promised himself. That should give her an incentive to move out of London. He was so immersed in his thoughts that he hadn't noticed there was someone standing right in front of him. Even then she had to say his name before she got his attention.

'Diane,' he said, looking up. 'What are you doing here so soon? I wasn't expecting you yet.'

She grinned and took off her rain-soaked jacket which she shook all over the floor. Then she moved over to the banquette where he was sitting.

'The plane was early,' she told him, 'but I'll go away and come back later if I'm putting you out.'

He moved up and made a space for her.

'You're not putting me out,' he said. 'Can I get you a coffee?'

She looked at her watch.

'Make it a glass of wine, it's getting on for twelve.'

He signalled the waiter for a bottle and two glasses. Then he turned to her.

'You said on the phone that you had something important to tell me.' He saw her hestitate as if she was frightened that what she was going to say next would upset him.

'Its about Sally,' she said, forcing the words out. 'I had lunch with her last week.'

David groaned inwardly. So she knows, he thought. And she's kicking up a fuss.

'Did she accuse you point blank of making off with me? Or did she try to worm it out of you?'

Diane smiled.

'Don't be silly, Sally doesn't know anything about us.'

He noticed how much it cost her to make light of the situation and he realised what he was putting her through. It must be hell, David thought, to have to go on pretending everything was the same as it always had been, when everything had changed. They were together again now, after years of living in the wilderness, years of being half starved for each other. But instead of telling the whole world about it, Diane was having to live a lie to protect his wife's feelings.

'How long are we going to go on keeping this a secret?' he asked.

She looked at him.

'Until Sally gets back on her feet.'

Now he began to feel impatient.

'Sally is on her feet. I made sure she could manage before I left.'

Diane pulled a face.

'Well, you didn't do a very good job. When we had lunch together, she told me how things really were, and I was horrified.'

He felt a moment of disquiet.

'Put me in the picture.'

She looked nervous.

'I don't think you're going to like this.'

David sighed.

'Probably not, but tell me anyway.'

'Sally's broke. She's having to sell up and move out of the house.'

'But that's not possible,' the words came out of him in an explosion. 'The business takes care of everything. Has she been gambling or something?'

There was a moment's silence.

Then Diane said:

'No, Sally hasn't been gambling. But I think Jeremy has. He's managed to lose most of the business you left. And now he can't pay Sally her share of the profits.'

David put his head in his hands and cursed his bad judgement. He had always known Jeremy was weak, but he hadn't taken him for a fool. With the team he'd put in, he should have been able to run Chandos standing on his head.

'Maybe it's a blip,' he said desperately. 'A lot of agencies go through a bad time when a principal leaves.'

'Stop kidding yourself,' Diane said. 'Jeremy's an incompetent with the brains of a flea. He'll never pull himself out of this mess.'

David pushed his wine away and took hold of the mineral water he'd been drinking previously. It took two glasses before his head cleared. Then he turned to Diane.

'How is Sally taking all this? She must be going out of her mind?

For the first time that morning, Diane smiled.

'Actually she's being remarkably cool. She's even threatening to run the agency in Jeremy's place.'

'She won't do it, will she?'

'I wouldn't be so sure. She pushed me into giving her a six-month extension on Chic.'

He looked at her.

'You didn't let her have it?'

'What else could I do? Sally was desperate.'

Now David really was worried. Losing Chandos was a big enough catastrophe. But for Sally to make a fool of herself into the bargain was unthinkable. Diane watched David as he wrestled with the problem and wondered when to make her move. Finally she said:

'What are you going to do about the situation?'

He looked anguished.

'What can I do, for Christ's sake? I'm out of it now.'

'You can go back.'

The violence of his reaction surprised her.

'You can't be serious. After everything that's happened you're asking me to put the new plant at Orly and my whole future on hold.'

There was a short silence.

'It wouldn't be for very long.'

He looked at her in disbelief.

'It would be a minimum of six months to turn the agency round and play in a new manager. And I haven't got six months. I haven't got six days. If I leave this operation now, I'm as good as dead.'

'So you're letting Sally die instead.'

He marvelled at her old-fashioned, sentimental loyalty. He'd left his wife for this woman, yet now she was prepared to send him back if it would get Sally out of a hole. He put his arms out and gently turned her round so she faced him.

'The way things are, one of us is going to suffer. And if it's Sally she won't be sad for very long. By next January I'll be making big money and I can help her out.'

Diane looked at her lover.

'You mean that, don't you?'

'You should know by now, I always mean what I say.'

Chapter Twenty Eight

Diane . . . London, 1992

She walked into the high-ceilinged lobby of the French Embassy clutching her gold-embossed invitation. There was a whole queue of people ahead of her, checking in at a desk manned by two very efficient debby-looking girls. Diane joined the end of it and wondered how long she was going to have to wait for her first glass of champagne.

It was a working evening, one of many that encroached on her time since she had joined Chic boutiques. Tonight the French textile industry was parading its wares. And she was there to cast an eye over them and talk to the salesmen who inevitably turned up at these dos. To a lot of people, a lot of her colleagues, it seemed like a fast ticket to boredom. But not to Diane. Ever since she started this job, she had lived and breathed it.

She cast her mind back to the moment when she knew she was going to succeed in the fashion business. Simon Moyses the managing director had picked her out from the other trainees and given her a few of his own projects. And after that there was no stopping her. She had worked every hour in the day, getting up early so she was first in the office and taking reading matter home with her.

From time to time Cissy, who worked on a glossy magazine in the West End, would express concern at the way she was spending her life.

'What about going to the odd party,' she would ask, 'picking up the odd man? You're not going to earn your own living forever.'

Diana would studiously ignore such questions, saying she wasn't interested in finding a husband. And in truth she wasn't. She had been disappointed in love so many times that she had become indifferent to men. She needed them for sex, of course. But that was easily arranged. London was full of married men on the prowl and little boys on the make. Diane could take her pick of one-night stands and she did whenever she could spare a little time away from Chic boutiques.

In a way it was inevitable that she would succeed. For most of the men and all of the women she worked with had lives away from the office. There were wives and boyfriends and young children to distract them and take their eye off the ball. But Diane never wavered from her ambition to reach the top. When there was a last-minute invitation to a trade party in Milan, Diane was always willing to go.

If a meeting went on beyond office hours, Diane was always the last to leave. And because she was so available and so wedded to her job, Diane was included in almost all the projects the boutique chain had on the go.

It took her two years to work her way out of junior management and into running her own section. Her colleagues, the ones she left behind, whispered behind her back, calling her a workaholic. But Diane didn't give a damn. If they wanted to waste their lives getting married and raising families, that was their lookout. She was on her way now and nothing was going to hold her back.

She was right, of course. When the marketing director's job came up, she was the obvious choice. And when she took her seat on the board it seemed as if she had always belonged there.

Now she had real power, Diane revelled in it. She was fêted by the fashion industry and kow-towed to by the same colleagues who used to whisper behind her back.

There was only one part of her life that didn't measure up to the rest, her sex life. She was over forty now and most of the available men were divorced with weekend children. And children, other people's children, she could do without. So she went on making do with one-night stands. It was a sordid way to conduct a sex life, and Diane sometimes wondered whether she had taken a wrong turning. She would get quite melancholy thinking about the life she could have had, the life she sacrificed in order to get the big job. Then someone would call and ask her to a ball in Paris, and she'd stop feeling sad about herself.

Now as she walked into the reception at the French Embassy she was surer than ever that she had made the right choices. The room, with its elaborate carvings and rich old oil paintings, soothed her nerves after a trying day of business. She accepted that she was going to be hassled by the French PR lady and the textile goons she had in tow. But that went with the territory. That was what she was there for.

She was just rehearsing what she was going to say to them, when her eye was caught by a face in the crowd. It looked uncannily like David Robinson, but it couldn't be. He was nothing to do with the fashion industry.

The PR lady had found her now and for the next five minutes she was bombarded with introductions to designers and marketing men. But she couldn't forget the man she'd seen.

As soon as her group were launched into their pitch, she sneaked another look across the room. He was still there, looking dapper and successful and talking sixteen to the dozen to the commercial attaché. He was using his hands to illustrate a point, as David always used to when he got excited, she couldn't resist any longer. She had to know if it was him. She turned to the official PR.

'Who is that talking to the attaché?' she asked.

The French woman peered across the room. Then she consulted the list she was holding.

'It looks like David Robinson,' she said. 'The PR man. I didn't know he was coming tonight. This isn't exactly his kind of crowd.'

So she had been right after all. And the realisation panicked her slightly. Ever since she had been in London, she had been avoiding this moment. For quite simply Diane never wanted to clap eyes on David again. He had hurt her too badly for her to forgive him. She often put her disenchantment with men down to their painful, disastrous affair. So when she came to London and found he was there in the thick of things, she had gone out of her way to keep her distance. If there was a gathering he might attend, she simply avoided it.

Not that there were too many chances for their paths to cross, for they moved in different worlds.

Until tonight. Just for a moment she felt curious. Despite what he had done to her, she had loved this man once. She needed to know if the years had altered him.

Excusing herself from the people she was talking to, she made her way across the room. As she did so, she was careful to conceal herself, moving behind large groups so that she was never in David's line of sight.

Finally when she was as near as she dared, she allowed herself a good long look. He had put on weight, she noticed. In her day, he had been lanky and intense. Now he was displaying a slight paunch and she put it down to Sally's influence. She was always such a dedicated cook, she probably stuffed David full of gourmet dinners the minute he came home at night. For no reason at all, she felt a stab of pain. I can't be jealous, she thought. Not now, not after all this time.

Before she had time to examine her feelings any further, the crowd in front of her started to clear. And she found she was standing just feet away from David.

Good God, she thought. He's going to see me. She put her glass down and started to edge out of the way.

But she moved a second too late, for David had come to the end of the story he was telling and was looking across the room. She'd seen him do it a hundred times before. Surreptitiously eyeing the crowd in case there was someone there he should move on to.

She knew he'd seen her, for all of a sudden his face changed: one moment he had been the grovelling courtier, his smile a permanent expression of flattery; the next he looked surprised, as if someone had bumped into him from behind.

Diane was a good two yards away from him now, and she knew that if she stood any chance of getting away, she would have to move fast. So she did something she hadn't done for years. She pushed her way through the throng of people, using her elbows. When she had covered the collections in Paris, the technique had worked a treat, and it didn't fail her now. She was out of the main door in minutes and racing towards the lobby. Out of the big glass door she could see several taxis waiting outside. And she knew everything was going to be alright.

She was going to make her exit without having to say so much as good evening to David Robinson.

His first thought was that she was so stylish. When he knew her in Manchester she was scruffy and poor, like all the other journalists. But something had happened to change her, for the Diane he was confronted with now looked like a socialite.

Just for a moment he wondered if she was the same underneath all the trappings. And in that moment all the memories he had so successfully suppressed came flooding back. She was in his bed again, teasing and goading and driving him wild. And in spite of the crowded room and the diplomat at his elbow, he felt his body start to ache for her.

I have to see her again, he realised. I have to go over right now and grab her by the arm and take her out of this place to somewhere quiet where we can talk.

The commercial attaché was asking his opinion about something and he realised he had lost the thread of the conversation.

'I'm sorry,' he said distractedly, 'It's so noisy in here I didn't catch what you were saying.'

He saw the dismay in the older man's eyes, so he remade his ground as best he could.

'Why don't I give you lunch,' he said, 'then we can carry on without being interrupted. I'll have my secretary call and fix a date.'

Out of the corner of his eye, he saw Diane moving away.

I've got to go after her, he thought. I've got to get away from this French man before I lose her. But the diplomat wasn't letting him go before the niceties were observed. He launched into long flowery thanks for the lunch invitation, and while this was going on David watched Diane slipping away. She'd seen him, he realised that now, but she didn't want to renew the friendship.

She was almost fighting her way out of the room and he felt a terrible sense of disappointment. She was probably off to join the new man in her life and he would never see her again, never tell her how important she'd been to him, never explain why he had to walk away and how he'd regretted it ever since.

The attaché was saying his goodbyes now in the same flowery, old-fashioned manner as he had offered thanks for being invited to lunch.

'Send my respects to your charming wife,' he finally said, shaking his hand. 'Tell her from me, I think you're a lucky man.'

It was the worst thing that could have happened, a sharp reminder that he was married to Sally and should be grateful for it. It made him feel guilty and ashamed about the plans he had been making.

Yet he couldn't help himself. Diane had put a spell on him a long time ago and it still had the power to draw him. He knew that now he had seen her again, he wouldn't stop until he found her.

And find her he would. For she had to live somewhere in London. She had the look of the capital about her and he guessed that he would find the clue to her whereabouts right here at this party. Her name would be on a list, somewhere along with a point of contact. All he had to do was get hold of one of the society girls who organised this bash and winkle the information out of her. Though it wasn't as easy as he thought it would be.

The girl in charge who was trying to clear up was irritated by David's request. All her papers were neatly packed away and she was planning to be out of the building in the next half hour.

'Can't it wait till tomorrow?' she asked crossly.

David hesitated for a second. Of course it could wait, but

by tomorrow his good sense might have taken over and Diane would go unclaimed. He leaned forward, concentrating all his charm on the organiser.

'It can't wait another minute,' he told her. 'The woman I'm trying to find works for an important client. I have to see her tonight.'

She looked doubtful, but David stood his ground and in the end the girl stomped off to find what he wanted. She came back five minutes later, clutching a business card for Chic boutiques of Brompton Road. On it was Diane's name, a phone number and a fax number. David decided to push his luck.

'Do you have her home phone, by any chance?'

The organiser frowned.

'We're not allowed to give out that sort of information.'

'But you've got the number?'

She sighed. It was becoming apparent she was never going to get rid of this man and she was meeting her boyfriend in fifteen minutes.

'If I give it to you, will you promise not to say where you got it?'

David grinned.

'Cross my heart and hope to die.'

She reached into her bag and extracted a bulky filofax, flipping the pages until she found what she was looking for.

'It's 589 3460.'

David took her by the shoulders and kissed her soundly on both cheeks. Then he took out his pen and made a note on back of his cheque book.

'I'm in your debt forever,' he said.

The girl looked at him sourly. She'd heard that promise too many times in her short career.

He rang the number from the phone in his car and Diane answered on the second ring.

'It's David,' he said. 'Why did you walk out on me tonight?'

He realised he had caught her off balance, for she didn't say

247

anything right away. Then when she came back on the line, she sounded wary and rather worried.

'I don't know what you're talking about.'

'Rubbish. You walked into the Embassy, took one look at me and ran for your life.'

He thought he heard her sigh. Then she said:

'What is it you want?'

David thought quickly.

'What about a quick drink after work tomorrow? I need to know what happened to you.'

'I can't do it.'

'You can't. Or you won't?'

'Alright I won't. I've got my own life now and there's no room for you.'

He laughed softly, the way he always used to when he was playing with her.

'We're only talking about twenty minutes, for heaven's sake. That's not going to take up very much space.'

He sensed she was hesitating, so he applied a little pressure.

'I'll meet you in the pub at the top of Sloane Street.'

'You mean the King's Head?'

'That's the one. How about meeting there at six?'

He didn't wait for her to say yes or no. He simply cut the connection and left her dangling. Diane would have to turn up now. From what he remembered of her, she was far too curious to walk away from unfinished business.

David arrived early on purpose, so he could be there when she walked in the door. He didn't want her changing her mind because she didn't like standing in a pub on her own. He laughed at himself. For all I know, Diane doesn't like standing in pubs at all these days. The way she looked last night she'd probably be more at home in the Savoy. He wondered if he should have made it somewhere smarter. Then he realised it probably didn't matter. If Diane wanted to pick up the friendship, she wouldn't give a damn where they met.

He went over to the counter and ordered himself a large

whisky. When it arrived, he took it over to a table in the corner. He could watch the door from there, and guard the space he had reserved. There was no way he was going to share Diane with the tourists and the shoppers who were slowly filling up the bar. For the next ten minutes, they were all he saw. And he wondered if she was coming after all.

She didn't owe him anything. All that held them together were a few sentimental memories. And they probably meant nothing to her any more.

The clock above the bar told him she was twenty minutes late and he was reminded of other times when he had sat and waited for Diane: the Midland Hotel bar, where she'd stood him up to teach him a lesson; that tacky nightclub where she made him sit around for hours because she insisted on staying late at the *Express*.

David began to feel as if he spent his entire life waiting around for Diane. And in some obscure way it increased his yearning for her. It was as if she was always just out of reach like a siren in some ancient fable.

He took a sip of his whisky and made an effort to be rational. If Diane hasn't arrived by the time I've finished my drink, he decided, I'll call it a day and get the hell out of here. It was all very well being made a fool of when I was a little boy in Manchester. But I'm beyond that kind of nonsense now. He drained the rest of the whisky in one gulp, and was getting out of his chair when he saw her.

She looked flustered, as if she'd been struggling against a deadline to make this date. And all at once he forgave her. Something important, something he didn't know about had slowed her down. He hurried across to where she was standing in the doorway.

'I'm glad you could come,' he said. 'I was worried you might change your mind.'

She made a face.

'I nearly did.'

'Is that why you're so late?'

249

He saw her nod and look embarrassed, and he knew he had to defuse the situation.

'I've been saving a table,' he told her. 'Come and sit down and have something to drink.'

She followed him to the cramped little space in the corner of the bar, but he could see she was still on edge.

'Why are you so worried about seeing me again?' he asked gently. 'I'm not such a monster, am I?'

She didn't answer straight away and while she was searching for what to say, David took the chance to study her. She had aged well. He guessed she was somewhere in her forties, and she didn't try to hide it. Instead she compensated by going all out for style. The silky dark hair which she wore on her shoulders now looked as if it had been cared for by someone expensive. The clothes were the same: dead simple, almost natural looking. But nothing that simple cost under a couple of grand.

He saw she wore no wedding ring and guessed she must have paid for everything herself. Then he remembered her business address, Chic Boutiques, and realised nothing had changed. She was still the successful career woman fighting her corner against all comers. If there was a man in her life, he probably took second place to her job and the idea gave him hope. It was shortlived.

'I didn't want to come here,' she told him, 'but I guess you know that already.'

'What's the problem?'

'Sally's the problem. None of this is fair to her.'

He faced her then doing his best to be reasonable.

'It isn't fair,' he said, 'but life doesn't work that way. If it did, I might not have listened to my father when he talked me out of seeing you all those years ago.'

He saw he had irritated her, for she pulled away from him.

'I didn't come here to rake up the past. You did what you did and you took the consequences for it. Anyway I bet it's no hardship being married to Sally.'

'It isn't, but it's not that interesting either.'

She grinned quite unexpectedly and it lightened up her face, taking ten years off her.

'I've known too many married men to let you get away with that one. Marriage isn't meant to be interesting. It's meant to be comfortable and secure and all the other suburban things people like you go in for.'

He was stung.

'How did you know we lived out of London?'

'It's written all over you. If you lived in town you'd do something about that paunch. And you wouldn't be quite so carefully turned out.'

She saw she had surprised him, so she hurried to explain herself.

'Looking at people is what I do for a living. It's my business to understand who people are and who they want to be.'

He took a sip of his drink.

'That explains your work address. Chic Boutiques.'

Now it was her turn to be surprised.

'How did you know that?'

'After your hasty exit from the Embassy I did some checking up on you, and one of the girls produced it.'

'So that's how you found me.'

'Would you rather I hadn't?'

She looked thoughtful for a moment.

'Yes,' she answered finally, 'I would rather you hadn't, because it's not going to end with a drink in a pub. Sooner or later you'll start calling me, and if I'm very foolish I might agree to see you again. And then Sally will be on my conscience.'

The ache he felt when he saw her last night was back now, stronger than ever. David felt whatever loyalty he had left for his wife slipping away from him.

'Why don't you think about us for a change,' he said harshly, 'and stop worrying about my marriage.' Sally has her own life in Oxford, looking after our daughter and cooking dinner parties. 'She doesn't give a damn about what I do or who I see when I'm in London. And that suits both of us very well.'

Diane raised her eyebrows.

'How very convenient. Where are you going to fit me into this neat little scheme?'

She was laughing at him now and he decided to put a stop to it.

'There isn't any scheme because I didn't think any of this out before I saw you tonight. All I knew is that I needed to hear your voice. To be with you. And that isn't a ploy or a married man's seduction game.'

She looked at him from under her eyelashes.

'I don't believe a word of it.'

Chapter Twenty Nine

David rang Diane at her office the following week and found he had to talk his way past a queue of secretaries and personal assistants before he managed to get hold of her.

'Just what is it that you do for Chic?' he asked her, suprised and impressed at the same time.

He heard her laugh on the other end.

'I'm the marketing director.'

'Are you telling me you hire and fire people like me?'

'That's about the strength of it.'

'Good, then you can take me out to lunch.'

She had protested she wasn't interested in his agency. But he took no notice. She was interested in him, despite her denials. And in the end she reluctantly agreed to stand him lunch at La Caprice.

It didn't start out as promisingly as he imagined. Diane was twenty minutes late and when she finally did turn up she offered him no apology. She was harassed and she had been working hard and what she wanted more than anything else was a cold glass of wine. They were in the cramped little chrome bar at the entrance to the restaurant and without any reference to him at all, Diane ordered herself a drink, then she called one of the waiters over.

'I'd like to go straight to the table,' she told him. 'My usual table by the window. And I want to order lunch as soon as I sit down, so don't keep me waiting around.'

It was like being with another man, a busy man who used

restaurants as conveniences rather than as somewhere to relax. The waiter, who turned up as instructed, was given a detailed list of what Diane wanted. When David slipped his order in at the end, the boy looked grateful that he had taken the trouble to be polite.

After he left, David turned to her.

'You don't have to be so hard on the boy. He's trying to earn a living the same as you.'

He saw her look stubborn.

'No way is he the same as me. My job is my life, whereas he's probably just filling in until he finds something better.'

'He still works.'

'It's not what I call work. While you and Sally were busy building a nest, I was skipping meals and going into the office at weekends to get somewhere. You don't think I made it by sloping off early, do you?'

He looked at her.

'You don't have the premium on hard work. Sally and I worked every weekend when we were building the agency. And our nest, as you call it, didn't exist until the business took off.'

'So Sally hasn't spent her entire life as a housewife?'

He grinned.

'No, just the important part.'

She caught his eye and saw he was teasing her, and they both started to laugh. As they did, the tension she had carried with her to lunch receded a little.

Now, as the food arrived, they started to talk as old friends, saying all the things they should have said to each other years ago, but somehow never did. David told her about the battles he had had with his father over her and over everything else in his life, and how in the end he couldn't go on being dictated to.

'It was either get out of Manchester, or get eaten alive.'

'You should have done it years before.'

He shrugged.

'I know, but I needed a reason to leave.'

'So what pushed you out in the end?'

For a moment David didn't say anything and Diane noticed

he looked worried, as if he was frightened he might offend her. Finally he looked up and met her eyes.

'Sally pushed me out. I wanted my own agency in London and father was dragging his feet over it. So in the end Sally dug into her savings and came up with the money to back me.'

If she was taken aback, she didn't show it.

'Why are you telling me all this?'

'Because I want to get things straight with you, for now and maybe for the future.'

He paused.

'Our problem was we never told each other the truth. We were both so busy playing games and trying to impress each other that we ended up miles apart. If I'd admitted just once that I was terrified of my father, we might have stood a chance together. But I was so busy being macho man in those days, I couldn't let my guard down.'

In all the years she had known him, this was the first time David had explained anything to her. It was almost an apology and it stopped Diane in her tracks.

She had come to lunch with her mind made up to turn him down; but now she hesitated. He wasn't pushing her the way she thought he would. He wasn't selling her a line about his wife not understanding him – though she doubted if Sally ever had fully understood him. Her old friend had been too trusting to see through David to the man he really was. So Sally had lived the whole of their marriage under the illusion that her husband was kinder, nicer, less ruthless than she knew him to be. Maybe David didn't want understanding, she thought. Maybe he married Sally because of her ignorance. But she knew that wasn't true. She had been wise to David from the start, but he had loved her nonetheless. Suddenly she was curious about what had happened all those years ago.

'What made you marry Sally?' she asked.

He passed a hand over his eyes.

'She made me feel important, and in those days I needed that.'

'You must have loved her too.'

'I suppose I did. But never the way I loved you.'

It was what she wanted to hear, for it excused everything she was going to do. David loved me first, she told herself. He loved me more. She reached out and took his hand and the touch of his skin tingled against hers, like a tiny electric charge. And all the things she had made herself forget came flooding back. Her heart yearned for him and her body yearned for him and she wanted to be lying somewhere naked beside him. They looked at each other then and she realised that everything she had been thinking had its echo in David.

'I could take you somewhere now,' he said.

And she nodded, pushing Sally and the guilt she felt about her out of her mind. David was rightfully hers, after all. She was only claiming back her property.

He took her to a hotel in the middle of the West End. It was one of those glossy impersonal places that businessmen used for conferences and shoppers met for tea. David had obviously been a client of theirs, for the porter didn't question him about his lack of luggage. He simply handed him a room key and took his credit card. It was all done so subtly that Diane wondered if David had other girlfriends he brought here. She looked at him, imagining him playing out this scene with someone else and she was gripped by an excitement so strong she could hardly conceal it. I want him because I can never really have him, she thought. It was always the same, even in the beginning. And for a moment she despised herself for the way she felt.

Then they were in the elevator, going up to the room, and there was no time for regrets. David had booked a suite, she discovered. As well as a bedroom there was a drawing-room overlooking the Park with its own mini-bar and fax machine. And Diane wondered if he was nervous. His cosy domestic life with Sally could have made him straight-laced. If she wasn't careful he might start averting his eyes while she took off her clothes.

She decided she couldn't let it happen. While he was rooting around the fridge, looking for a bottle of wine, she reached up to her waistband and unhooked her skirt.

When David turned round he saw Diane in her stockings and garter belt. She had left the top of her business suit and hadn't bothered to take off her high heels and he realised she hadn't changed. She still liked her sex dirty. He was outraged and excited all at the same time. But he couldn't let Diane see that. Not yet.

With a certain difficulty, he put the wine down and went over to where she stood. Then he took hold of her shoulders and pulled her up against him. It had been years since he had felt her body close to his and just her nearness aroused him. Then he kissed her, and in that moment he knew they weren't going to make it to the bedroom.

'I want you,' he said, pulling away from her.

And she undid the top of her suit and took off her bra and came back to him. Just for a moment he wondered why Diane hadn't got rid of the garter belt and the stockings and the lacy underpants. He had been deprived of her for so long he wanted to see all of her and feel all of her. Then he remembered that wasn't her way. Instead of simply making love, she'd want to go through the full erotic sideshow, building up to the act itself as she built his appetite.

He started to take his clothes off, lowering them both onto the carpet as he did so. This was one occasion when Diane didn't have to make him ready for her. She had his full attention right this minute. So he undid the garter belt and pulled down the panties and parted her legs. Then he found her and pushed himself into her, and in that moment David realised that since Diane had left him he had only been half alive.

I've come home, he thought, feeling young and free and unfettered from responsibility. I can be myself again.

They saw each other as often as they could, meeting in restaurants and ending up in her flat. And everything about Diane delighted David. He loved the way she lived and demanded to know how she had furnished her modern white apartment. Where did she find her abstracts? What part of Italy had she hunted down the graceful sculpture that adorned the surfaces?

And when she admitted she'd used an interior decorator, he felt briefly sorry for her. Poor girl, he thought. Furnishing a home was about the most creative thing a woman could do. Certainly when Sally had decorated the Oxford house, she was walking on air for months.

But Sally was lucky, of course. She had him to look after her, to take on the headache of earning a living. Diane had to go into an office every day and he wondered whether she chose to live the way she did or whether circumstances had pushed her into it.

Since that first lunch, they rarely talked about each others' lives, preferring to concentrate on the present. And David vowed the next time he saw her, he would try to draw her out about her single state. He didn't get the chance, for three weeks into the affair, Sally found Diane's business card. He must have tucked it into a pocket after the party at the Embassy and totally forgotten about it.

When Sally greeted him in the evening, brandishing the thing, he was astonished, though he did his best not to show it. Instead he pretended to be bored, dismissing Diane as part of the past he wished to forget. Not that it convinced Sally at all. She insisted they made contact again and if Diane had been in her office, she would have picked up the phone then and there.

As it was, she had to wait till the morning, but it still didn't give him time to warn Diane what was happening. When he got into the agency, he found three messages from her, all of them urgent. Christ, he thought. The shit's really hit the fan. He went across to the interconnecting door of his office and shut it firmly. Then he dialled Diane on his private line.

'You've had a call from Sally,' he said before she could sound off at him.

'You bet I have,' she said, sounding furious. 'Would you mind telling me what's going on?'

David sighed and wondered how much had been said. If he was lucky, Sally had dispensed with a cross-examination and simply invited Diane to lunch. If he was lucky. He lit a cigarette and started asking questions.

'Did my wife tell you why she was calling?'

Diane sighed lustily over the phone.

'She gave me some cock and bull story about finding my business card in one of your jackets.'

'That's exactly what happened. Sally wanted to know where I got it and I told her I'd run into you at a party.'

There was a silence while Diane digested this piece of information.

'Then what did you say?'

But he wasn't going to be sucked in as easily as that. He was the one who was asking the questions.

'What did Sally tell you I said?'

'Something really ridiculous. You hadn't bothered to get in touch because you were feeling guilty about what you'd done to me years ago.'

David laughed, mostly with relief. Sally had repeated his excuse word for word, and he didn't think for one moment Diane had filled her in on the truth.

'I suppose Sally wanted to put things right by having lunch?'

'How do you know that?'

'I do talk to my wife occasionally.'

'Well, if you talk to her,' Diane said tartly, 'you might have told her I didn't want to be friends again. How do you think I'm going to cope with girly lunches when I'm seeing you behind her back?'

He felt suddenly helpless, as if events had run away from him and were veering horribly out of control.

'You didn't say that.'

'Of course I didn't. I'm not a fool. I made a date for next week, only I don't suppose I'll keep it now.'

Oh yes you will, David thought. You'll keep it and you'll do your best to play the innocent, otherwise we're all sunk. Aloud he said:

'Darling, I think we should meet today. Is there anything you can get out of?'

He heard her laugh softly.

'What about my panties?'

* * *

259

Diane refused to listen to David. She liked Sally and she had respected her once. And now, just because she'd been put out to grass in the suburbs, there was no reason to make a fool of her. Anyway she didn't like the fact that David was so enthusiastic about them all being friends. He was behaving like a pasha with a wife for high days and client meetings and a mistress for sex. It would be healthier if Sally and I were at each others' throats, instead of best pals. She told David this after one of their lunches which had ended up in bed, and she thought he was going to have a heart attack.

'Don't you give a damn about Sally,' he screamed at her. 'She's not a woman of the world like you. If she knew what was going on, it would knock her to pieces. She wouldn't be at your throat, she'd probably be in a clinic having a nervous breakdown.'

David's outburst sobered Diane, but she still stood her ground. Her secretary was cancelling lunch that very day with an excuse that Diane was in New York on business.

'I'll just avoid her,' Diane said. 'In the end Sally will get the message.'

But she didn't. Two weeks later, Sally walked into Chic's Knightsbridge offices. The first Diane heard of it was when her secretary told her there was a friend waiting for her in reception.

'Does the friend have a name?' Diane asked.

'Sally Robinson. Apparently you ran into her husband a few weeks ago.'

Diane felt slightly faint. This was a nightmare that wouldn't go away. And now it was pursuing her into the sanctuary of her own office. She was tempted to send a message out that she was in a meeting and wouldn't be available all day. Then she thought, if I do that, Sally will only turn up again and I'm back where I started.

She cleared the pile of papers in front of her into a drawer. Then she asked her secretary to show Sally through. She would be cold and distant with her, Diane decided. She would make it quite clear that she hadn't got time in her life for old friends any more. Then Sally walked in and all at once she felt like a bitch. She had obviously come up for the day to shop, for she was clutching a big leather holdall and wearing flat shoes.

'I hope I haven't interrupted anything?' she asked.

Diane looked at her old friend and noticed the changes time had made to her. She was heavier than she used to be and there was a look about her that reeked of the affluent suburbs. There was too much shiny lipstick and the hair was too blonde and too perfect. Diane remembered a word her mother used to use: bandbox, that was it. It summed up Sally perfectly. She looked over the top of her papers and saw Sally was still rooted to the spot, hanging on like grim death to her shopping-bag.

'For heaven's sake, sit down, will you?' she said, indicating a chair. 'It's really great to see you.'

Sally looked slightly less nervous.

'As long as you've got time,' she said cautiously. 'I know how busy it gets when you're working.'

There was a wistful quality in her voice. She was obviously bored with being a housewife. But it was more than that. The fact that she didn't work had made her into a second-class citizen. Despite herself, Diane felt sorry for Sally. She glanced at her watch, all her previous intentions flying out of the window.

'Do you have time for a drink before you catch the train home?'

Sally looked faintly more cheerful.

'I'm not going home tonight. David's got a big client dinner so I'm staying in the London flat.'

For a moment, Diane was surprised. David had a flat in London? She didn't know that. Why didn't he tell me, she wondered. Then she thought, what's it to do with me? Sally's obviously up and down all the time. He wouldn't want me stopping by to say hello. She started to gather her papers together.

'So you are free for a drink then?'

Sally nodded.

'I'd love that.'

Half an hour later when they were sitting drinking ice-cold

dry martinis in the bar at the top of Harvey Nichols, Diane started to wonder why she had been so worried about Sally. There wasn't the slightest awkwardness between them. They'd even slipped back into their old roles with Diane acting like an elder sister, and Sally doing her ingénue bit.

She had been right about Sally being bored, but wrong when she assumed her friend didn't like being a housewife. Sally thoroughly enjoyed the round of drinks and parties and entertaining that went with being the consort of a successful businessman. She liked being a mother, too, and Diane was subjected to the usual snapshots that proud mothers always seemed to carry around in their handbags. Staring at Annabel standing in the garden of their Oxford house was the one bad moment Diane had.

The girl was the image of David. She had his curly brown hair and his gobstopper eyes. She even had his build, for she was already taller than Sally.

'You must be very proud of her,' Diane said, knowing how banal she sounded.

But Sally took everything at face value. 'I am proud of Annabel. She drives me crazy at times, but she's got David's charm, so she always manages to get round me.'

Diane decided she didn't want to talk about Annabel any more. She was a part of David's life that threatened her. She could just about cope with Sally, but a child who seemed so uncannily like him was a different proposition. If he was ever called on to choose between her and Sally, then Annabel would tip the balance. She steered the conversation into more general areas. But Sally seemed hell-bent on talking about children.

'I suppose you're wondering why I didn't have a bigger family?'

Diane did her best to look unconcerned.

'Not really.'

'Yes you are. Everyone we know has asked me that question at one time or another.'

Diane sighed. She was about to get some confession about David's ability as a parent, or Sally's. And she didn't want to know. She didn't want to know anything about this marriage. But Sally wasn't letting her off the hook.

'We both wanted more children,' she confided, 'but having Annabel messed me up inside. I couldn't do it again.'

She sounded completely gutted when she said it, as if she'd failed to clear one of life's major hurdles. Diane looked at her friend, wondering how she could get her to talk about something else.

'There's no point in feeling sorry for yourself,' she said finally. 'Look at me, I haven't got children at all.'

Sally put her drink on the counter and looked stricken.

'You must think I'm very selfish,' she said. 'All I've done since we got here is to talk about myself and my problems. I haven't even started to ask you about your life.'

Diane started to relax.

'There's not much to tell. I left Manchester three or four years after you did to join Chic. After that it has been hard slog and not much else.'

'Was it worth it? I mean now you've got to the top, are you sorry you didn't have time to do all the normal things?'

Diane smiled, but it was a bad-tempered smile.

'You said just now people were always asking you why you didn't have any more children. Well I get asked why I don't have a life. And I make a point of avoiding the question.'

'Even with me?'

'Even with you.'

After that the conversation was stilted. Sally had got the message that Diane was not interested in going back to the old days when they could say anything to each other. And Diane was relieved she had managed to make herself understood. She was prepared to pay lip-service to a friendship with Sally, but she wouldn't go any further.

As long as they both knew the rules, nobody was in any danger of getting hurt.

Chapter Thirty

David realised he had to do something about Diane when she cancelled a dinner date with him. It wasn't a particularly special dinner date. They usually managed at least one evening together during the week. But David had come to depend on this time out of time, for Sally was beginning to make him feel shut in.

He hadn't noticed how domestic his wife become. Her life revolved around running the house and looking after Annabel and when he came home at night he felt almost like an intruder. It was as if they lived two separate existences, he in London, Sally in the country. And unless they were entertaining clients there was almost no common ground.

So when Diane called and told him she had a last-minute emergency in the office, David didn't go back to Oxford. He decided to tough it out and spend the evening alone in town. I'll go back to the flat and get a takeway Chinese meal, David thought. Then I'll put my feet up and watch television.

His mind strayed back to the conversation he'd had earlier with Diane. Her American associates were in town and she had been pressed into taking them out for dinner. It annoyed him how people did that to Diane. They thought just because she was single, they could intrude on her personal time and it wouldn't matter. Well it did matter and he had told her so. And it had precipitated a row.

'You don't own me,' she had shouted at him.

'And Chic does, I suppose?'

There was a silence while she turned that over in her mind.

'Chic pays me a damn good salary,' she said emphatically.

He hadn't gone on with the argument, for he knew Diane would never back down. When her mind was made up about something it was like hitting up against a steel fence. So he put the phone down and rang the Canton place round the corner from his flat. He'd pick up dinner on the way home.

He realised it wasn't one of his better decisions when he opened the foil containers in his kitchen. The waiter had somehow managed to get his order wrong and he was stuck with a congealed-looking chop suey and wilted portion of spring vegetables. He threw the whole lot down the waste disposal unit. Then he stomped into the next room and rang his wife. He needed reassurance tonight: reassurance and consolation, and Sally was good at that.

He dialled his Oxford number, expecting it to be picked up on the second ring. But nobody answered for a good three minutes. What on earth is keeping her? he wondered. When she finally did pick up the phone, his mood had got worse.

'You're not busy, are you?' he asked nastily.

Sally didn't seem intimidated by his bad temper.

'I am actually,' she said coolly. 'Annabel invited a couple of her friends round to supper and we're all playing Monopoly.'

If he had been spending the night with Diane he would have been mightily relieved his wife had found something to occupy her time. Now he was all on his own, he was irritated with her. How dare she be enjoying herself when he was feeling miserable?

'I hope you had a good supper,' he said sulkily. 'My Chinese takeaway was filthy.'

Sally sounded concerned.

'You really should learn to cook for yourself. Marks do all sorts of things you can heat up in the microwave.'

For a moment David was tempted to tell her he couldn't work the microwave because he always ate out when he was in London. Then he thought, what's the point in making Sally suspicious of me? I've got the perfect arrangement with Diane, why rock the boat.

'Don't fret about me, love,' he told her. 'there's some cheese in the fridge that should solve my problem.'

She seemed relieved.

'Then I'll get back to the girls. I'm holding up the game.'

When he put the phone down, he felt even worse than he had done before. Everyone seemed to have something better to do than worry about him. Even his wife. And he felt as if the whole world had abandoned him. In desperation he turned on the television, but after an hour of flicking from channel to channel he realised it bored him. He was too edgy to sit around doing nothing.

His thoughts wandered to what he might have been doing if the evening had gone right. He and Diane would be finishing dinner by now and thinking about going on somewhere. There was an enormous choice of late nightclubs in London, but only one in which he really felt at home, and they always seemed to end up there.

Annabel's, David thought. What I wouldn't give to be sitting in that crowded, dark, warren of a place. As he thought about it, he could almost hear the insistent throb of music coming from the tiny dance floor and smell the expensive perfume from all the expensive girls.

It occurred to him that he didn't need to sit at home thinking about Annabel's. If he wanted to he could pick himself up and go there without Diane's or anyone else's permission. I am a fool, he realised. I should have thought of it in the first place.

He got to the club in Berkeley Square around eleven thirty and made straight for the bar. It was empty and the bartender was glad to see him.

'What will it be, Mr Robinson? Your usual, or something stronger?'

He started to feel more secure than he had all evening. In this dark cosy corner of the world they knew his name and his taste in booze. They probably knew his taste in women as well, though unless he made it known he needed one at that moment, they wouldn't come up with any helpful suggestions.

He settled back against the glass circular bar and watched

the action. The usual hooray henries were in tonight, probably after some deb dance, David thought. Car dealers and traders from the Middle East were also making a showing – all of them jangling gold jewellery as if it was solid proof of their success in the world.

But the men didn't hold his interest. It was the girls who came here that he liked to watch. They all made an effort for Annabel's. They piled up their hair and clinched in their waists as if this was the one place in London where they could show their sex and not get into trouble for it.

There was one girl on the dance floor that caught his attention. She was very tall and slender with jet-black hair twisted into sleek chignon. She had her back to him, so he couldn't judge whether she was gorgeous or just acting the part. But from the look of her dancing partner he had a pretty shrewd idea she had something special. He was whispering something in her ear and David guessed he was probably telling her what he intended to do when he got her into bed. Lucky sod, David thought. If things had been different that could have been me.

The couple turned round a little, allowing him to get a better look at the girl. And that's when David froze. For his earlier assumption proved totally correct. He could have been on the floor with his arms round this beauty: she was none other than Diane.

She lied to me, he thought. She pretended she couldn't see me because she had some business party, and all along she had a hot date with someone else. For the first time since he had started this affair, David realised he could lose Diane. Who could blame her if she didn't want to sit around on her own on the nights he spent with his wife?

But I'm not with Sally, he thought. I'm totally available tonight and still she doesn't want to know. He turned round and took a gulp of his cognac. Then he asked the barman for a cigar. He always thought best when he was lighting up a Havana. And he needed to figure this one out.

What had driven Diane to do this? he wondered. I thought she loved me. He laughed at his own naivety. She never said she loved me, he reminded himself. She said she wanted me often enough, but not once has she gone further than that. She respected the fact that he was married with a child and responsibilities so she never pushed it.

In the years he had been taking her to bed, it was the thing David most liked about Diane. Now he wasn't so sure. She's behaving like a man, he thought, keeping me on the side because I'm solid and dependable and seeing other, more available men when I'm out of the way.

He looked at the pocket handkerchief dance floor and saw they were still there. Diane was whispering in her partner's ear now and he realised with a start this wasn't a new suitor. He and Diane had been around together for some time. She wouldn't be so at ease with him otherwise.

How many lovers does she have? he asked himself. Is this clown the only one, or does she have a different escort for every night of the week?

He finished his cognac and signalled for a refill. Another drink might give him the courage to go up to her and ask her what the hell she was doing on the night she should have been with him.

If he hadn't glanced up, the whole course of his life might have been different. But he did. And it was then he caught sight of himself in the mirror over the bar.

For a moment he didn't recognise the man he saw. For this middle-aged stranger wasn't David Robinson at all. His suit looked tired from being worn all day, and there were pouches under his eyes he hadn't seen before. I look like a loser, he thought. If Diane was to see me now, she wouldn't feel guilty at being caught with someone else. She'd simply feel sorry for me.

The thought that he might make a fool of himself was too much for David. He pushed the untouched cognac away from him, and prepared to leave. But before he did so, he checked out the dance floor. Diane was still clinging to her partner, oblivious to anything or anyone else. In a miserable sort of way, he was glad of it.

If he walked out now Diane would never know he had been in Annabel's at all that night.

Diane looked out from the bright circle of the dance floor and saw David get up from the bar. He's leaving, she thought. And she felt miserable and guilty all at once. I shouldn't have put the office before him, she thought. I don't have to allow some visiting salesman to hold me too close.

All at once she was seized with the compulsion to rush off the floor and explain herself to David. She'd been wanting to do it, ever since she saw him five minutes ago. But she'd left it too late. He was leaving the club and walking so quickly she could never catch up with him.

Damn, she thought. I'm sure he's seen me and he's never going to believe in a million years I was just doing my job.

Diane couldn't believe what she was hearing. 'I thought you and Sally would be together for life,' she protested when David told her he was considering leaving home.

'What brought this on?'

They were having a drink in a wine bar near Diane's office two days after the Annabel's episode. Neither of them had admitted to seeing each other in the nightclub. And now David was discussing breaking things off with Sally, Diane decided he probably wasn't going to bring it up after all.

For once she was wrong.

'I knew I had to leave Sally when I saw you with someone else,' David said. 'I dropped into Annabel's on the night you were meant to be working.'

Diane was nonplussed.

'But I was working. The man I was dancing with was one of the Americans who was visiting the office.'

David looked at her and marvelled at her capacity to lie. It was perfectly obvious that she had been with a boyfriend, but she wasn't going to admit it. He decided to let her get away with it. If this boyfriend had been important to her, she wouldn't be pretending he didn't exist. He smiled.

'I don't really care who the man was,' he told her. 'The fact you could be in Annabel's with anyone else was enough for me. I knew I had to do something or I'd lose you.'

'So you decided Sally had to go.'

He started to feel irritated. Diane wasn't meant to react like this. Any reasonable mistress would be ordering champagne and thanking the Lord that he had finally seen sense.

'What's got into you?' David demanded. 'I thought you'd be pleased I was leaving Sally.'

She grabbed hold of his hand and gave it a squeeze.

'I am pleased,' she said. 'But I'm worried too. What's Sally going to do after all these years? She'll be rudderless without you. She won't know how to put one foot in front of the other.'

David felt guilt eating into his resolve. He had agonised for days over Sally before reaching this decision. For she hadn't been such a bad wife to him. And it really wasn't her fault that he'd grown out of her.

He turned to Diane:

'If it makes you feel any better I'm paying her off,' he said. 'She'll get the house and my share of the business so she won't be destitute.'

'She'll be pretty cut up, all the same.'

David sighed.

'She might be if I told her the truth, but I'm not going to do that. I'm going to say the agency is getting me down and I need a bit of time off.'

'Do you think she'll buy it?'

He shrugged.

'Not all of it, but enough to salvage her pride. I expect she'll think I'm having some kind of mid-life crisis and she'll feel sorry for me.'

Diane looked doubtful.

'It all sounds a bit brutal.'

David ran his hands through his black spikey hair.

'It would be worse if I said I was having an affair with her oldest friend.'

She noticed he said he was having an affair, not that he was in love. And she began to feel frightened. If she went on putting doubts into his mind, he'd start thinking she didn't matter all that much after all.

She went up and put her arms around him. 'I'm sorry I've been a bitch,' she said. 'It can't have been easy deciding to leave Sally.'

'It was the toughest decision of my life,' he said, looking agonised. 'But I took it because I want you and I don't want any more of your boyfriends getting in on the act.'

She was about to go on protesting her innocence over the Annabel's episode. But she changed her mind. She'd been altogether too lenient with him in this relationship. If she hadn't looked as if she was just about to be swept away by somebody else, David would still be treating her like a mistress. And she didn't want to go on in that role.

She was sick and tired of pretending to Sally that she was her best friend, when she was anything but. And she was even more bored with being hidden away. What she really wanted was to be able to go anywhere she pleased with David and not worry that he might see someone he knew. She wanted to see him on Sunday afternoons. And she wanted to introduce him to her friends.

For a moment she thought of Sally and wondered if she was being selfish, then decided she didn't care if she was. Sally was selfish once, when she married David knowing what it would do to me. Now it's her turn to suffer.

Chapter Thirty One

After he had looked at his bank account and checked his portfolio of stocks and shares, David was forced to the reluctant conclusion that he was not a rich man. He had never put anything aside for a rainy day, because he truly believed his life would never change. In his estimation he would go on running his agency at a profit for years to come. And when he retired he would keep his majority shareholding and let his subordinates support him.

Now he realised he had been naive. He had tied himself into his one asset, his agency. And now push had come to shove, he had nothing else. If he needed more money to pay off his wife, he was going to have to sell a chunk of Chandos.

The thought filled him with trepidation. He didn't want a partner coming in and turning over his systems. It would unsettle the staff and poison the clients. So he racked his brains for a way out of it.

An idea came to him in the middle of the night. It was so simple, he wondered why he hadn't thought of it before. He didn't have to do a deal with another public relations outfit. He could sell out to an advertising agency. Most of the big American conglomerates had their own PR arm. This practice was becoming increasingly popular with major clients who liked all their services under one roof. If David could find an up-and-coming agency who wanted to expand he would be quids in because he would still be running his own show.

The next morning, he put his plan into action, sifting through the advertising industry until he had a list of agencies without their own PR arms. Some of them were too small, and some of them didn't want to get involved in public relations. In the end he was left with the American partnership of Steiner, Morris & Black. Walt Black ran the UK operation and he arranged to meet him.

They lunched at Rules in Covent Garden, where Walt announced he had been considering taking on a public relations agency for some time. The news didn't surprise David at all. Walt, a tall patrician American with a shock of white hair and a permanent suntan, made it his business to keep in touch with current trends. He wasn't a particularly talented advertising man, but it was his astuteness that kept him in employment long after retirement age.

And now Walt's beady, experienced eyes were giving David the once-over. They had discussed balance sheets and client conflicts for the best part of two hours. But Walt still wasn't entirely satisfied with what David had to tell him.

'If I was in your shoes,' he said, stirring saccharine into his after-lunch coffee, 'there's no way I'd want to sell out to anyone else. You're making a healthy profit and it's getting bigger every year, so what do you need partners for?'

David recoiled slightly. He had been prepared for every question about Chandos, except for the most obvious of all. And because he hadn't prepared a pat answer, he was forced to fall back on the truth.

'I need the money to pay my wife,' he said, looking uncomfortable. 'We're talking about splitting up.'

Walt went on stirring his coffee as he absorbed this information. So David Robinson was using his business to buy his freedom. He had experienced similar situations, of course, many times and on both sides of the Atlantic. Because he was familiar with negotiations for paying off unwanted spouses, he made a mental note to check on what happened after the deals were done. Did newly divorced managers go on working with their former enthusiasm for a business that was no longer theirs? Or did they slack off and take a back seat?

Before he took on Chandos at the price David was asking,

he had to know what kind of future he was buying for Steiner, Morris & Black.

He looked at David.

'I'd like to think the whole thing over,' he said.

'I'd also need to sound out my partners in New York. So it might be a good thing if you gave me something in writing.'

David nodded.

'That shouldn't be any problem. When can I expect to hear from you again?'

The elderly American thought for a moment.

'Give me a couple of weeks. After that we should have something to talk about.'

The two men parted outside the restaurant, where Walt's chauffeur was parked and waiting for him. David didn't ask for a lift and Walt didn't offer him one and it was with a sense of relief that they went their separate ways. Whatever happened next was in the lap of the gods.

Exactly two weeks later Walt rang David.

'I got back from the States last night,' he told him. 'It looks like we're in a 'go' situation.'

For the first time since he opened this negotiation, David began to hope.

'When do you want to meet?'

As soon as we can set it up. I can be free at the end of this week?

They made a date for Friday and when David put the phone down, he was jubilant.

'I've done it, he thought. I've actually raised the money to get out of my marriage without having to get out of my business. He imagined the deal would be finalised in a matter of weeks. Then he could tackle Sally.

This part appealed to him least of all, for he couldn't bear the idea of hurting her. She might not be Diane, but he had loved her once and the thought of the inevitable tears and bitter recriminations filled him with horror. What appalled him even more was the fact that Sally would soon find out about Diane. For the minute the dust had settled, they

274

would want to move in together, and that would really tear Sally apart.

David sighed and set his face. He'd managed to get rid of his business elegantly, hadn't he? There had to be a way of doing the same thing with his marriage.

Steiner, Morris & Black occupied one of the spacious office buildings in St James's Square. In the adjoining streets that fanned out from the square were some of the most expensive restaurants in London – a fact not lost on the senior staff at the agency, who liked to take clients and important contacts for lavish lunches as often as their expense accounts would allow.

As David drew up outside Steiner, Morris & Black he reflected that soon he too would be ordering oysters at Wiltons, and the realisation gave him heart. He had lived a double life for nearly three years now and he'd be glad to see the end of it. The money will heal a lot of Sally's wounds, he thought as he walked through the revolving glass doors, and Walt Black has more than enough of it.

When he got into Walt's office on the fifth floor, he knew his instincts had been right, for no expense had been spared to make it look like Manhattan. Plate-glass windows ran floor to ceiling on two sides and the remaining walls were covered in the sort of splashy abstracts you find only in the best Cork Street galleries.

When Walt finally walked through the door five minutes later, David was more than ready to talk turkey. Walt felt the same way, for before he'd even sat down behind his desk, he was already naming his price. He was prepared to pay the kind of money David wanted over a period of five years. David heaved a sigh of relief. He could pay Sally out over five years and still have enough left to live on. He was just about to start talking contracts, when Walt interrupted him.

'There is one other thing,' he said. 'We'll want to bring in one of our own men from the States.'

David tensed. Walt had mentioned that possibility before, and he wondered what was going on.

'What do you need to do that for? I've been running Chandos at a profit for years now.'

Walt looked sad.

'I know that and you know that, but over in New York they got insecure. Unless one of their men is in the agency, calling the shots, they won't feel comfortable.'

As he spoke, Walt looked at David sitting opposite him. The guy looked as if he'd been hit by a thunderbolt, and he really couldn't blame him. But he couldn't blame his colleagues either. They saw a soon-to-be divorcee, who in their experience would take the money and run. They had to protect themselves.

He saw David turn to him and wondered what he was going to say.

'Does this American have a name?' he eventually enquired.

Walt smiled.

'He's called Irving Preston, Irv to his friends. We hired him a few years ago from a big public relations outfit in Cincinnati.'

A vision of Irving came into David's mind. He'd be Middle America personified, with all the rigidness that goes with learning the business away from the capital. He'd probably instigate office systems as his first move. Then he'd want to know which clients played golf. And before he could do anything about it, Chandos would be transformed into another boring American agency.

It was then he realised he couldn't go ahead. He couldn't allow the business he'd built up from nothing to be turned into dogfood. Not for Walt. Not for Diane. Not for anybody.

Before he could have second thoughts, he stood up and made to leave.

'Thank you for your generous offer,' he said, 'but I'm going to have to say no. In the end I don't think Irv and I could live together.'

Walt eyed him curiously.

'I wondered if you'd buck at the last fence. We all did.'

'But you thought I'd come to heel in the end.'

The white-haired patriarch sighed.

'You have to. There isn't any other way.'

* * *

Now he was pushed into a corner, David's nerve went completely. He felt as if was somewhere between the devil and the deep blue sea and he took it out on everyone around him. He yelled at his secretary. He yelled at Walt Black when he called to find out if he had decided what he was going to do. And he even started in on Sally, whom he blamed for all his current misfortunes, sulking when he was at home and biting her head off when she asked him if anything was the matter.

He was no better tempered with Diane, who didn't take his moods as a matter of course.

'You're behaving like a bloody bore,' she told him one evening. 'What the hell is the matter with you?'

It was then he came out into the open about the proposed takeover from Steiner, Morris & Black.

'It would solve all our problems on the Sally front, but I don't know if I could live with the idea of answering to somebody.'

To his surprise Diane backed him up. 'I don't think you should have to live with it. There has to be another way to raise some money.'

David looked weary.

'Don't you think I haven't gone through all the possibilities,' he told her. 'I haven't slept for nights worrying about it.'

'Then stop worrying this minute,' Diane said. 'Let me put my mind to the problem.'

Chapter Thirty Two

Two weeks later, Diane invited him to lunch with a friend of hers from her days on the *Express*. His name was Leslie Pickett and he owned a hair care clinic.

'I think you'll find he's an interesting man,' Diane told him, 'with plenty to say for himself.'

David was bemused.

'I don't need lunch with an interesting man. I've got enough friends already.'

She looked at him in despair.

'I wasn't trying to improve your social life. Leslie has an idea that could solve your money problems.'

Oh no, David thought, she's gone and taken what I told her to heart and now she's going to try and rearrange my life. His spirits sank. For much as he loved Diane, he resented her interfering in his private business. He had never liked the women in his life knowing too much about his day-to-day affairs. Even Sally had to be despatched from the agency when she got too close to the centre of things. And now Diane was getting in on the act. He looked cross.

'I can't see how some hair doctor could be any use to me whatever.'

Diane smiled.

'Then maybe I'd better explain about Leslie.'

She paused, wondering how best to present him. Should she say he was a whizz kid, or an entrepreneur? Or would that frighten David off? No, she thought, I'll just start at the beginning and tell it the way it was.

'When I first met Leslie, years ago,' she told him, 'he was another East End boy trying to make good in the rag trade. All the fashion girls liked him because he didn't try to push his line down our throats the whole time. He showed us the goods and let us make up own minds.'

'Did you like what you saw?'

She shook her head.

'Leslie didn't have a flair for clothes. He understood what made women tick, but he couldn't seem to apply what he knew. But he wasn't a quitter. He sold his fashion business, then he took all his specialised knowledge and applied it somewhere else.'

David looked at her.

'He opened a tricology clinic.'

The way he said it made Diane feel David simply wasn't taking any of this seriously. She decided she'd better get to the point as fast as she could.

'If Leslie had opened the clinic and stopped there, I wouldn't be talking about him. But he did something extra. He developed a range of shampoos and hair treatments that could take him into the big time.'

For the first time David looked interested.

'He'll need a very big promotion if he's going to take on the rest of the market. He'll need advertising too.'

Diane interrupted him.

'Leslie doesn't want to talk about PR or advertising. What he's got in mind is much wider ranging than that. But I'll let him fill you in about that over lunch.'

Leslie Pickett arranged to meet them in a Chinese restaurant in South Kensington. David knew from experience that the food was pretty inedible, and the only thing he imagined it had to offer was privacy. No-one much went there, so his host could discuss all his secrets quite openly with no danger of being overheard.

He realised he had been right when he walked through the door and saw Diane sitting all alone in the restaurant. He hurried across to join her.

279

'I see we're the first,' he observed. 'Would your friend mind if I ordered myself a scotch?'

Diane shook her head.

'Go ahead. I think I might do the same.'

She's nervous, he thought. Diane doesn't usually look at hard liquor until after she's left the office at night. He ordered the whiskies and settled back in his seat. Leslie Pickett had better be the hot shot she made him out to be, otherwise they were both wasting their time.

Twenty minutes later the man came through the door, out of breath and full of excuses. They came tripping off his tongue, each one more unbelievable than the last.

David took an instant dislike to him. It wasn't just the obvious lies about his lateness that did it. It was Leslie Pickett's whole appearance. He was a small, round butterball of a man with black crinkly hair and a high colour. Nature hadn't created him a gentleman, and he didn't fight it. Instead of a sober suit, he wore a loud check jacket and a bow tie which made him look like a bookie. David almost expected him to be taking bets for the two thirty at Epsom, and when he didn't he was almost disappointed. He wouldn't have objected to Leslie if he had been a bookie. It was the fact that he was masquerading as a businessman that got on his nerves.

Almost as soon as Leslie sat down, he went into his pitch. The shampoos Diane had been talking about were called 'Nourish' and had been developed by some boffin who had found a formula to make hair thicker. David had heard it all before of course. The big manufacturers were always coming up with some new gimmick, though Leslie's product sounded as if it had mileage in it.

He turned to him.

'You must have had a queue of bidders for 'Nourish' he said.

Leslie shook his head.

'Not really. The majors had a stack of their own shampoos on the shelves. They didn't want a product that would compete with them.'

Diane interrupted then.

'All Leslie's first approaches were from companies who wanted to buy him out and suppress the shampoo.'

David looked at her.

'But you didn't let him do it.'

'You bet I didn't. I told him to look around the smaller manufacturers, who might be hungrier.'

Leslie beamed at her.

'I was glad I listened. If I hadn't, I wouldn't have found Chemico and I wouldn't have got rich.'

The food started to arrive then, steaming plates of pork and seafood all covered in a grey glutinous gravy. The sight of it revolted David. Almost as much as the sight of Leslie Pickett, who was digging in as if it was his last meal on earth. I've got to wind this up, he thought. People getting rich out of shampoos are all very well, but it's not my field and I don't want to get involved.

He ploughed his way through the indigestible Chinese food with as much grace as he could muster, all the while listening with half an ear as Leslie went into raptures over his new backers.

Chemico, it appeared, was a down home Kentucky company whose main products were bath additives. A shampoo was just what they needed for their range, and they had ambitious plans to launch Leslie's brainchild, first in Europe, then in America. I'm pleased for him, David thought. But if I listen to much more of this, I'll go stark, raving mad.

The minute the waiter came to clear away the dishes, David was on his feet.

'I'm fascinated by what you have to say,' he told him insincerely, 'but I have to rush.'

Leslie looked disappointed.

'Aren't you going to ask me what the plans are for Nourish?'

David shook his head.

'I don't think I'm all that interested. I can't see a future there for me.'

Now Leslie looked crafty.

'Not even if it's running the whole show?'

He hesitated for a moment. So this was the big opportunity Diane had been hinting at. Before he turned it down, he needed a few more details.

'Why would Chemico want me to run the show? Surely they'd go for an American?'

'If they had a choice in it they probably would. But they don't. Part of my deal with Chemico was that I could choose the new manager.'

'And you choose me?'

'Why not? You're a friend of Diane's and I hear you've got contacts in Europe, which is where we're starting.'

David considered the prospect. He could set up a sales operation on his ear if he decided to. But I don't want to sell hair products, he thought. It would bore me silly inside six months. For the sake of politeness he asked where Leslie was thinking of setting up.

'We decided on Paris. Communications are easy from there and there's a factory outside Orly that's going cheap.'

Now he knew he was off the hook.

'I couldn't do it,' David said. 'It would mean giving up my own business.'

Leslie looked at him.

'I'd make it worth your while. There's half a million on the table for the first year, rising every year as the profits increase. If you're as good as Diane says you are, you could end up a rich man.'

It was a preposterous idea. Walk away from Chandos and start again in a foreign country as a shampoo salesman? He almost dismissed it out of hand. But the money was tempting. If he worked flat out for the next ten years he wouldn't see more than a hundred and fifty a year. And that was before tax. In Paris, with the right kind of advice, he could probably put half a million in his pocket with no questions asked.

Diane reached out and touched his hand.

'If you take this,' she told him, 'Sally won't have to know

about us. You could just disappear overseas. Then when the dust settles we could move in together.'

He realised she must have been thinking about this for a long time. The scheme was almost perfect. His main worry had been hurting Sally, but now he didn't have to. He could tell her anything he liked and there would be no evidence to the contrary.

He turned to Leslie, who was watching them both out of beady black eyes.

'I don't want to rush into anything,' he said. 'But it wouldn't do any harm to give me the name of your lawyer.'

Chapter Thirty Three

Sally . . . 1995

The worst day of Annabel's life was when she left her home in Oxford. She knew they couldn't stay there, of course. Mummy had made that more than plain. She knew that moving to Fulham was the sensible thing to do, but it didn't stop her from hating the move. What kind of life was she going to have in Fulham? she wondered, as she watched the removals men piling furniture into the van parked outside. She'd already guessed they wouldn't be moving to anything that remotely compared with the house she was used to.

They were leaving behind most of their furniture – the heavy oak table and high-backed chairs were waiting to be collected by Sotheby's, as were most of the antiques in the living-room and all the paintings. Annabel had never really liked any of the opulent pieces, but now she was saying goodbye to them, she reconsidered. They were part of her background, her style almost. She didn't want to get used to stripped pine and small rooms. That was for plebs and she had no intention of becoming one.

She was about to tell the removals men to start loading up the dining-room table, when she saw her mother coming down the stairs.

'I see we're nearly ready now,' she said briskly, 'at this rate we'll be in London by teatime.'

Annabel turned to face her.

'Do we have to do this?'

Sally saw the rebellious glint in her daughter's eye and braced herself for trouble. She'd done her best to talk sense into the girl, but she knew that when she saw how final things were, she wouldn't leave without a fight. This is all I need, she thought, though she did her best to be kind.

'Darling, I hate it too,' she told her, 'but we don't have any alternative. If we stayed here and stuck our heads in the sand, sooner or later the bailiffs would turn up and take everything away. This way, at least we're getting out with our pride in place.'

The girl sighed and looked at the floor.

'I know,' she said. 'But it's so unfair.'

Sally grabbed hold of her hand and pulled her towards the door.

'Life's unfair,' she said. 'But there's no point in brooding about it.'

It had been a long, slow journey. Roadworks that had been there for months reduced the traffic to single file and Sally and Annabel sat in a jam for most of the day. Neither of them spoke much. And by the time they got to World's End, they had little energy left. Sally looked wearily at her daughter.

'We'll be arriving in about ten minutes,' she told her.

Annabel looked out of the window with the first stirrings of curiosity and saw a mass of tiny winding streets all snaking off the main road. Every street had its own row of houses, but they were such shabby houses, she couldn't imagine anyone actually living in them. She was about to say so, but her mother looked so bone tired that she didn't have the heart. Instead she went on looking at the landscape. It didn't change for the better. As they drove deeper into South West London, everything seemed more delapidated. Torn fly posters hung off the walls they passed and the only bright spots were the smart antique shops that seemed to follow the main road.

They got to their destination just before dark. And Annabel realised that their new house wouldn't be any better than all the others she'd seen in this district. Her eye picked out a furniture van in the middle of the street and she prepared herself for the worst. This is it, she thought. This is where I'm being sent to die. It was only when she got a bit closer that she realised things weren't as bad as she feared.

The new house had a bright red front door, newly painted. And whoever had lived in it before had cared about the garden, for there was still a bed of busy lizzies all in flower under the window. She felt a bit better when she saw that. The place was still the pits of course. But if she tried, she might just be able to put up with it.

As soon as her mother parked the car, she jumped out of the front seat and ran across the street. She had to inspect this new home of hers, so she could give it her stamp of approval.

The front door had been left open by one of the removals men, so she took a deep breath and stepped inside. The room she walked into took her by surprise, for although it was clearly the main drawing-room it didn't have a hall. You came straight into it from the street. Though on further inspection she could see things hadn't always been that way.

The last people had knocked the hall through and she could understand why: it made the narrow corridor of a room that little bit bigger. She walked through to the far window and stared out into the back garden. It was a decent size for London, she supposed, and overgrown with roses and vines. Not bad, Annabel thought. Not a patch on Oxford, but not bad.

She took the stairs to the next floor with a lighter heart. There were two quite decent bedrooms overlooking the garden. And she knew without being asked which one she was going to take.

Then she saw something that really turned her off. On a tiny landing above the bedrooms was a bathroom. She guessed it was the only bathroom in the house. She and her mother would have to take it in turns to use the shower and Annabel felt slightly sick. This was positive proof that they had come down in the world. All her life she had lived with en-suite bathrooms, one for every bedroom. She sped down the stairs, wondering what other surprises this house had in store for her.

When she got into the big basement kitchen Sally was already preparing tea. She'd brought up a hamper with her from Oxford, as if she knew Annabel would be in need of consolation. On the big pine kitchen table she saw her favourite fruit cake, three different kinds of jam and the silver tea service Sally used only for best.

It was the tea service that did it. Her mother knew how this move was hurting her, so she brought along the silver to remind them they had seen better days.

Suddenly she felt small for hating the bathroom. Her mother had probably been round every place in their price bracket searching for somewhere halfway decent and this house was the best she had been able to find. She sat down on one of the kitchen chairs and helped herself to a slice of cake.

'It's not that bad,' she told her mother. 'Once we've got our things in, it could be quite homely.'

Sally pushed the tangle of blonde curls out of her eyes, and felt slightly reassured. She had been dreading this moment even more than she had been dreading leaving Oxford. Things were turning out better than she expected.

'You have been right upstairs?' she asked cautiously.

Annabel nodded.

'And I've seen the bathroom, so you can stop panicking.'

'You mean you don't mind sharing?'

'Of course I mind sharing, but I expect I'll get used to it.'

Chapter Thirty Four

In Sally's second week at the agency, when she was struggling to make sense of the chaos Jeremy had left behind, she had an unexpected visitor. He marched right into David's old office which she had taken over, and plonked himself down on the chair in front of her desk.

'You might say you're pleased to see me,' Albert Robinson said, 'I've had a hell of a time tracking you down.'

Sally looked at her father-in-law and felt beaten. She had managed to avoid him for months now, ever since David had made his dramatic announcement and walked out on her. It seemed he had repeated the same announcement to his entire family for she was besieged with calls from Albert, from Rose, from his two brothers and the various cousins she had been subjected to over the years.

She had dealt with them all the same way, thanking them for their concern, assuring them she was surviving, and promising to call the moment she had got over things. She hadn't called, of course, and everyone had given up on her, except for Albert. He was in the habit of phoning her for no apparent reason and threatening to drop in on her, but she always had a ready excuse. She was visiting friends in London. She had a hairdresser's appointment. It was Annabel's sports day.

It wasn't always easy to get rid of Albert, for he was very persistent, but she kept on fobbing him off because she knew very soon she would be leaving the marital home and her old in-laws would never find her where she was going. But she had been wrong. There was Albert, all done up in a tight brown suit and a felt trilby, sitting in front of her desk as if owned the place.

'How did you know where I was?' she asked, intrigued in spite of herself.

Albert grinned.

'Easy peasy. I rang the bank and they gave me your new address.'

'I didn't know banks were allowed to do that.'

'They're not. But I pulled a few strings.'

Sally had no doubt that he had. Albert had friends in the most unlikely places and he was not averse to using them outrageously. She looked at him.

'I suppose Annabel told you I was here when you rang the house?'

He nodded, looking pleased with himself.

'You've turned me into a regular Sherlock Holmes.'

Quite suddenly she was exasperated. When she and David had been together they had never been particularly close to his family. So why was it so important to make contact now?

'I don't know why you went to all this trouble to see me,' she said.

Albert took out one of his thin, evil-smelling cigars.

'I had to see you. We have things to discuss.'

Sally sighed. There was no way she was going to rake over why David left her again. She'd put herself through that inquisition too many times and now she wanted to get on with her life.

'If it's about David, I don't want to know.'

Albert took his time lighting up, then he fixed her with his shrewd hard eyes.

'It's not about David. I've given up on David. It's you I'm concerned about.'

'I can look after myself.'

'I don't think so. You're a clever girl, but you're not that clever.'

'How do you know?'

'Because I know people. My guess is you can do half the

289

job that needs to be done here. You probably sweet-talked a few accounts to stay with you till you sorted yourself out.' He paused. 'But now you've got it all nailed down, you can't put one foot in front of the other.'

Sally regarded her father-in-law with deep suspicion. He had always meddled in David's affairs until their move to London. And now history was repeating itself. She stood up behind her desk.

'You're wrong about me not being able to cope. I know exactly what I'm doing, but I'm not going to be able to do it with you cluttering up my office.'

She was being rude and she knew it, but short of throwing the old man out, there didn't seem to be any other way of getting rid of him. Not that he made any attempt to get moving. He simply stubbed out his cigar in her expensive china ashtray and leaned back in his chair.

'You're making a big mistake,' he told her. 'If you listened to what I had to tell you, you might learn something.'

'About public relations? Give me a break – you don't know the first thing about it.'

'Of course I don't know about public relations. I never said I did. But I do know about running a company. I was doing it before you were born.'

She shouldn't have listened to him, she knew that. Albert was definitely more trouble than he was worth. But he did have an uncanny habit of being right. She remembered the trouble she and David had had getting Chandos off the ground when they started, and how Albert had interfered and told them they were finished because they didn't have any friends down South. The old man might have put it badly, but he was spot on. They needed people to know who they were. Once they had solved the problem by throwing a party, they had never looked back.

His instincts are all there, Sally thought. He could probably sort this office out in no time at all, if I gave him half the chance.

'Why are you doing this?' she asked, still wary.

'Because I don't think you deserve what David did to you.'

Sally looked scornful.

'You want to help the little woman back to her feet.'

'If that was all that was on my mind, I'd offer you money. But I think you're better than that. I saw how you worked when you were in the agency. You were damn good, you know. Better than David gave you credit for. If you'd stayed on, you might have been serious competition for him.'

Nobody had said that to her before. Diane had told her she was out of date. Even her own daughter doubted her ability. But this difficult, tetchy old man was rooting for her. She knew at that precise moment, she wasn't going to turn him down after all.

Albert spent all week in the agency. And what struck Sally immediately was that he was completely ruthless. If he thought something was wrong, he simply ploughed in with little regard for anyone's finer feelings. She had the financial director threatening to resign almost as soon as he had spoken to her father-in-law, which didn't seem to bother Albert one little bit.

'The man's an incompetent,' he said. 'You'd be better off with a good firm of outside accountants.'

Her landlord was the next person to complain. Apparently the old man had been to see him, protesting about all the unused office space.

'He had the temerity to suggest we leased some of it back.'

Privately Sally thought this was a good idea.

'What are you doing about his suggestion?'

'We've been forced to go along with it. My company lets a lot of factory space to him in Manchester and he threatened to cancel the contract.'

She had to smile at Albert's antics. The man's only experience was running factories, yet he had managed to tune into the wavelength of her public relations business and make everyone stand to attention. He had even taken it upon himself to interview every single member of her staff, in order to sort out who should go and who should stay. She rather wondered how he'd get on with this weeding-out process and she didn't have too long to wait before she found out.

Towards the end of the week, her father-in-law presented her with his blueprint for her new re-vamped agency. She had no accounts department any more. She was operating in half the floor space. And apart from Heather, David's old secretary, who she had promoted to office manager, she was left with only three executives.

'How am I going to run an agency with nobody in it?' she screamed.

Albert stood his ground.

'The same as you did in the beginning. You'll have to work harder.'

She had no answer for that one, so instead she enquired who Albert had allowed her to keep. He came back with three names, only one of which was familiar to her. Sue Phillips the solid, dependable former *Vogue* editor who was virtually wedded to the Chic account. Sue was irreplaceable, which is more than could be said for the other two, both of whom were juniors. Fred, the dark lanky one, had come to them straight out of college. And Jim, the neurotic red-headed one, didn't look old enough to hold a driving licence.

She was glad they were sitting in her office with the door closed when she started to quiz Albert about his choices. For she didn't bother to flatter either of them.

'I don't need those little boys working in my business,' she told him. 'Neither of them looks older than Annabel.'

The old man perched on the edge of her desk and took out a cigar.

'Those two little boys, as you call them, are the only executives you've got that are worth anything.'

'What makes you say that?'

The old man smiled.

'Market economy,' he said. 'Both of them were leaving for other jobs with your rivals. Everybody else is nosing around for a move, but these two were the only ones with definite offers.'

Sally looked at him sharply.

'How do you know that?'

Albert allowed himself to look smug for a moment.

'Why do you think I went to the trouble of interviewing your entire staff? It wasn't to find out who could do their job the best. I wouldn't know the difference anyway. What I wanted to know was who had the gumption to get off their asses and get out while the going was good. And you'd be surprised how many of your loyal employees were willing to dish the dirt on Fred and Jim. They accused them of leaving you in your hour of need. Not that they would have been averse to walking out if they had anywhere to go.'

She started to feel worried.

'If it's common knowledge we're on the slide, why on earth would those two want to stay?'

He gave her an old-fashioned look.

'Money, of course. I promised them more money if they made the agency work.'

A horrible suspicion began to form in her mind.

'More money that what?'

'More money than they'd be getting if they took the jobs they were offered.'

She ran her hands through her short blonde hair, feeling faintly desperate.

'Even with your outrageous cuts, we're still going to be struggling. How am I going to find the extra for their salaries?'

There was a silence while Albert took out a cigar and lit it.

'You're going to motivate these two young hot shots to go out and find it for you. There's plenty of business out there. All it needs is the right kind of attitude to bring it in.'

The way he said it, it all sounded so simple. But why shouldn't it be simple? Sally asked herself. David had always shrouded the business in clouds of mystery, allowing no-one, particularly not his father, anywhere near it.

Now she realised her husband had been wrong all along. Albert has set Chandos back on its feet by applying a little common sense and his own native intelligence. And she felt sad that David had misjudged him all these years, shutting him out because of some private resentment. She leaned over to the edge of her desk and planted a kiss on his cheek.

'I don't know how to thank you,' she told him. 'I could never have done any of this on my own.'

Albert puffed contentedly on his cigar.

'I told you that in the first place. But I haven't finished with you yet.'

'You mean there's more?'

'Only one thing. But it's going to make a big difference to your cash flow.'

He paused, trying to make it sound as simple as he could.

'One of the reasons Jeremy got into such a muddle was that he never put his bills in on time. So the money was always late and he got deeper and deeper in debt to the bank.'

Sally smiled.

'It shouldn't be a problem now, surely?'

'You don't understand,' Albert said as patiently as he could. 'Because of Jeremy, you still owe too much money. The only way you're going to change things is to put your bills in ahead of time.'

'You mean before we deliver the work?'

'Three months before. Other companies do it.'

She looked at him, wondering which firms Albert knew with such chutzpah.

'None of our clients will wear it,' she said eventually.

'How do you know? Have you asked them?'

She sighed.

'No, and I wouldn't dare.'

Albert regarded her with shrewd old eyes.

'You dared almost everything else. You're not going to fall at this fence, are you?'

She started to realise why David had resented his father so much. You did your damndest to please the old man, but try as you might it was never enough. He just went on pushing until you were at breaking-point.

'What if they say no and fire me?'

'They won't fire you. The worst that will happen is they say no.'

So she did it. With Albert standing over her, Sally wrote to each of her clients and told them about her new accounting system. Bobby Brown's and Inca replied by return of post, approving the new arrangement. Diane replied by phone, asking her what the hell she was thinking of.

She was tempted to explain about Albert moving in on her, but she resisted. They may be friends, but Diane was her client now and she couldn't afford to look as if she wasn't on top of things. So she simply told her that the agency would run better if they billed ahead.

Diane wasn't convinced and in the end Sally had to compromise. If Chic decided to renew their contact in six months, then they would do things Sally's way. But only if they were still in business. When Sally told Albert about Diane the old man wasn't impressed.

'She's behaving like a bitch. I wouldn't trust her.'

'She's my oldest friend,' Sally protested.

Albert shrugged.

'She's not behaving like your oldest friend. But who am I to criticise? I'm just an interfering old bore who doesn't know the first thing about the agency business.'

It was an act of course. Albert always pleaded stupidity whenever he knew he was right. And Sally let him get away with it. He was leaving for Manchester in the morning and there was no point in falling out over Diane, though she did make a mental note to get closer to her. She had been so busy with the move and the new agency that they had not seen each other for weeks now. And they were in danger of losing touch with each other.

I'm not going to allow this to happen, Sally decided. When things have settled down a bit, I'll invite her to dinner. It's high time she saw the new house and paid a little attention to Annabel.

Chapter Thirty Five

Of the three executives Albert had chosen for her, Jim Morrison proved to be far and away the best. He had an aggression about him that reminded Sally of David in the early days. There was no account he wouldn't go after, and even when he got turned down and ridiculed for aiming too high, he didn't seem to get discouraged. He just tried harder the next time.

Jim's sheer nerve landed them three new accounts in the first six months. They weren't blue chip accounts. One of them was a chain of betting shops, but they were new business and they gave everyone in the agency a renewed confidence.

When Sally had taken over, nobody knew from one day to the next whether they were going to survive or not. And even Sally herself, sometimes lay awake at nights worrying about the bailiffs coming in.

Only it hadn't happened. Jim, aided and abetted by Sue and Fred, had carried her through the crisis.

Even Heather had pulled with the team and Sally was glad she had promoted her to running the office. She wasn't young or glamorous, the way you needed to be in public relations. But she had a direct line into the hot new firm of accountants they'd taken on. At any time during the day she could give Sally an instant update on the firm's financial situation. This invaluable information enabled Sally to control the business: if things were tight one week, she put a curb on Jim spending money chasing accounts; when things were easier, she let him have his head.

And it was when they were feeling flush that Jim got American

Hamburgers on the hook. He had got a tip that the country-wide chain was changing hands and looking for a new agency. And he had spent a fortune buying lunch and drinks for his friends in the business so that he could get his foot in the door. It had paid off. On Monday morning, Jim walked into Sally's office and announced he had managed to get them a meeting with American Hamburger's new chief executive.

'I'll make the presentation,' he told her, 'but I think you should come along as head of the agency.'

She nodded her agreement, making a mental note to do some homework on the fast-food business.

'Does the new man have a name?' she enquired.

Jim nodded.

'He's called Brad Hastings and from what I can find out, he's a bit of a tycoon in America.'

Sally leaned back in her chair and realised that for once, they stood a fighting chance of landing this account. It was way out of their league, of course. In the normal way of things she would have let Jim go ahead with his presentation, while preparing him and everyone else for a resounding defeat. Only now she suspected she wouldn't have to do that, for she knew Brad Hastings believed in her.

When she first met him, he had urged David to send her back to work. And when she ran into him in Langan's, seven months ago, his confidence in her ability had clinched the deal with Diane. Brad Hastings is lucky for me, she thought.

I'm going to enjoy meeting him again.

Brad had been in London for three hours, during which time he had showered, breakfasted and talked to his lawyer in New York. Yet he still wasn't functioning as well as he would have liked. It was always the same when he crossed time zones. His whole system got out of synch, not that any of the executives he was meeting today would make allowances for this fact.

He was a big boy in a big business with big responsibilities to honour. He mentally ticked them off as he sat in his five hundred pounds a night suite at the Savoy. He still had the hotel group he started out with, but he had added to it with an orange grove in Florida, a packaging company in Detroit and his latest acquisition, American Hamburgers.

It all keeps me busy and makes me rich, he thought. Pity it doesn't make me happy as well. Though even as the thought crossed his mind, he realised he was falling into the trap of feeling sorry for himself. I'm not the only man who lost his wife, he thought. The world is full of men cast adrift from their family lives for one reason or other. But they didn't see them murdered, he reminded himself. They didn't have to identify the bodies down at the city morgue. The memory of his dead wife, his dead children burned into his brain.

It had been six years since the murders yet they still haunted him. For the whole thing had been so senseless. A street gang, one of dozens roaming the city at night, had gained access to his apartment building and had chosen his family to rob. They could have pushed on any other bell, but some quirk of fate had made them lean on his bell. The same quirk of fate had sent him out of New York that night, visiting one of his hotels.

What could I have done if I'd been there? he asked himself. They were armed, so fighting wouldn't have made any sense. I would have just died along with them. Yet a part of him wished he had died. For living since the tragedy had been a hollow experience.

He thought about the girls he had dated on and off: nice, bright, beautiful girls, his for the taking; but he didn't want any of them. At first he put it down to his loss. But as the years went on, he realised he was kidding himself. He wasn't interested in any of the girls he met, because they were so unlike his wife.

Amy had been an old-fashioned small-town girl with old-fashioned small-town ideas. He had met her in high school and right from the start she had made it clear what she wanted out of life. While all her friends were talking about fancy careers and running away to New York, Amy stayed right where she was and dreamed about the family she was going to raise.

If he hadn't loved her, he might have encouraged her to try

298

her wings before settling down. But he did love her, so as soon as they graduated he married her and did his darndest to live on next to nothing.

Brad remembered their early struggles. If they hadn't been so poor, he might not have succeeded as well as he had. But Amy was the kind of woman men fought wars over. She didn't ask to be protected, but there was something about her that brought out that instinct in men. I always wanted to bring home trophies for her, Brad thought: first the hotel manager's job that meant we could afford a baby; then running the group which we celebrated by making another baby; then the big prize – raising the loan to buy the group. He remembered how proud she had been of him when he pulled that deal off. They had two toddlers then and were living in an apartment in downtown Houston and suddenly he had the clout to change their lives.

'I'll take you to New York,' he promised her. 'We'll live the way I always wanted us to live.'

He had too. He had rented a huge apartment in the best part of town, where the buildings had porters and security men. Yet it hadn't helped any of them in the end. The men who murdered his family had simply found a way past the uniformed guards. In the end he thought, all the money in the world wasn't enough to protect his wife.

Brad looked at his watch and realised he'd wasted too much time dwelling on the past. For the present was about to walk into his hotel suite any minute now. Ben Bradley, his marketing chief, along with Simon Best, the managing director of American Hamburgers, were due any minute now. They were coming to talk about his new acquisition and the image they wanted for it. And he knew without a shadow of a doubt that they would recommend firing the existing public relations outfit.

An hour ago, he'd had Ben on the phone telling him there were a couple of hot new agencies he wanted him to see today. He was about to tell Ben he was moving too fast when he heard the name Chandos. Normally one PR agency was much like another to Brad, but Chandos rang bells. Sally Robinson, he thought, remembering the last time he saw her in Langan's. Didn't her old man own an agency with a name like that? And wasn't she talking about going back to work for them? He made a mental note to check Chandos out the minute Ben got there.

Ben and Simon arrived ten minutes late, apologising about the traffic. There had been a demonstration at Hyde Park Corner which had slowed everything down.

Brad listened for as long as he had to, then he brought them both back to the business in hand.

'You wanted me to look at some agencies,' he said. 'How many have you got lined up?'

Ben, the marketing man, resplendent in a Ralph Lauren blazer, brought out a typed schedule from his briefcase.

'You're seeing two this morning and one around teatime.'

'What time is Chandos coming? And who are we seeing from there?'

Ben, who had no idea that Brad knew any of the British agencies, looked puzzled.

'Why the sudden interest in Chandos? It's not the place it used to be. In fact I've only asked them in because the eager beaver managing director chased me all over town for an appointment.' He glanced down at the schedule. 'His name's Jim Morrison, since you ask.'

Brad felt suddenly let down. He'd wanted Chandos to be run by Sally, the way he had it in his imagination. But he must have got the name confused. She probably worked for Shandwick or Sandown, and he cursed his inefficiency for not making a note of the name and bringing it with him.

It would have been the easiest thing to tell Ben to put Sally's agency on his shortlist. Now he'd probably never get another excuse to see her again. He sat down heavily on the bouncy hotel sofa and looked at his two executives.

'Run through your marketing plan for American Hamburgers,' he told them. 'I need to know what you have in mind before I start listening to agency pitches.'

The morning went predictably enough. Both agencies were big blue chip shops and they came through with the sort of conservative thinking of which his old agency had been guilty.

Neither of them would do, of course, and he was tempted to cancel his afternoon appointment. If Jim Morrison was anything like the others he had seen he was going to be wasting his time. Then he thought, what the hell. I'm going to be here for a few weeks. If Chandos doesn't pan out, I've got time to look around.

The Chandos team turned up on the dot of four. A tall, red-headed young man led the way. And behind him, looking slightly nervous, was Sally Robinson.

So I was right, after all, Brad thought. She does run Chandos. Jim Morrison must be her second-in-command. He grinned as she walked into the hotel room and stationed herself by the window.

'So you meant it when you told me you were going back to work.'

She nodded.

'It was a question of having to. David decided to do something else.'

A million questions went through his mind. Why had David left the agency? And was it just the agency he had left? Or was it Sally as well?

He looked at the blonde, middle-aged woman standing in front of him and realised with a start that he found her attractive. He obviously had done all along, only like most things to do with women he had shut it out. Now he wasn't fighting it any more. So he decided he would ask her for a drink after Jim Morrison had done his stuff.

He went and sat down, preparing to listen to his third presentation of the day. It wasn't anything like he expected. For a start, Jim Morrison hadn't brought any charts with him. In fact he hadn't brought any aids at all. All he relied on was his ability to conjure up images. Yet the picture he painted of American Hamburgers was the most exciting thing he'd come up against all day. It seemed this red-headed young man didn't think in any of the orthodox ways. And when Bill and Simon started to cross-question him, he put up a good fight defending his ideas.

Sally backed him up of course, the way a good agency chief should. But Jim was obviously the star of the show. Then he paid a bit more attention to what Sally was saying and realised she wasn't just echoing Jim Morrison. She was leading from behind, building a platform for him. So when he made his final pitch for their account, he looked older and more experienced than his years.

Sally's given him gravitas, Brad realised. But she's done it so subtly that most people would think it all came from Jim. He thought about all the sassy women executives he had met over the last few years. None of them could do what Sally had done today, because deep down they were all too insecure. It took a lot of confidence to allow a junior to steal the show, let alone help him.

He began to look forward to the drink he had planned. He would take her down to the American bar, Brad decided. The atmosphere was more social than it was in the suite.

When Jim had finally wound things up, he turned to his team.

'Will you stay around for a drink?' he asked his two executives. He said it very unconvincingly and they took the hint and invented other appointments.

'How about you?' he said to Sally. 'Will you join me for a glass of wine downstairs?'

She hesitated for a moment, then she said:

'I can't. I have to get home to my daughter. But I expect Jim's free.'

So Brad ended up in the American bar with a twenty-three-year-old red-head who wouldn't stop pitching for his business. In the end, just to keep him quiet, he made a half promise to consider Chandos in the final line-up. But it wasn't good enough. Jim wanted to know who else he had seen and who he was planning to see.

Brad thought about the two boring agencies of that morning and was half tempted to give in and tell Jim Morrison he was home and dry. He would have done too if it hadn't been for the fact that he was still interested in Sally. If I make it too easy for him, Brad decided, he'll stop trying to please me. Then I won't be able to find out a damn thing about his delectable boss and the state of her marriage. He put his drink down.

'I'll have some answers for you in a couple of days,' he said decisively. 'In the meantime there are a couple of things I need to know about your agency.'

'Fire ahead.'

'What happened to David?' Brad asked. 'How come he jumped ship all of a sudden?'

There was a moment's embarrassed silence while Jim struggled to figure out what to say.

'I don't know the details,' he said, blushing bright scarlet. 'But I think there was a problem between him and Sally.'

'What kind of problem?'

Jim sipped his Bloody Mary and wondered if he could bullshit his way out of this one. Then he saw Brad staring at him and realised he couldn't.

'They decided to split up,' he said eventually.

'David wanted to go and work abroad, so he left the agency in Sally's hands.'

Brad leaned back in his chair. So that was what happened. When he'd run into Sally in Langan's he'd thought it was strange that she was going back to the agency. Particularly since her husband had been so adamant about her staying at home and not working. Arrogant bastard, he thought, remembering David and not liking what he remembered. He keeps his wife away from the agency while it suits him. Then when he decides to walk out on her, and he was pretty sure David had done the walking, he dumps the whole business in her lap.

He remembered Ben telling him that Chandos had been on the slide recently. And now he realised why.

Taking over a full-blown business when you haven't been on the scene for a few years was a hell of a challenge. Sally must have had her work cut out, just keeping her head above water. He suddenly had an insane desire to make things easier for her, so that she wouldn't have to take on the world single handed. He turned to Jim Morrison, who was looking decidedly nervous.

'You can stop worrying about Sally and whether or not you've said too much. I've had a rethink about my business and I'm giving it to Chandos.'

He caught sight of the boy's exultant expression and held up a warning hand. 'I'll need to square it with the old agency and my own people before I can make it official. So keep quiet about it till next week.'

Chapter Thirty Six

Sally received Brad Hastings' news with less enthusiasm than he expected, and the American was strangely disappointed. Chandos was a hungry agency fighting its way back from financial ruin. Why wasn't the woman in charge inviting him round for champagne in the boardroom?

He almost regretted giving her this boost and told Jim Morrison as much when they got together to talk about the business.

'Sally behaved as if I was giving her a routine chore, instead of a quarter of a million pound account,' he complained.

For the second time since they met, Jim was put on the spot. For he knew why Sally was so down; her divorce had just become final. She got the papers a few days before Brad called her, and she had been impossible to deal with ever since.

He wondered whether to admit that his boss was so knocked for six by her private life that she didn't have time for the agency. Then he thought, there's no need to alarm this important client so early in their relationship. Sally will get herself together before much longer. When she does she can make up for lost time with Brad Hastings.

As things turned out, it took several weeks before Sally saw straight again. And what finally brought her back from the dead were the increasing demands of her agency.

For winning American Hamburgers had raised their profile. Chandos had stolen the account from Hill and Knowlton – a big established agency and it made the industry sit up and take notice. Clients who wouldn't have even considered them a few months ago were eager to do business with them now, and Sally found herself pitched into one new business presentation after another.

It was like the early days back in the seventies when the agency was just taking off. And despite herself Sally caught the mood of exhilaration and ran with it. She had mourned her lost marriage long enough, she realised, after the fourth new account had walked through her doors. It was time to start living again.

She arranged drinks with her five newest clients, starting with Brad Hastings, who she knew she had neglected. To her dismay she found the American difficult and resentful. Like all successful tycoons he didn't like being taken for granted. And Sally had to work long and hard before she had his confidence again.

After that they became friends. Brad started to tell her about his other businesses, and as she got to know him, Sally realised that work was the driving force in his life. He woke up with it in the morning and went to bed with it at night. And Sally suspected it filled the space left by his dead wife. Not that he ever talked about that part of his life.

For both of them it was easier to stay on the neutral ground of business. And Sally welcomed this, for she was picking things up from Brad that she couldn't have heard anywhere else.

Brad had a genius for running companies. He understood people management down to the last clerk in the post room. Yet at the same time he didn't let go of the bigger picture.

As the months went on, Sally realised Brad was helping her think like an agency chief, and she began to rely on him. If she had a problem at Chandos she couldn't handle, she'd bring it up at one of their lunches and they'd work through it together. It was an unorthodox way to run a business, but ever since her father-in-law had stepped in and pointed her in the right direction, she had no compunction about picking other people's brains.

She had learned from David when she started in public relations and she realised she would probably go on learning as long as she stayed in the business.

She wondered who her next mentor would be, for it was perfectly obvious Brad wouldn't be around for too much longer. In a month or so, American Hamburgers would be up and running and he would go back to New York.

Just for a moment she felt genuine regret. For she had come to depend on the American's bearlike prescence. It was an illusion, of course, but when he was around, she felt as if there was someone there to protect her. I shouldn't need protecting, she reminded herself sternly. I'm an independent career woman now. If Diane knew I was looking for a man to lean on she'd be scandalised.

As if by some telepathy her phone started to ring and she picked up and found Diane on the other end.

'I'm round the corner from you,' she said. 'I wonder if you've got time for a quick glass of wine?'

Sally guessed she'd had a meeting that had finished earlier than expected. Diane had a habit of calling on the off chance, expecting her to fit in with whatever plan she presented. And for a reason she didn't quite understand, Sally felt cross about it. I haven't seen her in ages, she thought. The least she could do was make a proper lunch date.

'I don't think I'm going to be able to do it,' she said. 'People are coming in to see me in fifteen minutes.'

'It doesn't matter then,' Diane said abruptly.

She was about to put the phone down but Sally wouldn't let her.

'When am I going to see you again?' she asked. 'We can't go on missing each other like this.'

Her question seemed to put Diane on the spot, for she started stammering out excuses about being rushed off her feet at work.

'When was it any different?' Sally teased. 'I'll tell you what. Why don't I cook you dinner next week? You haven't been to Fulham since we moved there and I'm dying to show you what I've done with it.'

She heard Diane hestitating.

'I'll have to look at my diary when I get back to the office.'

'That's OK. Call me when you've found a free evening.'

She didn't hear from Diane that day. And she was so busy herself that she didn't remember to call until she got home. They were both full of apologies when they eventually spoke.

'I meant to call,' Diane said, 'but it went out of my mind.'

'You were probably busy,' Sally replied.

'Not especially. I've just got a rotten memory. Hang on while I get my book.'

She was back minutes later saying she could make the following Friday evening. The two women arranged to meet at Sally's new house and after Diane had taken down the address, they both signed off.

'I'm really looking forward to this,' Sally said as she put the phone down. 'We've got a lot of catching up to do.'

Chapter Thirty Seven

The house had changed since they moved in last year. The walls had been painted in subtle expensive colours that made the rooms look less mean. Little things like door handles and light fittings had been changed as soon as Sally had any spare cash. The finishing touches had been made possible when she won the hamburger account. Sally could suddenly afford to pay herself her full salary and on the proceeds she had had all the wooden floors sanded and polished and bought bright oriental rugs to cover them.

Now the little terraced cottage had an elegance about it that made both Sally and Annabel feel more at home. It could never come near to the place they had in Oxford, but they could live in it for the next year or so without feeling too much like poor relations.

Sally felt glad she'd held off inviting Diane to dinner for so long. In its original state the house would have evoked pity and that was the last thing she needed. Now, she thought, I can sit her down in my country kitchen without feeling the least bit apologetic for it.

When Friday came, Sally decided to leave the office early. She wanted everything to be perfect this evening. So she stopped off in Soho to buy the ingredients for the elaborate meal she had planned. It took her over an hour to get everything and she was so weighted down with carrier bags that she had to splash out on a taxi to get her back to Fulham.

Annabel was waiting for her when she got in, sitting at the

kitchen table behind a huge pile of homework. She had decided to do her A Levels after all, and had surprised both of them by settling in at Holland Park Comprehensive and coming near the top of her class. Now the sight of all the bags and packages that her mother was piling up on the table banished any thoughts of revision. There was a feast-in-the-making right before her eyes. And she guessed Sally was going to need a bit of help.

'You're going to a lot of trouble tonight,' she said as she lifted out a huge pannier containing fresh mussels.

'I hope Diane appreciates it.'

Sally sighed.

'So do I. This whole thing is going to take hours.'

She was right. The three elaborate courses she had planned took her with Annabel helping, the best part of two hours. And just for a moment she missed being married to David who would always insist on buying in an expensive caterer when they were entertaining clients.

But Diane isn't a client, Sally reminded herself. She's a friend. So why am I treating her like a client with all this food? If it was just friends, I'd rustle up a steak and salad and not give it another thought. She might have argued with herself all night, but her feet hurt and she longed to sink into a hot bath. So she instructed her daughter to set the table and started to make her way up the stairs.

It took Sally longer than she thought to get out of her office clothes and start coming back to normal. Her eye make-up seemed to have slipped halfway down her cheeks and she had to cream everything off and start again. Then her hair, which was doing a good imitation of a haystack, needed attention. And when she finally made her way down to the long, thin drawing-room Sally knew she was in trouble.

Looking at her watch, she realised she had under ten minutes to make the house look presentable after a week of late nights and snatched meals. The place looks like a tip, she remembered, *panicking as she rushed downstairs.* Then she stopped in her tracks, for some invisible fairy had put everything to rights. All the old newspapers and unanswered letters had been magically tidied away. Surfaces had been wiped, cushions plumped, carpets hoovered.

'Annabel,' she called down to the kitchen, 'what on earth have you been up to?'

Her daughter came into the room bearing a tray with drinks and glasses.

'I've been holding the fort,' she said innocently. 'Somebody had to.'

Sally went over and took the tray out of her hands. Then when she had set it down on a table, she put her arms round her daughter.

'I don't know what I did to deserve you,' she said, holding her close.

The girl disentangled herself, looking embarrassed. She had got to the age where outward displays of affection made her feel foolish. But she loved her mother, so she went over and opened the wine, pouring her out a glass which she imagined she probably needed.

'I'm not that wonderful,' she said gruffly, handing over the wine. 'I still bitch about the bathroom when I get in a bad mood.'

Sally smiled, remembering the last few months. Annabel had taken a hell of a long time to settle into Fulham. And if she hadn't been so happy with her new school she might have taken even longer. For she had never lived in a house where there was no cleaner and no-one to do her washing. Housework was a whole new experience for Annabel and she hadn't liked it one little bit.

In the end she and Sally had come to an agreement. As long as the rest of the house was tidy, Annabel could keep her room any way she wanted. And it seemed to help the situation. They both took it in turns to pull their weight in the house and at least twice a week it almost looked respectable.

Sally looked across at her daughter and saw to her surprise that she looked almost looked respectable too. She'd changed out of her habitual blue jeans into a skirt and sloppy jumper, though she hadn't shed her trainers. I suppose that would be expecting too much, Sally thought.

On impulse she turned to Annabel and asked if she wanted a glass of wine. She occasionally allowed the girl to join her in a drink and she didn't see why she shouldn't indulge her just this once.

An hour later, they had demolished a whole bottle between them and were feeling no pain.

'Do you think she's forgotten about tonight?' Annabel asked.

Sally frowned.

'She's never done anything like it before. Diane's far too organised for that.'

'So why isn't she here?'

Sally put down her glass and went over to the phone.

'I don't know. But there's no reason why I shouldn't try and find out.'

No-one answered Diane's number. Instead on the fourth ring the phone connected to an answering machine. Sally slammed the receiver down.

'She's got to be on her way,' she said. 'She's certainly not sitting in her flat.'

Half an hour later, when Sally had switched to coffee in an attempt to stay sober, the phone went. Annabel raced across the room to answer it, only to find the caller wasn't the one they both expected.

'It's a man called Brad Hastings,' she told her. 'He says he wants to talk to you.'

Sally suddenly looked serious.

'It's a very important client,' she whispered, 'give me the phone.'

As lightly as she could, she said:

'I hope there's not a problem on American Hamburgers?'

Brad's laugh came reassuringly down the line.

'Does there always have to be a problem when I call you at home?'

Now it was her turn to relax.

'I'm sorry,' she said, 'I've had a bit of a fraught evening. A friend I was expecting for dinner hasn't turned up.'

'Then it's my lucky night.'

'How come?'

He paused a moment, then he said:

'If you've been stood up for dinner, maybe I can step into the breach. The maitre d' at the Gavroche would be delighted to see you.'

Sally smiled. It didn't occur to Brad to invite himself round for dinner the way a dozen other men might have done. But it would be such a waste to throw all that expensive, carefully prepared food in the trash bin.

'Could you bear to come round here?' she asked. 'My daughter and I have been slaving away making a feast and I can't leave her to eat it all on her own.'

'If you put it like that, how can I refuse? Though what if your guest turns up when we're halfway through everything?'

Sally looked at her watch and saw Diane was an hour and a half late.

'I can't see that happening now,' she said.

When Brad's taxi turned into Cranbury Road, his sense of curiosity increased. He hadn't expected Sally to live in the shabby suburbs. When he'd envisaged her at home, he'd constructed a picture of an elegant little pad in Chelsea or Knightsbridge. She would have her food delivered, of course, or cooked for her by a Filipino maid. And her daughter would be magically absent when he came to call. Brad laughed at himself. Real life wasn't like that.

He stepped into the street and paid the cabbie. Then he walked up to the narrow terraced house with the red-painted front door and rang on the bell.

The door opened inwards to reveal a tall voluptuous teenager with Sally's dark blonde hair.

'You must be Brad,' she said with just the slightest trace of shyness.

He walked into the house wondering what to expect and was

313

immediately welcomed by Sally. The first thing he noticed was that she was wearing hardly any make-up. When he'd met her during the day she was done up to the nines in chic little business suits and glossy paint. At home she shed all that and reverted to being a housewife. The full-skirted shirtwaister she wore made her look positively matronly. And to his surprise, he found it endearing. The woman in front of him was as real as the shabby street she lived in. After years spent in hotel rooms and expense account restaurants, being here was like coming home. Just for a moment he thought of his first home, the one he had had with Amy. Then he banished it from his mind.

Sally was asking him if he wanted a glass of wine before dinner. And the mention of dinner reminded him that he was ravenous. He'd been in meetings all day with only a ten-minute break for a snatched sandwich and a cup of coffee. Before he'd even got here, there had been dry martinis with his marketing team and now he couldn't face any more alcohol.

'Would you mind very much if we went straight to the table?' he asked.

Sally took his arm and guided him down the steps to the kitchen.

'I wouldn't mind at all,' she said. 'It's way past our dinner time.'

The big square table where they sat down to eat fascinated Brad, for it was totally out of keeping with the rustic kitchen. The way it had been set up reminded him of dinner parties in grand houses in the Hamptons.

Then he remembered that Sally was recently divorced. He guessed her spiv of a husband got all the assets, leaving her with the trinkets. He picked up a monogrammed silver serving spoon and helped himself to a heap of mussels in cream sauce. As soon as he started eating, he realised the fish had been cooking for too long – for it was rubbery and slightly tasteless.

He smiled across at Sally.

'My compliments to the chef. This is absolutely delicious.'

It was Annabel who smiled back.

'I did the mussels,' she admitted. 'I'm glad you like them.'

With a certain amount of effort Brad swallowed a mouthful and did his best to look as if he was enjoying it.

'I hope your mother's proud of you.'

'Of course she is. Do you have children?'

The question caught him off balance. Normally the friends he had avoided the subject of his family. But he was in another country now with people who didn't know his story. So he was bound to give them an answer.

'I had children,' he said, hearing his voice coming out all stiff and formal. 'But they and their mother got killed in a robbery in New York.'

He saw Sally looking at him.

'David told me you were a widower after I put my foot in it and asked about your wife. Now my daughter is doing the same thing asking about your children.' She put a hand on his arm. 'I'm really sorry Brad. You must think we're savages.'

He realised he'd overreacted. The murders had been over six years ago. Everyone he met knew about them and pussyfooted around him as if he was some kind of invalid. And now he was making Sally and Annabel do the same. Grow up, he told himself. Asking for pity all over the place isn't going to bring Amy back. She's dead and gone now. They all are. The time has come to let them rest in peace.

He forced himself to smile.

'It was all a very long time ago,' he said. 'I've learned to live with it.'

Sally looked at him.

'I don't believe you.' she said. 'No-one learns to live with a thing like that. You cover it up. You try not to dwell on it, but it's always there like a sore place. And all we've done tonight is tweak it.'

If anyone else had said it, he would have walked out. But there was such understanding, such compassion coming from Sally, that he stayed right where he was. She knows what I've gone through, he thought, because she's had her own pain with David.

Brad considered the three of them sitting round the table: the little girl who had lost her father when she needed him most; the grown woman who had been cruelly abandoned; and himself, the grieving widower. But we survived, he thought. Despite all the misery fate decided to throw at us, we're still here eating dinner and acting as if nothing had gone wrong in our lives.

Suddenly he didn't want to talk about the past anymore, and he searched his mind for something, some diversion, to bring them all back to where they were. The food was the obvious choice.

'Is there any more of this fabulous dinner?' he asked. 'You were boasting earlier you'd cooked up a feast.'

Mention of dinner galvanised them into action, and both Annabel and Sally jumped up and started to organise the main course.

Annabel was over by the stove, getting out a casserole dish and Brad hoped against hope that whatever was in it was more edible than the mussels. He was in for a disappointment. The main ingredient of this dish had once been lamb, but it had been stewing so long that it was falling apart. He pushed the congealed mess around his plate and hoped no-one was looking. Then he glanced across at Annabel to see if she was enjoying her dinner and noticed she had eaten very little.

'You're not on some kind of diet, are you?' he teased.

The girl pulled a face.

'Not really. I just don't feel very hungry.'

Sally pushed her plate away.

'I'm not hungry either. This food is terrible.'

The three of them stared at each other, not knowing what to say.

Then Sally started to laugh. She'd bust a gut trying to impress two of her most important clients to no avail. One hadn't shown up. And the other found himself faced with an overcooked dinner.

'I'm so sorry,' she spluttered, 'I didn't do this on purpose, I promise.'

Annabel looked severely at her mother.

'It's not funny,' she said. 'Think of what we've wasted.'

Brad got out of his chair and started stacking up the dishes.

'The hell with the waste, let's just get this out of the way.'

'Then what?' Annabel demanded, still mortified. 'All we've got in the fridge is a bit of old cheese.'

He turned to her.

'Have you got any bread to go with it?'

The girl nodded.

'Then we're in business.'

Sally looked on helplessly as Brad and her daughter took over. In the old days she would have been doing her best to make amends, phoning for takeaways or organising omelettes. David would never have allowed her to neglect her duty regarding a client. But David wasn't here any more and the client didn't look as if he was having too bad a time. He and Annabel had come across half a Stilton as well as the remains of the cooking Cheddar and the expression on their faces told her they'd won the jackpot.

Things are getting out of hand, she thought, looking at her best china piling up in the sink. This isn't how I planned it at all. Brad caught her expression and wanted to know what was bothering her. Sally took her time before answering, then she said:

'I can't help thinking I've let you down.'

It was incredible how someone as bright as Sally could get it so wrong. He hadn't come to her house to be dazzled by her cooking, or her décor, or even to meet her daughter. He'd accepted her invitation tonight because he was curious to know who she was when she left off the glossy professional mask. And now he knew, now she'd revealed herself to him, he was totally intrigued.

'You didn't let me down tonight,' he told her. 'I'm having a wonderful time.'

Chapter Thirty Eight

Diane . . . Paris, 1996

Charles de Gaulle airport was hell on Friday night. All the weekend tourists on cheap packages came flooding into the main hall, clogging up the baggage reclaim and forming great queues at passport control. When she finally struggled her way to the taxi rank, Diane felt as if she'd done a whole day at the January sales.

I could have been in London, she thought, as the cold wind penetrated her fine wool coat that had felt so cosy when she put it on that morning. I could have been sitting in the warm, having dinner with Sally and Annabel. Then why aren't I? She asked herself for the umpteenth time since she left London. Why did I suddenly take it into my head to do a runner without even leaving a message? She had avoided facing the truth of what she had done all day. But now with a huge throng of travellers in front of her, she had no choice but to stand and think. It would be a good half hour before she got near a taxi. She pulled her flimsy coat around her and made herself go back over the muddle of the last few months.

She had started feeling guilty about Sally ever since David left. In the beginning she could cope with it, because of the Chic business. She genuinely felt she was helping Sally survive, which excused her for stealing her husband. But as time went on, and Sally turned out first-class work, she realised she hadn't done her any favours at all. In an open competition Sally would have won the boutique account hands down.

The guilt intensified then. She would sit in a meeting with Sally and find she couldn't quite meet her eye. Or they would have lunch together and she'd be struggling for things to say. In the end she went out of her way to avoid her. Not that Sally took the hint. All she did was think she'd done something wrong and lay out an invitation for dinner.

She'd felt such a fool when Sally called her at home last week and asked why they hadn't seen much of each other. After that little speech she was almost obliged to accept her gracious invitation. Until the time came near, she actually believed she could handle an evening with Sally and her daughter.

Then on Wednesday she started to have doubts. She pushed them to the back of her mind, but her conscience wouldn't leave her alone. What if I make a mistake and she finds out I've been seeing David? she fretted. I can't talk my way out of that.

By Thursday she was walking around in a cold sweat, wondering how to put off dinner. And on Friday, when she got up in the morning, she knew that she would change her Saturday ticket to Paris for that evening. Once she was on a plane, she was safe from Sally, safe from accusations, safe from her guilty conscience.

So here I am, she thought, freezing my butt off in a taxi queue, hoping that David will be pleased I've come a day early. Just before she thought she would die of the cold, her turn came for a taxi and she gave the disgruntled-looking driver David's new address.

He had recently moved into a new apartment just off the Champs Elysées and she rattled off the street number in her best schoolgirl French. The driver appeared to understand her and she collapsed onto the back seat, rubbing her hands together to get the circulation going again. She started to feel more human as they approached the suburbs. And when they got to the Round Point, she started to feel excited as she always did when she came to see David.

There was something perfect about the arrangement they had.

She could live her life during the week, immersing herself in her job, catching up with old business friends. Then, come the weekend, she was off on a mini-holiday. She had forty eight hours when she drank wine and made love and forgot about reality completely.

She would have been quite happy to go on living like this forever. But David wanted permanence. This new apartment was the first signal that he wanted to settle down, for it was bought with two people in mind. There was a huge country kitchen with a separate dining-room leading off it. The main bedroom had a big double bed and an en-suite bathroom. And the drawing-room was grand enough to entertain the French Ambassador.

Diane sighed. Things had seemed so simple when she fell into bed with David three years ago. Now her whole life was theatening to change course, and she wondered if she was going to be able to cope with it.

She let herself in with the key David had given her and saw immediately he had been to the market. The main room was full of fresh flowers. Lilies and out of season roses and great bunches of winter-flowering jasmine. And she knew without having to ask that he had got them for her.

She called out his name then, hoping she hadn't come on an evening when he was out seeing friends. But her luck was in and she followed his answering call to the kitchen. He was overjoyed to see her, gathering her up in his arms and kissing her so thoroughly she wondered whether they would end up making love on the kitchen floor. But he let her go just before the moment of no return.

'Why are you here so early?' he asked when they had both recovered their breath. 'I didn't expect you till the morning.'

She looked shamefaced.

'It was all a bit of a muddle, actually.'

He went over to one of the big wooden cupboards and found a bottle of wine. When he had opened it and filled two glasses, he looked at Diane.

'Suppose you tell me about your muddle?'

She didn't say anything for a bit, then just when he was going to prompt her again, she came out with it.

'It's to do with Sally,' she told him. 'I was meant to be having dinner with her tonight, but I couldn't face it.'

'So you came to Paris early as a way of avoiding her.'

Diane looked at her lover.

'What else could I do? I've done my best to stay out of her way until one of us could tell her the truth. Only it never seems to happen. So I lie to her and pretend we're buddies, when I know that was over years ago.' She sighed and took a sip of her wine. 'It got to the point when I just couldn't go on doing it.'

She saw her words were having an effect, for he looked stricken.

'Poor Sally,' he said softly. 'Poor innocent, stupid Sally. She's probably cooked up a storm for you tonight. She and Annabel will be all dressed up waiting for the honoured guest. And you let them sit there like dummies because of a sudden attack of guilty conscience.'

Diane couldn't believe what she was hearing. She'd been through all kinds of unhappiness for David, and all he could do was castigate her for not being nicer to his ex-wife.

'The trouble with you,' she said, taking a swig of her wine, 'is you want everybody to love you. You can't bear to tell Sally about us, not because you're frightened of hurting her feelings, but because you're frightened she'll think you're a shit.'

He turned on her then.

'What about you?' he demanded. 'You could have faced her just as easily as me.'

Diane smacked her wine down on the expensive wooden surface, knowing the splashes would stain it beyond repair.

'What you seem to forget,' she said, 'is that your precious Sally is in charge of my public relations business.'

'Whose fault is that?'

'It's both our fault, Diane sighed. 'It's your fault for leaving her with a business that was going broke. And it's my fault for taking pity on her.

'Look', she went on after a pause, 'we could go round

in circles about this all night. But it's not going to solve anything.'

She looked very intense as she said it, and David was overcome with a wave of love for her. She had done her best for him all the way along, finding him this high-flying job in Paris when there seemed there was no escape from his marriage. And he had done nothing for her in return except spend his weekends with her. I can't go on using Diane, David thought. I have to bring things out in the open and commit myself once and for all. And if that means upsetting my daughter, my parents and Sally herself, then we're all going to have to live with that.

He reached out and drew her close, wondering why he had taken so long to make up his mind. Diane was meant to be his wife, right from the very beginning.

'I want you to stop worrying about Sally,' he said, nuzzling her ear and inhaling the delicious musky scent of her. 'My ex-wife is my problem and I'm going to have to deal with her.'

Chapter Thirty Nine

Annabel read her father's letter with mounting disbelief. Then she went back to the beginning and read it again. There was no mistaking it. He really did want to see her again. After all these months he wanted her to get on a plane and come to Paris and spend the weekend with him.

She put the letter down, wandered over to the window and stared disconsolately down at the overgrown garden. The whole idea of letting her father back into her life unsettled her. For she was fearful of what she might find. It wasn't just the prospect of a girlfriend in tow that deterred her. It was her father himself, for he wasn't the man she once imagined he was.

While she was growing up she had regarded him as the one being in her life on whom she could depend. While her mother disciplined her, Daddy doted on her, buying her expensive presents on her birthday and taking her out for forbidden treats. It was as if she was his most precious possession and she always felt he would protect and defend her against the world.

Only she had got the whole thing horribly wrong. The minute she and her mother didn't suit him any more, he didn't give a damn about what happened to them. He just upped and left.

She had written to him about having to move out of their house in Oxford. And even though it was disloyal to her mother, she had given him a good idea of where they were living now. But he hadn't come back and put things right. He had simply written and told her that life was full of changes and she would see it was all for the best in the end.

Platitudes, she thought scornfully. As far as Daddy's concerned it's all for the best because she wasn't his responsibility any more and he could do what the hell he liked.

She thought of writing back and telling him to stuff his Paris weekend. She didn't want see his flat or his new girlfriend. Only it wasn't true. She was dying to know what was going on with her father, even though she was furious with him.

She walked back to the desk where she had been reading the letter and folded it up before putting it in its envelope. She would talk to her mother about the invitation before she decided to do anything. Mummy would know exactly how she should handle this.

When Sally got home she was in the mood for celebration.

'Annabel,' she called up the stairs, 'Annabel, darling, come down, I've got something to tell you.'

Three seconds later, the girl who looked suspiciously as if she lying in wait for her, came flying into the living-room.

'What's all the fuss about?' she asked, seeing how flushed and excited her mother looked. 'Don't tell me we've won the lottery?'

Sally laughed.

'Not the lottery,' she told her, 'but something nearly as good. *Campaign* magazine has nominated our Chic promotion for an award.'

There was a slight lull in proceedings and Sally realised she had failed to strike a chord in her daughter.

'A *Campaign* award is about the best thing that could happen to the agency,' she said, doing her damndest to communicate her excitement. 'It means we count for something in the industry.'

'But you haven't won it yet,' the girl said, looking at her feet.

If Sally had been less wound up she might have noticed that Annabel looked slightly down. As it was, she simply thought the girl was being obtuse and went on explaining the importance of what had happened.

'Winning isn't the point,' she said. 'The fact that Chandos

has been shortlisted means we're doing good work and there's no way they can consider moving to another agency.'

Annabel looked at her.

'I'm very pleased for you.'

'What's that meant to mean?'

'It means I'm glad there's something in your life that makes you happy for a change.'

There was an edge to her voice and for the first time since she came in, Sally realised something was amiss.

'What is it?' she asked, suddenly concerned. 'You don't sound a bit like the daughter I used to know.'

For a moment Annabel didn't say anything, then she went over to the desk where she had put the letter.

'Daddy's been in touch,' she said without meeting Sally's eye. 'A letter from him arrived this morning.'

'Do you want to tell me what he had to say?'

'I've been waiting to tell you for the last five minutes,' Annabel said, exasperated, 'but you've been so busy talking about your precious agency, I couldn't get a word in.'

Sally realised she'd been selfish and she wondered if by going out and working she was somehow failing her daughter. When she had been at home, full-time, she had been there when Annabel needed her. For a moment she felt worried. These are her most difficult years, Sally thought, and she'll have to get through them with no-one to hold her hand. She turned to her daughter.

'Can we start again?' she said. 'You had a letter from your father.'

The girl was holding the airmail envelope in her hand, turning it over and over, as if its contents were somehow explosive. In the end, Sally took it from her and opened it herself.

'It says here,' she said, as calmly as she could, 'that Daddy misses you and wants you to come and see him. Is that what you wanted to talk about?'

Annabel nodded.

'I don't know if I should go.'

'Why, because you're angry with him for going off?'

She'd touched a nerve, for Annabel went bright scarlet.

325

'How did you know I was angry?'

Sally reached out and stroked her daughter's bright blonde hair.

'It wasn't difficult to work out. You were always Daddy's favourite girl and now he's found another one. Anyone would be angry.'

'You're not.'

She did her best to smile.

'I was, but I got over it. And you're going to get over it if you know what's good for you.'

She paused. 'You've only got one father and though he might not be everything you expect, he's still your father and you can't ignore him.'

'So you think I should go?'

'Of course I do. You'll kick yourself if you miss this chance to see him.'

Annabel digested this for a moment, then she tested her mother one last time.

'What about the girlfriend? How do I cope with her?'

Sally shrugged.

'I haven't got the foggiest idea, but you're bound to think of something.'

Chapter Forty

When she got into the office the next day there was a message waiting for her from *Campaign* magazine. The awards were going to be judged at a dinner at the Dorchester in Park Lane. They wanted to know whether she would take a table. Sally thought about it before calling back. It would cost a bomb, of course, but could she afford not to go? What if we won, she thought, and nobody was there to pick up the prize? She decided that whatever she had to to pay it was worth it and she asked her secretary to reserve the smallest table going.

Then she started to plan who she was going to take. Sue Phillips, her account director, would have to be there, probably with her husband. She'd better ask Sue's assistant as well, for Sally knew that she had done all the running around on the new promotion. And of course their client needed to be represented, which meant Diane.

The thought of sitting across a table from Diane made Sally's lip curl. She had not heard from her since she stood her up for dinner, neither a phone call nor a letter. Even when the awards had been announced, Diane still hadn't been in touch. Have I done anything to upset her? Sally wondered.

Then she thought about it and realised it wasn't a possibility. When Diane let her keep the Chic business, they had made it a rule to be straight with each other. If there was a problem, even a small one, they talked it out there and then.

If I'd upset her, Sally thought, I would have known all about it. Only I haven't upset her. Diane's upset me and now she's too much of a worm to pick up the phone and say she's sorry for what she's done.

She set her face. I'm not going to call her, Sally decided. And I'm not going to invite her to the awards dinner either. The agency will just have to come up with a replacement. She buzzed through to Sue Phillips, who ran the account and asked her to step into her office. Then she told her why she wanted to see her.

Seconds later, Sue was standing in front of her looking worried. She was a short, rather dumpy woman, who at first glance nobody would have connected with a chain of fashion boutiques. Yet it was Sue's expertise that had put Chic on the map originally, when David was in control. And it was Sue's work which had got them the nomination for the *Campaign* award.

'You can't just ignore Diane,' she said now, settling into a chair. 'She's the most senior person at Chic.'

Sally shook her head and looked stubborn.

'Diane is not the most senior executive at Chic. She's just the most senior one we deal with.'

Sue sighed.

'That still leaves us with a problem. If we invite any of her deputies, we're going to look as if we're in trouble. Here we are, nominated for a top award, and head honcho at the client can't even put in an appearance.'

Sally began to get impatient.

'For the tenth time, Diane is not the head honcho. Steve Blake, the managing director, is the man with the power at Chic.'

'So what? We can't invite him.'

There was the briefest of pauses.

'Who says we can't invite him?' Sally replied. 'He might just jump at the chance. It's a pretty prestigious party.'

Now Sue began to feel uncomfortable. Any minute now, her boss was going to tell her she was going to have to put herself on the line and call Steve Blake.

'If I go over Diane's head,' she said, 'she could make things difficult for me.'

'I know,' Sally said, 'which is why I'm going to do the inviting.'

Sue hesitated.

'What if he turns you down?'

Sally got up, indicating that the meeting was at an end.

'If Steve turns me down, we'll survive. He won't be the first man who has said no to me.'

Two days later, Sally got a call from Steve Blake's secretary saying he'd love to come to the *Campaign* dinner. She also asked if Steve could bring his wife. Sally said that would be fine and made a mental note to get Sue's number two to bring along her current man.

That left her with another problem. Now everyone was going to be paired off, who on earth was going to escort her? Since David had left, she hadn't looked at another man, much less dated one. It crossed her mind to call one of the model agencies and hire someone for the evening, but the prospect struck her as a little sordid. I might as well go to an escort agency, she thought. It would be the same thing.

Out of the blue, she had an idea. Why didn't she take her daughter as her escort? It was the most natural thing in the world to have her child with her to share her success. And it would be good for Annabel too. Taking her to an official office party might stop her feeling so shut out.

She waited impatiently for the girl to get home from school. Then on the dot of four, when she was sure she'd be there, she rang home. When Annabel picked up the phone and found her mother on the end of it, she sounded slightly put out.

'Why are you ringing me so early?' she demanded. 'I thought you were meant to be in meetings all day.'

Sally laughed.

'I had a spare minute. Anyway there was something I wanted to ask you.'

'Don't tell me, let me guess. You want me to go to Sainsbury's.'

'You're wrong for once. I want you to do something much

329

nicer than that. My awards dinner is on the 30th and I thought you might enjoy coming with me.'

There was a groan.

'Mum, have you any idea where I'm going on the 30th?'

Sally could have kicked herself. Of course she knew where Annabel was going. She was off to Paris to see David. The date was ringed in red in both their diaries and the calendar they kept in the kitchen.

'Darling, I'm an idiot. How could I have forgotten?'

'Maybe you didn't want to remember,' her daughter said cryptically. 'Anyway, its all set and there's no way I can back out of it now.'

Sally felt defeated.

'I know that. I'll just have to find someone else to take.'

'That shouldn't be too difficult. You know plenty of people.'

'I don't know plenty of men.'

'Yes you do. What about Brad?'

'He's a client,' Sally said quickly. And I'll be at the dinner representing another client.'

Annabel considered this for a moment, then she said:

'I don't suppose Brad gives a stuff about who you're representing. I got the impression he was a friend more than anything else.'

She was right, of course. The formal relationship they'd had before he came to dinner had almost totally disintegrated. Now when they went out to lunch, they talked about David and her divorce and business was the very last item on the agenda.

'If I ask Brad to this dinner,' Sally said thinking aloud, 'won't it be a bit like inviting him out on a date?'

'What if it is?' Annabel interrupted. 'You want him to come, don't you?'

'Of course I want him to come. I just don't want to sound forward.'

'Don't be silly, Mum,' the girl said impatiently. 'You're asking him to an agency jolly, not some intimate evening.' She paused. 'You're not frightened of Brad, are you? If it's difficult for you, I can always ring him up.'

She realised things were getting out of hand.

'I can handle this perfectly well on my own,' Sally said crossly. 'I am a grown woman you know.'

'You could have fooled me.'

After she hung up on her daughter, Sally flipped through her index until she found American Hamburgers. If Brad was in London she was bound to find him there. Then she spoke to his secretary and realised she was out of luck. Brad had left for America three days ago and nobody knew exactly when he would be back.

'Can I ask what it's about?' the girl enquired.

Suddenly Sally felt flustered.

'Not really, it's a personal matter.'

'I can get hold of Brad in New York, if it would help.'

'It wouldn't help at all,' Sally said, feeling more foolish than she had in years. 'Why don't I just leave it till he gets back?'

Ingrid sounded reluctant.

'If you're absolutely sure. It wouldn't be any bother to call him in the States. I talk to him twice a day as it is.'

'I'm absolutely sure,' Sally said firmly. 'What I want to talk about is nothing to do with the account.'

Twenty minutes later Brad rang Sally in London.

'What do you have to say to me that's so secret you can't tell my secretary?' he asked her.

Despite herself she laughed.

'I don't want to disappoint you, but it's no big deal. I'm up for an award and I was casting around for someone to escort me to the industry dinner.'

'When is it?'

'On the 30th, but you probably won't be here then.'

'Who told you that?'

Sally started to feel impatient. She'd already expended far too much energy organising this party. The last thing she needed was to argue about dates with Brad.

'Ingrid told me,' she said shortly. 'I assume she keeps your diary.'

'Then you assume wrong. I keep my diary and the way

331

business is looking right now, I should be in London in time for your party.'

Sally was nonplussed.

'So you'll come?'

'That's what I was trying to tell you.'

If she had all the time in the world, Sally would have booked herself a hairdresser's appointment for the night of the awards. She would have also invested in a facial, a manicure and a professional make-up, because she knew that looking immaculate put her ahead of the game. In David's day she went through this ritual every time they had a black-tie dinner. But it wasn't David's day any more. It was her day and she was just too damn busy to fritter her time away trying to look like an ornament.

So she compromised. She went to the hairdresser's a week early and got him to cut her blonde curls into an urchin cut she could manage herself. Then, because she looked like a boy, she went out and bought herself a long tuxedo jacket which she teamed with a pair of skinny silk pants. When she examined the finished result in her bedroom mirror, she was surprised at how much she had transformed herself. She was used to looking pretty and appealing, but this new look robbed her of those qualities. She didn't look like someone's wife any more. She looked tough and a bit frightening and she knew for sure this was exactly what the managing director of Chic would expect of her.

Just for a moment she thought about Brad. Would he like this new persona she'd invented for herself? Or would it frighten him away? She made a face at her reflection in the bedroom mirror. I'm too old to start chasing after men, she told herself, too old, too newly separated and too shaken up to consider anything more than a sedate friendship.

She made a mental note to explain all this to Brad when they saw each other on Friday the 30th.

Chapter Forty One

It was not the sort of crowd you would normally find at the Dorchester. The women were comparatively young and unconventional and the men looked more like actors than the sort of businessmen who went to dinners like this. Brad saw several of them were wearing pony tails and rings through their ears and guessed they probably worked in the creative department of one of the big ad agencies.

Most of the awards tonight were being handed out to the advertising industry, with public relations taking second place right at the end of the ceremony. Sally would go almost unnoticed among the copywriters and the art directors, but Brad didn't think that was such a bad thing. She was making her début in a business that was competitive at best and small-minded and bitchy at worst. It was better she didn't expose herself to the public relations mafia en masse until she'd found her feet. Tonight enough of her peers would be represented to put her on her edge. And if she succeeded and walked off with an award she would be perfectly equipped to walk on a bigger stage.

Brad went over to the bar, got himself another scotch, and went on thinking about Sally. She was an extraordinary woman by any standards. Even in America, where women habitually fought their way to the top, she would stand out, mainly because she hadn't lost sight of the rest of her life. Too many divorcees abandoned their domestic personas the minute they went back on the job market. But Sally hadn't done that. He suspected she had enjoyed being married, even if it was to the wrong man. So she went on being a housewife when she wasn't in the office.

He remembered the little house in Fulham where she lived with her daughter. For the same money she could have bought a service flat in a better area. But she didn't want those sort of trappings and he realised he had started to fall in love with her when he discovered that. If he had been younger and less damaged, he might have pursued her. Except he knew it wouldn't have been any use. You didn't have casual affairs with women like Sally. You committed yourself to them, heart and soul and Brad wasn't sure he was ready for that.

So what am I doing here? he asked himself. Why did I come charging over to London, where I have nothing very much to do, as soon as Sally picks up the phone? He might have gone on beating his brains against a brick wall if he hadn't seen her come into the room.

All his doubts and fears went into rapid reverse at the sight of Sally. She had done something different to her hair, he noticed. He wasn't quite sure what it was, but it made her look sleeker, more like an agency chief. And she'd completed the effect by wearing a severe, mannish suit. On another woman it might have been off-putting, but he wasn't put off by Sally tonight even if he found her new boy-woman look strangely disturbing. As he went forward to greet her, he did his best to put a rein on his emotions.

Then he saw she wasn't alone. A tall, greying man was with her and by his side was a hard, rather overdressed blonde. Brad guessed the couple were probably clients of Sally's. And as she introduced them, he realised he'd been right.

'Meet Steve and Betty Blake,' Sally told him, 'our most important guests.'

Brad smiled his agency dinner smile. 'If you're that important, you must be from Chic.'

Steve nodded.

'I'm the managing director,' he said a little selfconsciously.

'Then we're two of a kind,' Brad said. 'I run American Hamburgers.'

He didn't add he was the major shareholder, for he realised it was more than his life was worth to make Steve look small tonight. Ten minutes later, when they all had drinks in their hands, they were joined by a small dumpy women trailing behind her a stately, spectacular blonde.

'Sue,' said Sally, her face lighting up, 'and Liz as well. I'm glad you're here at last.'

Sue turned out to be Sue Phillips, the account director who worked on Chic. Liz Atkins the breathtaking blonde was her assistant. Their husbands were lining up with the coats and were expected any minute. Career women, Brad thought. There's no way either of them would have left me to look after the coats. He wondered whether Sally would start picking up their habits now she was getting successful. He hoped she wouldn't. She had too much going for her the way she was.

They all trooped into dinner and for the first and last five minutes of the evening, Brad managed to get a few words out of her. After that she joined in the general conversation. It was a frustrating experience, as he had a hundred and one things he wanted to tell her and no chance at all of getting even a minimal hearing.

Sally was here tonight to justify her existence and he remembered all the other nights when he had been in exactly the same situation – hosting a dinner when he had to be on show and his date had to take second place.

He was suprised at the sudden reversal of their roles, yet strangely he didn't feel threatened by it. In a perverse way he was proud she had come so far, and honoured to have been partly responsible for Sally's success. He had influenced several of her key decisions and as the agency grew he'd helped her steer a steady course. She didn't fully realise it, of course, and he would never tell her just how much he had done because he knew it would be bad for her. When you were on the way up like Sally, you had to believe totally in yourself.

He sat back and watched his protogée in action. She was a cool operator, he had to hand it to her. Any other agency chief would have dominated the dinner table, making quite sure the client she was entertaining knew exactly how clever she was. But

335

Sally didn't play it that way. Every time Steve Blake rhapsodised about the work that had got them all to this dinner, she made a point of bringing Sue Phillips into the conversation. Sue and Liz were here tonight not as window dressing but because they had both worked like dogs on the Chic account. By the time the plates were cleared away, nobody was left in any doubt about their contribution.

Brad wondered whether she was overdoing the shrinking violet routine, but he didn't get a chance to voice his doubts for the awards ceremony took over. The head of a well-known London ad agency had got to his feet and was starting to list the winning categories. There were half a dozen advertising awards, as he had expected, and just two public relations prizes. At any other trade party, the host would have got on with the business at hand. But this was a media affair so there had to be a speech praising the assembled talent.

Brad groaned inwardly. He had been to dozens of these dinners in his working life and they all seemed to follow the same pattern. Boredom, followed by self-congratulation, followed by relief when the last winner collected the final prize. Tonight wouldn't be quite so bad, he thought – at least he had a vested interest in one of the nominees.

After an hour of watching the advertising industry collecting the honours, it was finally the turn of public relations. Brad saw Sally sit up straighter as the contenders for the best corporate campaign were announced. She wasn't in the race, but she was going to try her hand at this kind of campaign one day. And she was interested to know who her peers were.

The prize went to an eye-catching press campaign for a South African hotel group, and Brad saw the agency chief get up to collect her award. He noticed, as did everyone else in the room, that Maureen Smith of the Communications Group was an extremely glamorous woman. With her manicured red nails and glossy hairdo, she was a walking endorsement for the agency she ran. And she knew it. Instead of taking the award and legging it back to her table, Maureen made a little speech praising her client and plugging a couple of her other accounts while she was about it.

Brad leaned back in his seat. It was an impressive performance, the sort of show David might have put on had he been here tonight. He wondered what Sally could possibly do to rival it. He didn't have to wonder too long. For the nominees for the best fashion campaign were already being read out.

Chic's name was one of three and Brad held his breath waiting for the final judgement. It came five minutes later when all three campaigns had been flashed up on a screen at the end of the room. He knew before they announced it that Chic had won the day, as Chandos's work was far and away the best.

As the winner was announced, Brad turned to help Sally out of her chair. But Sally was whispering something in Sue Phillips's ear. After a brief exchange of words, it was Sue who got up and walked towards the top table.

'What made you send her up there?' Brad asked Sally. 'You should be collecting the prize.'

He realised he had embarrassed her, for she reddened.

'It's not my style to take credit for other people's work,' she told him.

'Maureen Smith didn't seem to have any problem with it.'

She turned to him and he saw she wasn't embarrassed any more. She simply looked pained.

'I'm not Maureen Smith,' she told him. 'I don't have her personality or her salesmanship. So there's no point in playing the agency supremo.'

'You don't have to hide either.'

Sue Phillips had got back to the table bearing the silver statuette, and the next ten minutes were spent oohing and ahing over the agency's success. Finally when the fuss was over and conversation returned to normal, Sally turned her attention to Brad again.

'I didn't realise you thought I was hiding tonight,' she said.

The American sighed.

'You've been keeping out of sight ever since we sat down.

Steve probably thinks you had nothing to do with the Chic win at all. It was all down to your staff.'

She picked up a bottle of mineral water and poured some into her glass.

'Steve doesn't believe that any more than you do. Terrific people need a good manager, otherwise they fall apart.'

She smiled, remembering the day she and Jim Morrison had walked into his hotel suite to pitch for his Hamburger account.

'Without me to hold his hand, Jim would never have landed American Hamburgers.'

I knew that, Brad thought. I saw it at the time. And as he adjusted his view of Sally, he saw himself in a totally different way. For Sally wasn't the only one who knew how to lead from behind. He had been guilty of the self-same thing when he took her in hand and showed her how to run her growing agency.

The party ended around midnight and he expected her to be wrung out. Yet Sally showed no signs of being tired at all, and he wondered if he dared ask her for a nightcap. It was a cliché she would recognise instantly. Men on the prowl always suggested a strong drink at their place when they were bent on seduction. But he couldn't think of anything else to suggest, so he took a chance.

To his surprise Sally went for the idea.

'A glass of champagne at the Savoy sounds like a great way to round off the evening.'

He took her arm and led her through to the pastel-coloured foyer of the Dorchester.

'If we hurry,' he told her, 'we might just manage to get away before the others decide to join us.'

She grinned at him.

'I think we're safe,' she said. 'Everyone in our party has got to rush home to deal with the babysitter.'

'What about you, won't Annabel fret if you stay out much longer?'

'Annabel's a grown-up girl. Anyway she's away seeing her father this weekend.'

Brad looked at her thoughtfully.

'So if you stay away till Sunday, nobody's going to make a fuss.'

The intention in his words was crystal clear. To her surprise, Sally felt her heart start to race. Calm down, she told herself, you've no business behaving like this at your stage of life. Yet for the first time ever she paid no heed to her inner voices. Instead she said:

'I'm not sure about Sunday. Can we take this one step at a time?'

They were standing in the taxi queue now and Brad let go of her arm and took a firm grip on her hand.

'We can take it at any rate you want,' he told her.

When they got to the hotel, she thought Brad would play the gentleman and suggest a drink in the American Bar. But he did nothing of the sort. Instead he led her over to the private lift that served the permanent suites.

'I do have a drawing-room,' he said gently. 'There's no need to look so worried.'

'I remember,' she said.

Then she kept her mouth shut, because she didn't trust herself not to sound foolish. There had been no-one in her bed except David for nearly twenty years. She had no idea how she was going to handle the rest of the evening. Brad must have realised what was going through her mind, for he changed the conversation to business. As soon as they got to the suite, he sat her down and demanded to know how she was going to capitalise on tonight's triumph.

Sally looked around the soulless hotel room and realised her reason had deserted her. All she could think about was kissing Brad. So she widened her eyes and told him the truth.

'I'm not all that interested in what Chandos does right now.'

He came towards her with a glass of champagne in each hand.

'What are you interested in?'

339

'You, if you must know.'

He put the drinks down on a side table and came over to where she was sitting. Then he pulled her to her feet and started kissing her. It was better than she had imagined, better than anything she had known before. And without thinking she let herself be led into the bedroom. Then, out of the corner of her eye, she saw the bed, and she panicked. For the hotel staff had been in that evening and turned the covers down. It wasn't Brad's doing, she knew that. But somehow she felt compromised. He seemed to realise it and let her go.

'There hasn't been anyone since your husband, has there?'

She shook her head, feeling about two feet tall.

'It's OK,' he said, 'I'm not a stranger you picked up in a bar. If nothing happens between us tonight, it won't matter at all.'

While he was telling her this, she noticed he was stroking her hair, as if she was a nervous puppy that needed calming. Brad kept animals once, she realised, family pets he fed and stroked and loved. The knowledge relaxed her, for it told her there was nothing cruel about this man. He wouldn't make love to her and walk out the next morning, the way David had done on his last night in Oxford.

She sat down on the end of the bed, pulling him with her so they were both wrapped in each other. In that moment, she wondered what all her worry had been about, for she suddenly felt as if she had been close to Brad all her life. And she relaxed and opened herself to whatever was going to happen. Brad responded, moving closer, undoing the buttons running down the front of her jacket. Her shoulders were bare now and Brad caressed them the way he had stroked her hair.

Sally felt herself starting to tremble. She had never known a man be as gentle as this one. He unlocked a warmth inside her she didn't know was there. And she reached out for him, undoing his tie, unbuckling his belt until the two of them were twined together among a pile of discarded clothes.

Brad pulled away from her, looking at the wreckage all around them. In one decisive movement he swept everything onto the floor. Then he turned to her and removed first her bra and then her panties.

'Now I can see you,' he said, running an experimental hand across her breasts.

Her nipples came erect almost instantly and Sally knew now she had reached the point of no return. She took hold of his other hand and guided it between her legs, then as pleasure washed over her she realised how starved she had been since David left her. She had done her best to pretend she was above this sort of thing. But now as she felt her body crying out for Brad, she knew she had been deluding herself. She needed a man in her bed. She needed this man. She only hoped that when it was all over, Brad would feel the same way about her.

Chapter Forty Two

The last time Annabel had been abroad was on a school trip. A group of them had gone to Florence to look at ancient churches. But their history teacher had been with them then, telling them what to do and where to be. So the expedition lacked the spirit of adventure.

Going to Paris on her own was another story altogether. The moment she got on the Gatwick Express she began to feel like a grown-up, for it was up to her to find her way through the terminals and onto the plane. And if she didn't, no-one was going to come and slap her wrists. All that would happen would be she would miss seeing her father this weekend. And there was no way she was going to risk that.

Hefting her overnight bag, she followed the signs that led her past a shopping village and into a steel tunnel where she caught a transit train. By the time she had her boarding pass, she knew she was well and truly on her way.

In an hour or so, she would be talking to David and finding out who the new girlfriend was. The prospect of coming face to face with her mother's replacement scared her a little, but she knew she couldn't go on pretending she didn't exist. Her father had someone else and she had to accept the situation and make the best of it. Though if she hated her on sight, it wasn't going to be easy.

I won't hate Daddy's girlfriend, Annabel decided. Or if I do, I won't show it, because I can't afford to. Daddy's such a coward that the least bit of unpleasantness is bound to drive him away.

She remembered the effect her tantrums had on him when she was a little girl. He didn't make the slightest effort to pacify her. He simply went into another room and ignored her until she'd recovered her temper. He'll be just the same if I fall out with his girlfriend, she thought, only instead of going into another room, he'll send me back to London. And she knew she couldn't bear it if that happened.

I need Daddy, she thought. Not as much as I need Mummy, but I still want him in my life, so the minute there's any mention of a girl, I'll be nice as pie and pretend I'm dying to be best friends with her.

Now her mind was made up, Annabel took her seat on the plane and let go of her worries. She even ate the plastic airline meal. And when they touched down in Paris, she was among the first into the terminal building at Charles de Gaulle.

The queues at passport control were longer than she remembered and by the time she'd picked up her case, she wondered if David would have tired of waiting for her.

He hadn't, of course.

She saw him the minute she got through the customs hall. He was leaning back against a desk, reading a copy of the *Herald Tribune*. Despite the hustle and bustle of the busy airport, David seemed perfectly at ease with his surroundings. Annabel knew that even if her plane had been late, he would have just finished his paper and gone and bought something else to while away the time. She felt a rush of affection for her father. No situation, no matter how uncomfortable or outlandish seemed to phase him.

She called his name to attract his attention, and he put down the *Herald Tribune* and held his arms out in welcome. She ran into them, surprised at how pleased she was to see him again.

They both had a million questions for each other and as they walked from the terminal building to the car park, they talked nineteen to the dozen. David wanted to know if Annabel had decided to go to University. When she told him she'd rather get a job, he seemed disappointed.

'I don't want to put another burden on Mummy,' she told him. 'She's had enough problems as it is.'

Her father looked at her warily.

'I heard you were a bit hard up, 'but that's all alright now, isn't it?'

Annabel wondered what to say. Did she skate over the horrors of the past year as she had in her letters? Or did she drop the whole thing in his lap? She decided he richly deserved the latter.

On the drive down the motorway into town, she filled him in on every detail, starting with the house being repossessed and ending with Sally's struggle to get Chandos on its feet.

'At the time I thought Mummy wasn't going to make it and I'd have to write to you begging for help,' Annabel said.

They were coming up to traffic lights and David took his eyes off the road and turned to his daughter.

'I knew all about your mother being in trouble,' he told her. 'I was actually planning on bailing her out, which is why I wrote to you once I'd settled in Paris. To be honest I was surprised that I didn't get a letter by return of post telling me you needed money.'

The girl did her best not to look smug.

'By the time we heard from you, half the battle was over. Mummy was actually able to pay herself a salary.'

David revved up the engine of his Porsche and followed the train of traffic into town. It was a few minutes before he spoke again. When he did, he sounded cautious.

'When will your mother be able to afford to get somebody else to run the agency?' he asked.

Annabel was startled.

'Why would she want to do that?'

David sighed.

'Because she needs to. I know Sally is fantastic in a crisis. She was when we ran the business together in the old days, but she doesn't have the flair to take Chandos onto the next stage.'

'How do you know what Mummy's capable of? Annabel demanded angrily.

'Because I'm in regular contact with one of her biggest clients.'

Now Annabel was intrigued. She was going to throw all Sally's success right back in his face, but now she held her tongue.

'Which client?' she asked.

David's expression didn't alter.

'Diane Craven,' he said shortly. 'She's kept me in touch with all your mother's movements.'

Annabel recalled the freezing-off of relations between Diane and her mother and wondered whether the reason wasn't sitting right beside her.

'What was Diane doing spying on us?'

She saw her father grip the steering-wheel tighter.

'She wasn't spying. She was keeping me informed.'

Annabel was tempted to make a rude noise. Instead she said:

'You can call it anything you like. I think she was bloody disloyal, considering she was Mummy's friend.'

She glanced across and saw David's knuckles had turned white.

'Diane is my friend too.'

'Since when?'

'Since before I met your mother. We both go back a long way.'

Nobody had told her that. All these years she had just sort of assumed Diane belonged to Mummy and Daddy tagged along for the ride. The fact that it wasn't so changed a lot of things.

'So when you dumped me and Mummy, Diane must have known all about it?'

David nodded and turned his attention back to the road. The dark, cluttered suburban streets were giving way to broad boulevards with rows of trees on either side. This was the Paris she'd read about in the tourist guides, but it failed to thrill her. All her emotions were taken up with Diane and Diane's treachery.

'If she knew what you were going to do,' Annabel went on, 'why didn't she say something? Why didn't she warn Mummy?'

She saw her father scowl and realised her questions were making him uncomfortable.

'Diane wasn't in a position to interfere,' he said shortly. 'She was caught right in the middle between the two of us.'

Annabel tried to visualise the chic, dark woman in a go-between's role, but the image didn't make any sense. Diane was a marriage breaker, not a marriage maker. And a suspicion began to form in her mind.

'Diane was your girlfriend in the beginning, wasn't she?'

David didn't say anything, pretending to concentrate on the traffic. But Annabel wouldn't be put off.

'When I used to see you together, I always wondered if you fancied her. And now I know you did all along. I bet you still went to bed with her now and then when you thought Mummy wasn't looking.'

David interrupted the outpouring.

'It wasn't like that.'

She turned to him, marvelling at how calmly he was telling her all this. They were talking about Daddy going to bed with Mummy's best friend, and all he could say was she didn't understand what was going on.

'Maybe you'd better tell me what it was like,' she said. 'You were having an affair with Diane, weren't you?'

She could see she'd put him on the spot, for he actually started to look embarrassed.

'It wasn't just an affair,' he said slowly. 'I loved Diane right from the beginning and when she came back into our lives I realised I still loved her.'

'What about Mummy? Didn't she matter at all?'

'Of course she mattered. She'd been loyal to me for years and it nearly killed me to do what I was doing. But I couldn't help myself. Love isn't something you can turn off when you feel like it.'

You seemed to do a pretty good job with Mummy, Annabel thought, but she refrained from saying so. Daddy was clearly trying to tell her something and to start berating him now would only put him off.

'Do you still feel that way about Diane?' she asked cautiously.

She saw her father nod and realised all at once that Diane was the girlfriend he had been talking about. They'd been together spying on her and her mother, observing how they weathered the storm, almost as if they were two animals in a laboratory experiment.

Just for a moment she wanted to tell her father to turn the car round and take her straight back to the airport. But she didn't do it. After months of living in no man's land, she wanted to know the whole story. She wanted to see Diane with her own eyes and listen to her explain herself. She turned to her father.

'I suppose Diane is waiting for us in Paris?' she asked, testing the water.

'She's in my flat, making us lunch.'

The girl smiled thinly.

'A sort of welcoming committee.'

The irony of her words was lost on David. He simply looked relieved that his daughter wasn't making a fuss and concentrated on his driving. Annabel stared out of the window as well, for they were negotiating the traffic round the Arc de Triomphe and the landmark roused her curiosity. She had expected something bigger, more awe-inspiring than this piece of masonry and she felt vaguely disappointed. It reminded her of a jigsaw puzzle and she suspected that everything in this town would let her down this weekend.

The Porsche pulled up outside a modern block of flats and David got out and opened the door for her.

'I've got to go and get rid of the car,' he said. 'If you take the lift to the second floor, my flat's facing you as you come out.'

He'd driven off before she could protest, so reluctantly Annabel made her way through the glass and chrome front door, towards the bank of lifts. When she got out, she saw the door to the flat was already open.

'Come on through,' she heard Diane call. 'I'm in the kitchen.'

She looked just the same as she had in London, all glossy dark

347

hair and red lipstick. And it set Annabel back on her heels. She had imagined Diane would have gone through some sea-change in Paris, love and her father mellowing her into someone softer, more girlish. But she had been mistaken. Things didn't happen to Diane. They happened around her, leaving her untouched.

She walked over to her and offered her cheek for a kiss. When the proprieties had been observed, she sat down at the rough pine kitchen table and poured herself a glass of wine from the open bottle she found there.

Diane was the first one to speak.

'I take it David told you about us.'

She sounded nervous when she said it and Annabel decided she liked to see this woman on edge. She knew better than to offend her this weekend, but she wasn't going to offer reassurance either.

'We talked about it in the car,' Annabel said, making sure to keep her voice neutral.

'You must have been surprised.'

The girl leaned back in her chair.

'Not really. I always suspected you and Dad had something going. I just didn't realise it would get this far.'

She saw the dark woman recoil slightly and she hoped against hope her father hadn't found a parking space yet.

'Do you mind things have got this far?' Diane asked.

The girl shrugged.

'I mind for Mum. Knowing you took my father away will hurt her.'

'But how does it affect you?' Diane pressed. 'Are you hurt too?'

Annabel looked at the immaculate older woman and realised she was feeling guilty as hell. What she wants, the girl thought, is for me to say it makes no difference; that I love my father and I want him to be happy. She took a sip of her wine.

'I'm not going to give you a hard time, if that's what you're worried about.'

She hadn't seen her father come in. She realised he was

there only when she saw him standing on the other side of the kitchen table.

'Diane isn't worried about you playing up,' he told her. 'What she cares about is what's going on inside your head. She wants things out in the open between you.'

She's got a fat hope, Annabel thought. Aloud she said:

'I haven't hidden anything. I'm a bit knocked for six at the moment, but I guess I'll get used to things.'

That seemed to satisfy them, for her father suddenly seemed very interested in getting her settled. He made a great to-do about showing her her room, which reminded her of an expensive hotel suite.

When she'd unpacked the few things she'd brought, she went back into the kitchen and saw Diane had been busy. The kitchen table was set with an assortment of pâtés and crudités. As a finishing touch Diane had made a vast salade niçoise which she set right in the centre of things. It was Annabel's favourite food and she suspected her father had remembered when he got Diane to lay on this feast.

As she took her place beside her father, she began to feel queasy. She was ravenously hungry, but she knew that if she took a mouthful of Diane's lunch she would probably choke on it.

Later on that evening, all three of them went to an expensive little restaurant on the Left Bank. It was one of those places which had a regular and very exclusive clientèle. Annabel wished her father had warned her they were going somewhere this elegant. She had only brought jeans and T-shirts with her and when they walked into the tiny mirrored dining-room, she began to feel like the poor relation. All the other women there were wearing diamonds and little black numbers. Diane was looking vixenish in low-cut green velvet, and Annabel wished she hadn't decided to tough it out.

There was no way Diane was going to tell her what they'd been up to behind her mother's back. All she was concerned about was her state of mind. Was she coping with the divorce? Could she handle seeing her father in love with somebody else?

349

They were such dopey questions, Annabel had been tempted to come out with the truth and tell Diane in no uncertain terms what a bitch she'd been. She didn't bother, for she knew that in any argument she was bound to lose. Diane had her father wrapped round her little finger. He'd back her to the hilt at the first sign of dissension. If I want to have any effect on either of them, Annabel decided, I'm going to have to box clever.

She waited till the waiter had shown them to a corner table dominated by an ornate candelabrum. She gave her father a docile little grin when he handed her the leather-bound menu. Then she started to talk about her mother. She sounded deliberately babyish as she did it and she saw David being taken in by it. This is going to be easier than I thought, she decided.

'I suppose you're wondering how we're managing without you?' she asked innocently.

David looked up from the long elaborate list of dishes.

'Not really,' he said. 'You told me you're keeping your heads above water.'

Annabel savoured the moment. Daddy was so obsessed with his boring new life in Paris, he hadn't bothered to check up on what was happening at the agency. What she was about to tell him would make him eat his heart out. He'd want to know everything and for an hour or so Diane would be right out of the picture while they caught up with each other.

She waited while the waiter lit the candles, then she said:

'Mummy got beyond breaking even ages ago. She's put on a lot of new business in the past few months.'

The girl saw her father look across at Diane.

'Did you know anything about this?'

For a moment she looked blank.

'I didn't actually. Sally and I haven't been in touch recently.'

Annabel turned to her.

'It's not for lack of trying on Mummy's part,' she said sweetly.

Diane put her menu down impatiently. The child was referring to the dinner date she'd ducked out of a couple of weeks ago.

She supposed she only had herself to blame for that one. She swivelled round in her chair so she was facing Annabel.

'I'll square things with your mother,' she said firmly, 'as soon as I get back to London.'

The two of them looked daggers at each other across the tablecloth and Annabel realised she was in danger of being diverted away from her original purpose. She was here to dent her father's confidence and make him question what he'd done. She'd deal with Diane another time. She turned back to David.

'Don't you want to know how Mummy saved the agency?' she asked her father.

She realised he was relieved there wasn't going to be a scene, for he seemed a little too anxious to hear about her mother's success. Annabel jumped in while the jumping was good.

'When Jeremy left we all thought Chandos would have to close because he'd left such a mess behind him.'

David nodded.

'I heard about that.'

'Did you hear who cleaned up the mess in the end?'

He looked puzzled.

'You just told me. Your mother did it.'

'She took her time before replying.

'Mummy didn't sort things out on her own,' she said finally. 'Grandpa came down from Manchester and helped her.'

'What the hell was Albert doing interfering in my agency?'

Her father was shouting now and several diners turned round to stare at him. Annabel smiled and pressed home her advantage.

'I don't think Grandpa was interfering,' she told him. 'From what I heard, he just fired a few people and rearranged things.'

'I bet he did,' David muttered, slightly calmer. 'I bet he gutted my brainchild and made it into his own image.'

Annabel saw Diane reach over and put a hand on her father's arm.

'He didn't change it that much,' she said, trying to reassure him.

But David was beyond reassurance.

'What happened after my father left?' he asked Annabel between gritted teeth.

She toyed with a piece of bread, tearing chunks out of it and leaving them on the plate.

'Nothing happened for a bit,' she told him. 'The executive he put in charge of things pulled in a few accounts. Then Mummy got lucky. Some American tycoon took a fancy to her and gave her all his business.'

If it was possible, her father looked even more put out at this piece of news than he had about his father.

'What American tycoon?' he demanded to know. 'Does the man have a name?'

She smiled sweetly, before putting the knife in.

'He's called Brad Hastings. I think you know him.'

She expected her father to lose his rag completely. After all, she knew from Mummy that he had tried to get Brad's hotel account and failed miserably. What a fool he must feel, she thought, now that he's been pipped at the post by her.

David regarded his daughter and felt an intense desire to smack her. She'd been goading him ever since they'd sat down and he'd let her get away with it because he needed to hear her news. Now he was up-to-date, he decided to get his own back.

'I've met Brad Hastings,' he said vaguely, 'but he didn't make much of an impression on me.'

Then as if Brad Hastings wasn't worthy of his attention one minute longer, David signalled the waiter to come across and take their orders.

Annabel had never seen her father make such a performance organising a meal. When they had gone out to restaurants in England, David usually told the waiter he'd have his usual and leave it at that. Even when Mummy was there, he never went on about the food. But Paris, or maybe it was Diane, seemed to have turned him into a gourmet. At one point when the waiter wasn't sure how long the filet de boeuf stayed in the oven, the chef was summoned.

Annabel thought she was going to die with embarrassment

when the man in the high starched cap went into conference with her father. What on earth did it matter how long the bloody beef was cooked? It was probably horsemeat anyway, Annabel thought.

When David had finally decided what they were going to eat, a fat old man with a chain round his neck came up to the table. Diane told her he was in charge of the wines. And Annabel looked on while the three of them went into a long session about château-bottled burgundies.

If she hadn't been so nettled by her father's put-down about Brad, she might have forgotten what they were talking about before. As it was, the minute the waiters left them alone, Annabel returned to the attack.

'You might not be impressed with Brad, but mummy thinks he's wonderful.'

It wasn't all that fair on her mother. But she felt the need to shock David all over again. She'd pulled him up short about his agency, now it was time she put him right about her mother. But her father wasn't taking the bait.

'I think Sally's very lucky to be able to pull in business with her sex appeal. I wish I'd been able to do that. The agency would have been twice the size.'

Annabel started to feel unsure of herself.

'Mummy didn't get Brad's business through sex,' she said angrily. 'She worked damn hard on the presentation.'

Her father smiled and looked across at Diane.

'The presentation of herself, or the presentation of the account?'

Diane preened slightly and Annabel began to regret she'd started on her mother. It was like throwing her to the wolves. But Diane didn't seem interested in scoring any points that evening.

'I'm sure Sally is worthy of Brad's business,' she said smoothly. 'Did you know she managed to get Chic shortlisted for an award?'

They talked about the awards dinner and Diane made a big fuss about the fact she hadn't been invited.

'I wonder who Sally will put in my place?' she said.

But Annabel wasn't playing. She could have told her about her mother inviting Chic's managing director, but she saved her breath. For the evening was slipping away from her. Diane and her father were so easy together, so completely relaxed in each other's company, that there was no way she could compete. She'd held David's attention in the first place only because she'd had bombshells to drop. Now all her weapons were spent and she was back to being in the cold again.

For she knew she was there on sufferance. She was just a leftover from an old life her father had no use for any more. Annabel sent up a fervent prayer that the weekend would pass quickly and she could go back to where she was wanted again.

Chapter Forty Three

Annabel was home in time for supper and she hoped her mother had remembered to get something in for her. As a rule the two of them had a scratch meal in front of the television on Sunday evenings, and she found herself looking forward to it.

She had probably consumed more gourmet treats this weekend than she had had in her entire life. But she hadn't really enjoyed any of them. What she really wanted was baked beans on toast and a great mug of tea.

Annabel smiled as she got her key out and fitted it in the lock. She was looking forward to the gossip they were going to have about Paris. As the door swung open, the first thing she heard was Sally talking. She imagined her mother was on the phone, then she heard a male voice and realised she had a visitor.

As she lugged her overnight bag into the hall, Annabel saw the visitor was Brad. He was sprawled across the sofa in an open-necked shirt and jeans. And she wondered what the hell was going on. There was something too relaxed about him, almost as if he had just got out of bed. Then she saw her mother and the whole thing became clear. For Mummy was wearing a towelling robe and her hair was wet from the shower.

'It looks as if I got home a bit too early,' she said, dropping her bag on the floor. 'Would you like me to go out for a bit while you make yourselves decent?'

She saw Brad and her mother exchange glances and she was reminded of Diane and her father. Adults, she thought. Leave them alone for five minutes and they start behaving like alley cats. She looked accusingly at her mother. 'Aren't you going to tell me whats going on?' she demanded.

Sally came over to her.

'I guess this must be a surprise for you. But it was for us as well. If you go and unpack, I'll make us some tea and try and explain things.'

Annabel looked at Brad.

'Is he staying around to explain things too?'

She saw him get up out of the sofa and make to leave.

'I know when I'm in the way,' he grinned, 'so I'm going to get the hell out of here.'

He turned to Sally.

'I'll give you a call first thing tomorrow.'

Before either of them could say anything, he was on his way out of the front door. And Annabel saw the look of loss in her mother's eyes.

She minds that he's going, the girl thought. She'd rather Brad had stayed with her and I'd been the one to push off. For the first time in her life, Annabel felt totally alone. Her father didn't need her any more, he had made that totally obvious all weekend. And now her mother was in danger of behaving the same way.

'How long has this been going on?' she asked.

Her mother had the grace to blush.

'Not long at all. Just this last weekend.'

Then there is some hope, Annabel thought. A weekend isn't very long. If I make a big enough fuss maybe I can put a stop to all this. But even as she considered the idea, Annabel knew she was on a loser. Her mother was well and truely hooked on Brad. You could tell it a mile off.

The girl looked at her again, noticing for the first time she was naked under her bathrobe. And she realised quite suddenly she couldn't bear to be in the same room with Sally. She didn't want to know about her new great love and she certainly didn't want to talk about it over a cup of tea.

She reached down and grabbed hold of her travelling bag. Then she slung it over her shoulder and started climbing the stairs to her room.

'Don't bother to get tea together for me,' she called back to Sally. 'I won't be coming down.'

Sally sat on the stairs outside her daughter's room and felt helpless. Annabel had been crying non-stop for nearly half an hour and there was nothing she could do about it. If I wasn't so terrified of making things worse, Sally thought, I'd break down the door and insist she listens to me.

She needs to know that Brad isn't a mistake or a one-night stand, that what we did mean something. She smiled and corrected herself: that what we're doing means something. For all over the weekend they had been making plans. She was going to fly to New York and spend a week with him there. The three of them were going away on holiday to the Caribbean later on that year. And Brad was even talking about renting a big house for when he was in London so that they could all be together.

She remembered feeling panicky when he started to talk about the house.

'Isn't this all a bit quick?' she protested. 'I've known you five minutes and already you've tied me up for the next five years.'

Brad looked at her.

'I love you,' he said simply. 'And it has made me hasty and selfish and clumsy as hell. Forgive me, darling, but I've been alone so long, I don't know how to behave in this situation.'

She smiled.

'You're doing fine.'

'Then you'll let me look after you. It's all I want to do.'

She laid her head on his knee, luxuriating in feeling wanted again. Brad was a good man. If she let him, he would provide for her and protect her – for the rest of her life. But she couldn't give in so easily. The last year had taught her to stand on her own feet and she discovered she had a taste for it. No, Sally thought, I'll let Brad into my life because I want him there, but what I'm not going to do is let him take it over. She sat up and looked at him.

'A long time ago, David said the same things you're saying now. And I was so grateful for being loved that I didn't think of what I wanted at all. I think that's half the reason things haven't worked out. If I'd only listened to myself I would have discovered that I didn't want to submerge myself completely in David. I wanted my own achievements and my own identity, and I could have had them along with my marriage if I'd been a little bit stronger.'

She saw the tenderness in Brad's eyes and realised that she was getting through to him.

'I'll do my best not to cramp your style,' he said, taking her into his arms, 'as long as you promise not to leave me.'

Sitting on the stairs outside her daughter's room, she found the memory of the last few days come flooding back, filling her with warmth and confidence and the knowledge that she could take hold of her own life and turn it into whatever she wanted. She wasn't a helpless housewife any more, terrified of people not liking her. And she didn't have to go on sitting on the stairs waiting for her daughter to calm down and listen to her.

She got up and knocked lightly on the bedroom door.

'I'm going to get dressed,' she said, 'then I'm going downstairs to open a bottle of wine. If you know what's good for you, you'll be out of your room in five minutes.'

Annabel took slightly longer than five minutes, but when she did appear, Sally noticed she had washed her face and pulled a comb through her hair. She looked so totally repentant that Sally's heart turned over.

'Come here,' she said, opening her arms, 'let me hold you.'

They flew to each other, each of them letting go of all the anger and hurt that had come between them. Annabel was a little girl again, a baby almost, and Sally was simply her mother. After a bit Sally relaxed her embrace and poured them each a glass of wine. Then she looked at Annabel.

'You don't have to be so upset about Brad, you know. It's not what you imagine.'

'You mean you're not having an affair.'

Sally laughed.

'Of course we're having an affair, but it's not a ten-minute wonder. We're both pretty serious about each other. Brad even wants to buy a house in London so we can all live together.'

Annabel looked at her mother and felt only dismay. She had been scandalised when she thought that her mother was behaving like a trollop. But now what she was telling her was much worse. Mummy was in love with Brad, which could only mean one thing: she was going to be pushed out all over again.

Sally caught her daughter's expression.

'What's the matter, darling? You don't look happy.'

'I'm not happy. How can I be, when Brad's taking you away from me?'

She sighed. So that's what was bothering Annabel.

'Who says Brad's splitting us up?' she demanded. 'It doesn't have to be like that.'

'You're saying that now, but wait till you get shacked up together. You'll be bored with me in five minutes.'

The way Annabel said it bothered her. This wasn't some sulky teenage whine – Annabel sounded as if she was speaking from experience. Sally remembered where she had just come from and decided it was time they talked about it.

'Did you have a bad weekend with your father?'

There was a small silence, then Annabel said:

'It was terrible. Daddy made me feel like a spare part. I was relieved when it was time to come home.'

She looked so pathetic, so utterly crushed, that Sally wanted to weep for her. How could David let this happen? she wondered. Had Annabel ceased to matter to him? She leaned across the sofa and stroked Annabel's hair.

'I would never do that to you,' she consoled, 'no matter what happened or who I was with. I don't know what got into your father.'

Annabel made a face.

'Diane got into my father.'

Now Sally was totally confused. 'Whats Diane got to do with it?'

'She was there in Paris. With Daddy.'

She saw her mother's startled expression and ploughed on before she lost her nerve.

'Don't you see? She's the girlfriend. She has been all along, only nobody was admitting it until now.'

Sally looked at her daughter and wondered if she was imagining things.

'Are you sure you're not jumping to conclusions? Diane could have been visiting for the weekend. She and your father go back a long way.'

'I know that. Daddy told me all about it when we were driving into Paris. He said he loved her in the beginning and when she came back into his life, he found he still loved her.'

Annabel sounded awkward when she said it, almost embarrassed.

Sally realised she had to be telling the truth. She felt something explode inside her head and realised it was pure rage. Christ almighty, she thought, all the time I imagined Diane was on my side, she was quietly fucking my husband. She remembered all the dinners in Oxford with the three of them playing at being friends. Then she thought about the girly lunches with just the two of them sharing secrets, her secrets.

She took me for a complete fool, Sally thought savagely. She sat and listened to me tearing my hair out over David, wondering why on earth he would just get up and walk out after all our years together. And all the time she knew exactly what was going on.

She turned to her daughter.

'No wonder your weekend was a nightmare. It's a miracle that you could cope with it at all.'

'It wasn't easy. I kept wanting to throttle Diane for being such a bitch. But I couldn't say anything because I knew Daddy would back her to the hilt.'

Sally breathed out slowly, feeling her new pain, the pain that came with betrayal, knifing through her.

'I'm glad you felt that way,' she told Annabel. 'I want to throttle Diane as well.'

Chapter Forty Four

When Sally got into her office on Monday morning, the first thing she did was summon Terry Jones, who she'd hired from Shandwick to be her new managing director. His appointment had been Brad's idea. Brad always seemed to know instinctivly when the moment had come to bring in some extra weight.

'You can't do everything on your own any more,' he had told her a couple of months before. 'Go and poach someone from one of the big firms.'

So she had poached Terry, who was making a name for himself in the industry. He seemed to have a talent for attracting business and every time Shandwick landed a new account, Terry was invariably responsible. A lot of other agencies were after him, of course. And Shandwick was pretty adamant about not letting him go without a fight, but in the end Sally had managed to lure him away with a huge salary and the promise of share options.

Now she was glad she had gone out on a limb for him. For at this moment in her life she needed to take advantage of all Terry's management experience.

He came into her office five minutes after she spoke to him on the internal phone. And as soon as she set eyes on him, she felt reassured. For Terry was all business: from his Saville Row suit to his polished loafers he exuded authority. If you were a client you knew you would be safe with Terry, because he took you seriously. Because he took the business seriously.

Sally looked at the new powerhouse she had invested in and

began to wonder how he would view her letting go of their most prestigious account. He'll probably think I'm a fool, she worried.

Then she straightened up remembering who was in charge. 'I'm thinking of dropping Chic,' she said.

Terry didn't wince the way she had expected him to. He simply picked up the intercom and asked his secretary to bring him the file. Then he turned to her.

'You must have a good reason for what you're doing.'

'I have actually.'

She was about to go on when the door opened and Terry's secretary came in.

'It's all up to date,' she said, handing him a thick folder. 'If there's anything else, I'll be at my desk.'

Terry drew up a chair and started to spread papers all over Sally's desk. The computer print-out was a complete record of the account's history with the agency. It showed regular yearly payments, and then, quite abruptly, two six-monthly payments. Terry pointed to the row of figures.

'How did that happen?' he asked.

Sally looked uncomfortable.

'When I took over, Diane didn't think I'd keep the agency afloat, so she hedged her bets and put us on six months notice.'

Terry screwed up his round face, giving him the appearance of a hamster.

'I can understand that. But why has she done it a second time? You would have thought it was quite obvious Chandos was going to survive by then.'

'She objected to me billing in advance.'

'That was her way of penalising you,' Terry said. 'Not very trusting behaviour for an client who you've done rather well for.'

Sally shrugged.

'That's what I thought.'

'But it's not the reason you want to fire Chic, is it?'

Sally regarded her managing director and knew she was going

to have to level with him. It was going to be painful for her, but it would be easier than lying.

'I found something out about Diane that I didn't know,' she said cautiously. 'It explains why she didn't want to commit for longer than six months.'

She fell silent for a moment, then she continued:

'Did you know Diane was having an affair with my ex-husband?'

If Terry was phased he didn't show it.

'I heard some sort of rumour it was going on, but I ignored it. There's so much gossip in this business, you'd go mad if you took any of it seriously.'

He was being tactful and she respected him for it. It was clear to her now that half the people she met knew all about David and Diane. And it hardened her resolve to get this false friend of hers out of her life for good. She turned to Terry.

'It's true about Diane,' she said. 'It's been going on for a long time, too long . . . I can't put a stop to it. But what I can do is put a stop to seeing her. Knowing what I know isn't going to make our meetings much fun.'

Terry looked at her.

'You're a brave woman,' he said, 'braver than a lot of executives I've worked with. Most of them would rather break bread with their mortal enemies than take a penny off the bottom line.' He shuffled through his papers again. 'I suppose I'd better put you in the picture about the bottom line. You stand to lose quarter of a million in turnover if you drop Chic.'

She looked at him with trepidation in her eyes.

'Can we afford that?'

He thought for a moment.

'If I'd been here six months ago, I would have strongly advised against it. But Chandos has picked up a lot since then. There are at least two other accounts that look like coming near Chic in size. And American Hamburgers is more than double that.'

'So we can do it?'

'If you insist. Though have you considered what it might do to your reputation?'

363

She looked embarrassed.

'You mean wronged wife fights back?'

'I don't mean anything of the sort. It might have slipped your mind, but you won an award for your work on this account. It's going to look strange if you throw it out because of a private wrangle.'

Sally thought for a moment.

'I can live with that,' she said.

She watched Terry gather his papers together and noticed he was still frowning.

'But can Chic live with it?' he said, almost to himself. 'If you get rid of them, they look like a bad client. And they're going to hate that.'

'I know,' Sally said.

She arranged to give Diane lunch in the boardroom at the agency. If things had been different she might have booked something feminine and trendy like La Caprice or Daphne's, but she wasn't looking to have a girly gossip. What she had in mind was strictly business, so she arranged for her secretary to set the whole thing up.

When Diane arrived at the agency, she would think she was there for a review of her account. She'll know something's up only when all she gets is me across the boardroom table, Sally thought. But by then it will be too late. Whether she likes it or not, she'll be forced to hear me out. And I've got plenty to say to her.

On the morning of the meeting, she put herself together with more care than usual, choosing a tailored dark suit and chunky gold jewellery. With her newly shorn hair, she looked every inch the successful executive, powerful and competent. All their lives Diane had managed to upstage her, and make her look small. Today it was going to be her turn.

When she arrived at the office, Sally told her secretary to block all her calls. There was no way she was going to be able to concentrate on anything until she'd seen Diane. So instead of tackling her mountain of post, she paced around her office rehearsing what she was going to say.

By the time twelve o'clock came, she was word perfect. The anger she had been bottling up all week was just about under control. And she knew that when Diane saw her, she would appear ice cool. The buzzer on her phone sounded and she picked it up to hear her secretary say that the Chic client was here and had been shown into the boardroom.

'I'll be there in twenty minutes,' Sally said.

The girl registered surprise.

'Do you want me to give her some excuse for your being late?'

Sally told her no.

'It will do her good to cool her heels for a while.'

Diane walked over to the bar at the end of the stark white painted room and wondered where everybody was. Normally when she was asked to an agency lunch there was a secretary dispensing drinks and at least two junior account men fawning over her. She frowned in irritation, sensing something was wrong. Then she thought, the hell with it. I'll pour my own drink while I'm waiting. She picked up a bottle of white wine and noticed that somebody had forgotten she liked Sancerre at lunchtimes. Now her only choice was a ghastly plonk which hadn't even been chilled.

She uncorked the bottle and splashed some of the wine into a glass. She'd make do with this until one of the agency minions could find something more to her taste.

Because she was alone, Diane made a cursory inspection of the room. It was barer than it had been in David's day. All the notices and tear sheets of his prize-winning campaigns had been taken down from the walls. In their place was the new Chic stuff that had got them that surprising award. And one or two other things she didn't know the agency handled.

She remembered David's precocious daughter boasting about all the new accounts her mother was pulling in. Out of curiosity she wandered over to look at some of the work:

she knew about American Hamburgers; but Vista double glazing and Universal petfoods came as a surprise. They were both substantial slugs of business and Diane wondered how Sally was building her agency. She refused to go along with David's theory that she was using her sex appeal to get clients. The nineties were too competitive for those tactics to succeed any more.

No, Diane thought, Sally must have hired some bloody effective staff. Or she must have come into her own at last. Neither prospect made her feel particularly happy. A successful, confident Sally was the last person she wanted to contend with. She corrected herself. A successful, confident Sally who knew all about her and David was the last person she wanted to contend with. And she had no doubt that Sally would be fully in the picture by now. Annabel would have wasted no time in spilling the story. She was probably halfway into it before she had put down her bag.

This was the main reason Diane had kept her distance. She didn't want to confront Sally's wrath while the wound was still fresh. She needed the whole thing to sink in, to be discussed and digested and finally seen in its right perspective. She and David had been meant for each other right from the start. They were like souls, two of a kind. When Sally sat down and faced that fact, she would realise it as well.

Diane was so wrapped up in her own thoughts that she didn't see Sally come into the room. Though when she finally caught sight of her, she registered her friend was a good twenty minutes late. She's nervous, Diane thought. She didn't have the courage to turn up on time because she couldn't face me about David. Despite the lack of account men and the terrible wine, Diane began to feel considerably better. She had the advantage, as she always had in the old days. Talking Sally round to see things her way was going to be easy.

She came towards Sally expecting to greet her with the usual air kiss. But Sally stuck out her hand instead, and she found herself on the end of a strong business-like handshake.

'What is this,' Diane began, 'some sort of top level meeting?' She saw Sally smile. But there was no warmth in it.

'You could call it that. You and I have a lot to talk about.'

So this is it, she thought, cards on the table time and not a moment too soon. She sat herself opposite Sally and watched her pressing the buzzer for lunch. Normally the agency came up with a plate of smoked salmon followed by an elaborate hot dish. We need to keep our strength up for the business we have between us today, she thought. Then she saw one of the assistants bringing in a plate of sandwiches and felt disappointed.

'Are you cutting costs?' she enquired. 'Normally the refreshments are better than this.'

Sally raised her eyebrows.

'I'm not here to curry favour today, I'm here to get a couple of things straight between us.'

Diane counted two beats, then she said: 'Like David, you mean.'

Her friend looked across at her, and Diane noticed she wasn't looking in the least bit nervous. She was looking very determined, almost tough in a mannish business suit. And she wondered if she'd misjudged the situation.

'I'll get to David in a minute,' Sally said. 'I'd like to get the business out of the way first.'

Diane looked around the empty boardroom table and was mystified.

'What business?' she asked. 'You need your account team to talk about Chic business. You don't even work on it.'

'I don't have to for the business I have in mind. I'm here to terminate your contract with the agency.'

For a moment she wasn't sure whether she heard it right.

'You can't be serious. Who on earth throws away quarter of a million?'

Sally unscrewed the top of a large bottle of Perrier and poured herself a glass.

'I'm throwing away quarter of a million,' she said, taking a sip. 'And not a moment too soon.'

'Have you lost your mind?'

'I don't think so. Not the last time I looked.'

'Then what the hell's going on?'

Sally had been rehearsing this moment not just in her office, but in her bath, in her car, in her bed before going to sleep. Now it had finally come, she leaned forward and gave it everything she'd got.

'What's going on,' she said, her voice dangerously calm, 'is that I found out about you.'

She paused, letting her words sink in.

'If you'd been having an affair with David and had nothing to do with me, I could have understood it. I wouldn't have been happy about it, but I guess I could have come to terms. What I can't cope with is the deceit. You were sneaking off with David, yet you were carrying on as if you were my best friend.'

Diane was momentarily shaken. She'd been expecting a tirade about what she'd done. But this attack was something different.

'You don't understand,' she said. 'It was very difficult for me. You made things difficult when you heard I was in London and wanted to get close again.'

Sally looked at her.

'You're not a little girl,' she said. 'You could have put me off. Or were you afraid that if you did you'd put David off as well?'

Now Diane was on ground she understood.

'You've got it all wrong about me and David,' she said with conviction. 'We weren't having a hole-in-the-corner affair. We were having a love affair that started years before he ever knew you.'

'And you thought that was OK, did you? You could take up where you left off without even considering that this great love of yours was married to a friend?'

Diane looked anguished.

'I thought about it. Both of us did. But we couldn't help ourselves.'

Sally regarded Diane in disbelief. She was talking like an old-fashioned movie script.

Any minute she expected her to say, 'this thing was bigger than both of us.'

'Come off it,' she said. 'If it was that good with David, he wouldn't have married me.'

'He shouldn't have married you. It was the worst mistake of his life.'

For a moment Sally thought she was going to slap Diane. She was so smug, so convinced she was right. And she realised then there was no point in going on with the discussion. She was never going to get any sense out of Diane. And she was too weary with the situation to listen to any more lies. No, Sally thought, I'll stick to business. At least I know where I am on that score.

'I'm not all that interested in talking about David's mistakes,' she said curtly. 'We're here to talk about my mistakes.'

'What mistakes?'

Sally looked savage.

'Trusting you just about sums it up. It was the stupidest thing I ever did, and I'm never going to let it happen again. From now on, I want nothing more to do with you.'

Diane looked at Sally warily.

'You're not still threatening to fire the Chic account, are you?'

'I'm not threatening. I'm stating a fact.'

She suddenly felt worried. She hadn't believed Sally when she talked about firing the account. Her feelings had been hurt and she wanted to make a stand. But nobody in in business kissed goodbye to solid turnover. Or did they? There was something dangerously determined about Sally today.

'What if I made it worth your while to keep the business?' Diane asked. 'I've been thinking about extending your contract to a year for some time now.'

'It wouldn't make any difference if you extended it to ten years. I don't want to deal with you any more.'

Diane's worry turned to genuine panic. Ever since the agency had picked up that stupid award, Steve, the managing director, had been singing their praises. If she came back to the office and told him they'd just been ditched by these stars, there would be hell to pay. Steve would have an immediate post mortem into why it happened. And it wouldn't take too long to find out she was to blame. Then it would be goodbye job, goodbye career, goodbye future.

Diane rummaged in her bag for a cigarette. She had to find a way of leaning on Sally, of pushing some magic trigger that would somehow diffuse her anger. She decided to dig up the past again.

'If it hadn't been for me,' she said lighting a filter tip, 'you probably wouldn't have an agency today. I know you think I've been a rotten friend, but I didn't let you down when it really mattered. I didn't pull my account out when I should have done. Anyone else in my position would have done it without hesitating.'

Sally weakened slightly. Diane was speaking the truth. When push came to shove, she'd backed her, knowing that if things went wrong she would be in trouble herself.

'You put yourself on the line for me, didn't you?'

'You bet I did. And I don't expect you to pay me back by dumping me. Steve would have a fit.

'I suppose you'd get fired?'

Diane nodded, looking pained. All at once Sally felt angry again.

'A lot worse happened to me,' she said. 'When you took David away I lost my home and my life.'

'But my job is my life.'

Sally was tempted to tell her to stop being so childish, but there was a better way to deal with her. She remembered the way Diane strung her along when she was desperate to keep the Chic account.

'How would you feel if I put you on six months notice?'

Diane winced.

'Does it have to be official?'

'Not if it's going to hurt you. We could keep the whole thing a secret between the two of us, and break the news only when you've got another agency lined up.'

Diane supposed it was better than nothing, though in the long run it wasn't going to save her job. Steve was set on using Chandos forever and a day. He wouldn't even consider going to anyone else. She lit another cigarette on the end of the first one.

'If I don't find anyone else, would you consider extending the six months?'

Sally had asked Diane the same question a year ago, with the same desperation in her voice. And now their positions were reversed, she didn't have the heart to turn her down.

'Why don't we cross that bridge when we come to it?' she suggested gently. 'A lot can happen in six months.'

Chapter Forty Five

Diane . . . Paris, 1996

Diane was woken by the sun filtering through the blinds. Without looking she knew she was in Paris. The light was different here; the air was different here. And if she stretched out her leg she could feel David sleeping soundly beside her. But Diane didn't stretch out her leg. Instead she lay there on her own, savouring the moment, feeling lazy and happy and free of the cares that dogged her during the week.

She wondered what it would be like to wake up like this every morning. There wouldn't be her job to look forward to, of course. But she hadn't been looking forward to that at all recently. The memory of the last few months came flooding over her, eroding her sense of well-being, casting a shadow over the morning.

It was all Sally's fault, of course. Ever since she threatened to fire the account the certainty had gone out of things. Now that she was unsure whether she would be staying at Chic, she worked less efficiently. And it was noticed. Once or twice Steve had pulled her up quite sharply over obvious, minor mistakes she wouldn't have made if she was in her right mind. She started to dread going into meetings, fearing she would make a fool of herself.

And her colleagues sensed her nervousness and preyed on it, making her feel increasingly as if she was walking on a tightrope. The story of her involvement with David was common knowledge now. And the gossips speculated, often to her face, whether Sally would put up with the current state of affairs. Not that Sally gave them any ammunition. When Diane went into the agency, her former friend was sweetness itself. Anyone looking at them talking business over the conference table would have imagined they were in complete harmony.

But Diane knew it was all an act. On the odd occasion when she had invited Sally to lunch or a quick drink after their meeting, she was met with frozen rejection. Sally didn't want to know her anymore. And she wouldn't want to know her in three weeks, when she went cap in hand and asked for a stay of execution.

Diane visualised Sally sitting behind her boardroom table, turning her down. She would be very nice about the whole thing, which would make it worse. And at the end of the day she would walk out empty-handed.

How can she do it, Diane thought. How can she go on punishing me for her disaster of a marriage, when it wasn't all my fault. David is as much to blame as I am, but she doesn't take it out on him. She doesn't come over to Paris and wipe the floor with him, the way any other deserted wife would do. No, she thought, it suits Sally to hold me to ransom for every one of her problems. And I have no choice but to take it on the chin and apologise for existing.

Her eyes were open now and she looked around the big sunny room and the man lying next to her. I'm happy here, she thought. I love Paris and I love David and if I had the courage I'd break away from what I have and make a whole new life here. She played the thought back over again. If I had the courage I'd break away from what I have. What did she have? A job that was coming to an end, an enemy called Sally and a guilty conscience that was threatening to destroy her. I don't need any of those things, she reasoned. So it won't take courage to leave them behind me. All it will take is commitment, commitment to David. For a moment she felt scared to death.

Until now, she had never been prepared to promise herself entirely to one man. She couldn't handle the responsibility and the headaches and the staying in one place for the rest of her life.

373

But I have to, she thought. If I don't settle for David, then I will have turned his life and Sally's life upside down for nothing. It was that which finally made up her mind. And now she knew where she was and what she was doing, she was filled with a new optimism.

She would find a job in Paris. The big fashion houses had been wooing her for years now. And she would make over the apartment. It was too masculine for a couple to live in. It needed lace curtains and a few decent antiques to make it homely, and that was only a start. The spare room would have to be altered to become her dressing-room. She would need a place for her word processor. And the cleaning woman would need a good talking to: she never seemed to dust in the right places and the way she ironed David's shirts was a disgrace.

She leaned over and shook him, impatient to communicate all her new decisions. But she got no response. All David did was groan and put his head under the pillow. And she knew him well enough not to press him. He would wake up of his own accord in about half an hour, when he would want coffee and croissants.

I'll slip out to the corner shop and buy some boulangerie, she decided. A decent breakfast will put him in the right mood for what I have to say.

Half an hour later, laden with bread and croissants and a punnet of strawberries from the local barrow, Diane pushed her way into the apartment. There was still no sign of David, so she put the water on to heat and started squeezing fresh orange juice. She was so engrossed in what she was doing that she did not see David until he was standing right in front of her.

He was wearing jeans and a shirt that hung half open and she saw he hadn't bothered to put on shoes.

'Are you up,' she enquired, 'or is this just a rehearsal?'

He plonked a kiss on the top of her head.

'Careful, you're beginning to sound like a wife.'

She turned round.

'I'm beginning to feel like a wife, that's what I want to talk to you about.'

To her surprise she saw him hesitate. And she realised that she had taken so long to make her mind up, he'd probably gone off the whole thing. She looked at David uncertainly.

'You do still want me to move in, don't you?'

'Of course I do. It's just that things have changed recently.'

Now she was really rattled.

'What things?'

He downed his orange juice in one gulp, then he went over to where the coffee was percolating.

'I've been putting this off for weeks now, because I wasn't sure what head office was going to decide. But I had a call from Leslie Pickett on Friday so I suppose I can talk about it now.'

He poured coffee into a large shallow cup and started tearing one of the croissants into small pieces.

'The thing is, Diane, I'm not going to be in Paris for much longer.'

She felt a frisson of alarm.

'Where will you be?'

He saw her pinched, worried face and wondered what was the best way to break things to her. He could tell it to her straight, he supposed. Or he could dress it up a little. Years of talking people round to his way of seeing things made him decide on the latter.

'Do you want the good news or the bad news?'

'Don't be silly. The good news, of course.'

He grinned.

'I'm glad you said that. I've just been promoted. As from next month I'm on double the salary and I've got a fancy new title to go with it.'

She put her coffee down and hurled herself into his arms.

'Darling, that's wonderful. I bet you're over the moon.'

He ran his hands down her back and over her hard, tight buttocks.

'You haven't asked me about the bad news.'

She pulled away from him, frowning slightly.

'I think I know it already. The new job means you have to move away.'

He nodded.

'As from next month I'll be based in Kentucky, running the American sales operation.'

Now she looked really dismayed.

'So I won't be seeing you.'

'Don't be silly. We can make it work for us.'

'How?' she asked bitterly. 'It's a rather long commute from London.'

'I wasn't talking about commuting. I was talking about you coming with me.'

She didn't know what to say. A few minutes ago she was making elaborate plans to move to Paris. But moving to Kentucky was in an entirely different class. She didn't know anyone in Kentucky. And she guessed that even if she did, they wouldn't be much use to her. Haute Couture wasn't all that strong in the Mid-West. They'd probably never heard of the idea.

He saw the doubt in her face and looked surprised.

'Don't you want to come with me?' he asked.

'Of course I do, it's just . . .'

'I know what your problem is. You don't want to go to the ends of the earth without it being worth your while. So I'm going to make it worth your while. Come to Kentucky as my wife, Diane. We'll get married in Paris, so we can invite all our friends. Then we'll arrive over there as Mr and Mrs Robinson.'

She should have loved the proposal. It was what she had been working herself up to all morning. Only things had moved on since she opened her eyes.

'This is all a bit sudden,' she said. 'Can we sit down and talk about it?'

Now it was David's turn to look dismayed.

'What's there to talk about? We love each other. We're been virtually living together for the last year. I thought you'd want to be my wife.'

'I do want to be your wife. All I want to know is what I'm letting myself in for.'

He smiled.

'What a tough little negotiator you are. You'll be asking next what kind of house I'm going to build for you.'

She thought about David building houses out in the Boondocks and everything she was screamed out against the idea.

'It's not about houses.'

David was undeterred.

'I think it is, so I took the trouble to visit a couple of estate agents the last time I was over there. I don't think you'll be too disappointed with what's on offer.'

He went through the door that connected to his study and returned five minutes later with a stack of papers. Right on top was a glossy photograph. David put it in front of her.

Diane saw a low ranch style house with a verandah running the length of it. What struck her about it most of all was not the size of it, or the fact that there was a swimming-pool glinting in the grounds. What scared the hell out of her was that the house was all alone. There was no comforting terrace of matching properties. There wasn't even an estate with other houses on it. All there was was this millionaire's residence in acres and acres of rolling lawns.

'Have you put in an offer for this? she asked nervously.

David hesitated.

'I wanted to know if you liked it before we did anything definite.'

She noticed he said we, not I, and she began to realise that this move and this marriage were almost a foregone conclusion. She looked at David.

'Show me the other houses you've been looking at?'

He leafed through his papers and produced another three glossy pictures, placing them all over the table so she had an uninterrupted view. None of them was any different from the first one. All the houses David had been selecting for their future life were in the back of beyond, miles away from a crowded street or a friendly face. She picked up the photos and placed them in a neat stack.

'Do you really want to live so far from town?'

David sighed.

'In middle America people don't live in cities – not the sort of people we are, anyway. All my fellow board members have places like this. It's a way of life.'

'I suppose they belong to the country club as well?'

'Of course they belong to the country club. It's the centre of the community.'

Diane suddenly had a vision of what she would become if she married David. There would be no job for her in Kentucky. And even if there was, she would be encouraged not to take it. Top executives in little American towns had their own code of conduct. And one of the first rules was that wives didn't work. She would be expected to join the tennis club and the golf club where she would spend the best part of her time.

Her home, one of those soulless ranch houses in the photos, would be the other centre of her existence. Here she would put on barbecues for David's colleagues and their families. Occasionally when they wanted to get away from the children, there would be formal dinners in local restaurants. But that would be the total of it.

In one stroke her whole life would move from the glamorous helter skelter she knew to the boring plod of small-town America. She wondered how David could endure such an existence. Then she remembered how he had lived in rural England and she realised Kentucky would be home from home. His house in Oxford hadn't been that dissimiliar to the places he was looking at.

And his wife, the woman he wanted her to become, would be exactly the same as Sally had once been: a home-maker, a hostess and a second-class citizen. Diane wondered whether all men needed their soul-mates to occupy this place in their lives. Then she looked at the stack of glossy ranch houses piled on the table in front of her and she supposed they did. It was one of the penalties of getting married. When you turned a lover into a husband, you turned yourself into a wife. Then you both embarked on your life together as totally different people.

She glanced up to see David staring anxiously at her. He was waiting for an answer, she knew that. He wanted to hear her say she loved the idea of settling down to married drudgery in suburban America.

Yet somehow her mouth couldn't find the words. David must have read her mind for he said it for her.

'You hate the houses I've chosen, don't you?'

She was suddenly overcome with guilt. David had gone out on a limb for her. It wasn't his fault that she didn't share his dreams.

'I don't hate the houses,' she told him. 'I just can't see myself in any of them.'

'Why ever not?'

'Because they're not me. Because my home has always been a place for sleeping and bathing and grabbing a cup of coffee before I rushed back into the real world. These places you're showing me are a world in themselves. They'll gobble me up and keep me prisoner and I don't know if I can live like that.'

She half expected him to compromise, to suggest taking an apartment in town while she got used to the change and the upheaval. But when David spoke next she realised it was a vain hope.

'You're beginning to sound like a little girl,' he told her, 'a little girl with a bad case of wedding nerves.'

Diane started to feel impatient.

'Not wedding nerves. Living nerves.'

David smiled.

'It's all the same thing. You'll get over it once we move into our new house and you start looking at colour schemes.'

Her impatience began to turn into panic, as she realised David didn't begin to understand her. The minute he'd decided to marry her, she had assumed a different identity in his eyes. Now she was a female who liked shopping for built-in kitchens and antique furniture. Any minute now he'd want to know who she wanted to invite to their wedding and whether she'd be married in white.

She felt a headache growing in the base of her neck and realised that unless she talked some sense into David, the headache would blossom into a full-blown migraine.

'I think you have to know right now,' she said as steadily as she could, 'that you're not going to bury me in the wilds. I've lived in cities all my life and I'm too old to change now.'

This time he didn't argue with her. Instead he put his coffee down and came over to where she was sitting. Then slowly and very deliberately he put his hands round her waist and pulled her to her feet. They were inches away from each other now and before she could say anything, he started kissing her. He was putting his heart into it, she could feel it. And she wondered why it left her cold.

She closed her eyes in an attempt to block out their differences and leaned her body against his so she could feel his solid, reassuring warmth. He took it as a signal and started to push the top of her track suit up above her breasts. Now his hands were on her, taking the tips of her nipples between his finger and thumb and massaging until they were hard. She started to undo his flies then, easing his pants down until his cock was in her hand. Then she leaned back against the kitchen table, pulling at her own pants until her sex was exposed to him.

This was the way they had made love the first time – hungrily, like animals. And she knew that if they could find some of that old passion, nothing else was going to matter very much. As long as there was heat between them, it wouldn't matter if they lived in a ranch house or a mud hut.

She felt his hardness against her now and she parted her legs expecting him to slide into her. Except it was difficult. The moisture she manufactured every time David touched her wasn't there any more. She was dry like an old woman, and she wondered what was happening to her.

Behind her on the kitchen table was the butter she had been spreading on her croissants. I would have done more good spreading it on me, she thought. And in that moment she realised what she needed to do. Diane reached behind her and dug her fingers into the block of butter. Then with her hand half full of it, she brought it to the lips of her entrance, smearing it inside and out.

She saw David watching her, mesmerised, and she realised he thought she was playing some new kind of sex game. Relief washed over her. She never wanted him to know what had happened to her just now. What she wanted him to remember, for the rest of time, was how much she desired him, how hot he always made her. She smiled and took his cock in her hand again and this time there was no difficulty at all. David thrust himself into her, right up to the hilt, grunting his pleasure the way he always did.

Now she relaxed as their rhythm took over and she felt her body finally respond. She had been quite prepared to fake it for him, but now there would be no need. She would feed on his desire, swelling and contracting until they both exploded into each other.

Then when it was over, she would kiss him and tell him he had been wonderful. And he would never know that she hadn't felt a damn thing.

Chapter Forty Six

Somewhere a long way off a bell was ringing. David stirred uneasily in his sleep, curling into the foetal position as if to avoid the nagging sound in the distance. But the ringing went on, growing steadily more insistent until sleep no longer protected him. His eyes came open then, focussing on the alarm clock which signalled the beginning of the day. He reached his arm out and turned it off. Then he rolled over in bed, searching for Diane. She wasn't there.

David shook his head in an effort to clear it. Then he swung out of bed and went through to the adjoining bathroom. She wasn't there either.

Now he was fully awake and ready for his first cup of coffee. And he knew it would probably be brewed by now. Diane would be perched at the kitchen table working her way through a full percolator while she waited for him to get up.

He smiled: she didn't know it yet, but she had the makings of a wonderful wife. He hadn't thought so in the beginning, but since they'd been together in Paris, he'd seen a difference in her. She seemed less selfish, less independent, though her last-minute nerves over the house bothered him. He got out of bed and shrugged on a dressing-gown. She'll come round, he thought. Once I put a ring on her finger and make her respectable, she'll change. Women always did.

He sniffed the air, anticipating the delicious smell of Diane's favourite coffee. But all he could detect was last night's cigarettes. So he hurried into the kitchen and saw the reason why. There was no percolator on the stove; no cups on the table; no Diane anywhere to be seen.

He wondered if she'd gone out. She sometimes took it into her head to go down the street for fresh bread and croissants. That's what it must be, he thought, Diane has decided to stoke up on breakfast before she gets the early plane back to London.

He went and turned on the stove, then started measuring out coffee grounds. As he performed the chore, he started to think. It wasn't like Diane to go out and get breakfast on a Monday morning. The moment she opened her eyes, she always started to fret about the office. More often than not, she skipped coffee altogether and set off for the airport early, preferring to make sure of her connection to London.

Maybe the prospect of getting married has calmed her down, he thought. Now she knows she'll be on a plane to Kentucky in three weeks, she's probably not so concerned about her job with Chic.

But even as it went through his mind, he knew it was unlikely. Diane was wedded to her career. She would probably work right up to the last minute, so no-one would be able to say she was less than perfect when it came to executing her duties.

He put the percolator on the stove and took stock of the situation. Diane wasn't there beside him when he woke up. She wasn't taking her usual shower. She wasn't making coffee. And though he didn't know for sure, he was reasonably convinced that she was nowhere near the local boulangerie.

So where is she? he wondered. There was no way she would pack up and go without saying goodbye. Or would she?

He turned down the heat under the coffee and went back into the bedroom, making straight for the wardrobe. Her cases were gone, as were the Carmen rollers she kept there permanently. And he could find none of her other things. What on earth is she playing at? he wondered. She must have got up at the crack of dawn to get away before I opened my eyes.

He suddenly realised he had trouble. Last night's wedding nerves were still playing on her mind, giving her doubts and second thoughts. Damn, he thought. Damn and blast. I can't even get to her to talk her round. She'll be halfway across the English Channel by now. He decided to tackle her when he got into the office. She might have calmed down a bit by then.

There was a mountain of mail waiting for him. It was only when his secretary asked if he wanted a car to take him to his lunch date that he realised the morning was nearly over. He glanced at his watch and saw it was nearly twelve thirty. Diane would be in London by now, sitting at her desk. It was high time he rang.

She sounded nervous when she answered the phone and he let her burble on for a bit, hoping she'd come up with the reason for her abrupt departure. But she couldn't seem to bring herself round to it, so he decided to give her a helping hand.

'What made you dash off so early today?' he asked. 'You didn't tell me you had an early meeting.'

There was the slightest pause, then she said:

'There wasn't an early meeting. I just needed to get away.'

Now David was all at sea. She wasn't a teenager, for heaven's sake, but she was both sounding and behaving like one.

'Could you explain to me why you needed to run off like that?'

There was another pause and when she next spoke David could hardly hear her voice.

'I realised last night,' she said, stringing out the words so she sounded as if she was underwater, 'that I couldn't marry you, only I couldn't tell you to your face.'

'So you buggered off back to London,' David said harshly. 'What were you planning to do, Diane? Send me a fax saying goodbye and good luck?'

His anger seemed to pull her together, for she now began to sound stronger.

'I was going to ring you, actually,' she said, 'when I'd worked out what I was going to say.'

'Well I've just saved you the price of a call. So go ahead. Tell me why you've decided to duck out all of a sudden.'

She sounded really miserable now.

'It's not as sudden as you think. If you'd bothered to listen

384

to me over the weekend you might have got the clue that things were going wrong.'

David sighed.

'You're not still harping on about not liking the house,' he said. 'It's hardly a reason to cancel the wedding.'

'It's not just the house. It's you. You expect me to change into somebody different when I'm your wife and I can't do that.'

She sounded very determined when she said it and David realised this wasn't just a show of temperament. For a reason he didn't quite understand, Diane was terrified about settling down. He had one last go at reasoning with her.

'Are you seriously telling me you want to be a single career woman for the rest of your life?'

'If it means I don't have to live in the country and cook barbecues for your clients.'

He knew at that moment he'd lost her. And when she cut the connection, he made no attempt to try and get her back. For this wasn't a simple case of wedding nerves. Diane had never seriously contemplated getting married at all. The realisation made him feel bitter, bitter and used. For he knew now that what she had wanted all along was a boyfriend she could spend her spare time with, the time she had left over from her job and her friends.

From out of nowhere a vision of Sally came into his mind. She would never have behaved like this, stringing him along, playing him for a fool. And he realised several years too late that he should never have left her.

Diane was perfectly happy being his mistress. They could have gone on forever with the arrangement and no-one would have been the slightest bit put out. He and Diane would have had their ups and downs. Of that he had no doubt. There would have been the occasional rival to fight off. She might even have got impatient now and then. But there was nothing he couldn't manage. While he was seeing Diane during the week in London, his obedient little wife would have gone on running his household in blissful ignorance in Oxford. He could have stayed in his comfortable house, gone on with the business he loved and watched his daughter grow up. Now that was all denied to him.

David had backed the wrong horse and was paying the price for it. He thought about the future with a foreboding he had never felt before. Selling hair-care products had been interesting for a while because he was setting up something completely new. But peddling Nourish hair thickener for the rest of his life didn't exactly thrill him. The money would make it easier, of course. He could have endured it with Diane by his side. But going it alone in middle America was his idea of a permanent jail sentence.

He wondered what on earth he'd done to deserve this misfortune.

Chapter Forty Seven

Sally . . . four months later

It wasn't a major problem. If Sally had been in London she could have handled it easily. But she wasn't in London. She was in New York with Brad on one of her increasingly frequent extended weekends.

So when Annabel's application to Edinburgh University got turned down, she was powerless to do anything but mouth platitudes over the transatlantic telephone.

'I should really be at home, ploughing through lists and talking about all the other places she could go,' Sally told Brad.

He looked at her worried face and felt a momentary irritation with Annabel. Why hadn't the girl waited a couple of days till her mother got home, instead of ringing up in the middle of dinner and ruining a perfectly good weekend?

Then he remembered his own children and knew it didn't work that way. If they had a problem they ran to you, irrespective of whether or not it was convenient. And something told him that unless he got Sally, Annabel and himself under the same roof, the whole thing was going to end in tears. He signalled the maid to clear away the dishes, then he turned to Sally.

'Why don't we have coffee in the drawing-room?' he said. 'There's something I need to ask you.'

'Ask me now. There's no need to wait for coffee.'

Brad looked at her.

'I'd rather wait.'

When they were settled in the low-ceilinged modern room that was the centre of the huge rambling apartment overlooking Park Avenue, Sally allowed her curiosity to take over.

'What is this big question you had for me?'

She saw he was finding it difficult to say anything, and she felt worried. Brad was never at a loss for words.

Eventually, when the silence had wrapped itself round the room, Brad found his voice.

'I wanted to know if you would marry me.'

She looked at him, knowing that he had wanted to ask her this for a long time but had put it off because her divorce had been too recent.

'What brought this on?' she asked, feeling foolish and unable to cope.

Brad grinned.

'The problem with Annabel, I suppose. She can't be expected to cope with you away half the time.'

'If she gets a place at University, she'll be away herself.'

'There's over a year to go until then. Anyway it's time we married. My nerves won't stand much more of this long-distance relationship.'

He was right, of course. Since she started falling in love again, her whole life had been in turmoil. She was never in the office when she was needed. And living out of a suitcase had done terrible things to the way she looked. But she lived with it, because the alternative scared her too much. She reached out and took Brad's hand.

'I'm sorry about your nerves,' she said, 'but I've got nerves too. And right now the thought of being married to anyone scares me witless.'

'Because of David?'

'He's a lot of it. When he dumped me for someone I thought was a friend, I got very cynical about committing myself again.'

'You're not worried I might do the same thing?'

Sally suddenly realised she was dangerously close to tears.

'I don't know what I'm worried about.'

She pulled herself together.

'Yes I do. I'm worried if I promise myself body and soul, I'll be opening myself to being hurt again.'

To her surprise, Brad looked sad.

'Don't you think it's the same for everybody? The minute I fell for you, I was racked with fear that something, some accident, might take you away from me. It happened once before, after all.

'But you can't live like that. Just because you've had one bad experience, you can't go on looking round corners waiting for it to happen again.'

'But what if it does happen again? What if I get ill? Or you go off with somebody else?'

He looked at her.

'So it happens again. It's the risk we all take. But if you don't take chances, you stop going forward.'

Sally thought about it. She could still pull back from the brink if she chose, if she was too frightened to commit herself to marriage a second time. But where would that get her? She'd go back to London and get on with her successful business. Then one day soon, Annabel would leave and she would be on her own again. I'll end up taking my work home at night for company. Or if I'm really unlucky, I'll be wheeled on at dinner parties to meet some suitable divorcee.

'If we do marry,' she said, feeling shaky, 'what am I going to do in New York? I can't run Chandos from there.'

'Damn right, you can't. You'll have to sell Chandos and find something else.'

Out of nowhere, she felt a tremendous sense of relief. Getting involved with Brad wasn't anything like tying herself to David. For Brad didn't want her to stop working at all. He knew how much she needed it, and he respected her for it.

'There's only one problem,' she said, looking at him. 'I don't know any PR people in New York. All my contacts are in London.'

He moved closer to her on the long white sofa and put an arm round her shoulders.

'You're forgetting something,' he told her. 'We're both in this together. You might not know anyone useful in New York, but I know dozens. I've employed countless agencies in my time and stayed on good terms with the ones I no longer use.'

She smiled at him.

'You know that's nepotism.'

'Sure I do. But if you can't help your family, who can you help?'

It was when he said 'family' that she melted, for she realised the one thing missing in her life since David left was a sense of belonging. Her father-in-law had been a support, but he was on his own. The rest of the Robinsons had studiously ignored her as soon as they knew about the divorce.

'Are there any other Hastingses besides you?' she asked, snuggling up to him.

'My mother's dead,' he said, looking serious, 'but I've got a father who lives in Connecticut and a younger sister in California who are both longing to meet you.'

So it all starts again, she thought. The father will spawn uncles for Annabel, and the sister will probably have children who will depend on me to come up with presents for Christmas and birthdays. All at once she felt terribly content. She'd found her independence since David deserted her. She knew she could stand on her own two feet if she needed to.

But she also knew that she had a far deeper need than mere survival. She needed to be connected to a clan. When she grew old she wanted to be surrounded by cousins and nieces and sisters by marriage. She needed to keep up with her own parents, instead of quarrelling with them the way she did. And she needed her daughter and the children she would produce.

She thought about Albert Robinson, who she knew she would fit into her plan somehow. And finally after she'd counted and re-counted her extended family, she turned to Brad.

'I'd love to marry you,' she said, 'if you can put up with an earth mother as well as a working wife.'

Chapter Forty Eight

Sally . . . London

Sally looked at the pile of clothes in the private changing-room and knew it was going to take her all afternoon to decide what to buy. Then she thought, what the hell, it's Saturday. I've got all afternoon. She took hold of a pair of tailored trousers and held them against her, observing her reflection in the triple mirror.

I've lost weight, she thought. It must be all this worry about selling the agency. For she had been back from New York for two weeks now and she still had no idea of how she was going to offload Chandos.

It was her baby. She couldn't just sell out to her managing director, Terry, because he didn't have what it took to be an agency chief. He was a wonderful number two, but left to his own devices, he would run the agency into the ground as surely as Jeremy had done.

Sally sighed, studying her reflection in the mirror. I have to pull my finger out and start talking to people, she decided. There must be some agency in London which would jump at the chance of taking over Chandos.

I'll start the ball rolling on Monday, she promised herself. But now it's the weekend and I need to make some serious decisions about clothes. She decided the trousers didn't suit her despite the weight she'd lost, and went onto a dressy suit with a long skirt which she liked a whole lot better. What I need, she thought, is to look at myself at a distance. There was a big cheval mirror in the main shop, so Sally walked out of her changing-room and went in search of it.

As usual, there wasn't a crowd. The women who bought their clothes here didn't browse through the rails. They knew what was in the shop because the sales assistant who looked after them had sent them a catalogue detailing the new collection. All they had to do was come in and try on the items they fancied, much as she was doing right now.

Sally glanced across to the long mirror that lived in the corner of the shop, expecting it to be free. But there was somebody hogging it. A tall woman with shiny dark hair was parading up and down in a blazer and trousers.

She looked as if she had been there a long time, wondering whether or not to buy the outfit, and Sally decided to go across and see if she could hurry her up.

As she came nearer Sally realised she had seen this customer somewhere before. Then she turned round and found herself face to face with Diane. She was so surprised, she said the first thing that came into her head.

'What on earth are you doing here?'

'I'm buying a blazer. What does it look like?'

Sally regarded the woman who used to be her friend and wondered if they had anything in common any more. Were they still up to girly chats in dress shops, or had David put an end to all that? She decided to test the water.

'I suppose you're on a flying visit,' she said, 'there can't be much to keep you in London these days.'

Diane looked surprised.

'I never left London.'

Sally felt suddenly foolish and small, as she often used to when she and Diane were talking at cross-purposes. But she wasn't going to be put off.

'I can't have got it wrong,' she said, 'Annabel told me you and David went to live in Kentucky.'

Diane crossed in front of the mirror and took Sally's arm. Then she propelled her towards the velvet sofa in the corner of the shop.

'I think you and I had better sit down and talk,' she said, suddenly turning into the big sister she had known in Manchester.

'Things didn't turn out the way either of us thought they would. They sure as hell didn't turn out the way your daughter imagined.'

Sally looked at her.

'You mean you didn't go to America with David?'

She pulled a face.

'We changed our minds at the last moment. So in the end David went on his own.'

Sally wondered if she was hearing right. Her entire life had changed course because this woman couldn't keep her hands off her husband, and now she was calmly announcing things hadn't worked out. As if she was talking about a lunch date that had stood her up.

'You can't be serious,' Sally said.

'I am serious; I've never been more serious. Do you think I wanted to stay in London after I lost my job at Chic?'

Sally felt guilty now. She'd been responsible for Diane losing her job, thinking it wouldn't matter with David around. But now he wasn't around. He'd gone off to Kentucky, leaving Diane to fend for herself.

Did he ditch her? Sally wondered. David had walked out of one life. She wouldn't put it past him to do the same thing a second time.

'Do you feel like telling me what happened?' she asked.

For a moment Diane didn't say anything, and when she did speak again she seemed to have lost the jaunty, who-gives-a-damn attitude she always carried around with her.

'The whole thing was mostly my fault,' she said sadly. 'I thought when I settled for David that we could go on living the same lives as we did before. But that couldn't have happened in Kentucky.'

Sally looked suprised.

'Why ever not?'

'Because David didn't want it that way. His idea of being married to me was to dump me in a big house in the middle of nowhere where I'd cook barbecues for the rest of my life.'

Despite the sadness of this confession, Sally couldn't help smiling. How typical of Diane, she thought. It didn't occur to her that if she had only met David halfway, gone along with him until she could see a way of changing things, they might have stood a chance. But Diane didn't function that way. Even when she'd first known her, she liked to call the shots in her relationships. Compromising even an inch would have meant losing control. And she couldn't do that, not even with David. 'You sound as if you've had a lucky escape,' Sally said.

Diane shrugged.

'You could call it that, though I'll probably end up a wrinkled old spinster all alone in my penthouse flat.'

You probably will, Sally thought, and all at once she felt terribly sorry for Diane. She didn't deserve her sympathy, of course. She'd behaved unspeakably towards her. Yet she couldn't help herself and she realised she'd stopped being angry with her. What a difference being happy makes, Sally thought. It immunises you against the past and all the people in it who hurt you.

She would have probably got up and gone back to her changing-room if one of the sales assistants hadn't come up and offered them coffee. The shop did this for their favoured customers and Diane looked delighted at the suggestion.

'Will you stay and have some with me?' she asked.

Sally hesitated. They weren't really friends anymore, just old acquaintances exchanging gossip. And she had heard all she needed to from Diane. Then she looked at her and saw the pleading in her eyes and realised there was still unfinished business between them.

'I'd love some coffee,' she said.

'Good, then you can tell me what's been going on in your life,' Diane smiled.

Sally wondered if she should. What if her friend got ideas about Brad? She laughed at her insecurity. Brad wasn't another David . . . Anyway, he was too far away to steal. She took a deep breath.

'I'm getting married again,' she said.

Diane started to perk up.

'Is it anyone I know?'

'I don't think so, though you met him once when we were having lunch. He's called Brad Hastings.'

'The American tycoon. Of course I remember him. He's incredible, a real powerhouse.'

She stopped mid-sentence and grinned. 'Is he letting you keep your agency? Or is he swallowing it up along with you?'

For a moment Sally felt indignant.

'Why should he do that?'

'Well, you're not going to go on living in England, are you?'

Sally remembered the promise she'd made to herself in the changing-room. She was going to worry about Chandos on Monday, when she'd finished shopping. But now Diane wasn't going to let her put it off that long.

She looked at her.

'Brad isn't going to swallow up Chandos. Anyway I wouldn't let him. It belongs to me.'

'So what will you do with it?'

'Sell it, of course. It's a going concern.'

She saw the interest in Diane's face and realised that the news had turned her on.

'Are you talking to anyone about Chandos?' she asked.

'Not right now, but I will be on Monday.'

'If I asked you, would you hold off for a week?'

Sally looked regretful.

'I haven't got that sort of time. Brad's pushing me to get over to New York as soon as I can.'

Once more Diane's new intensity reached out to her.

'What I'm going to say could help both of you. If I raise the money, I might be interested in Chandos.'

Sally did a double take.

'Come off it, you don't know the first thing about public relations.'

There was a silence, then Diane said:

'With my style of business I don't really need to. What I'm

good at is running things, and talking to the top people. I leave the creative stuff to other people.'

She was reminded of her father-in-law who had roughly the same philosophy, and she had to admire it – they were effective, these high-powered executives. They saw something they wanted and they went for it, oblivious of the pitfalls along the way. Diane will probably be very good at running my agency, Sally thought. She'll work at it day and night. And she'll care about it too. There won't be a man who merits the same attention.

Just for a moment Sally saw the irony of the situation. They had changed places once in their lives before, and now they were doing it again. She was going back to being married. And Diane was going back to what she did best – working.

'If you do take over Chandos,' she said curiously, 'will you keep in touch with me? I'd like to know what's going on with the agency.'

Diane turned at her.

'You don't really want to do that, do you? Aren't you better off putting everything behind you and starting again without memories?'

She's talking about David, Sally thought. She still thinks I'm mad as hell about it. For a moment both women looked at each other, remembering the friendship they had had before David came along and soured it.

It was then Sally knew she wasn't going to walk away.

'I'm very attached to my memories,' she said, looking at Diane. 'They're a part of me.'

'Even the bad ones?'

'Particularly the bad ones. You learn from them.'

Diane looked wry.

'What the hell did you learn from what I did to you?'

'Forgiveness,' Sally said. 'I learned forgiveness.'

Neither of them spoke after that, for each was engrossed in her own thoughts, marvelling at what quirk of fate had brought them together in this shop on this weekend to make this unlikely peace.